PRAISE FOR SO YOU
MATCH

"Michelle Hazen is so wickedly funny you'll think that you don't need anything more than her rapier wit. But then she goes and drops sex scenes that will make your toes curl. I now have the book hangover of the century." -Devri Walls, international bestselling author

"Complex characters strive with serious issues, and yet the story glimmers with charm, romance, and laugh-out-loud humour. This is a book that will make you think - and feel - and care about where it's taking you on the page and in your heart." -India Holton, author of *The Wisteria Society of Lady Scoundrels*

"Romance readers used to the typical one-dimensional fling will find far more simmering beneath the surface of *So You Think You're a Match*.

Underneath its romp through romance lies a thought-provoking consideration of what makes opposites attract, how beliefs and values are changed by circumstance and romance, and wherein lies the boundaries in a love connection." -Midwest Book Review

"Michelle Hazen is the queen of flirty banter. The chemistry between responsible Harlow and quicksilver Bishop is delicious and sizzling. You'll have a smile on your face for the whole read." -Kristin Wright, Amazon-bestselling author of *The Darkest Flower*

"Between clutching my heart and snort-cackling, I couldn't turn the pages fast enough in this one-of-a-kind rom-com. Opposites don't just attract in *So You Think You're a Match*. Harlow and Bishop collide in a burst of sparks, showering the reader with their electric chemistry." -Kelly Siskind, award-winning author

"With sizzling chemistry, hilarious banter, and heart-tugging stakes, this story had me alternately swooning and frantically turning the pages. So You Think You're A Match truly puts both the *rom* and the *com* in rom-com." -Alanna Martin, author of *Hearts on a Leash*

"If you're looking for well-developed characters that are brimming with humor and authenticity, then look no further than this friends-to-lovers romance.

Hazen is a master at creating a story that's deeply rendered and honest. You'll be swept off your feet when Bishop (a modern day Robin Hood) meets his match in honest, hardworking Harlow. Their chemistry crackles on every page, reminding you that friends really do make the best lovers." -Elle Berlin, author of the *Flambé Series*

SO YOU THINK YOU'RE A MATCH?

MICHELLE HAZEN

For Katie Golding

This is your Austin tribute series, because you love your Texas so much. I stuffed as many stars and tacos as would fit, plus John Cena with a goat!

DEAR READER

Dear Reader,

The inspiration behind a book can be a magical, unpredictable kind of thing. This one began when my credit card got stolen.

Someone used my card to pay for their Netflix subscription, which I felt was the height of ridiculousness. I commented on Twitter that it seemed like such a mundane (and easily traceable!) thing to use a stolen card for. This led to a flood of stories of all the bizarre items other peoples' stolen cards had been used for, the strangest of which was a subscription to a dating app. Someone else said, "Imagine if they matched with the girl whose card they stole. Wouldn't that make a great rom-com?"

Here's where it gets weird.

Two months *before* my card got stolen, I was driving home from the gym, and a character fell fully-formed into my head. Here's what I knew about him:

-His name was Bishop

-He had messy black hair and always wore a fedora

-His little sister had cancer and he stole credit cards to pay her bills

No story. Just a character. But when my card got stolen and I had that Twitter conversation, I got immediate chills. I already *had* a character who stole credit cards, and now I had the book idea to match.

Today, I'm delighted to be able to share with you the book born from that moment of serendipity. If you enjoy it, I hope you'll leave a review online. It helps authors more than anything, and I absolutely love to hear from my readers.

Happy reading,
    Michelle

CHAPTER 1

$\mathcal{B}$ishop Riley needed to get his stealing done for the day before his little sister came out of chemotherapy.

The laptop sat crookedly on his wide-sprawled knees as he navigated the website he'd just hacked. He tapped more keys, starting to download their clients' names, addresses, and credit card numbers to his hard drive.

"Come on baby," he murmured. "Show me the money." Daisy's chemo treatment was going to be done any minute, and he was fresh out of credit card numbers to cover her co-pay.

Fraud detection systems were quick on the draw these days, so he only got one or two uses out of each number before it passed into the great credit card graveyard in the sky. He'd used the last of his stockpile yesterday. The last time he'd come up short on the co-pay, Daisy had been so worried that she sold her school textbooks on eBay and proudly handed over the cash to the receptionist at their next visit. He couldn't let that happen again, because he'd be damned if *both* Riley kids were going to end up loser dropouts.

The door to the treatment rooms gave the deep whirring that signaled its automatic opening and he crossed his fingers.

"Anybody but Daisy," he muttered under his breath. "Anybody but

—" The small figure in the wheelchair had a magenta-pink wig on. "Crap."

Looked like he was about to be damned, after all. No surprise there.

Daisy's least favorite nurse—the one who called her sweetums— wheeled her over in the office-policy wheelchair. Bishop uncrossed his fingers and clicked to minimize the tab where the new credit card numbers were downloading, pulling up the tab for his cover story job instead. He began energetically clacking the keys at random. He'd written three jokes earlier, so if his nosy sibling peeked, he'd be covered.

"There ya go, sweetums." The nurse patted her shoulder. "You take it easy for the rest of today, okay?"

"No aerial yoga, check," Daisy said. "Can I at least make the kegger tonight?"

Bishop wagged his finger at her. "C'mon now, sweetums. We discussed this. No keg stands on chemo days."

A smile tickled the edge of Daisy's chapped lips, but she'd never abandon a deadpan, especially not before the nurse stomped off in a huff of offended teddy-bear print scrubs. Which she promptly did.

"What are you doing?" Daisy asked. "You better not be looking at dirty pictures in the hospital waiting room."

He grimaced. "Please don't tell me how you know laptops have dirty pictures in them."

"I'm eleven, not four." She narrowed her eyes at him, which only made them seem more sunken. Her skin was one shade lighter gray than he'd come to expect and her sarcasm got sharper when she was nauseous. This wasn't his first rodeo, though, so he'd already claimed a seat closest to the trash can and didn't need to move. The status bar said ten more minutes to download all the stolen numbers, and more importantly, Daisy looked like she was going to need at least nine of those to sit very still if she wasn't going to lose her lunch on the way to the parking lot.

"I'm working, if you must know."

She went a shade paler, making the vivid color of her newest wig stand out even more. "Are we picking up an Uber person on the way home?"

"Nah, other job. Joke writing one."

"I still don't understand why a dating app needs jokes." She eyed the trash can. Yup, stalling was definitely in order here.

"I'll show you." He pulled up YouTube and found the latest commercial. Three minutes, fifteen seconds. Well, that was at least a third of the time they'd need, and cleaning up the inevitable vomit would probably use up the other six. Win/win, and then they'd be able to go home without washing dishes to cover their bill. If that was even an option in hospitals. Wait, *was* that an option in hospitals? He made a mental note to check as he spun his laptop around and hit play.

The dating app name zoomed onto the screen in pink cursive letters.

So You Think You're a Match?

"The hottest new dating app on the market!" the voice-over proclaimed. An animated hand popped up holding a phone with a slimy-looking blond guy on it. "Swipe right for yes, left for no, and wait for a verdict!"

The animated thumb swiped left, and a comment bubble popped up on the screen.

"The nose, right? It was totally the nose."

A canned laugh track played and Bishop tried not to wince. He really wished they'd cut the laugh track.

The thumb swiped right on a square-jawed dude with dark emo-adjacent bangs and the comment bubble followed.

"Oh yeah, this is the one. This is the guy who will finally respect you, love you more than his mother, and not leave his toenail clippings on the coffee table."

Bishop took a breath to brag that they'd chosen one of his jokes for the commercial but Daisy interrupted.

"Ew! Do boyfriends really leave their toenail clippings on the coffee table?"

"I don't know what boyfriends do. I tried playing for that team and they benched me."

She sniffed. "I still don't get what the jokes are for."

"Keep watching." He hit play again and the picture expanded to show a cartoon girl out with her friends at a table littered with wine and martini glasses.

"This is the one," she squealed, clutching her phone to her chest. "I just know it."

"He may not be Prince Charming," her phone's voiceover piped up, "but by the look of that selfie, he's at least the Crown Prince of the Ab-Roller."

Her friends erupted into laughter and the picture zoomed out to the app's logo again.

"Taking love a little less seriously, because it's not life and death... it's just dating!" the commercial proclaimed.

"Why wouldn't people take love seriously?" Daisy asked. "I mean, you don't want to end up married to just whoever, right?"

Bishop was still trying to figure out a way to work into the conversation that he'd written that last joke as well. He had no idea how many freelance joke writers the website had, or what the odds were they'd use two of his jokes in a single commercial, but he'd be lying if he said that wasn't why he chose that particular commercial to show to his sister. But she wasn't acting particularly impressed anyway, so he gave it up as a loss.

He spun his laptop back to face himself. Down to five minutes and they'd be able to pay and get going.

"You'll understand when you're older and infinitely more jaded. With those apps, people get all up in their head about it. There are thousands and thousands of people on them and it's pretty easy to start thinking every one's your soulmate. Adding the jokes reminds people it's only a date, not a diamond solitaire." He waved a hand to indicate the waiting room. "Like this place."

Daisy nodded, her face shrewd. She was a prodigy at not taking things too seriously. She'd been diagnosed when she was so young he wasn't sure she remembered what it was like to be a kid without cancer, but she hadn't spent much time crying about it. He'd never been sure if that was because she didn't understand what death was, or because somehow, she knew she wasn't going to die. Though before her surgery when she was nine, even the doctors hadn't been so sure about that one.

What he did know was whenever he took her to chemo, she was always teasing and joking with the other kids, trying to take their mind off the nausea. He liked to think she got it from him. After all, it wasn't like anybody else in the family had a sense of humor.

"Does it help?" she asked.

"Hmm?" Four minutes and ticking down fast.

"When you're using the app, do the jokes make you feel better?" She was looking at him particularly earnestly. Her blue eyes were bright, even after chemo, not dulled by pain and pills like their mom's. He had the same eyes, though Daisy claimed his were more electric Kool-Aid and hers were more summer sky. He was pretty sure they were the same color and girls just liked to believe their eyes looked like the sky instead of sugary, over-processed beverages.

"I don't use the Match app. I just write their jokes." He pulled a pack of wintergreen gum out of his backpack. It was the only thing that reliably settled her stomach after chemo, and took the weird taste out of her mouth that she always complained about. "Gum?"

She took the gum, but still frowned. "Why wouldn't you sign up?"

"What, and take shit from myself?" He snorted. "I can dish it out, little sis, but you know I can't take it."

"If it's an app all about not taking things so seriously, then it shouldn't be that big of a deal. Besides, you need a date," Daisy said.

Bishop crossed his arms, smirking openly. "Do tell, Queen Daisy. For what?"

"To buy you dinner and tell you you're pretty." She nodded firmly. "That's what people do on dates."

He tipped his head. "Well...yeah." That actually did sound pretty good.

Dating had kind of fallen by the wayside for the last few years, because he needed every dollar he could get for deductibles, co-pays, and out-of-network costs. He didn't have the room in his life, wallet, or heart for any female except his baby sister.

On the other hand, he loved dating. The flirtation, the thrill of first dates and first kisses and second times in bed...it was his favorite rollercoaster ride. His future wasn't something he'd foist on some unsuspecting female, but so many women in Austin these days were too busy with their jobs and school to get serious. A lot of them were probably looking for casual, just like him. Also, his sister was looking expectantly at him and he needed to stall until the program finished.

"Okay, you sold me. I'll make my profile right now."

Bishop typed his name into the app, flicked his way through all the toggle switches for preferences and gender identities, and added a two-sentence bio. Doffed his signature fedora and ran a hand through his black hair, then stuffed it back onto his head and gave the camera a twinkly-eyed smirk as he snapped a selfie.

"Ugh, comb your hair first," Daisy complained. The gum seemed to be working, though, because her face was getting its color back.

"Shows what you know. Women like their men's hair messy and their smiles crooked. Do I *need* to read you the whole Twilight series again?"

She lit up. "Yes! Would you?"

"Absolutely not." That was three months of his life he was never getting back. Her face fell and he improvised. "At least not unless you want to trade me reading aloud for you making me omelets. Not plain cheese ones, either. That's cheating."

"You don't even let me come to your apartment anymore."

That was because a methhead had moved in next door and he was a little afraid he might become the neighborly victim of some bath-tub-chemistry explosion. Daisy had enough health challenges without adding a meth lab mishap to the list.

"Well, I would invite you over more if you'd make me omelets," he lied. The program chimed completion, and he tilted the screen away from her before he opened the results. "Besides, I don't want you stealing my wallet and using it to go on an American Girl doll buying spree. Again."

"Whatever. That was years ago and it was *one* doll."

"One doll that cost more than a pony."

"You said I could pick my own present! You didn't say I couldn't get an American Girl doll."

He didn't answer her, because his screen was full of delicious credit card numbers. Solvent again, and it felt oh so sweet. He clicked on the top one and entered the information into the new app profile on his phone.

Thank you, Harlow Rimes, you generous soul. You don't even know it, but you may have helped a man find true love. Or at least free dinner.

He wouldn't mind being called pretty, either. An ego had to eat, too.

The credit card didn't decline, so he used it to make a quick donation to his favorite LegUp charity campaign, the one for the cat with the tragic paw accident. LegUp was the Swiss account of internet piggy banks. It didn't ask questions and it transferred anonymously to anywhere, so you could "fundraise" for any cause you wanted. He punched a button on his phone, opening it to the PhonePay that linked to all his phony LegUp accounts. Take that, exorbitant chemotherapy co-pay.

"You ready to drive, Miss Daisy?" He pushed out of his chair. "Because I am all signed up and ready to take love a little less seriously."

CHAPTER 2

$\mathcal{H}$arlow Rimes hauled open the glass door and then shook out her hand with the quick reflexes of a Texas-born girl used to sun-scorched metal door handles. Inside, she was greeted with a blast of air conditioning that carried the scent of kale, dirt, and the astringent bite of eucalyptus.

Harlow hadn't exactly gotten off work on time, so her two best friends were already inside and waiting in line, even the perpetually late Sadie.

"I've been wanting to try this place for weeks. What do you think?" Sadie beamed up at her, hair held back in an elaborate crown braid and dark eyes shining.

What she thought was that the juice bar smelled like a farmer's market had a love child with an essential oils counter, but she didn't think that would be helpful to say. "When I said I wanted to go out for a drink, I wasn't expecting quite…this."

"I'm on an alcohol cleanse for 30 days," Sadie said. "You should try it. It's a great way to get your life back in alignment with your intentions."

Her life and intentions were pretty far out of line right now, but

SO YOU THINK YOU'RE A MATCH?

that had a lot more to do with her embezzling boss, curses be upon his name, than it did with drinking.

"Plus, alcohol is loaded with sugar."

"So is fruit juice," Alice pointed out, and Sadie frowned at her taller friend.

"They have vegetable juices, too!"

"Juice is fine," Harlow said, interrupting the burgeoning argument between her friends. "With all the sad desk lunches I've been eating, this'll be the first time in weeks I've been within biting distance of a vegetable."

At least the cream-colored walls with their arched nooks were soothing, even if she'd like the flickering electronic pillar candles even better with a sidecar of whiskey.

"I saw the press conference." Alice silenced a reminder on her ever-chiming phone and stuffed it back into her purse. "They haven't found your boss yet, huh?

"Oh, they found his plane ticket easily enough. Window seat all the way to some little island nation where the tourist trade is booming but the government is so dysfunctional they're never going to get around to our extradition request."

The line moved forward toward the counter.

"So what's going to happen to all those people who already put the money in to buy houses in the subdivision you guys were building?" Sadie's shoulders cringed under her sleeveless blouse.

"Hopefully our liability insurance will cover it, but an entire development's worth of money is a huge claim. I'm sure the insurance company is going to try to find some embezzlement loophole that will make it our problem." And then they'd go bankrupt.

She was only a junior associate without a stock option in sight, so in that scenario, all she'd lose was her job. And oh, yeah, the three years of unpaid internships, dues paying and coffee fetching she'd given to this company after grad school, hoping to earn a spot in the corner office. Namely, the office Hank just ditched for a beach chair, a margarita, and his younger, about-to-be divorced secretary.

"So what does that mean for you getting promoted to run Sunny-brooke?" Alice asked, zeroing in on the heart of the issue.

"The bad news is, the whole plan of me being his co-designer for the next neighborhood is clearly in the trash can. The good news is, the whole position is now up for grabs, not just the co-chair."

Sadie perked up. "So this might actually help you?"

"It could, except I'm still young for the position, and Hank was the one who'd promised it to me. Now that he's gone, everybody knows me as the assistant of that guy who screwed the company over. Not the best look."

The line cleared and they stepped up to the counter. The options felt too dizzying to analyze after the emergencies she'd been juggling all day, so Harlow just ordered a lavender lemonade.

"Add an extra stress-relief booster to that lemonade," Sadie advised the clerk, then glanced at Harlow. "Actually, make that a double."

"You're the one giving all the press conferences and keeping that place on its feet." Alice scanned the menu. "Maybe they'll remember that when they're passing out promotions." She turned to the clerk. "Dark kale and beet juice please, and add an energy shot. The caffeine one, not the gingko one."

"That'll be $36.14," the clerk piped up after taking Sadie's order, too.

Harlow cringed. She should at least catch a buzz for that kind of investment. She dug in her shoulder bag anyway. "Let me get it. You girls deserve some kind of compensation for listening to all my whining the past few weeks."

"Don't apologize. It's been shitty." Alice skewered her with a look from under razor-cut bangs. "You deserve that promotion. Don't forget it, no matter what those suits decide."

"Um, I'm sorry, but this card has been declined?" The clerk offered her credit card back to her.

"What?" Harlow frowned down at it, then rolled her eyes. "Oh, I'm sorry. Wrong one. I had to cancel that one." She swapped it for her debit card.

"What happened? Are they having trouble making payroll?" Sadie accepted a seashell from the clerk that was apparently their juice bar stand-in for an order number, and led the way to one of the round booths, with their white pegged leather seats and gleaming black granite tables.

"No. In the midst of all this other crap, my credit card number got stolen somehow. It's really my week." She tucked the credit card in with her cell phone so she'd remember to cut it up later.

"Oh wow, you're so pretty!" A perky redhead interrupted. "Are you two sisters? You could be models."

Harlow collapsed into the booth. *Not* the sisters thing again. As if that weren't bad enough, hearing your friends described as models while you lurked in the background was a special little moment of its own. She knew she probably looked tired, but she'd hoped her press conference makeup would cover up a bit of that.

"Nope, not sisters," Alice said. Her voice was tight, but she left it at that. The redhead was getting off easy. When Alice and Rob were in an off-again phase, her normal saltiness got even sharper and anything could happen. As long as it was bad.

"Oh..."

The trail off was ominous. Harlow held her breath and hoped the other girl wouldn't go there.

"But like, where are you two from?"

Harlow stared up at the clueless redhead. People. As if her ex-boyfriend, Chad, hadn't been enough, this week was doing its best to destroy her faith in humanity.

Alice ripped a pen out of her purse, pulled a napkin from the holder at the center of the table, and scrawled four quick shapes on it. "Recognize these?"

"Um, that's Texas. And...New Jersey?"

"This is Sweden, where Harlow's family is from. China, where my family used to live." Alice snapped the pen against the next shape. "This is Korea, where Sadie's great-grandparents immigrated from. This is Texas, where *we* are all from." She crumpled up the napkin and dropped it in the redhead's empty juice cup. "And none of that is any of your damn business."

The redhead gawked and Sadie scooted further into the booth, eyes down like she could disappear if she tried hard enough.

"Bitch," the other girl muttered under her breath and flounced away, flinging her cup at the trashcan and missing.

Alice stiffened, and Harlow tried to remember if she had enough in her checking account to cover a bail bond.

But instead of going after her, Alice just tossed out, "Yeah, you kind of are."

She dropped into the booth.

"Sorry," she said to Sadie. "I know you hate making a scene, but sometimes I can't help it."

Sadie gave her a wavering smile. "That girl was cruising for it. I can't blame you; it just makes me...tired." She turned to Harlow. "So, did they get much off your credit card?"

"Once I reported it as fraud, I'm not responsible for the charges. But they were for the weirdest stuff! The person used it to sign up for a subscription to that new dating app, So You Think You're a Match." Her phone chimed, and she ignored it. "And to donate money to a LegUp for a pawless cat."

"That poor kitty!" Sadie's hands flew to her mouth. "Maybe it's a really nice thief, then."

Alice made a choking sound and Harlow elbowed her before she said something too sharp. "It's not a real cat. The description said it lost its paws in a tragic meat slicing accident and most people don't have a meat slicer anywhere cats are allowed, so..."

"So it's probably a way to funnel money from cards into cash, so they can buy drugs or hookers or something," Alice said. "Signing up for a dating site seems weird, though. Can't they trace the account to the thief really easily?"

"You'd think. I mean, it's all screen names, but the GPS has to be turned on in your phone to find matches in your range, so I bet they could follow it right to the guy. I made a report to the website and got this canned response." She shook her head and wished for a glass of wine instead of a stress relief booster that was probably going to smell like her eucalyptus foot soak. "I bet they don't do a thing."

Her phone chimed again.

"Do you need to get that?" Sadie asked. "We can wait if you need to put out a few work fires."

"It's just that dating app. I got nervous and needed a distraction while I was waiting to go on for the press conference, so I swiped a whole bunch of profiles and I've been popping up new matches like crazy."

"Do you really have time to date right now?" Alice pulled a lip gloss out of her purse. "I don't even feel like shaving my legs when I'm working the kind of hours you are."

"Yeah, but it's been months since Chad, and more of the good ones are probably getting snatched up every week."

"And you don't want to die alone." Sadie nodded.

"It's not that. I mean, dying's probably going to be pretty sucky no matter who's there. It's all the time leading up to it that bothers me." She slumped, dropping her face into her hand. She'd been thinking about this way too much lately. "I want, I don't know, to be the kind of spunky old lady who would own a wacky parrot. The parrot would say all this random stuff that made no sense so me and my husband would be the only ones who could decode his little phrases. Because I want someone who loves my weird parrot, too. Like, how empty would the world start to feel after a while if nobody else understood what your parrot was saying but you?"

They both stared at her for a second, then Alice said, "Is the parrot a sex metaphor?"

"Ugh, no." She rolled her eyes and pulled out her phone to silence it. "Never mind."

"C'mon, let's see the goods." Alice beckoned, her slender gold watch gleaming.

Harlow shrugged. "Okay, but don't blame me if the goods are odd." She clicked on the notifications for new matches.

Alice leaned in to see the latest one. "Lacrosse Boss, who is fit but trying a little too hard to be sporty." She scrolled past him. "Playa62. Nice pecs but a weird nose and he already messaged to ask what you were doing and oh! You just got a new message."

"From which guy?"

"Hottie with the *eyes*, wow. He calls himself Professional Joker, whatever that means. Hopefully a comedian and not a Dark Knight reference. Fifth new match on the list."

Sadie had pushed up onto her knees by now and was leaning across the table to see. She inhaled audibly. "Is he real? I read sometimes these dating apps put in fake profiles of models to try to make their site look like it has tons of hot people. I know the last girl I went out with from the app looked *nothing* like her picture. The guys I've tried have been more honest about their pics, but not by much."

Harlow tugged her phone away from them and remembered the guy at once. She'd had a similar thought when she'd swiped right on his profile earlier.

Caribbean blue eyes and a mischievous smirk that made her tingle. Messy black hair spraying out from under the edges of a battered charcoal fedora. Weird backdrop choice though, since he was surrounded by industrial-looking chairs and ugly carpet. Most people took their profile selfies out at the beach or the gym or something.

"You've got to double-filter to get eyes like that," she agreed, but her fingers were clicking through to his message as if they didn't share her cynicism.

Professional Joker: Hey, is this thing on?

She smiled. That was a change from the usual Wat up? Or UR so pretty. Or the ever-classic Heyyyyyys or the Heeeeeeeeys. She still wasn't sure which she hated more: the drawn-out y's or e's.

Development Diva: It is indeed on. You type into the tiny rectangle, and hope the genie who lives inside grants your wishes.

Why had she said genie? Now he was going to make a joke about rubbing his "lamp" and she was going to have to block him.

Professional Joker: Dear Rectangle Genie, I would like three million dollars, for my landlady to stop boiling sauerkraut, and to take you out to dinner.

She snorted a laugh.

"I'm going to go see what's taking our drinks so long," Alice said. "Text Blue Eyes something witty from me, hmm?"

Professional Joker: (You of the golden hair and stuffed narwhal you, to be clear, in case the genie is a separate entity.)

Harlow's hand rose to her hair, still smoothed back in its careful press-conference-on-TV-look-older bun. He thought it looked golden? It was on her driver's license as brown, though it was light-ish, and in the summer sometimes it sun-bleached to where she could almost claim blonde, though not without a twinge of imposter syndrome. More tellingly, he must have already dug into the other pictures on her account, not just her profile pic. There was one of her hugging her stuffed narwhal, Henry, that she'd put in because she was laughing and she thought it would make her look fun.

"What did he say?" Sadie had given up leaning and scooted her way around the round booth so she could see.

"He asked me to dinner." Harlow set down her phone, hoping the heat she felt wasn't showing in her cheeks. She'd been in the office so much this summer she barely had any sort of tan to cover it.

"Whoa, already?"

"Too soon." Alice set down a trio of compostable plastic cups.

"I know, right?" Harlow said, stealing one more wistful glance at his profile pic. "He only has one picture up, we've only been chatting for a minute, and he's already skipping coffee and shooting straight for dinner."

"If he only has one pic up, he could be catfishing you with a cologne ad. Did you Google Image search that pic?" Alice took a slurp of her dark green juice.

Harlow grabbed for the purple-tinged cup. "No, but...I don't know, I kind of like that he's not messing around. Plus, the backdrop is too weird for that pic to be an ad. It looks like he's in a doctor's office."

"Maybe he got diagnosed with a fatal illness and you're his YOLO bucket list girl." Sadie smiled over her mega-sized juice. "You'd totally be my YOLO girl, if I were dying."

"I thought Henry Golding was your YOLO guy if you were dying."

"I get both, duh," Sadie said. "I'm the one fictionally dying here."

Harlow laughed, but she was only half paying attention. She didn't want to say no yet, so she messaged back to stall.

Development Diva: Usually people ask the genie for a million. Why triple?

The three dots barely started to bounce before he hit her back.

Professional Joker: Inflation.

Professional Joker: Probably I should have asked for three dates, too, just to be safe. But I figured one date was the wish currency equivalent of three million dollars, so I probably couldn't afford the upgrade.

A laugh tickled at her throat.

Development Diva: But one date with me is also equivalent to the wish currency of changing your landlady's sauerkraut habits?

Professional Joker: You don't understand: there are gallons. Gallons and gallons of sauerkraut every week. I can't prove it, but I think she may be selling commercial without a sauerkraut permit. Also, wish currency exchange rates are complex.

"Let us see," Alice interrupted. "I can spot a scammer a mile away through his DM's."

"Sorry, we were joking about…sauerkraut." That sounded way stranger out loud. Harlow passed over the phone to them with a twinge of reluctance. "Here. What do you think? Is it charming he's moving faster than weeks of digital small talk, or creepy?"

Sadie's eyebrows popped up. "Whoa, these are in complete sentences. *With* punctuation. Oh my God, Harlow, you've got to set a date." She scrolled up. "He used a full colon in its correct context!" She clutched the phone to her chest. "If he whips out a semicolon, I'm gonna put a ring on it, dibs or no."

Harlow extricated the phone from her friend, swapping an amused glance with Alice. "Second opinion?"

"This is the first time I've seen you stop worrying about work in weeks." Alice's voice was gentle. "I'd take it."

Harlow gulped a breath and went for it.

Development Diva: Okay, in the case of gallons of illegal sauerkraut, I'll accept that wish currency exchange rate. Cash flow for

the rectangle genie is not so great right now, so the three mil might take a while. But I think I could deliver on that date. This week maybe?

Was that too pushy? She didn't have much time to think it over, because Professional Joker had fast typing thumbs.

Professional Joker: You free tomorrow? We can meet in the park, and I'll bring dinner.

A few seconds later, a pin popped up with the GPS location of the park.

"He sent GPS." Alice chuckled, reading over her shoulder. "I might as well start shopping for bridesmaid dresses."

Harlow hesitated. Tomorrow. Most guys were afraid of looking too eager, which might mean he was desperate for a hookup, or he might be a freak, or both. She liked that it wasn't the standard date-at-a-restaurant template, though. Her gut said it was fine, but she'd make sure to transfer her pepper spray to her smaller, date-night purse. She took one more glance at his profile picture and her stomach tingled as she began to type.

Development Diva: Your wish is my command.

CHAPTER 3

*H*arlow stepped out of her SUV and smoothed her shorts. The sun was warm against the skin left bare by the silky, boat-necked top that skimmed her elbows. This wasn't her favorite of the local parks in terms of how they'd done the layout, but she liked the big old oaks on the south side, and it was nice to breathe air that hadn't been cooked stale by her office ventilation system.

She started a lap around the edge, looking for her date. By the playground, birds hopped around, competing to peck at the Cheerios thrown by a laughing toddler in his stroller. A smile tickled her lips, and then she spotted Professional Joker shaking out an old quilt under the biggest of the oaks. She registered a lean build, slim hips and quick movements, but it was the orange argyle fedora that made her certain it was her blind date. As soon as he turned around, she caught a toe in the grass and stumbled. No wonder Alice had thought his profile picture was stolen from a cologne ad.

That ridiculous hat lounged in his messy hair like it had been invented to do just that. The narrow brim framed his sharp cheekbones and graceful jawline, his eyes sparkling as his face burst into a grin.

Nobody should look that good in an orange hat.

He started toward her, which was when she realized she had forgotten to keep walking.

"Development Diva?"

She cringed. "I really need to change my screen name. Extra points for saying it with a straight face." She was never sure how to greet app dates. A hug felt like too much, a handshake too little.

He laughed. "Well, we can never get married now. Otherwise, the first words I ever said to you will go down in our personal history as Development Diva."

"Don't DM's count? Then your first words would be something about sauerkraut. Which reminds me, how many gallons did your landlady make today?"

"Enough to fill the trunk of a Honda Civic. Why, can you smell it on me?" He lifted his black tee shirt, pretending to take a sniff, and she got a peek at the sleek abs beneath. He wasn't crazy tall, but he had a few inches on her, and an agile way of moving that made it easy to picture him on a snowboard, or maybe a dance floor.

"Well, I assumed that's why you wanted to meet outside. Living in a sauerkraut factory takes a little airing out."

He winked. "You caught me. Plus, even cheap food tastes better in the fresh air. I hope Thai is okay."

"Thai is perfection." Especially since she'd worked through lunch to get off in time for this picnic.

He tipped a hand toward the quilt and cooler he had laid out, his opposite fingers just brushing her shoulder as he guided her that way.

Even in the heat, her skin tingled with goosebumps, and she realized they'd bantered right through the hug/handshake dilemma. She'd say this for the guy—he was easy to talk to. Maybe it was the argyle hat.

"So should we exchange real names now," she asked as she settled herself on the quilt, "or are you one of those who holds off until no-stalker potential has been clearly established?"

"Wait, I was sort of hoping for stalker potential. Are you saying you aren't interested in stalking me?"

"I mean, you haven't inspired my undying love just yet, so I don't want to necessarily commit to burning the gas money. Plus, do you know what they charge for those big cameras with the stalker lenses? Ruinous."

"There are always clearance sales." He sat cross-legged on the blanket and stuck out his hand. "Bishop Riley, un-inspirer of undying love and procurer of Thai food."

"You lost me on all those double negatives. But I'm Harlow Rimes. Planner of neighborhoods and devourer of Thai food."

He frowned, his hand lingering on hers but softening from their first firm clasp. "I swear I've heard that name somewhere."

Her smile faded. "Probably on the news. My boss got our company into a real mess and I've been left picking up the pieces."

"Damn. Isn't that always the way it works, though?"

She shook it off. "I didn't come here to talk about my work drama, though. If my friends could hear me, they'd be rolling their eyes that I made it less than five minutes before bringing up the catastrophe."

"Drinks, then. I mix a Moscow Mule specifically calibrated to erase work-related stress." He flipped the cooler lid open and took out a chilled metal water bottle. "Your cup, milady." He filled her a travel mug with a wild floral pattern and swirly lettering that proclaimed, *Give me tea or give me death!*

"Uh..." Harlow had a quick internal debate. She didn't want to be that girl and kill the mood, but she really didn't want to be *that* girl who got roofied in a park. "Sorry, but I'm really not going to take an unsealed drink from a guy I just met."

"Oh!" He'd already poured his own into a black mug that said *Pinkies up, bitches. It's tea time.* He looked at it, then traded her cups.

She hesitated.

Bishop smiled. "But clearly, you cannot also drink the drink in front of me, because a roofier would have predicted that you would switch. Of course, you would have predicted that I predicted that, so clearly you cannot drink the drink originally in front of you."

"Inconceivable!" she quoted, relaxing again. "Do you have that whole *Princess Bride* skit memorized?"

"Please. I have a younger sister. I've read the book aloud, memorized the movie, and dressed in its costumes for Halloween. Also, to be fair, that was heavily paraphrased."

"Are you a Westley or an Inigo?"

"Rodent of Unusual Size, unfortunately. Much less dashing."

She choked on laughter, and he rescued the mug from her hand right before it started to tip. He took a drink from both, then offered the choice of mugs to her.

"I've also got bottled water, if you'd rather. Like I said, I have a little sister. If I ever saw a guy drugging a woman, I would invent a machine of inconceivable pain specifically for him."

It wasn't just the hat that was making her comfortable, she decided. It might be the eyes, too. His lashes were dark and velvety, framing bright blue eyes she couldn't stop stealing peeks at. She took the cup and squeezed it, trying to ignore the tingles that ran from her fingers all the way down into her heart.

It was way too early to decide she liked this guy. Even if he did happen to be just the teensiest bit charming.

Bishop did not remember first dates being this fun. He remembered the kissing part being fun. He definitely remembered the hooking up part being a great time. But he hadn't met a girl who made him laugh so easily in years, much less one who could keep up with his jokes.

He could get used to that.

"So is the Thai food in there, too?" She peeked toward the cooler and took a sip of her drink, which made his chest flex with masculine pride. It was probably stupid to be glad that she trusted him not to roofie her, but he liked it when women got comfortable. That's when they were the cutest: all messy ponytails and yoga pants and soft eyes. Now that he was thinking about it, he missed that part of dating, too.

"Nope, food's coming courtesy of Door Dart. Figured it'd be warmer that way." And unlike restaurants, the online delivery services let you keep a credit card number on file without producing the physical card. Hence the "romantic" date in the park that *was* actually turning out to be a little romantic.

It didn't hurt that Harlow Rimes was glowingly pretty.

She was all gold. Long, light brown hair in shades like a wheat field, eyes one shade warmer. Slender legs and competent fingers with one tiny ring with a rough-cut rock of crystal on a twisted rose-gold band that graced her right hand.

While he was lost in thought, those golden-brown eyes had wandered from him and now were narrowing on the nearby playground.

"You know if you keep staring at those kids, the parents are going to get nervous."

She flushed. "Sorry, occupational hazard. I was thinking how stupid it was that they put the shade structure over the playground and left the benches out in the full sun so the parents would fry while they were waiting. When they could have bumped them back a few feet and had them under the branches of those trees."

"Harlow Rimes, neighborhood planner," he remembered. "Does that include designing playgrounds?"

"It includes designing most everything. I work for a developer and we create planned neighborhoods." She broke off as if she'd been about to launch into a longer speech and toyed with her drink instead. That probably meant some self-centered douchebag had said her job was boring at some point. But the idea of creating neighborhoods felt warm to him, like a sip of hot chocolate.

"How does that work? Are you designing the houses, or the parks, or the streets, or…?"

"Some of all of it. The architects do the blueprints, but we can give feedback on the big picture. For instance, we did an outdoor-themed community and I made sure all the floor plan options had a mudroom where you could store boots and jackets, add a rack for mountain bikes, that kind of thing."

He stretched out on his side and propped his head up on his palm. "That's smart. I never would have thought of that."

She waved a hand. "Eh, it's kind of my job."

He almost frowned. Who had knocked down her confidence so much that she downplayed a career that she obviously loved?

"So how would you have done this park differently, other than the benches?" he prompted.

Her gaze flicked across the scenery, and she twisted to see behind them. "Well, I would have moved the bike rack to the edge, not the center, so bikers could use it to access local businesses, too. For this close to the college campus, I probably would have put a Frisbee golf course in that back corner instead of soccer fields, because there are already soccer fields in this neighborhood. Plus an acoustic wall so we could have attracted more music-based events." Her voice had dropped, becoming more earnest, and her eyes were far away. "The more opportunities you give a community to come together, the closer people get and the better the whole place works."

"There's a lot to this stuff. I wouldn't have thought about it that way." This was only one park. He couldn't even imagine how much went into planning a whole neighborhood. This woman was not just sharp, but *wicked* smart. Fuck, he was so here for that he was all but panting.

"A bit, yeah." She blushed. "So what do you do?"

Aaand that was the slap in the face that he needed to remind him of his less-shiny reality. He plucked a few strands of grass, piling them at the edge of the blanket. "Actually, I write jokes for a living."

"You're a stand-up comedian? Like Dave Chappelle?" She lit up.

"Not exactly." Doing stand-up comedy was a career that required planning and ambition and a whole grab-bag of other things his class clown childhood hadn't prepared him for. "You know those little messages you get on the app when you swipe a new picture?"

"You write those? No way!"

He'd had regular jobs, of course, but he'd lost one after another thanks to his erratic schedule of driving Daisy to chemo or doc appointments. And the times he had to stay at the house for a few days if she was doing bad when Dad was out of town for work and Mom was down with another migraine.

Now that he'd hacked his way into a felonious new source of

income, his freelance gig was a cover story so he had an excuse for where his money came from, and a clean way to pay for his apartment. Rent and utilities were two of the only things you couldn't pay with anonymous online accounts. Unfortunately, jokes didn't cover a whole apartment with the rising Austin prices, so he Ubered, Lyfted, and managed other peoples' WebBnB listings for a fee.

"So how did you—" she began, and thankfully, a skinny guy with two white paper bags approached just then.

"Are you Bishop?"

"I certainly am, my good man." He completed the transaction on his phone with a generous tip courtesy of somebody who was about to get a fraud alert phone call, and got to work laying out the food.

"Red pepper chicken or pork pad thai?" Her eyes darted back and forth between the containers, and he nearly groaned when she took the chicken. His willpower only lasted about two minutes before he snagged a piece.

"Oh, you started it now." She leaned over and stole a bite of his pad thai, wrapping the rice noodles around her fork with an expert twist before she dropped them into her mouth. "Your food is never going to be safe from me."

He grinned. "Maybe I don't want it to be." He always wanted to try everybody's food. It had driven his mom and a couple of his ex-girlfriends crazy, but apparently not this woman. Bishop was trying very hard not to imagine how Harlow would look in a pair of yoga pants.

She cocked her head at him, her ponytail falling to skim her right hip. "So, do you get an employee discount on your Match account for writing their jokes?"

"Actually, this is my first date off the app."

"What? More of a Tinder person, then?"

"I've been off the market." Ah, how to put it? Mention of his sister's tumor surgery killed any conversation dead. "Didn't want to subject poor women to these devastating good looks." He grinned outrageously so she'd know he was joking. "Left a trail of hearts through my college career and my karma's still healing."

"Through college? Oh God, how young are you?"

"Twenty-three. Not even close to jailbait, no worries. You?"

"Twenty-seven."

"Bah." He waved his fork. "Not even enough of an age gap for you to count as an affair with a more experienced woman. My loss."

"Is that your type? Older, sexually predatory women?"

"If it's not yet, it should be." He winked. "What's your type?"

She snorted. "Well, my last boyfriend did nothing but sit on my couch and play video games. He'd always swear he was looking for jobs all day and could I spot him his half of the rent this one time? While my boss got me to do all the work and took all the credit so… yup, that's apparently my type. Which is why I'm on the app, looking to start fresh."

"Oh, I am so your type." He stole another bite of her chicken and laughed. "I'm a broke college dropout living on side-hustles." He flared his eyes at her. "Are you swooning yet?"

She choked, sputtering with laughter until she had to grab another sip of Moscow Mule. "My taste is so consistent, it's terrifying. Wait, are you joking? You're not joking, are you?"

"Want to see my student loan statements? Bet they're even bigger than your ex's."

"Oh my gosh, we really are the worst match ever, aren't we?" She covered her mouth with her hand, eyes dancing.

"The worst. We're the modern version of star-crossed lovers. You're a very competent woman and I'm a deeply incompetent gentleman."

Which was probably why he found her so mouthwateringly sexy. Ah well, life wasn't fair, but it was frequently funny. He could roll with that.

A bee landed on her travel mug and he waved a hand to warn it away. "Clearly this date is going to end in the Fake Friendzone, so you might as well relax and enjoy the food."

"What's the Fake Friendzone?" She shifted on the quilt, and it was probably just his wishful thinking that was reading disappointment in her expression.

Didn't every guy think he'd found his dream girl on the first date?

He'd been spending too much time watching Disney movies with Daisy if he had forgotten for an instant that reality was anything but a cold, con-artist bitch. The truth was that Harlow was a career woman with a brain as big as his student loans, and he was just the wannabe comedian who could never aspire to be more than her couch-surfing ex.

"That's when we say we're going to be just friends, agree warmly, and never call each other again." He held up his mug for a toast, ignoring the squeeze in his chest that was probably only heartburn from the Thai peppers. This app dating thing had only been for casual fun anyway; long-term girlfriends were a luxury afforded only to people with no ongoing felonies to hide.

Harlow pursed her lips and considered him. "You're not even in for group brunch two weeks later? Because I thought that was the agreed-upon transition into the friendzone, and boyfriend potential or not, we were getting along pretty well."

He zeroed in on her, his heart literally skipping a beat. "Wait, did you say brunch? Are you a brunch person?"

She scoffed. "Is that even a question?"

"I love brunch," he declared, sitting up so he could wave his cup for emphasis. "Brunch does not love me. Why didn't we meet for brunch? Then I could at least justify it to myself as overspending to impress a girl."

"I thought you were trying to friendzone me. Are you trying to impress me, instead?"

"Clearly not, or I'd have taken you to brunch!" he sputtered, and she burst into a fresh round of giggles.

By the time it was starting to shade toward twilight, Bishop's stomach hurt from laughing and he'd decided his little sister was completely right about casual dating. It was fun as hell and he intended to do a lot more of it. Especially with incredible, multi-talented women like Harlow who would immediately write him off as unsuitable so he wouldn't have to let them down later.

She helped him fold up the blanket, and he walked her back to her car.

SO YOU THINK YOU'RE A MATCH?

"Milady," he said and bowed over her hand, laying a kiss on her soft skin that made electricity spark and sizzle all the way down his back. "Your company was a pleasure, and it will be an honor residing in your Fake Friendzone."

She grinned, her eyes lingering on him a little longer before she opened her door. "Goodnight, Bishop."

"Goodnight, Harlow." Her name rolled off his tongue, as curvy and golden as the rest of her, and the sound seemed to knock something loose in his brain.

His eyes widened, and as soon as she drove away, he turned and broke into a jog. When he got to his car, he opened his laptop on the passenger seat and clicked on a password-protected spreadsheet.

He didn't even have to scroll because her name was sitting right on top of the new batch of credit card numbers, an X next to it to show the card had already been used up and cancelled by its rightful owner.

"Well, shit." He shoved a hand back through his hair, knocking his hat onto the ground. Thank God they'd friendzoned each other. Because he was worse than a deadbeat boyfriend: he was a thief. *Her* thief.

CHAPTER 4

*H*arlow hauled her purse out from under her desk and hooked it over her shoulder, then smoothed the slacks she always wore on visitation days, even in the heat of the summer.

"You taking off early?" her office-mate, Emilia, asked without looking up from her screen.

"Dentist."

Emilia swiveled in her desk chair, feathered earrings swinging. "You have the cleanest teeth of anybody in this office, I swear. What is that, your third cleaning this year? Fourth?"

Harlow's fingers inched toward the bullet journal in her purse, but she couldn't check it for last month's excuse while Emilia was watching.

"You're sneaking out early for a date, aren't you?" Emilia grinned and gave her desk chair a kick that rolled her across the room closer to Harlow. "I've seen you swiping up a storm lately."

The last thing she needed was any hint of impropriety at work right now, with the big Sunnybrooke presentation coming up on Monday. HR had approved her for flex-time and she came in early on these Fridays so she could leave early, but reputations were built on rumors, not on reviewing her time cards. Harlow made a snap decision and nodded, not having to fake her blush.

"Yup. A Krav Maga instructor I met on that new app."

Her date was actually tomorrow night, but if Emilia felt like she was getting the inside scoop, she'd be less likely to go snooping about the fake dentist appointment. Harlow had never really gotten too into app dating, mostly only picking up a date here and there when she was bored. But her picnic in the park with Bishop the other day had sparked something. If there were guys that cool on the app—genuine, actually honest guys—maybe it was worth weeding through a few first dates. Even if not all of them led to something, Bishop had proved to her that it didn't have to be awkward or all full of pressure. It could just be...fun. Hence why she already had another match set up so soon.

Emilia pointed at her.

"I want all the details on Monday. Text me over the weekend if it's really juicy."

"Got it. But not a word about me sneaking out early." Harlow laid a finger across her mouth.

Emilia mimed locking her lips. "Nobody wants to have to report to Bill Dumpling for the Sunnybrooke neighborhood. Jeez, that man is boring. I'll do anything I can to keep you looking squeaky clean for that promotion."

Harlow smiled her thanks, and then hurried out down the corridor. Normally, she loved strolling these halls, with their big framed prints of sunny neighborhoods and playgrounds and forest walking trails. It was the world she helped build, and the three-dimensional embodiment of the childhood she had always wanted to have. The hallways of her office were like a bridge between her fantasy world and her reality. But this was the Friday of the month when the unframeworthy parts of her reality intruded the most undeniably into the better life she'd tried to build for herself after it all came apart senior year of high school.

Her destination was an hour's drive away and when she got there, she parked in the same far corner she always parked in, trying to keep her pristine paint protected from people scratching it by throwing their doors open and leaving in a huff. It was the kind of place that encouraged a stressful afternoon.

She kept her head down as she hurried up the sidewalk, leaving her purse behind because it would make her trip through security quicker.

Inside, it sounded as industrial as it smelled. Everything echoed because it was a square building full of square rooms without a single soft surface anywhere. Which was maybe why her whole apartment was a sanctuary decorated in Crate and Barrel throw pillows and artfully draped blankets in blues and creams. Not a single shade that was found in the industrial tiles and Formicas of this place. Buzzers blared from deeper in the building as doors were electronically opened and closed. As she navigated the corridors with the handful of other people here for the same thing, she couldn't ignore the ticking of the round plastic clocks they used in every room.

She imagined if she was stuck here, those clocks would underline every second of her punishment, rubbing like jaggedly-ground rock salt into the open wound of her failure. Harlow took shallow breaths, trying not to appear nervous. She would never have to be trapped in a place like this. All she had to do was follow the rules. Anybody could do that. It was as simple as making a sandwich.

When she got to the visiting room, her dad was already waiting at one of the round, cheap tables. He lit up to see her, his neatly trimmed beard and bright eyes looking as glowingly healthy as they always had. It seemed like he should be bedraggled, with bloodshot eyes mirroring the suffering of nearly a decade in prison. It wasn't as if the cafeteria served the organic vegan food he preferred, though they did have an inmate gardening program he'd practically been running since his first summer here.

"Hey, love bug!" He beamed.

She hugged him, aware as always of the guard's eyes scrutinizing their embrace. "Hey, Dad. Everything going okay?"

"Well, my radishes could have turned out better, but…" He shrugs. "They don't let me order the fertilizers that would really work."

"That's too bad. Budgets and all, I'm sure. Before I forget, what do you have for Mom this time?"

She pulled out the scrap of paper and guard-approved crayon she brought for her monthly visit. She always visited her Dad before making the drive to Mom's prison because Dad was usually either genuinely cheerful, or made an effort to fake it. Whereas Mom hated her daughter visiting her in prison. It nearly always ended in tears, and Harlow's inadequate attempts to comfort her. But then, lying and saying it was all okay and didn't bother her…she didn't think it fooled either of them. If she went to see Mom first, she would never have had the emotional energy to visit Dad afterwards.

"Oh, I've got a good one this week. Let me know when you're ready."

Her parents had earned the warden's permission to exchange letters between their prisons, but Dad always liked to send a little message along to Mom through her—their messed-up version of family bonding. Sometimes it was a song or a riddle, but most often they were bad jokes.

"Fire away." She kept her crayon poised.

"What does a vegetarian zombie eat?"

She scribbled it down and waited, only belatedly realizing he was waiting for her to play along. She crossed her legs more tightly and tried not to look at the loudly ticking clock. "What?"

"GRAAAAAAIIIIIIIINNNNNSSSS," Dad zombie-moaned.

Her lips twitched toward a smile, then she remembered where they were and glanced around, blushing to see if anybody was bothered by their noise. Dad had always had a horrible pun on hand to make her smile when she was growing up. She hated the way it cheapened those memories to have him tell her jokes here, with all the guards watching to see if she'd aid and abet some kind of criminal enterprise.

But of course she wouldn't tell him to stop, not when the jokes always made Mom smile. It was so rare these days to see a couple who'd been married nearly thirty years, and her parents had managed to make it, even with spending the last nine years locked up apart.

Mom saved every message in Harlow's careful crayon handwriting like they were some sort of arts-and-crafts project.

"I'll make sure to do the voice for her," Harlow promised as she tucked away the message and straightened to face him. "So, what have you been up to lately?"

"The usual. The garden's nearly all harvested for the season, so I've been reading quite a bit. I've come across a lot of really great stuff about permaculture and rotational crops to rejuvenate your soil. I was thinking, when I'm out next summer I can try some of them on a smaller scale, in flower beds until we're able to get some acreage again."

She stared at him. "Wait, you've been reading all these books so you can start—" She almost said "growing pot" before she realized that the guards could overhear. "*Gardening* again?" she hissed under her breath. "Are you kidding me?"

"A lot of things have changed, sweetheart. They're decriminalizing all over the country, and it's recreational legal in more states after every election."

She couldn't believe he was openly admitting it. To her, and especially in front of the guards, even if there were only two of them, looking half-asleep as they slumped on the far side of the room.

"Of course, I wouldn't grow until it was legal here." His smile pulled tight. "The garden's helped, but it's not as if I've enjoyed my time here quite *that* much."

She didn't believe him. Her dad had never been able to let go of a project until it was done. If he was researching this much, he was planning on doing it whether it was legal or not, and she knew good and well he and Mom would never move out of Texas if she was still here.

"Haven't you? Because it wasn't enough that you've missed my entire adult life, my graduation from high school *and* college, that I had to spend my senior year living with strangers because you and Mom were both in jail? After all that, you'd still risk it all for a *plant?*"

His jaw tensed. "It's not evil, Harlow. It's a million times better than alcohol, with so many applications to help people, and alcohol is perfectly legal. Aren't you old enough now to stop being so judg-mental about all of this?"

She coughed out a disbelieving breath, the tears welling up despite her attempts to blink them away.

"Ahh, honey, don't cry." He scooted his chair. "Listen, I wasn't plan-ning to jump back into anything. Let me explain—"

"No." She shot to her feet. "If that's how you're still thinking, after all we've been through because of a stupid 'plant,' then we have nothing to say to each other. You can follow the laws and have a family, or you can break them, and you can have *this*." She threw her hand out at the industrial room and uniformed prison guards. "You pick."

She whirled away and headed out of the room, pretending not to see how the guards straightened up and eyed her like she might become a security risk. She'd worked so hard for her entire high school career. Done all the AP classes, all the extra-curriculars. Followed every rule and kept her clothes in the trunk of her car so they wouldn't pick up the scent of her parents' grow house.

If you played by the rules and planned ahead, you got the life you wanted. If you let the wrong people into that life, they ruined everything.

She swept out of the prison and out into the sun, yanking the note and her last crayon out of her pocket and chucking them in the closest trash can. No way could she face visiting her mother after all that. They'd just end up fighting, and crying, and if Dad already planned on growing again, Mom probably did, too. They were like peas in a pod, they'd been married so long.

But screw them. She had a life now, a home that couldn't be confiscated by the cops as evidence, and she was *thisclose* to getting promoted into her dream job. She had a sudden urge to knock on wood. What if Emilia told someone she ditched work early to go on a date? She was perfectly within her flex hours to leave early today, but so much of this promotion rested on office politics that even gossip could sink her.

She hurriedly unlocked her car and scrabbled for her phone. There were only two notifications—one a get-them-girl good luck text from Emilia, and one private message on her So You Think You're A Match app. From Professional Joker.

A bolt of heat washed through her, taking her dress-code-approved cardigan from uncomfortable to stifling. She flung it into the back seat before she clicked into the app. Why was Bishop messaging her, after he'd made a point of joking about how they'd never talk to each other again? Had he changed his mind? Maybe hadn't been able to stop thinking about her... They *had* gotten along really well, and the chemistry was—well, but he was the sort of guy who probably had chemistry with an umbrella stand. She shook off her fantasies and opened the message. It was probably going to be a dick pic, thus destroying all her newfound faith in decent men having dating app profiles.

Professional Joker: You have done me a disservice, ma'am.

Was he actually mad? The ma'am sounded kinda flirty.

Development Diva: Oh? Do tell.

Professional Joker: Exhibit A.

A second later, a picture appeared on her screen. It was a Post-it note, in loopy feminine handwriting, that said: *This is where we'll cuddle on the couch, watching the holographic Matlock reboot together when we're old.*

Development Diva: That is...the strangest accusatory IM and Post-it I've ever received.

Professional Joker: Oh, it gets better. This is the one I woke up to. Enjoy Exhibit B.

This picture was a new Post-it, same handwriting, this time centered on a pillow on an unmade futon. *This is where we'll rip the pillow having our first wild time in bed together.*

Development Diva: Okay, rewind, rewind. I'm assuming this is your apartment, but Bishop, you don't think I actually found your place, broke in, and left you a bunch of stalker Post-its, do you?

Her head was starting to hurt. This day was really not going her way. If Sadie was still on her alcohol cleanse, maybe Alice would get a real drink with her. She cranked on the car engine and turned up the

AC, hoping the cessation of heat would help. Even in early September, the Austin sun had her car hot enough to bake brownies in the glove box.

Professional Joker: Oh no, I know it wasn't you. Though your crime was nearly as bad. You made me think app date women were sweet, unthreatening. Not even the least bit Post-it stalkerish. So I ran right out and tried a second app date and BAM. Post-it hell. Plus, she used all my Post-its so now I have nothing to write on to remind myself to buy more Post-its.

Harlow scoffed out a laugh, smiling as she typed.

Development Diva: Double Post-it hell.

Professional Joker: Exactly!

It was kind of cute that she'd inspired him to date more, too, despite their amicable friendzoning. Though wow, he was definitely a fast mover if he'd already met someone else he liked enough to take back to his place. Why hadn't he tried to take her back to his place? Not that she would have accepted on the first date, but still.

Development Diva: So you took an app date home, and she did...this. Except where were you? How did you not notice her rampaging with the Post-its?

Professional Joker: Well, we met for drinks, she wanted to watch a movie but said she hated the theater, cited fears of popcorn lung. So I gallantly offered my place for the little watch party, but I was up late working last night because the golden hour for writing jokes is like 3 am with a fresh pot of coffee. And I own it, I was an asshole, I fell asleep on her halfway through the movie.

Harlow shut her car door so the cooler air wouldn't escape, but before she could respond he hit her back.

Professional Joker: Apparently, she was watching me sleep and she was...overcome by romantic feelings? I don't know how, I'm not a handsome sleeper. Just ask my little sister.

Development Diva: Was she still there when you found all the Post-its? What did she say??!

Professional Joker: No, she let herself out. We didn't even kiss! Not even a walk to first base, and somehow it led to this:

This picture was of a refrigerator, with a half-empty bottle of generic OJ and a Post-it reading: *This is where I will put my juice next to your juice.*

Harlow burst out laughing, picturing his wide eyes upon finding this really very bold juice proposal.

Development Diva: I guess now wouldn't be the right time to remind you that you told me you were hoping to inspire stalker potential.

Professional Joker: Cold. So cold, Harlow. Especially since I was hoping for stalker potential in YOU, my poster child of charming, non-psycho-eyed playground-planning app date normalcy. Not stalker potential in actual stalkers.

Development Diva: You Fake Friendzoned me first!

She glanced out the window, fighting a smile even though there was no one watching. Maybe he hadn't thought she was too gross to ask back to his place. Not that she cared. Still, it was nice to know he had been as genuine as he seemed when he declared them a match made in hell.

Professional Joker: It was for your own good. You really need to set your dial higher than broke-asses like me. Unless you get turned on by guys asking for a loan because rent is coming up really fast and Ms. Post-it Proposal ordered a twelve-dollar cocktail for our get-to-know-you drink last night.

Development Diva: Nah, I'm good. But definitely hit me up the next time I'm doing laundry, to see if I want to haul 3 loads of yours all the way to the laundromat, down the elevator from the parking garage and around the block, to just "throw it in" with mine. Three loads. Zero quarters ponied. Stain remover necessitated.

Professional Joker: That did not really happen to you. Tell me that didn't happen to you.

Development Diva: Ex-boyfriend...I think it was 4 guys ago? Yup yup.

Professional Joker: You're so lucky I Fake Friendzoned you. It's super close to laundry day. Though I feel honor-bound to state that

nothing in my basket requires too-intimate stain removering. I may be a deadbeat, but I'm a hygienic deadbeat.

Development Diva: A hygienic deadbeat with a shiny new fiancé, I'm afraid. Have you checked your left hand for territorial Post-its?

Professional Joker: I've checked all my private areas for Post-its, Harlow, and it's been very traumatizing. Which is why I blame you personally for the disservice of setting my guard so far down after my first app date.

Development Diva: After that story, I am almost sorry.

Professional Joker: At least tell me you're off having some glorious date in a French restaurant dripping with crystal chandeliers, so I know the app isn't a total failure.

Her eyes stung anew, reminding her of how crappy her day had been before his dating bloopers had provided some much-needed comic relief.

Development Diva: Visiting hours at the prison, actually.

Professional Joker: Whoa, your dating situation is even more dismal than mine. Which makes me feel...better? No, worse. Definitely worse.

Development Diva: It's nbd. I've got a date with a Krav Maga instructor tomorrow. No matter how crappy it is, it's gonna feel like a success after hearing about your Post-it anti-love story, so thx for that.

Professional Joker: Happy to be of service. If there's one thing I excel at, it's setting the bar comfortably low for others. ;)

Development Diva: What about you? What are you going to do about your Post-it soul mate?

Professional Joker: Delete the app. Change my locks in case she made a copy of my key while I was sleeping. Repent of all my life choices.

If he deleted the app, that meant they'd never talk again. It's not like she had his phone number. Harlow looked up from her phone, staring out at the barren expanse of sun-scorched parking lot. Which was fine. Staying friends after one date was something you said, not something anybody did.

Development Diva: Sounds smart. Well anyway, it was nice knowing you! Make good choices, and don't let strange women into your apartment with Sharpies and stationery.

Professional Joker: Ah, and where were you with your sterling life advice yesterday? Good luck with the Krav Maga instructor. Break a...well, whatever intimate parts you break for good luck in a dating scenario.

She didn't realize she'd been smiling at his texts until she clicked off her phone and the expression started to fade. She hadn't thought she'd hear from him again even once, but his timing was amazing because she'd really needed that laugh. And actually, she was feeling a little better. Maybe she'd still visit her mom today after all.

CHAPTER 5

*B*ishop knew he was a bad person. He'd known this for quite some time. Good people did not hate their parents when their parents hadn't, for instance, locked them in the vegetable drawer or forced them to take viola lessons.

Good people did not steal. Especially not repeatedly and with only fleeting and momentary remorse.

He flipped his phone up into the air, caught it, and stuffed it into his pocket before sinking onto his unmade futon, shoving both hands back through his hair with a groan.

Good people did not text women from whom they had stolen. Not even from the safety of the friendzone. Not even when they were alone in a shitty apartment with a late rent notice taped to the door, surrounded by psycho girl Post-its.

He hadn't intended to ever message her again. He'd had one of his rare pangs of conscience over their date, and the irony of her money paying for his dating app subscription, while someone else's stolen card had paid for their Door Dart dinner. Even this morning when he woke up to the first Post-it, he'd thought, "Shit, that's weird," and dashed out to clean one of the WebBnBs he managed for extra cash.

But then he'd gotten home, his back aching and hands smelling of bleach, and found five even creepier Post-its around his apartment.

It was one of those moments where he was either going to get really depressed, or find a way to laugh about it. He'd been thinking about Harlow, and how differently *their* date had gone, and had a feeling she'd get a kick out of the pictures. Which she had, but he really needed to leave her alone now. He snatched a Post-it off his crumpled pillow and folded the comforter away so the futon would look like a regular couch again. Passed his card table "dining room" with its curbside reject office chair and snatched another Post-it off its water-damaged cushion. He'd already tossed the one from inside the fridge, along with last week's Chinese takeout. But when he reached the one on top of his cinder-block-and-boards shelving unit, Bishop stopped, his fist curling closed around the yellow paper.

How fucking lonely was this Post-it woman that her fantasy life included moving into *this* dump? Especially after only one date that he'd mostly slept through? He'd been nice to her, of course, flirting over drinks and letting her set the pace of any contact during the movie. Now, seeing the desperation in the notes she'd left him, it made him wish he'd been extra sweet to her when he had the chance. Not that he intended to see her again. He was brave, but not *that* brave.

How could she look at this place and see any kind of future? He sure didn't. He'd given up on the kind of life where you planned for the future right around the time he cashed his financial aid check during senior year and gave it all to Daisy's surgeon.

He'd tried once, a while later when he was dating Maggie. She was a nursing assistant with a strawberry blonde ponytail all the way down to her ass and a huge laugh. They used to go to open mike sessions on the weekends because she was trying to break into stand-up comedy. He'd dated her after the six months of sleeping in his car, when he realized no job he could get was enough to pay his bills when his wages were garnished so heavily for all the debt that was starting to go to collections. It took him a minute to realize he could code his way out of sleeping in his car if he was willing to steal other people's cards, and another minute to figure out how to funnel the money through LegUp and PhonePay.

However, he hadn't been that good at covering his tracks, because Maggie had started to get suspicious about why he could take her out —but only to places that took PhonePay—even when he could barely pay his rent. That was when he stopped trying to have friends.

Plans and futures and lives with decorated apartments were for women like Harlow. She wouldn't be on this dating app for long. He'd bet his laptop that if he looked for her profile next year it'd already be deleted. He just hoped she wouldn't run into too many dick-pic-sending idiots before then. Or Post-it stalkers.

The vague smell of sauerkraut and mildew was tormenting him again. No matter how much he scoured this place, he'd never managed to knock out the source of that smell. Time to get the hell out of the house before he got mopey and was tempted to start text-flirting with out-of-his-league women again.

He snatched up his gym bag and headed for the door.

After a couple of pickup basketball games and a hard sweat, he felt a whole hell of a lot better. Bishop jogged back to the sidelines, snatching up his water bottle and draining it. One of the day's team-mates followed him over, the one who'd made that nothing-but-net shot that ended the game. Dude had a couple of inches on him and tattoos ringing both biceps—some classy art, though, not those old barbed wire tats he saw some douchebags sporting. Tats slapped him a high five before going for his own water bottle.

"Good game."

"Damn right." Bishop shot a glance to make sure the rest of the guys weren't within earshot. "Well, for us anyway."

The other guy snorted a laugh. He was the only one who'd scored a point all night, other than Bishop. That was the crapshoot of a pickup game. Sometimes you grabbed a player that wiped the floor with you and sometimes you spent all night slow-jogging around behind the paunchy middle-aged set, wishing you could pour a Red Bull down their throats to make things more interesting.

"Hey, man," Tats said. "A group of us plays on Wednesday nights.

You should come. Maybe we could finish with a decent score for once."

Bishop hooked a thumb at the court. "Not if you've got many of these clowns playing."

The taller guy laughed. "No shit. But only one of these guys is part of that group, and he doesn't always suck as bad as he did today." He held out his hand. "My name's Samwise. You can just call me embarrassed for short."

Bishop gripped his hand. "Nerd parents? Say no more, Sam. I'm Bishop."

"Chess nerd parents?"

"Nah, think they just had hopes I'd turn out a lot more holy than I did."

Sam smirked and slung his gym bag over his shoulder. "Wednesday nights, seven or so. I'll see you there."

"Yeah, maybe." His smile faded. The kind of friends you saw on a regular basis were for other people. Law-abiding people with nothing to hide. "Not sure I'm free on Wednesdays, but we'll see."

CHAPTER 6

*D*evelopment Diva: You have done me a disservice, sir.

Professional Joker: Krav Maga instructor date was a bust, eh?

Professional Joker: Were there Post-its? We could get the two of them together, leave a trail of Post-its right to a wedding chapel. Lure them into their stalker soulmate happily ever after.

Development Diva: By the power invested in me by the Match app, I bind these two in holy matrimony. Using very light adhesive.

Professional Joker: Wait, are you already home? By 7:30 on a Saturday night? That *is* bad.

Development Diva: No, hiding in the bathroom because I need a break. He spent the first fifteen minute explaining his knee problem, then his gastrointestinal struggles, then this rash he's been having.

Professional Joker: Did you wash your hands?

Development Diva: Twice.

Professional Joker: I'm not sure what disservice I did you, though, because there's no way dating me set your expectations for app matches too *high*. My superpower is kind of the opposite.

Development Diva: But you were funny! And not disgusting!

Professional Joker: LOL See, I told you I set the bar low.

Development Diva: Not low enough.

Professional Joker: Can I interest you in hearing about my food allergies?

Development Diva: LOL!

Professional Joker: Want me to come get you? I can play a mean Uber driver...

Professional Joker: Mostly because I *am* an Uber driver

Development Diva: No, I should give him a second chance. I'm probably being too picky. I mean, twenty minutes isn't long enough to really get to know a person. He does teach women's self-defense classes. Anybody who does that can't be too awful.

Professional Joker: Okay, but if you need a rescue, our secret signal is "Would you like to schedule a ride?"

Development Diva: Very subtle. They'll never guess.

Professional Joker: And I'll feel virtuous for working on a Saturday night.

Development Diva: Win/win

Professional Joker: Go get 'em, Tiger.

Development Diva: Mayday, mayday. Schedule a ride. SCHEDULE A RIDE!

Professional Joker: Um, you may have mistaken which app you were supposed to do that in.

Development Diva: So you chat up all your old app dates in hopes of drumming up ride share business? Seems kinda labor intensive in terms of marketing strategy, but okay.

Professional Joker: No, that was a joke. I do really drive for Uber but I wouldn't actually charge you. You were joking, too, right? Do you really need me to come get you? Did he try something?

Development Diva: Nah, I'm already home. I was joking, too.

Professional Joker: Wow, I need to change my screen name.

And profession. First rule of comedy is if you have to say "Get it?" the answer is no.

Professional Joker: You kind of got my pulse going with the caps lock, though. Dude who teaches Krav Maga could be a real handful if he turned out to be a douche.

Development Diva: No, sorry. That was a joke, too. Fortunately landing a punchline isn't a requirement of my screen name or profession.

Professional Joker: Thanks for the free cardio, though. I take it he moved on from rashes to discussions of oozing sores?

Development Diva: Nope, dove right into quizzing me on all my past relationships and why they didn't work out. Straight up asked me why we broke up. Not just for my last boyfriend, but like, the full catalogue all the way back to sophomore year of college.

Professional Joker: He stopped before freshman year? Everybody knows freshman breakups are the real measure of whether a woman is meant to be the other half of your wedding napkin monogram.

Development Diva: He probably would have gone there. I left after sophomore.

Professional Joker: Yikes. Guess there was no need to ask why *his* past relationships didn't work out.

Development Diva: Yup.

Development Diva: Wow, there's nothing to make you feel quite so much like a failure as having your romantic history judged by a guy who brought his own bib to dinner.

Professional Joker: No.

Development Diva: Yes.

Professional Joker: Pics or it didn't happen.

Development Diva: Wow, now I wish I did take a picture. I was worried about being rude and in retrospect...

Professional Joker: Please tell me it was a crab shack. At *least* a bbq place.

Development Diva: French-Asian fusion

Professional Joker: And he was...dissatisfied by the quality of bibs provided by your eating establishment?

Development Diva: He was worried about being exposed to the chemicals used to launder commercial napkins, so he brought his own napkin. Which okay, maybe he had an allergy. Except he also brought a bib, which he put on as soon as he sat down. Forty minutes before the food came.

Professional Joker: Wow, that really needs to go in the app. Swipe left: Yeah, that guy looks like he brings his own bib.

Development Diva: You'd really write a passive aggressive joke into the app for me?

Professional Joker: You've got friends in high places, baby. Don't let all that power go to your head.

Development Diva: Oh, I'm irrevocably corrupted now.

Professional Joker: *[Three dots bouncing. Disappearing.]*

Development Diva: *[Three dots bouncing. Disappearing.]*

Development Diva: *[Three dots bouncing. Disappearing.]*

CHAPTER 7

On Monday, the conference room was full of the sounds of rustling papers and tapping keys, burnt coffee odor mixing badly with the scent of industrial carpet. Harlow straightened the pile of folders next to her laptop and folded her hands in her lap, looking toward the executives at the head of the table instead of the four co-workers she'd be competing with today. The edges of her fingers were already chapped from fidgeting, and she wished she'd put on more lotion before leaving her office.

"Look, most of the work Hank already did on Sunnybrooke probably disappeared with him, so as soon as we appoint a lead designer, we need to start delegating the grunt work," Ellen said. She was the senior vice president, one of the executives who'd swooped in to handle the mess after Hank dined and dashed with the company accounts. "We can't afford any more delays."

Harlow took a deep breath. "Actually, I did a lot of the early work on Sunnybrooke for Hank, and I have all the documentation you need."

It was a calculated risk, reminding everyone of her close mentorship beneath the traitor who'd absconded with all the money for their last development project and nearly bankrupted the company. But the meeting today was to narrow down the five candidates who were up for lead designer of the Sunnybrooke Development, and she needed to be bold if she wanted to win it.

The CEO looked up, his mustache twitching. "Zoning approval?"

"Already done." She plucked the fourth file in her stack and pushed it his direction.

"Floor plans? Finishes?"

"Tentative floor plans are in the queue at the architect's, waiting to be finalized. I actually already have all the finish choices picked out." She pulled another file and spread a few paint swatches, flooring choices, and pictures of countertops across the conference table.

Ellen swapped a glance with the CEO and she clicked her pen closed. "Well. This meeting will be a lot shorter than I thought, if we don't have to play so much catch up."

"Are those all the finish choices?" Bill Dumpling reached across the table and picked up what she'd provided, looking under them for more.

Harlow struggled not to scowl at him. He was her primary competition, a fixture at the company who had managed at least twenty different developments, albeit their lowest price point neighborhoods. He was also married to the CEO's little sister.

"People like a lot of choices," Bill said. "It's how you talk them into shelling out for this cookie cutter bullshit. Slam 'em with a whole cereal aisle's worth of different wood-grain flooring choices so they think they're getting their dream home instead of a glorified box in twelve different shades of beige."

If that's the way he thought, no wonder his developments were forgettable, and usually took years to fill. She pressed her tongue to the roof of her mouth so she wouldn't grind her teeth.

"Actually, studies show that people are less satisfied with the eventual outcome when presented with too many choices," she said. "I based our finish choices both on what was selling best through our vendors and on the optimal number of choices you can provide before satisfaction starts to drop off."

"Hmm," the CEO said. His name was Tony, but everything from

his gray suit to his gray mustache said CEO, so clearly he should just change his name to the acronym.

"Well, since the preliminaries are handled, why don't you tell us your big-picture plans for the development?" Ellen smiled and flipped to a new page in her leather folio. "After that, we'll move on to the other candidates."

"Pretty simple, actually," Bill began.

"Actually, why don't we let Harlow continue?" Ellen interrupted him. "Since she's already been speaking."

Bill snapped his mouth shut with a grimace like he'd taken a swig of coffee with chunky creamer floating on top. Harlow struggled not to laugh, but as soon as she stood up and took charge of the remote control to the PowerPoint screen, the laughter in her chest dissipated in favor of nerves.

This was it. Her chance to finally move past paper shuffling and into a position where she could design the kinds of communities people really wanted to live in, instead of watching Hank take bows for ideas that had all been hers to start with. If she didn't make it this time, their money problems and reduced production schedule meant it'd be another two years before they started a new development she might have a chance to manage.

The CEO checked his watch, and she clicked into her first slide, trying to move quickly through her many ideas for the development.

Walking trails.

Food truck hubs, connected by the walking trails.

Garages all opening onto shared alleys where cars and trash cans could be kept out of sight.

Recycled water fountains and water features that helped clean gray water while also providing habitat for migrating ducks.

A park with a stage for outdoor concerts in the summer and a safe, floor-level fountain kids could play in while their parents watched the show.

"Food, music, and family." She smiled. "It's everything Austin is known for, and we're going to have it all in our new neighborhood. As you can see, I also—"

The CEO interrupted before she got to her final slide. "This is all great, but this is a mid-priced neighborhood. I don't think we can afford these kinds of amenities with our current…situation." The light flickered as one of the overhead fluorescents buzzed, and Harlow struggled to keep her focus.

"Actually, the amenities more than pay for themselves in the increased home prices we can ask for. The price point we're aiming at is millennial with young families, and that demographic has started to shift to apartments and condos in the urban core. In order to talk them into taking on the additional debt of a house, you have to sell a lifestyle." She smiled. "Urban living at rural prices. That's our hook."

"Right, except it's so far out in the sticks they're going to spend too much of their lives commuting to enjoy any of this fancy shit," Bill said.

Harlow shuffled her papers. "Commute times should be well within average specs. I have them right—"

"The development down the street from there, Lenwood, I think it's called. Went in a few years ago. It's going to weeds because they can't get lots sold."

Shit. She hadn't expected Bill to do his homework.

"Right, but they went live before the grocery store came in." She turned to Ellen. "An HEB grocery store is going to be opening up three months before our Phase I goes live. It's perfectly timed. Also, with the office park I'm proposing we put on site, people won't need to drive far at all to drop off their kids at day care, or go to the dentist. Instead of being a commute to the suburbs, with my timing and planning it becomes its own destination." Harlow smiled, delivering her closer. "People aren't just looking for a house, they're looking for a whole habitat where they can thrive."

"Wow. You've put a lot of work into a program that you were supposedly only an assistant on," Ellen observed. "Tony, do you have any questions before we move to Bill's plan?"

Harlow took a half-step forward. She hadn't gotten to pitch them her plan for long-term customer retention. She had four slides—but no, CEO Tony was checking his watch again. She folded her hands in front of her and prayed she'd get another opportunity to show them how many ideas she had to get this company at the forefront of the Austin building boom.

Bill leaned back in his chair, not waiting for his brother-in-law to answer or for Harlow to sit down. He scratched the buttons over his gut.

"We build houses. We sell them to people. No studies required. It's simple, and I won't steal the company's money. I've been here for thirty years, which is longer than you've been alive, young lady. Any questions?"

Tony chuckled. "Well, you're a straight shooter, Bill. I appreciate that. You've done a lot of solid work for us over the years."

Ellen scanned the table. "From what we've heard today, we're a lot further along on the Sunnybrooke project than we anticipated, even though Hank left us in the lurch. In light of that, I think I'm going to dismiss the other three candidates from consideration. My apologies, but I think Harlow and Bill are the only two with the experience to pick this project up mid-stream without too much transition time."

Harlow's cheek twitched, and she stole a glance at her co-workers while they made genial team-player noises to cover their disappointment.

"Listen, the PowerPoint was nice," the CEO said. "But honestly, what we need now is some way to cut this budget by fifteen percent. Why don't the two of you adapt your plan for that, and we'll move forward on making a decision about the lead designer job from there?"

"I'd like to see a map of your proposed neighborhood and amenities as well." Ellen closed her folio and capped her pen. "Thank you both so much for your hard work on this."

She moved over to Harlow and put out her hand.

"It was lovely to meet you."

Harlow shook it and didn't correct her, though she'd met the woman at least twice during her years with the company.

"Well done," Ellen said in a lower tone. "I'm impressed with your preparation and creativity."

Blood rushed to her face so quickly she felt faint. Her skin tingled as she shook the older woman's hand, trying to rein in her smile. "Thank you. That means a lot to me. I'm so sorry about what happened with Hank. I was um...grateful for everything I learned from him and so shocked about what—"

Ellen's smile went distant. "Yes, we were all shocked. Anyway. We'll be in touch."

She left and Harlow grimaced as she watched her go, uncertain if she should have skipped that opportunity to try to spin her whole messy work history. But it was her only chance, and she'd be damned if Hank was going to take off on the promotion he'd been promising her for years and then screw her all the way from whatever island nation he'd run away to. She'd played by the rules, and that *had* to pay off. All she needed to do was work hard and keep her head down and eventually she'd get her dream job, her don't-die-alone parrot, and, with a bit of luck, the man who understood his weird parrot language.

She gathered up her laptop and stack of folders and juggled them back to her office.

Her phone beeped when she was halfway there, but she couldn't even look until she dumped the stack on her desk.

It was a text from Alice.

Alice: How did the presentation go? Did they kill Bill on the spot and give you a raise?

Alice: BTW if they didn't, it now occurs to me we should probably watch Kill Bill while cursing his name for catharsis.

Harlow: I think I nailed it!!!

Harlow paused, bouncing on her toes and glad Emilia wasn't there to see how drunk on excitement she was.

Harlow: They cut three of the candidates and narrowed it down to me and Bill Dumpling. Not in the bag yet, though. I think the senior VP was on my side. But the boss man seemed to be strangely into Bill's complete lack of fucks given.

Alice: You think that's maybe because Bill's married to his sister?

Harlow: My ego would like to think that, yes. Just in case I don't

get it, we should celebrate now, because I KILLED that presentation.

Alice: You got it, girl. Dinner?

Harlow: OOOH

Alice: You are...really excited about dinner.

Harlow: No, I just remembered! The Tipsy Taco is doing mimosa fountains all month. 5 flavors! It's pricey so I've been looking for an excuse and this is it. Any chance you can hold onto your celebratory mood all the way until weekend brunch?

Alice: I will do my best. And I'll text Sadie.

Harlow put her phone down, her mood ebbing a little when she remembered Sadie wasn't going to be interested in mimosa fountains because she was on an alcohol cleanse. Alice had been so supportive just now, but she'd been pretty sharp-tongued all month—the Alice version of breakup depression. She needed to forgive Rob already, because being apart from him was making her far more miserable than his screw-ups ever had.

Harlow sighed. She could invite Emilia. She was one of the assistants who was going to be working on the development, so she had a vested interest in celebrating any possibility of Bill not getting it. But she'd been to a couple of happy hours with Emilia and both had ended up with puke in the gutter. An unlimited mimosa bar was not the place for her office mate.

She clicked her phone back on. Fortunately, she just so happened to know somebody who was fun, not an alcoholic, *and* who loved brunch.

CHAPTER 8

*D*evelopment Diva: **Hey, wanna impress a girl?**

Harlow's DM pinged on Bishop's phone, and he looked up from his laptop to check it. He'd stopped halfway through cleaning this WebBnB apartment so he could use the free Wi-Fi. He needed to code a few bug fixes for the malware software he sometimes used to steal credit card numbers, and also check the latest sports scores.

Somehow, he did not think this would impress a girl. But he could never resist a little texting banter, so he found himself responding anyway.

Professional Joker: It is my heart's fondest desire.

Professional Joker: Has been ever since I tried to impress Bonnie Blythe in second grade with my knowledge of esoteric dinosaur species. She called my bluff on the steglociraptor, so then I had to stay up all night hacking my stegosaurus and velociraptor stuffed animals apart and safety pinning the two mismatched halves back together, to provide supporting evidence.

Development Diva: LOL!

"Ah, hell," he muttered, scrubbing his hand over his two-day growth of stubble. Women who laughed at his jokes were his Achilles' heel. And he really needed to cool it with texting this particular woman. But her question had him wriggling on the hook of curiosity and now he couldn't keep coding until he found out who she wanted him to impress.

Professional Joker: Why do you ask? Are you in the market for a plush evolutionary disaster? Because I'm crap at planning playgrounds and I know that's what turns you on.

Darn it, now he was flirting. He could not be trusted. Bishop got up and banished his phone to the tiny galley kitchen, turned off his ringer so he wouldn't be tempted, and went back to coding. He'd been known to sink into a computer for up to twenty-nine hours at a stretch, when he was really into a project. Today, he only lasted two minutes before he started wondering if she'd answered.

If she was annoyed with him for not texting her back.

Harlow was sweet. She didn't deserve to be ignored, even if it was for a good cause. He'd just peek, and then wrap it up. But when he looked, all he saw was his *other* Achilles' heel.

Development Diva: I hear brunch is the ticket for impressing girls.

"Not brunch," he groaned to the empty WebBnb. "I call foul play."

He couldn't see Harlow again. He was a thief, a bad person, and also, he should not be blowing money on brunch. Then again, if the restaurant took PhonePay, he could funnel from one of his fake LegUp ideas and pay with stolen card money…but no.

Texting was nothing. But seeing a woman in person that he'd knowingly stolen from was gross. Like taking twenty bucks out of her purse after sex or something.

He grabbed the mop and started scrubbing at the kitchen floor, trying to distract himself with good, clean hard work.

This was just bad karma coming back to torture him, because he'd paid for his dating subscription with a stolen credit card.

Wait.

He dropped the mop, letting the handle rap against the floor as he crossed back to the table with his laptop and pulled up his stolen card spreadsheet. The day he'd bought the dating subscription was the day he'd gotten this latest batch of numbers while waiting for Daisy at chemo, so the card he'd used should be right at the top—damn it. It was *Harlow*'s card he'd bought the app subscription with.

His Match account was definitely cursed. That explained the Post-it Stalker, and why he kept finding himself texting a woman he knew was out of his league after the first date *and* turned out to be one of his marks.

But he had free will, and at least some moral fiber left. One or two fibers, anyway. He wouldn't go to brunch with her or see her again, and he should probably delete his account before his sauerkraut-swilling landlady's head started spinning around or whatever other demonic nonsense happened around people who were cursed.

His phone dinged again.

Development Diva: I know you said we were Fake Friendzone material, but I think we could be real friendzone material, and the agreed-upon transition for that is brunch two weeks later. I'm already going to brunch this weekend with friends at the Tipsy Taco to celebrate a big promotion I maybe sort of might get, so all criteria would be fulfilled.

No. Not the Tipsy Taco. Why would she take the name of his favorite brunch place in vain like that? Bishop started to sweat, and he dashed across the WebBnb and went back to mopping his ass off. In his vigor, he bumped a side table so hard that a decorative accent bowl tipped and a wicker ball rolled out onto the floor.

As he was chasing down the stupid wicker ball, his phone dinged once. Twice. He didn't mean to check it. He just had to pass the table to put the mop away and get the vacuum and he happened to see her words.

Development Diva: All you can eat tacos, even breakfast tacos.

Development Diva: They do a kale, goat cheese, and bacon taco with a charred white corn shell that you wouldn't even believe.

Development Diva: 5 flavors of mimosa fountains.

Development Diva: Basically, it's the brunch of kings and I feel like you're the only one besides me who would appreciate the sacredness of a brunch this good.

Bishop vacuumed ferociously, even pulling off the hose and doing all the cracks of the couch as penance. He hadn't really stolen *from* her. She'd cancelled the card, and all fraudulent transactions went to the great write-off pool in the sky, hanging on the bank's tab, not hers. Which was exactly why he did this the way he did.

It wasn't the shiniest of Robin Hood stories, but he was definitely stealing from rich bankers, and *he* was definitely the poor. If he occasionally paid for a dating app or a brunch with his ill-gotten gains, it's not like it would land him any deeper in hell than he already was for the tens of thousands he'd put into his sister's medical bills.

When he turned off the vacuum, there was another new message from Harlow.

Development Diva: Bishop? You still there? You didn't delete your account like you said you were going to, so I figured that meant you were still okay with me DM'ing you. I freaked you out coming on too strong about brunch, didn't I?

Her honesty pinched at his heart until he couldn't help but answer.

Professional Joker: No, I was paralyzed by my love of unafford-able brunch and frantically trying to justify going anyway.

It was a group date, not a *date* date. Totally platonic, even if it was with a pretty girl. He could go on a group outing with an attractive female without hitting on her. He wasn't that ruled by his hormones, and his self-respect rested on it staying platonic.

Stealing was a douchebag move. He got that. But he'd take a bullet for his little sister, and his parents had nearly lost the roof over their heads trying to pay for her treatments, so swiping a couple of credit card numbers to keep the family afloat? Not even a question. The necessities of keeping his secret had started to create more and more distance between himself and the people who used to be his friends, but he still managed to sleep at night.

However, stealing from a woman was a second-degree douche move.

Stealing from a woman you were dating was felony douchery.

If he wanted to play at still being the kind of person who had weekend brunches and regular text chains, then he could not compound the sin by letting things get any further out of hand with Harlow.

As long as the money came out of her bank's pocket, not hers, and she was just a friend, not a girlfriend, it wasn't really that much worse than any of the other credit card numbers he'd stolen. Besides, he'd make it up to her. She'd never have to find out it was him, *and* he'd make sure to be the best darn platonic guy friend she'd ever had.

Professional Joker: I'm in for brunch. Now, tell me more about this promotion you're totally going to bag.

Bishop sat down in front of his lines of code. He had work to do, to try to dig his karma out of the gutter.

Credit cards weren't attached to gender information, but if he screened out the 200 most common female names, it'd be a start on his new resolution of not stealing from women.

Of course, even as he was doing it, he couldn't help but think that not even his new and improved name-screening program would have kept Harlow out of his life, because her name was so unusual.

Did that make it fate?

CHAPTER 9

*H*arlow edged sideways between the tables on the sunny patio at the Tipsy Taco, her thighs brushing the jacket draped over the back of another woman's chair. She was five minutes early, but she'd told the hostess she was meeting friends because Alice would probably have—yup, she already had a table. Score.

"I adore you." Harlow hooked her purse over the back of the chair across from her friend, who looked up from her phone with a smile.

"Because I scored us a river-view table during prime-time Sunday brunch?"

"It's even in the shade! Mostly." Harlow squinted against the one bar of bright sunlight that was sneaking between the sail-shaped shade canopies that crisscrossed atop the patio.

"Wait five minutes." Alice gestured toward the western movement of the sun. "Then we'll get a full hour of shade before the next tarp gap hits us."

"It's so clear why we're friends."

Alice smiled and tucked her phone away, but her eyes still had that distant reserve that had dogged them for weeks, along with the dark circles that were almost but not totally covered up by her makeup.

Harlow took a breath to ask how she was doing, but then their friend showed up.

"I can't believe this!" Sadie appeared next to them and tossed her purse across the table, landing a nothing-but-net shot in the empty seat next to Alice. "I got up early, got ready early, and didn't even hit traffic so for once I could look like I have my shit more together than you guys. And you *still* beat me."

"We camped out here, Harry Potter release style," Alice said. "Been here since last night."

"Tents. Sleeping bags. We're brunch super fans." Harlow's eyes lit up. "Oh my gosh, look at those. I've got to get a picture."

The mimosa fountains were set up in the shade with the river stretching out in the background, the fountains ranging in color from deep red through all the citrus tones and ending in a pale yellow. The middle three bubbled roundly down from layer to layer like chocolate fountains, and the outer two were set up like water-falls, circumscribing a river that arced around the outside of the table and met in the middle, where the pool sank down to be pumped back to the top.

"Are you ladies doing the buffet brunch today?" The waitress offered menus and Alice waved them off.

"We don't need those. Buffets all the way around. Wait, Harlow, will your friend want a menu?"

"Let me just text him really quick and—you know what, no. He'll definitely want the buffet. Can we do separate checks, though?"

The waitress smiled. "Absolutely. Plates are at the buffet, so help yourselves whenever you're ready."

Alice's chair scraped on the concrete as she pushed it back, but Sadie caught the arm of it. "Sit your butt down. No way you're going to get food now and waste the prime gossiping time before Just Friends Guy shows up."

Alice immediately scooted her chair back in. "Yes, please! We definitely need to hear more about this man you've been texting nonstop but inexplicably don't want to date."

"Is it pimples?" Sadie pulled out her phone. "I saw an ad on my

Instagram yesterday for some prescription pimple stuff. The before and after video was incredible."

"It's not pimples." Harlow laughed. "He's not serious boyfriend material, but he's fun. We probably could have had a fling and an awkward breakup first, but we decided to cut straight to the good part."

They'd exchanged numbers and switched from DMs to texts since she'd taken the official friending step of inviting him to brunch. She'd had three more Match dates this week, and he'd been on two. She'd actually taken the third date more because she wanted to hear what jokes Bishop would crack about them than because she was interested in the date itself.

Even when they weren't making fun of their respective dates, he'd been surprisingly attentive, asking all about her upcoming promotion and wanting to hear about her friends and where she'd grown up. He'd been so nice, actually, it was almost like he was making a conscious effort. Though she couldn't figure out why he would do that, since he didn't seem at all interested in her romantically.

"The 'good part' is the friendzone now?" Sadie cringed. "How bad have your app dates gotten?"

Harlow took a breath to reply and then stopped. Actually, Sadie had a point. How cynical had she gotten that she was weirded out by a guy being nice to her when he wasn't gay *or* trying to get in her pants?

She waved a hand. "You know how it is trying to make friends once you're out of college. If you find somebody new, it's cause for celebration."

"What are we celebrating?" Bishop tossed her a grin as he approached, then swung around the back of her chair, giving her a quick shoulder squeeze before dropping into the spot next to her. "Did they announce the promotion early? Did good ol' Bill Dumpling get fired?"

Bishop had a charcoal gray fedora today, his hair messy and damp where it sprayed out from under the edges, like he'd just gotten out of the shower. He had maybe a day's worth of stubble on a jaw so sharp she caught herself staring. *Wow*, had he been this cute on their first

61

date? She'd gotten used to him being the guy who lived in her DMs and was good for a laugh. She'd sort of forgotten how electric blue his eyes were.

"Nope, still only celebrating that I made the first cut. Bishop, this is—"

"No, no, don't tell me." He held up a palm to stop her. Today, he had a thick bronze ring on his longest finger, which made his hand look graceful, like a pianist or an artist or something. He gave her friends a crooked smile. "She told me a few things about you two, so I want to see if I can guess."

He leaned forward, studying them intently. He had on one of those movie star tee shirts, the ones made out of thin, expensive-seeming fabric that draped just so to show off tight biceps and intriguing shoulder muscles.

Harlow blinked and reached for her water glass. If he caught her taking that long a look, he'd be the one thinking she was secretly trying to get in his pants.

Bishop was still perusing her friends in uninterrupted silence. Alice met his eyes dead on, unaffected. Sadie glanced away, flushing slightly under his scrutiny as she tucked her hair behind her ear.

"Got it." He rapped out a little three beat drumroll on the table and pointed. "You're Sadie." He half stood to extend his hand across the table to her.

Sadie laughed, her eyes brightening as she took it. "How did you do that?"

"Stalked Harlow's social media, most like," Alice said, but she shook his hand, too, in what looked like a deliberately firmer hand-shake than Sadie had given.

"Two seconds and she's already calling me on my bullshit." Bishop flopped back into his chair, grinning. "I bet you and Harlow have been besties since the womb."

"Just since college," Alice said. "We met because we dated the same guy, actually. I was the ex, but she dumped him, too, once we decided we liked each other better. Anybody ready for food? I'm starving."

Harlow turned to Bishop. "Have you been here before? *Wait* until you see the taco bar."

"I'm going to get mimosas first so I can have both hands free to load taco fixings. I'll grab you one. What color do you want?" He waited for Harlow to stand, then scooted her chair in so he could get past.

"Mmm, surprise me, I like them all." Her friends had already made a beeline for the French toast, so Harlow paused and tossed a narrow look over her shoulder at him. "Did you really look them up on my Instagram?"

"No, I really did guess! I just figured Alice wouldn't believe me, and I didn't want to argue since we just met. But frankly, I was sort of proud."

"Okay, that is a little impressive and you're totally right—Alice never would have bought it." She laughed and headed for the tacos.

They made it back to the table with full plates before Sadie and Alice. Bishop sat down first and pulled her chair out since her hands were full. He pointed to the waiting mimosa glasses. "Meyer lemon, or pomegranate. Take whichever you like best and I'll take the other. I'm not picky when I'm day drinking."

"Lemon, please, and thank you." She reached across him and plucked it.

He passed her a set of rolled silverware. "What happened with stockbroker guy last night? You never texted me."

"He didn't do anything worthy of mocking."

Bishop quirked an eyebrow. "Nothing mock-worthy? That's a first. Do we have a winner?"

Alice watched their conversation as she set down her plate. "I haven't heard about any stockbroker. How do you know more about her dates than we do?"

"I should be *screening* her dates. Her standards aren't high enough." He stole a strawberry off Harlow's plate.

"Clearly not, I dated you."

Sadie laughed, edging behind Alice to get back into the table. "Ooh, burn."

"*Barely* dated." Bishop bit into the strawberry. "You got one dinner out of it and busted the grading curve for my app dates forever. Thanks but no thanks for that."

Harlow took a sip of her mimosa to cover whatever expression was on her face. He couldn't really be saying she was the *best* of what he'd met. Was he flirting?

"What happened with Krav Maga instructor guy?" Sadie said. "Was he hot?"

"He was hot on talking about himself," Bishop answered for her. "He's last week's news."

Alice was wearing one of her unreadable Mona Lisa smiles. "Is he?"

"He better be, because stockbroker guy and I have a second date tonight," Harlow said.

"Two dates already!" Sadie brightened. "That sounds serious."

"I don't know, maybe? He was handsome, no red flags, didn't seem like too much of a wildcard. I don't know if I have the energy anymore to go through a bunch of super fun, hot flings that don't go anywhere. I'm kind of looking for long-term potential these days. Somebody I can count on." She stopped talking, feeling a little self-conscious talking about husband material in front of Bishop. "But shh, no counting chickens. I don't want to jinx it."

"That's silly." Alice scooped blueberries onto the top of her waffle and then smashed them with the bottom of her spoon, mangling bread and berry alike. "If high expectations could jinx a relationship, Rob and I would have been safe forever. Nobody expected anything out of us."

Harlow focused on taking a bite of her taco without letting all the goat cheese roll out the back. She really didn't want this to turn into another Rob-bashing session, since she'd spent all last weekend at Alice's while she cried over him. It was easy to tell he was on her friend's mind today. Alice had that…brittleness she always got when they were in an off-again phase.

She hated to think of what her friend might turn out like if years ended up passing this time without the softening effect Rob always had on her. But there was no denying what he'd done. Or the fact that if Alice wouldn't have taken him back the first time, he never would have gotten a chance to hurt her again.

"You're doing the right thing," Harlow said. "Remember, when someone shows you who they really are, believe them. Don't forgive them just so they can show you a second time. Rob had his chance and he blew it."

Bishop glanced between Alice and Harlow. "Sounds like there's a story there. Did he cheat?"

"Rob?" Harlow said. "Fat chance."

Sadie offered Bishop a smile. "Yeah, not really his style."

"Doesn't need to be. He has plenty of other faults." Alice stabbed her fork into her eggs.

"Ah, I gotcha." Bishop nodded knowingly. "Kind of guy who really brings his own bib?"

Harlow choked on her mimosa.

"Don't laugh! I'm gonna make this one happen. They'll be selling it on tee shirts by next year, bet me."

Her friends were looking back and forth between then, waiting for the punchline.

"The Krav Maga guy brought a bib, and then the next guy had this really wide ascot that looked—" Harlow broke off because her friends were starting to glaze over. "Doesn't matter. It's just one of our running gags from making fun of our app dates."

Bishop slanted her an amused glance. "We're basically the Mystery Science Theatre 3000 of internet dating."

Harlow erupted into giggles. "Oh my gosh, we so are."

"At this point we should just get our own reality show and let other people do the dating."

"And we can do the mocking."

"I'll have my people call your people and then your people can call Netflix."

"My people will get right on it." She scooped up a chorizo and mozzarella taco.

"I think Netflix would dig it." Sadie propped her chin in her hand, grinning at their back and forth. "Everybody knows what it's like to go on a terrible first date."

"It's how I'll make my first million. Harlow'll probably be on her third by then." Bishop took a sip of his mimosa and then blinked. "Oh, damn, that's good. You've got to try the pomegranate next. It kills."

Harlow wrinkled her nose. "I don't know. Sometimes I love pomegranate stuff, and sometimes it's kind of chemical-y."

"Here, try mine. Then you don't have to risk it." He passed over his flute.

Harlow took a sip and then caught Alice staring at her.

"What?" She double checked the glass. "Did a fly get in it?"

"Nope." Alice had the too-smooth upper lip she got when she was trying not to smile. "So, Bishop, how do you feel about pets? Ever had say, a parrot?"

CHAPTER 10

*B*ishop: Hey, Harlow, are you busy?

  Harlow: Not for a minute, what's up? Did your stalker come back? Need me to come defend your virtue?

Bishop: Is there any way you'd let me ask a favor? I'm so sorry, I'm screwed here and I can't believe I don't have anybody else to ask.

Harlow: What's wrong? Are you okay?

Bishop: My driver's license got yanked. There were extenuating circumstances and I thought I was going to win my hearing, and I didn't. Wasn't expecting it, and my little sister has to get to chemo today, and I've got no way to get her there. I know this is not your problem. I'm an ass for even asking you. Fuck.

Harlow: I'm so sorry! I had no idea your sister was even in chemo. I'll be right there.

Bishop: Thank you. Seriously.

Harlow: Seriously, it's not even a problem except I don't know where you live.

Bishop: *Google Maps pin* It's a great neighborhood, just swerve around the rats, haha.

. . .

67

Harlow was pretty sure the rats were a joke, but she did have to swerve around a few potholes before her phone navigation system announced her arrival. She pulled to the curb next to an old triplex with peeling vinyl siding and a sun-faded garden gnome marooned by one of the stoops. The wind gusted and clouds swam across the sun, sliding a pattern of dappled light across the brown patches in the lawn. She started to check the numbers to find his door, but then Bishop came out of the one in the center. He jogged up to her SUV and propped his arm above her door, then waited while she rolled down her window.

She'd never seen him without a hat before. When his hair poked out from under the edges, it always looked shaggy, but now she realized it was in a surprisingly sophisticated cut that fell just right for mouthwateringly mussed.

"Have I told you this week that I worship you?" He held out a yellow scrap of paper between two fingers.

She reached out, but then hesitated when she realized it was a Post-it. "Should I be afraid?"

"I bought more. It's not from my Post-it stalker." He turned the paper so she could see the I.O.U. written on it. "No expiration date, open-ended for whatever you want. I could probably soup up your computer to run faster if you want. Write you a program to get rid of spam emails for good. Or clean your apartment. Ask WebBnb, I'm a 5-star janitor."

Well, that was an interesting selection of skills. Harlow folded the paper back into his hand, closing his fingers over it. "How much of an asshole do you think I am that I need you to do me a favor in exchange for helping your sick sister?"

"In exchange for helping *me*, because I fucked up and let my sick sister down," he corrected. "So speaking of..." His hand started to tap a too-quick rhythm against the roof of her car. "Would you be cool to take my car? She gets pretty sick after chemo and nothing says 'thanks for helping a guy out' like vomit in your backseat." He flashed a quick, tight smile, and it sent a pinch of pain through her chest.

She'd never seen him look so tense.

"If that would make you more comfortable, of course." She rolled up her window and locked her SUV, slinging her bag over her shoulder as she got out. "So, is your sister inside?"

"No, I live alone. Luckily for my sister." He gestured to the triplex. "Home sweet home: meth lab on the left, sauerkraut factory on the right, and me in the middle of the worst sandwich on earth." His eyes swept over her leggings and tank top, and her skin prickled with that awareness she'd desperately tried to ignore all through their brunch together. But he glanced away too fast to have been checking her out. He grimaced. "Made you miss yoga, too, didn't I?"

"Yet another reason I'm happy you called. Guilt-free excuse to skip a workout." She smiled, trying to tease him back into their usual easy rapport.

He led her to the car parked in front of hers, which had stickers in the back window for two different rideshare companies and was painted a blaring magenta. He headed for the driver's side, checked himself, then held the door open for her instead.

She bit her lip, trying not to laugh, because it really didn't seem like the moment. "Um…"

"What? Do you not drive a stick shift? Crap, I didn't even think of it. You seemed like you would— But it's fine, we can take your car, I can just bring some plastic and maybe a trash bag. She knows when it's coming and she's gotten really good at only puking once she's got somewhere to aim it."

Harlow touched his arm to stop him. "No, I can drive stick. Just the car caught me off guard."

"Oh, the color?" That brought the light back into his eyes for a second. "Funny story, actually. I'll tell you on the way."

"Does it have a back seat or do we have to put your sister in the trunk?" It looked like a Miata, or an MG or something, but she hadn't checked the back for the model name when they walked up.

"It does indeed have a back seat—barely. It's so small if you try to make out in it, you might sprain your tongue."

She gave a laugh with a catch to it, and told herself not to look at his lips. Crap, she was looking at his lips. Was it possible to be around a guy this cute and not feel every inch of her body like it had been manufactured new in the last thirty seconds? She slid into the front seat, annoyed with herself as he closed the door behind her. It took her a second to get the seat pulled forward far enough so she could reach the pedals and adjust his mirrors down to her level.

He set up their destination address in his phone and clipped it to the dash mount by her steering wheel.

"Oh, thanks. That was thoughtful."

"Uber driver habit."

She winced. "Guessing that's not going to go over too well with the whole revoked license thing."

"It is not."

She was feeling increasingly horrible about inviting him out to a fancy buffet brunch last weekend, but he hadn't acted like the price was a big deal. He'd even forgotten his wallet and for a second, Alice got that "Oh really, another freeloader?" unsurprised look on her face, but fortunately the restaurant took PhonePay, and Bishop was able to pay for his meal without a problem using his phone.

She had so many questions. What he was going to do for work now, how he was going to pick up his sister after today, how long had she been sick, was it terminal? Of course, none of that was really her business, so she just asked, "Does your sister live alone? I have to imagine it's tough to find roommates when you're sick."

"Daisy's eleven. She lives with our parents." He propped his elbow on his door, his fingers picking at the rubber seal along the glass. "Sorry to drop the cancer kid bomb on your day. It's always a crowd pleaser."

Harlow gripped the steering wheel tighter, checking the directions on the phone and the traffic around them before stealing another peek at him. He was always so upbeat and quick to laugh that they'd never actually *had* a serious conversation for more than two sentences. She wouldn't have guessed he was going through something like this. Then again, maybe this is what he was hiding from when he turned everything into a joke.

"But then why wouldn't your parents…"

He let out a short laugh. "Right. You'd think, wouldn't you? Except Dad's too busy traveling for 'work.'" He threw up sharp air quotes. "Mom said she couldn't get the shift off. Which fine, maybe they really wouldn't let her. Or maybe she didn't ask. She hates taking Daisy to doctor's appointments. She cries through the whole damn thing, and that starts Daisy crying, and it's a total shit show." His knee started to bounce, the movement catching her peripheral vision.

Harlow thought if her eleven-year-old daughter had cancer, she'd probably cry through every doctor's appointment, too. Though she also wouldn't let any boss on earth tell her she couldn't leave when her kid needed a ride to chemo.

"Sorry. I know I sound like a dick right now, but things are complicated with my mom. That's why it's always me and Daisy for all the appointments, is what I was trying to explain. Clearly I have no room to get judgy at my mom, since I never plan ahead enough to show up on time, which is why I keep ending up speeding, which is why I got another damn ticket."

She held her silence, letting him rant. As crappy as his situation was, part of her thought he should have thought of all that before he broke the law. There was a pretty simple solution to keep from getting speeding tickets: don't speed. Then again, if her family had thought about how it might affect her before they broke the law, she'd still have parents she got to see outside a prison visitation room. In her experience, people mostly didn't think about how much it would cost them to break the rules until it was already too late.

He shoved forward in the seat, yanked at his jeans, then flopped back with his fingers drumming a harsh rhythm against his thigh. "Now I'm out all my rideshare jobs until who the hell knows when, and might have to drop some of the WebBnbs I'm managing, too. Which, fine, I could get a day job with regular hours now that I don't need flexibility to run Daisy around all the time except oh wait, how the fuck would I get there?" He shook his head. "Stupid. I was so freaking stupid and now we're all fucked because of me."

"Yeah, it was stupid." Harlow clicked on her turn signal.

"What?" His head jerked her way.

71

"Seriously, you fucked up. It's going to suck for a while now until you get it straightened out." It was a crappy situation, and she felt a little bad for him, and a lot worse for his sister, but Harlow wasn't about to help him pretend it was anybody else's fault but his own. "That's what happens when you break the rules. You have to pay the consequences."

She stopped at a red light and looked over.

Slowly, a smile crept across his face, lifting the side of his mouth. "We interrupt this pity party to bring you these sponsored messages. Get your shit together, Bishop, because you're the one who messed up." He laughed. "Aren't you supposed to lie to make me feel better? Tell me it was a simple mistake, people make them, all that jazz?"

She arched an eyebrow at him. Said nothing.

He laughed even louder, slapping his palm across his leg. "Damn. I like you, you know that? You are a hell of a woman."

She shrugged. "It wasn't a mistake. You knew what the speed limit was. I guess next time you'll follow it."

He snorted, leaning back more casually in the seat now. "I guess I'd better."

The light turned green; she shifted in her seat and picked at the steering wheel. Maybe she shouldn't have been so blunt. He was stressed about a lot of things today, and they really hadn't known each other for that long. She wouldn't hesitate before laying it down like that to Alice or somebody, but it was different once you'd been friends for years.

Harlow cleared her throat. "So, I believe I was promised a funny story. Something about why I'm driving a bright fuchsia car right now. Is one of your side hustles selling cosmetics for Mary Kay? Because I've heard you can become a six-figure earner, right out of your own home..."

"Think the cars they give away are a different pink. Not as eye-shattering as this." His knee stopped bouncing. "Yeah, so when Daisy first started going to chemo, she was way more freaked out about the whole thing. Would cry sometimes even when Mom wasn't there to get her all upset. She's fine now, doesn't even want me to hold her hand in the treatment room anymore. Kids adapt, and Daisy's tough as nails. But in those days, to distract her on the drive there, I sort of got her hooked on radio gambling."

"Radio gambling? What even is that?"

"This story was a lot funnier before I realized you were going to call me on all my bullshit," he said. "Now, it just sounds sort of sleazy."

"You've got five minutes before we get there." Harlow nodded at the navigation app on his phone. "Let's see how much sleaze you can pack in."

"Basically, what we'd do is cruise all the radio channels for whoever was doing a giveaway or trivia and call in. Didn't matter if we knew the answer. We'd call in and google it while we were on hold, or just make a wild guess. We did it enough that Daisy actually got picked a couple of times when we didn't have the right answer, so we sort of lost by default. Still, it gave her a kick, the thrill of the chase and hearing her voice on the radio and all that, so it was fine."

"That's really cool." She ran her thumb over a worn smooth spot on his stick shift, starting to smile a little in spite of herself. "You're clearly a natural at babysitting."

"Don't think it counts as babysitting when it's your own family. Anyway, one time she was the eleventh caller, and she won a paint job. Kid didn't have a car, obviously, and this one looked like junk even back then, so she gave the prize to me. Problem was, I was always egging her on with these things, saying she could pick where we went if we won the trip around the world, or dress me up if we got the concert tickets…"

"And you said you'd let her pick the color."

He dropped a finger in her direction. "You got it. Though it made her laugh every time she got in the car after that, and it's an ice breaker on dates, so win/win. Plus, hey, free paint job."

She didn't think most guys would be so relaxed about having to paint their cars bright pink, but she didn't get a chance to say so because they were pulling up in front of a small ranch house. The vinyl siding on this one was in much better shape than Bishop's triplex. The lawn had long since gone to crab grass and dandelions, though somebody was apparently still mowing it. Sometimes.

The front door opened and a preteen girl in a glittery blue wig came out, hooking a messenger bag over her shoulder while an older woman looked on.

Wow, so much for his mom's "had to work" excuse. Harlow shot a glance at Bishop, but he didn't seem surprised, or affected. Maybe she worked from home?

"Hey, real quick." He coughed. "On the way there, you can talk about anything but cancer. She hates being known as the sick girl." He popped the door open and got out. "Hey, there's my ugliest sister!"

"Still hotter than you." She stuck out her tongue at him.

"I thought I told you weren't allowed to use the word hot until you were sixteen. And then only if you gave me a frontal lobotomy first."

"What's a lobotomy?"

"I'll tell you when you're old enough to be hot." He turned and swept an arm out toward the car. Harlow had rolled down the window but now her hand hesitated on the door handle, not sure if she should get out to meet his sister. "This is our chauffeur for the day, my friend Harlow. Please treat her with all the respect for your elders that you have saved up from years of never giving any to me."

"Shotgun!" Daisy shouted right over the last part of his statement, and he scoffed.

"You could at least try to pretend you care about something in life other than getting shotgun. Art, literature. The anarchist sentiments embedded in rap music. Dates to the Sadie Hawkins dance. Anything striking a chord here?"

Daisy was already most of the way to the passenger door. "Who's Sadie Hawkins?"

"I'll tell you once you're old enough to hate literature." He held up a finger toward Harlow. "Give me one sec, okay?" He jogged up to the house, where the woman was still waiting in the doorway. Apparently parental introductions weren't on the menu.

Daisy poked her messenger bag into the car, and then got in.

"Hi, I'm Harlow," she said, not sure what else to open with.

"I know about you." Daisy smiled, shyer than she'd been with her brother. "You're his favorite."

His favorite what?

Also, she hadn't expected he would have told his sister about her. Well, of course he'd probably texted to say someone was giving them a ride, because having a stranger poke their nose into your chemo was probably kind of an intrusion. Except the way Daisy phrased it made it sound like she'd known about Harlow for a while. But before Harlow could think of any subtle follow-up question, Daisy had pulled a phone out of her bag and was already glued to the thing.

"Look, I know it sucks. And I'm sorry. But we're stuck with the situation for now."

Bishop's voice drifted across the lawn to her. Harlow pulled out her own phone so she wouldn't be sitting there awkwardly, not sure where to rest her gaze.

"Most days, if you can pick me up first, you can drop us off at the doctor's and I'll stay with her. Or honestly, there's probably no point. She has so many friends going to the center right now that she doesn't even want me going back into treatment with her anymore. So you could drop her off and just go in to pay when you pick her up. She won't care, and if you think it might be easier on you, you could do that. Or I could take her using an Uber, but if she's feeling sick, she's really not going to want to get into a stranger's car."

Harlow stared blankly at her Twitter feed. How did he think he was going to afford Ubers when he'd just lost two out of God knew how many of his jobs? Maybe his parents could pay, though it seemed extravagant. She couldn't hear the mom's response, but a second later, the door slammed and Bishop was back.

She was his favorite *what*?

"You gonna let me ride along, or did you already ditch me for Harlow?" he prompted his sister.

Daisy hopped out and dug under the seat for some kind of hidden lever that moved the seat all the way forward. Harlow threw a skeptical glance into the tiny backseat as Bishop moved aside a plastic trash can and a roll of paper towels and stuck one long leg in, hunching as he squeezed in behind the seat.

"Are you even going to fit back there?"

"He'll fit," Daisy said. "But he'll whine about it all the way to the treatment center."

Harlow snickered, and Bishop looked put out. "I do not whine. Whining is for girls. I protest in a masculine and understated way."

Daisy locked the seat into place and then moved it forward to leave room for her brother. She moved it so far up there was barely space for her own skinny legs under the dashboard until she pulled her messenger bag into her lap. Harlow pretended her heart wasn't melting at how considerate the siblings were of each other, even in the midst of all their bickering.

"Put the address in Google Maps for her, squirt."

"I'm not that short for eleven," Daisy complained, taking his phone out of the holder by the steering wheel and typing into it. She settled the phone back in its holder and said, "I have cancer, you know."

A choked sound came from the back seat. Then, "Don't be a dick, Daisy."

Harlow threw a quick scowl over her shoulder at him for swearing in front of a child. Then she pulled to a careful stop at an intersection and looked both ways before continuing, her mind racing as to the right way to handle this. Bishop said his sister didn't like to talk about it, but this felt like a test. Harlow really, really hated to fail tests.

"Oh, really? I thought we were just going to the chemo center for free ice cream."

"I wish." Daisy snickered. "But if they gave out ice cream, we'd probably all yak it up afterwards, so they don't want to waste the money."

Yup, she'd definitely inherited her brother's tendency to laugh off the tough stuff. Harlow stole a glance, wishing she'd have asked Bishop more about her prognosis when she had him alone. But the girl seemed blunt to a fault, so maybe the best thing wasn't to tiptoe around it. "You at least have one of the good kinds of cancer, right?"

"I'm not dead yet, so I guess so." Her smile deepened, a pair of perfectly matched dimples peeking through.

Even with the sallow, unhealthy cast to her skin, Daisy was adorable. Light freckles dotted her heart-shaped face, and she had her brother's clear blue eyes, only in a softer shade that looked unexpectedly great with her blue wig. Harlow wondered what color her hair had been before the chemo started.

"Did Bishop tell you I'm going to Austin Walker Stalker this year?" Daisy was apparently done with the cancer talk already.

"Um...that's..." Harlow fumbled. Daisy seemed excited about it, but Harlow wasn't sure she should be supporting anything that had "stalker" in the title.

"It's a fan convention." Bishop leaned forward between the seats. "Do you watch the Walking Dead?"

"I do. Though I almost stopped watching when they killed—" She stopped herself. "Wait, no spoilers. But you guys are probably caught up, right?"

"Who do you think is more badass, Carol or Michonne?" Daisy wanted to know, but hardly waited for Harlow's response before she began explaining the merits of each choice.

While their passenger chattered away about her favorite female characters, Harlow stole glances at Bishop in the rearview mirror and tried not to worry about how quiet he was.

Of course he was quiet—he had some serious problems to solve. But they were *his* problems, not hers. He was good company, and pretty adorable as a big brother, but he was also every bit as irresponsible as he'd joked about on their first date. She wasn't a naive teenager anymore. She'd already learned her lesson about having the wrong people in her life, ones whose bad choices could overshadow all her attempts to keep her life clean and uncomplicated.

If there was a tug in her chest that ached for his impossible situation, and how scared he must be for his sister, then she just needed to ignore it. Bailing him out today was one thing, but it was no secret what kind of guy he was. Dropout, no steady job, impulsive enough to get multiple speeding tickets. The type who was probably always borrowing twenty bucks off his friends and never paying them back: a deadbeat like he'd laughingly warned her, who would end up in bankruptcy or living off his girlfriend. She tried to ignore the part of her that was a little endeared by his honesty, because it didn't change the fact that he'd been right.

Friends was all she should be with that kind of guy. But even knowing that, she couldn't help sliding just one more glance into the backseat to see if he was okay.

CHAPTER 11

ishop leaned his elbows on his knees and stared at the too-familiar gray tones of the waiting room carpet, his knee jiggling so the strings from his hoodie bounced. He watched them, trying to think of something to say to keep Harlow entertained. He already owed her, and the last thing he needed was for her to get depressed by the admittedly not-so-uplifting atmosphere of the pediatric chemotherapy center.

"You cold?"

He looked up, confused by the question. "It's Texas in September. Who gets cold?"

"That's what *I* thought." A little smile played around her mouth and damn it, she was cute.

Her long, golden-brown ponytail fell in loose waves over her shoulder, and he was a shallow bastard for feeling worse about begging favors from a hot girl than from a plain one, but…yup, he was pretty much a shallow bastard. He should have taken Samwise up on that weekly basketball game. If he was just going to go making friends he'd have to run from as soon as they started suspecting where his money came from, he'd rather be a dick to sardonic, tattooed Sam than pretty, ponytailed Harlow. Then again, if he was any good at planning ahead, he'd still have a driver's license.

"But then you grabbed a hoodie out of the car," Harlow continued, "so I figured you must be the only person in Austin who gets cold in September."

"Oh, this?" He looked down at the soft cotton he'd forgotten he was wearing. "Right. There's a method to my madness. Daisy gets chilled sometimes after chemo, and she gets pissed off that I'm hovering and treating her like a baby if I remind her to bring a jacket. If I have a hoodie, she'll let me loan it to her. Except if I'm not wearing it, and she thinks I brought it just for her, she gets pissed all over again."

Harlow looked down at her lap, a strange, soft look on her face. He didn't want to analyze what she might be thinking right now, so he looked away and clasped his fingers together so he wouldn't fidget. He breathed shallowly, because the industrial cleaner they used in this place always left a tickle in the back of his throat like he needed to cough.

"You don't have to wait with us if you don't want to. If you've got stuff to do nearby or wanted to go grab a coffee or whatever, I could text you when she gets done."

"Could I ask you a question instead?"

This would be a lot easier if her voice weren't as soft as her melted-caramel eyes. Everything about her fell in shades of perfectly toasted food items, which was probably why his mouth started watering every time he looked at her.

"After how completely you saved my ass today, you can ask me anything, including my social security number and banking password if you want." Not that either would do her much good, unless she wanted to see how low a credit score could plummet before it burned up in the fiery center of the earth.

"Why don't you have anyone to call? I mean, you seem like a pretty friendly person. Not my first guess for a shut-in."

"You mean why don't I have any friends, to the point that I need to hit up my app dates for rides to the doctor?" He swept his hand around the gray-toned waiting room. "I mean, have you seen the glamorous and fun places I hang out? There's a line out the door waiting to spend time with this guy."

And now he was being a sarcastic asshole.

Bishop scrubbed his palm over the back of his neck and tried to swallow the pride he hadn't realized he still possessed. "Sorry. Honestly, brunch the other day and the picnic in the park before that was the most I've gone out in years. I told you that was my first app date, right?"

"Yeah, but…"

"Yeah, but I probably say that to all the girls? Not so much. That was me trying to dip my toe back into the land of the living."

In a way that would allow him to have a little fun and companionship without leading anybody on, giving away his more felonious secrets, or bringing them into the mess he'd made of his life after Daisy's surgery. But somehow his toe dip had led to him cannonballing back into the friendship pond, where he was now dragging Harlow underwater with him. The least he owed her was an explanation.

"It's been since I left college, really. You're looking at the only valedictorian senior year drop out the UT computer science program ever had. Hook 'em, horns!" He half-heartedly threw up the school's mascot symbol.

"Valedictorian?" She stiffened and backpedaled. "I mean, I just—"

"Surprised?" He smirked mirthlessly. "So was everyone else. It was…awkward hanging out with my college buddies once I wasn't in college anymore. Couldn't talk about classes. I wasn't going to the same parties anymore, wasn't living in the same buildings everybody else was, or eating in the caf. They felt weirded out because I used to be the one everybody went to when they couldn't figure out some glitch. I loved coding. Fucking lived for it. And suddenly they were moving on and getting head-hunted for jobs after graduation and I was…not."

He lost his dorm along with his financial aid, so he'd also been sleeping in his car because he couldn't get along well enough with his mom to move back home, but he didn't necessarily love the idea of telling a woman that.

"I told a couple of friends the truth—that my sister had rhabdomyosarcoma and she had to get this huge expensive surgery, and she might die. Those friends became even harder to talk to than all the rest. It was like they thought they had to be sad with me all the time and couldn't bring up girls, or play video games together, or anything anymore. I was living in waiting rooms and on WebMD, learning everything about her diagnosis and trying to hold it together for Daisy because my parents were both wrecks. I was a full-time resident of cancer country and they were in Keg-landia, and suddenly, I didn't have a passport to get me across the border."

He flicked a hand out at the room, like where they were told the whole story.

"So I stayed in cancer country."

The door to the waiting room opened and Ricky and his dad came in. He lit up when he saw Bishop and waved. Bishop gave him a deft two-finger wave and dug a pack of gum out of his hoodie pocket, tossing it across a few rows of seats to the kid. Ricky fumbled the catch, but grinned when he picked up the gum. He was only a year older than Daisy and they'd had a little crush going for a minute there, but then Ricky got worse and they hadn't seen him for a while and it kinda fizzled out.

"I just…" Harlow's forehead was wrinkled, like she was struggling not to look pissed. "You had parents. Where were they?"

"They were actually really good, back then. Best they ever were, in the days after her diagnosis. My dad came back in off the road and they really tried. But after a while, the shock wore off and they kind of drifted back into old patterns." His dad back to his mistress and his mom back to her pills and her friends.

"What do you mean?"

"My mom gets migraines. I mean, I think she really does, sometimes. But a lot of times, she's just taking the pills, or staying home from work, and I can tell she doesn't really have a headache. She's pretty busy, you know. Calling all her friends and going to all her support groups to tell them how hard it is to have a kid with cancer." He looked away. He couldn't keep the bitterness out of his voice anymore, and it felt too exposed for her to know how much this bugged him.

"Um, Bishop? No offense, but it kind of is hard to have a kid with cancer. I think I'd want a support group, too. Or twelve."

"Yeah, no shit." He straightened up as soon as he heard himself, and reached out and touched her knee. "Sorry. I didn't mean it like that. I'd just have more sympathy if she spent as much time taking care of Daisy as she does telling her friends about how hard she's working. Whenever I'm there, Daisy's dragging herself around the house getting her own stuff, and Mom's on the phone or across the street at Mary's. And Mom was always like this, honestly. Before the cancer, she was bitching to her friends about how out of control I was, what a wild and crazy teenager." His knee started to jiggle again. "I mean, it could be worse. She could be an alcoholic, or abusive or something."

He yanked at the sleeves of his hoodie, too hot but not wanting to take it off in case Daisy came out early and saw that he wasn't wearing it.

"Talk about damning with faint praise," Harlow said, and chuckled darkly. "Actually, my parents are okay but not super great, too. They love me, don't get me wrong. But not enough to not screw up my life with their shitty choices. Which I think is supposed to come with the whole being responsible thing."

"You'd think, right? Or like at least that if your kid got cancer it would change everything, but I don't know. For them, they were just the same okay-but-not-super-great people only with a lot more debt, stress, and doctor's appointments to juggle." He paused. "Though Dad could have left us. Daisy's on his health insurance and at least on paper, he's stayed with us. So, I'll give him that."

Daisy getting sick hadn't changed his parents in any of the ways that mattered, but for a second, Bishop stopped to consider if it had changed *him*. Hell, if anything, Daisy getting sick had made him a lot worse. He had a future before that. He was going to have a career and a degree and he wasn't a thief. So maybe he didn't have a lot of room

83

to get bitter about his parents not being that great. When he looked at it from that angle, they were coping better than he was.

"Hey…" Harlow laid a hand on his arm. Even through two layers of fabric, it felt soft and he stilled. How long had it been since somebody touched him that gently?

All the way back to the last time he'd had a girlfriend, probably, before he'd had to break up with her because she got suspicious about him using PhonePay for everything.

Bishop didn't want Harlow to move her hand, but he could feel her eyes on him, and she wasn't saying anything. He risked a glance. "What?"

"You ever realize you've been a judgy little asshole?"

He coughed out a laugh, then realized she was talking about herself, not him. "Yeah. About thirty seconds ago, actually." But then his throat went sour when he thought of all the things he wasn't telling her. "It's only judgy if you're not right, though. I'm fair game for judging. If I were really screening your dates, I would have screened myself right out."

"Uh…" Her eyes twinkled. "You kind of did."

"Oh, right." That actually did cheer him up a little. "I did warn you I was an unsuitable deadbeat." He grinned. "Maybe I'm not so bad after all."

"You know what this means, don't you?"

He cocked his head. "Actually, no."

"Group brunch two weeks later, favors and secrets exchanged." She clucked her tongue. "We went from fake friendzone to real friendzone all the way to real friends."

She took his hand, and it felt even softer without the fabric of his hoodie to buffer it.

"It also means you should call me when you need help, and not apologize twelve times for it." Her eyes gentled from melted caramel all the way to honey-brown. "Besides, it sounds to me like you have a shortage of people in your life that you can count on."

His thumb played with the twisted-rose gold ring she wore, with that tiny chunk of uncut crystal in it. He didn't want to let go of her hand, and that was kind of messed up when she was holding it because she thought he was a platonic friend. He'd been trying so hard to play that role the best he could, but that was before, when she wasn't *touching* him. Bishop tried to think, but all he could manage was to lay his thumb over that pretty little ring of hers.

Her phone beeped and she pulled away, bending down to retrieve it from her bag.

"Everything okay? Do you need to go?" He could still feel the ghost heat of her hand against his palm.

"Nah, it's just Andrew."

"Andrew?"

"Stockbroker?" she said absently, typing a text. "We've got a third date in a couple of days. Oh my gosh, he got a puppy!" She squeaked. "Look!" She turned the phone around and there was a soft-eared black Labrador sleeping on a sofa cushion.

It was good she was hitting it off with a decent guy. With a solid job. And an adorable puppy. "Great. Cute." He forced a smile, but he could still feel the ghost of her hand on his.

CHAPTER 12

*H*arlow: Hey, what are you up to?

Bishop: Considering burning my apartment down.

Harlow: And I thought I was having a weird Friday night. Any reason in particular for this recent urge to arson?

Bishop: Found ANOTHER one. *Image of an empty drawer with Post-it reading: This will be my drawer.*

Harlow: It's been weeks! How did you not find it until now?

Bishop: I mean, it's an empty drawer! I never open it.

Harlow: Or maybe she came back and left it later. Uh, you really got that locksmith, right?

Bishop: Yeah, I looked at how much they charged to change the lock cylinders and that wasn't happening. Now I just sleep down the hall in the janitor's closet so she can't show up at night and Post-it herself right in next to me. It suits my lifestyle. I find the smell of Pine Sol soothing.

Bishop: Anyway, I'm glamorous. How's your Friday night?

Harlow: Ugh, you don't want to know.

Bishop: Please tell me this isn't another visiting hours at the prison thing.

Harlow: No, I'm just sick of my own company but too tired to go out and actually do anything. Or make conversation with real people. I'm basically just a heap of a person in sweatpants.

Bishop: Too tired to go out and too bored to stay in is the entire reason they invented Netflix and chill. Want me to come over? I do a mean binge watch.

Harlow: Isn't Netflix and chill code for sex?

Bishop: I think it's normally code for too cheap to shell out for dinner but still want to hook up. But for you, my favorite brunch partner in crime, I can be my best, cleanest, Netflixiest self.

Harlow: If your best self includes bringing Chinese takeout, here's my address. I'm starving.

Bishop: I'll Door Dart it ahead. Should be there about 10 minutes before me, if the buses are running on time.

Harlow: Want me to come pick you up?

Bishop: Nah. Defeats the whole point of a night in if you have to go out. Besides, I'm a wiz with the bus schedule. Ordering now.

Harlow: Extra egg rolls!

Bishop: It's like you don't know me at all.

Harlow: I love you.

Bishop: Hey now, I already said I wasn't putting out.

Harlow opened the door while she was still chewing. "Don't hate me, but I might have eaten all the egg rolls."

"Is that the last bite in your hand right now? Because I don't think that means you've eaten *all* the egg rolls." He dropped his chin and gave her the saddest puppy dog eyes she'd ever seen. Especially since he was wearing a dark beanie that somehow only made his blue eyes glow brighter. Harlow glanced from him to the bite of egg roll, then slowly extended it. He nipped it straight out of her hand, leaving her fingertips tingling where he'd grazed them with his teeth. Then he held up his hands, both of which were full of offerings.

She burst out laughing, though that was mostly at his pants. "What's all of this?"

He had a bottle of white wine in one hand, a pint of Ben and Jerry's in the other, a ripped TOOL tee shirt that was too tight on his shoulders, and a pair of duck-print flannel pajama pants that barely made it past mid-calf.

"The PG-13 version of Netflix and chill. I figured if you were texting me that you were too tired to hang out, what you really wanted was a girls' night of wine, pj's, and pretending the other two were the ones who ate all the Chunky Monkey, but your girls were too busy."

She bit her lip and let him inside. "Well, I mean, I wasn't sure that you'd be interested in that kind of thing." She hadn't actually called Alice or Sadie. Anything but texting with Bishop felt like too much work. Of course, she hadn't expected him to actually come *over*. Now that he had, it would be weird if she admitted she hadn't tried anyone else first. So she covered by teasing, "Are you offended that you're my third choice?"

He gave her an incredulous look. "I've met your friends. I'd be my own third choice if I had those two on call. I already want Sadie to be the best woman at my wedding, and I want Alice to be my dominatrix."

She covered her mouth, her eyes widening. "You did not just—"

He pointed at her. "Girls' night confidentiality privilege. You can never tell them I said that."

"Okay, but can I at least tell them about the pants?" She gestured to his outfit, losing the battle against a grin.

"I don't actually wear pj's," he explained, "so the best I could do were some lounge pants my sister stole from my mom and then left at my place. Pretty sure ducks are unisex."

Well, that explained how tight they were on his ass. She tried to hold back a giggle at the sight of him in duck-print pajama pants, but then she thought of him in bed at night with no pajamas at all.

Boxers? Naked?

She cleared her throat. "How much do I owe you for dinner and everything?"

He gave her a dirty look.

"What? I know losing your license put you in a bind."

"Not your problem. I'm here to eat, drink, and be merry. I just have to decide which to do first. Nice place, by the way."

He nodded to her apartment with its soft blue throw pillows in the window seat, honey-oak floors, and couch with an overstuffed ottoman and more blue and cream pillows thrown haphazardly over its surface. The coffee table held her tea from earlier and her phone. His gaze lingered on her roll-top desk in the corner, and hers lingered on his shoulders, which looked wider than she remembered under that too-old tee shirt. The fabric was stretched tight enough she could see the individual bumps of muscle in his arms and—

"Here, let me take those." She grabbed his offerings and pretended to check out the wine to get her too-hormonal mind back on track. Trying to do casual get-to-know you dating during her horniest week of the month was basically hell, and pjs and wine really were exactly what she needed to get her mind off the sexual frustration. Until she actually read the label.

She peeked up at Bishop. "You brought Chardonnay? Are you really straight?"

"To my sister's everlasting chagrin, yes."

"And you like Chardonnay?"

"Hate the stuff." He commandeered her chopsticks and went after the broccoli beef. "Last I checked, girls' nights always included Chardonnay."

"You're a walking stereotype, and I hate white wine."

"Okay, then what are we drinking?"

"Uh…" The other problem with the horniest week of her month was that she'd already drank all the red wine in the house. She opened her stash cupboard and started digging. "I have whiskey and… ooh! Some whipped cream-flavored vodka left over from my last girls' night."

Bishop finished the broccoli beef and grabbed both bottles. "Whipped whiskeys it is."

He went to the cabinet over the sink, pulling out two glasses without having to ask her where they were, and started pouring a very specific mix of whiskey and whipped cream vodka into each glass. She watched him warily.

"That looks like the worst idea ever."

"Mmm, I'm famous for those. But my bad ideas are usually more fun than you'd think." He held out a glass. "Try me."

She took it, her fingers brushing his, and wrinkled her nose, bracing for a flabbergastingly awful taste. Instead, it went down smoothly. *Too* smoothly. She took another sip. Charred oak, both sweet and savory vanillas, a light kick at the end. "Hell," she muttered and took a third sip.

Bishop laughed and stole the glass back from her. "Let me finish making them before you go overboard, cowgirl. Now, what are we watching? I'm thinking the staples for girls' night have got to be Sex and the City, Friends, maybe the Office. Gilmore Girls? I don't know, everything I can think of is pretty outdated." He eyed her thoughtfully.

She wrapped her hoodie more tightly around her, self-conscious for the first time about her baggy flannel pajama pants. She should have put on her more flattering yoga pants when she realized she was going to have company.

"No," Bishop decided. "Veronica Mars. She's two steps ahead of everybody, and falls for all the wrong guys. It has your name written all over it."

"Never seen it."

He handed her a glass. "It's gonna be your new favorite. Plus, it'll be more fun for me, because she's cute as a shiny button and as competent as Ruth Bader Ginsberg." He blew out a breath like it got him hot just thinking about it. "My dream girl."

Harlow glanced away, wondering if he noticed that he described the TV character as being just like her, *and* his dream girl. She should be more careful with him. He was so easy to be around, she let her guard right down. Case in point; she hadn't thought to put a bra on before he came over.

She also got that same soft tug in her chest that always got her in trouble with guys, every time he talked about his little sister. And then just when she'd think of taking a step back because she liked him too much, he'd make her laugh or tell her heart-wrenching stories about his parents and she just…couldn't bear to push him away.

She took another sip of her delicious whipped whiskey, vowing to be more aware of her interactions with him. This might be a girls' night in, but he was very much a guy. A very cute, very inappropriate guy.

Bishop scanned the configuration of drawers in her kitchen before choosing the right one on his first try, and taking out a spoon. "Since you're not a stereotype, you probably don't want any of this ice cream, right?"

"Dream on, duck pants boy." She dove for the Ben and Jerry's.

CHAPTER 13

*H*arlow felt *great.* By the third whipped whiskey, all the tension from her long week of work had drifted away. By the fourth whiskey, her stomach hurt from laughing at Bishop's joking patter about the show they were watching. By the fifth, the buzz of egg rolls and ice cream had settled into the perfect contented vibration in her body, singing in harmony with the alcohol until her body hummed like a tuning fork.

Which got her thinking way too much about how irresistibly horny she got during this week in her cycle. She shifted on the couch, bringing her knees up higher and curling her toes into the cushions. Bishop glanced over and flicked a corner of the chunky knitted afghan they were sharing so it covered her feet again. She'd worried she should have been more careful about inviting him over, especially late at night in her pj's, but he'd been a perfect gentleman.

Except as great as his company had been for taking her mind off things, he was still very much a member of the opposite sex and she was increasingly focused on how tight the muscles in his forearms were. She kind of needed him to go home so she could do whatever damage control she could with her vibrator. Even though during this week of the month, toys were never quite enough to satisfy her the way an enthusiastically vigorous full-bodied man could. Also, she wasn't sure *how* he was going to get home. Bishop was as drunk as she was, it was too late for the buses to still be running, and she knew he couldn't afford an Uber. Or dinner, which she really shouldn't have let him pay for.

She poked at the pillow behind her back, then zipped her hoodie over her too-sensitive nipples, trying to think of a way that she could cover his Uber without him becoming all uncomfortable and emasculated about it.

"Why are you getting all squirmy? This isn't even a horror movie." He gestured at the screen, which was showing teenaged boys doing backflips off the bleachers, then snorted when one of them hit his head and started bleeding.

She closed one eye so she could see him better. God, he was pretty. All bright eyes and lean muscles and that *smirk* of his. Bad-boy movies were invented for crooked smirks like those. She wished this night was a movie so she could drag him into her bedroom, fuck him until she could think straight again, and then just delete that scene from the reel so they could go back to what had become their normal. Brunch, jokes, him loving her friends and never asking for money, or for her to work less hours, or any of the inconvenient things her boyfriends usually wanted.

Suddenly, she realized he was looking at her while she was looking at him. And he had one eye playfully closed to mirror her. As soon as she noticed, she flushed and he burst out laughing. "Harlow Rimes, are you drunk?"

"No!" She pulled a blue pillow from behind her and threw it at him.

He nabbed the pillow easily. "Well then catch up, because I am. Do I have ice cream on my chin or something? What were you looking at?"

"No, you're good." She flopped her legs off the couch and reached for her drink, hugging her free arm in tight around her waist.

"Seriously, you're *so* squirmy. I'm never giving you sugar again."

She scowled at him and his expression shifted.

"Wait. Are you…horny?"

Her eyes flew wide. "No!"

"You are, aren't you?" He threw the pillow back, snickering.

Of course he could just tell. Coming from the guy who'd guessed where her glasses were kept, and her silverware, and had suggested this TV show she'd never seen and already adored. She should probably be blushing, but he didn't seem embarrassed, so she shrugged and went with it.

"Come on, my last boyfriend before I got desperate enough to go back to app dating was…" She started counting the months on her fingers, but then, her last boyfriend had been *Chad*. So really, it wasn't like she'd been satisfied back then, either.

He reached across and caught her hand, halting her counting. "Stop, that's making me way too sad. Do you want me to go down on you?" He held up his palms. "No strings attached. So many women in free porn clips have helped me out over the years, I figure this can be my attempt to balance the karmic scales."

Her mouth hung open. "You did not just say that."

He shrugged, shifting back to his side of the couch and un-pausing the show. "Just saying. I know you weren't asking, but if you were, my karma is at your service. I have a lot of guilt to work off. Misspent youth, unsavory life choices. You know how it is."

Harlow tried to watch Veronica Mars taking a teenaged boy to the hospital, but her mind was racing. Bishop had offered in less than a heartbeat, like it was no big deal at all to give somebody an orgasm when you weren't even a little bit together. There was no way oral sex fit into the definition of platonic friends. Not even when her downstairs was tied up in so many knots she could barely follow the plot of a TV show meant for teens.

Bishop was so unexpected in every aspect of how he went about his life. But even he couldn't possibly really mean it, that he'd just *do* that and it would be fine.

She curled her legs up beside her on the couch. That was the kind of stuff people fell for that ruined friendships. They'd known each other only a few weeks so it wasn't like she'd be throwing away a relationship she'd had since childhood, but she *liked* him. It had been years since she met anyone she got along with so effortlessly, and he was good comic relief. God knew her life needed more comic relief.

Unfortunately, God knew she needed other things at the moment, too. Or, hopefully, God didn't know, because her thoughts were sincerely not church-appropriate.

Oral sex was so personal. He couldn't really mean that he wanted to... She shifted on the couch. "I haven't even showered," she muttered.

Bishop glanced over, his eyebrow arching. "I bet I can find a work-around to that." He reached across the space separating them, his fingers brushing the waistband of her loose pajama pants just above her hip bone.

Her breath hiccupped and when it started again, it was coming way faster than she'd like. "You're just trying to get in my pants." This was about him, about getting sex. Had to be. He was a nice guy, but who was *that* nice?

"Eh." He waved her off. "Can't. I'm too drunk to consent."

She smirked, the glow of the alcohol making that way funnier than it probably was. "Is that a euphemism for whiskey dick?"

"I think that's a myth. My dick loves whiskey."

Her heart rate jolted into a higher bracket. "Why would you tell me that right now?" She scrabbled on the ground for another of her couch pillows and threw it at him. She really couldn't afford to be thinking about his dick right now and how hard it might or might not be. Or how big it was. Her thin hoodie was suddenly stifling hot.

Bishop eyed her, another of his calculating, electric blue sideways looks. "How horny are you? Scale of one to ten."

Her inner muscles squeezed just at the question. And at the way he was looking at her.

Yeah, her vibrator was so not going to cut it tonight. Though neither was the hand he was offering. She wanted full on, hard-driving sex, the whole weight of his body behind every thrust. She wanted to be kissed. Not those super self-conscious do-I-like-this kisses you got at the end of a date. She'd had a handful of those lately and even when they went well,

95

they were just…fine. She wanted the kind of kisses you got when you'd been dating a while. Wild, forget-yourself, only-for-sensation kisses. She wanted bare skin, and muscles and—this was definitely not helping.

They were supposed to be just friends, but she didn't even care right now. She'd ruin their friendship. Even knowing this would set her up for a terrible "let him down easy" call later in the week when she had to reiterate that one hookup did not a relationship make. She was drunk, she'd earned some fun after battling office politics and Bill for that promotion all week, and she needed more than batteries could provide. "I'm at a nine. Point one."

"A nine?" He blew out a breath, looking like he might be getting overheated, too.

"Throw on the Vampire Diaries and I'd ping to ten in a heartbeat," she joked, pretending to fan herself.

"Stefan or Damon and if you say Stefan I'm leaving," Bishop shot back and she grinned. Damn it, he was good company.

"Is that a joke? Damon is obviously the sexy brother. Stefan is just the soulfully hot guy friend I wish I could have had in high school."

"Can *I* be your soulfully hot guy friend?"

"You can if you come with benefits…" she angled. Why were they still talking? He'd offered, she'd basically handed her panties over on a platter with admitting she was a nine point one on the horny scale, and he hadn't done anything about it. Maybe he'd been joking after all. She played along, mostly to save her dignity in case he hadn't been serious. "Though to be honest, you're more sharply handsome than soulfully hot."

"I have soul! Loads of soul. I had a psychic tell me I was an old soul once. Right before she picked my pocket."

She looked at him, and she couldn't pretend she wasn't picturing him without that shirt on. She wasn't hearing a word he said.

Alice could never know about this. Alice never bent her principles for anything, and would never want something so badly that she stopped caring about the consequences.

Bishop's gaze fell to her mouth, and he licked his lips. "Harlow, no.

I cannot in good conscience. I'm too good a friend to let you fuck another deadbeat when you've been downing whipped whiskeys all night. Even if that deadbeat is me. And even if those whipped whiskeys whipped my dick up something fierce."

She groaned.

"Okay, okay, I'm not a monster. I can get you off, but strictly as a friend, and strictly if you promise not to take advantage of my inebriated state."

She squinted at him. "If you're too drunk to consent to sex, how are you sober enough to consent to perform sex acts?"

"Wait, are *you* too drunk to consent?"

She considered. She'd been horny way before he came over. She was sober enough to know this was a terrible idea and it was going to destroy their bantery friendly dynamic, but she was also drunk enough not to care. "Absolutely not."

"Is that what a too-drunk-to-consent person would say?"

"Yes."

"So how can I..." He hesitated.

"Oh my God, that's it." She snatched up the remote and flicked from Hulu to Netflix, hunting for the Vampire Diaries. "I'm turning on the Denver episode and taking care of it myself."

He inched closer on the couch. "Am I going to step on any stockbroker toes here?"

"We're not exclusive. We've been on three dates but I can't just... booty-call him." Harlow fidgeted with the remote.

"Incorrect. All men love to be booty-called, at any time for any—okay just for the one reason. So, if you've had three dates that weren't even mock-worthy, what are you doing here with ol' Duck Pants? When you could be over there with...whatever kind of fancy pants stockbrokers wear?"

She stole back one of the pillows she'd thrown at him and hugged it. "Okay, I joke around but I can't get naked with someone I barely know. I don't—it's just not fun for me. I know everybody's doing it now, and it's no big deal, and when you need to get laid you can't wait around until you find some long-term relationship material, but that's me. As much as it sucks sometimes."

"C'mere." His voice was soft now.

She glanced at him. She couldn't believe she'd admitted that, even to him, and now he probably felt sorry for her that she was such a prude.

Bishop opened his arms for a hug. "Seriously. C'mere."

She crawled across the couch and he kicked his legs up across the cushions and leaned back, pulling her up onto his chest. He rubbed circles on her back and she huffed out a breath. "It's not stupid. And you're kind of killing me right now, making me think about you trying to force yourself to get naked with some guy you barely know."

His fingers moved lower, skimming the bare skin just above her waistband. Tingles exploded through her stomach and she sucked in a breath. That felt way, way too good. Did this mean…was he really going to…

"Tell me to stop if this starts to get weird, okay?" he said.

She nodded against his chest, her heart pounding. Could she do this? Her inner muscles clenched and she really, *really* wanted to, but also holy shit, what was she doing?

He kissed the top of her head and slipped his hand down the back of her pajama pants, smoothing his palm across the curve of her bottom, over the top of her panties. It was a sweet touch, almost inno-cent, and he didn't go further than that. Just kind of petted her, his hug a slumberous sort of warm while her heart tried to pound out of her chest because he had his hand—that quick, long-fingered hand —*inside of her pants.*

Bishop tucked her head closer into his neck, letting her hide her face against him, and wow, he smelled nice. Like really good body wash, or fading cologne he'd put on so many hours ago that it was only a teasing hint she wanted more of.

"Is your arm going to sleep?"

"Nu-uh," she reassured him, her hands tucked up between them. She was actually really comfortable and it was kind of sweet that he'd asked. His hand on her butt felt nice. Nothing like the wild fantasies she'd been having, but more like the kind of casual intimacy she hadn't had in a long time. He reached lower, trailing down the bare skin of her leg and she shifted against his chest. He tugged at the back of her knee, bringing one bent leg up next to him on the couch.

Jeez, she was already drenched. It was going to be embarrassing when he realized how turned on she already was, without him having to do more than stroke her like a cat. Harlow didn't realize she'd started to squirm until he tensed his thigh, raising it so it rubbed right where she needed it. Oh fuck, that felt nice.

He kept petting her ass and her legs, his fingertips toying with the edges of her panties until the dividing lines between fabric and flesh all seemed drawn in red-hot lines of oversensitive awareness. Harlow really, really needed him to go faster than this. As good as it felt, she needed hard and deep and friction and—

His hand slipped down and right across the center of her panties. Just a brush where she needed it the most, but she jerked, pushing toward him for more as her breath stuttered to a complete stop. Responding to her silent plea, he came back for more, rubbing light circles right between her legs, still over her panties.

She was breathing raggedly against his neck, and he smelled so good. She wanted to kiss him, let his tongue and teeth distract her from the torment of how much he was giving her right now, and how little. But he hadn't kissed her first, so maybe that wouldn't be a part of this.

He hooked a finger inside her panties, his knuckle skimming past her soaked opening.

"Fuck, you're wet," he rumbled. "Ah, that's hot."

He reached deeper into her panties, curling around to the front of her but couldn't quite reach all the way to her clit, even when she wiggled, trying to get his hand there.

"Mmm, can I roll you over?" He changed his grip on her, letting her turn over until her back was to his chest. Her head hung back off his shoulder at a weird angle but she really, really didn't care. His hands were out of her pants and she hated it.

His chest flexed beneath her and she gritted her teeth with the frustration of the delay right before he managed to retrieve a pillow off the floor, tucking it under her head.

"Better?"

"Not yet," she practically hissed.

He chuckled and wrapped one arm around her, sort of hugging her and spooning her all at once. His erection was a blunt line against her ass, and her head swam as she realized this was arousing him, too. Maybe she should reach back and rub him a little. He'd said he was too drunk to consent, but had that been a joke, or was he serious about this being no strings attached, just something he was doing for her?

Bishop nuzzled his face against her hair and something in her chest snagged, then fluttered. He was being so fucking *nice* about all this. He was a fantastic hugger—all cuddly and warm, his chest as safe as a bed full of pillows. His free hand was rubbing her legs over the top of her flannel pants with slow, easy sweeps that got her skin rippling with sensation. She squirmed, deeply conscious of his arousal against her bottom.

"Bishop, please," she gasped, not able to take his slow warm up any longer.

He pushed his hand into her pants, under her panties, and she moaned without meaning to, all her muscles tensing. Even then, he didn't rush. Just cupped his hand over her center and went quiet, waiting for her to get used to his touch. She couldn't hold still, and started rocking against his hand with convulsive little clenches of her ab muscles. Sweat broke out across her forehead and her nipples pebbled so hard that she could see them through her thin hoodie and wondered if he could, too. She wanted him to look, with a hazy-eyed pull of desire she didn't entirely understand herself.

The sight of his tightly corded forearm disappearing under the waistband of her pajama pants was driving her mad. She rocked more forcefully because if he wasn't going to move, she was. That movement got his fingertips wet, the slick slide of them down low on her making another moan rise in her throat that she swallowed back.

His fingers moved lazily, drawing the slick moisture up to the hard knot of her clit. He didn't hit it directly, just circled softly around the edges.

"Breathe, Harlow. I'll make it better. Just lay back and trust me."

She was tensed up and stiff all the way down to her toes with need, but she made the effort to relax, her head falling back next to his on the pillow he'd gotten her. A soft kiss pressed against her temple, and his cradling arm enfolded her more securely, his thumb skimming soothing lines against her ribs.

He wasn't teasing anymore. Instead, he rubbed perfect, glittering circles exactly where she needed them so sensation glimmered through her whole body and she couldn't think at all.

It felt so good but she could tell it wasn't going to be enough to make her come. It was that exact kind of pleasure that would stick her on the edge until she'd go mad with it. She clenched, her hips rising up to meet his hand until she was arched completely off his lap, seeking more pressure from those unhurried, gentle fingertips.

He ducked his head, nuzzling her hoodie away from her neck. Her skin was so sensitive right now it felt amazing and she began to whimper, hoping he'd use his tongue against that place on her neck and—he bit her. Blunt and hard, right where her shoulder curved up toward her throat. It bolted her into orgasm before she even felt it coming. He thrust two fingers deep inside her, the hard jab of them catching the first wave of her release as she squeezed tight against the invasion of him.

Harlow squeaked, her whole body twitching as her hips rose, and he used the hard heel of his hand to push down against her sex so her release spooled out and out and out instead of slacking off after the peak. It almost started to ebb, and then he rubbed his fingers inside of her, curling them to hit that spot that had been utterly neglected until now. She squeezed down around him again, gritting her teeth against a rough groan, because she couldn't tell if she was peaking all again or if it was all just one glorious, messy storm of pleasure.

When she went limp, she couldn't think at all. She gulped a breath and licked her dry lips, tasting sugar and whiskey. His hair tickled her cheek and he must have lost his beanie somewhere in the middle of that. He was still rampantly hard against her.

Bishop slipped his hand out of her panties and tugged the waistband of her pants back into place, smoothing it against her belly with a soft touch as he wrapped that arm around her to match the first, cradling her from both sides now.

Should she get up? Return the favor? Maybe say she had to go to bed, that she had to go in to work a few hours on Saturday morning. She tensed to sit up and he squeezed her a little tighter.

"Cuddle me for a minute or I'll feel cheap," he teased, and she snorted.

But his thumb was rubbing against her hoodie-clad arm, and that felt good. As good as the afterglow of that truly spectacular orgasm that was fading through all her limbs. She really didn't *have* to get up for anything, if he didn't want to. And Bishop gave the nicest hugs.

She nuzzled her head more closely into the pillow, resting it next to his. Her mind drifted for a second and before she knew it, his breaths had gone long and steady and he was asleep beneath her.

CHAPTER 14

*W*hen Harlow woke up the next morning, Bishop was gone. She flipped the throw blanket away from her face and squinted around. "Fleeing the next morning awkwardness," she mumbled. "Smart."

She hauled herself off the couch, rubbing her forehead. Her eyelashes clung gummily when she tried to blink and her mouth was dry, but she wasn't nearly as hung over as she should have been. Huh. Her feet scuffed against her hardwood floors as she stumbled into the bathroom. She flipped up the toilet lid, hooked her thumbs into her pajama pants to pull them down…and screamed.

There was a man in her bathtub. She jerked away, knocking something off the bathroom counter as he shot upright, clutching his head.

"Owww…" Bishop complained. "Party foul. No screaming while hungover, please."

She bent to retrieve the hairbrush she'd knocked onto the floor. "What are you doing in my bathtub?"

"Uh, it's kind of amazing, hadn't you noticed?"

She had noticed. It was the whole reason she'd rented this apartment actually. The tub was a deep, free-standing basin tub with a modern silhouette. Both ends were high and sloped back for leaning against so she could share a romantic bath with someone, if she wanted. Though she still hadn't made use of that particular feature. There was no water in the tub, though, and her houseguest was still wearing his clothes, which confused her already-muzzy brain even further.

"Woke up about four a.m. feeling not so great about all those whipped whiskeys." He shoved his shaggy black hair back out of his eyes. "No offense, because you barely weigh anything, but the barely anything of you was all on my stomach and the stomach did not appreciate any interference. So I got you settled on the couch again and slept in here. I was afraid I might get sick and didn't want to do it on your area rug."

She crossed her arms over her belly. "Okay. That was...actually really thoughtful. Though I probably owe you a chiropractor visit after a night in the tub."

"Could be worse. I'll get out of your way so you can pee." He climbed out of the tub and stretched, his old tee shirt pulling up to give a peek of abs. Ugh, she should be way too hungover to notice that. She stepped back to let him out of the bathroom, staring pointedly at the floor.

She was not supposed to think of him like a real guy. She wouldn't have let a real, datable guy see her in her baggy pajama pants, or come over last night when she was too tired to be witty, or gotten that drunk after they'd only been on one official date... Oh and the twelve other reasons she knew better than to date him in the first place. Except now, she couldn't un-know what an incredible lay he was, even only using his fingers. Jesus.

He closed the door behind him and she sat down on the toilet. As soon as she started, he said through the door, "Just so you know, I'm not going to be weird just because I got you off last night."

She buried her face in her hands. "Oh my gosh, Bishop, I'm *peeing*. Can you not listen, please?"

"Everybody pees, who cares? You're already giving me the shifty eyes, so I thought I'd better cut you off before you spiral halfway to Mars."

She flushed and stood up to scrub her hands. "Okay, well thank goodness you're not going to make it *awkward* or anything."

He chuckled and she snatched the towel off the rack, ripping open the door so she could glare at him while she dried her hands. His eyes were bloodshot but sparkling. It was kind of annoying that he could be hot with bedhead and a whiskey hangover so bad that he slept in the bathtub in case of unexpected vomiting.

"I don't think we're dating now or anything. You were in a bind. I offered, I enjoyed myself, I'm pretty damn sure *you* enjoyed yourself, we're still friends, and if you want breakfast I'm cooking."

She propped her hands on her hips, the damp towel dangling. "It's horrifying how chipper you are right now. Aren't you hungover?"

"Desperately hungover. Though you're not, are you?"

"No…" she said slowly. "How did you know that?"

"Orgasms. The endorphins cure headaches and hangovers." He gave a longing look to her bathtub. "I should have jerked off in the tub last night, then I wouldn't be feeling so gross. Plus, that tub is totally sexual fantasy worthy."

She flicked him with the towel. "You're disgusting."

"Truer words and all that." He cupped a hand around the nape of her neck, stepped close, and dropped a kiss onto her forehead. "Lucky for you, I'm not your boyfriend, so it's not your problem. And just for the record, you're ridiculously fun in bed. Or in couch, as it were."

He grinned, his eyes flaring so bright she couldn't look away.

Then he let her go and sauntered down the hall. "You want eggs or waffles?"

Sadie: So, you're just pretending it didn't happen?

Harlow: Yeah, but pretending so well that it feels like it didn't. Like, everything is the *same*. No awkwardness, same text frequency. Yesterday, he went with me to that free concert series I was thinking about duplicating for the Sunnybrooke community

events, and we had a great time. But like...I know. And I can't not know.

Sadie: Right?!!!

Harlow: Sometimes when I'm with him I'll look over and think about the way he held me. Because he held me, you know, while he was doing it. He didn't have to do that.

Sadie: You don't think about the sexy times part?! It was good, though, right?

Harlow: Yeah, but of course it was! A guy that cute, no way he doesn't know his way around a woman's body.

Sadie: Uh, no. A guy that cute doesn't have to know anything to get laid.

Harlow: True.

Harlow: But it's that hug I can't stop thinking about. It was like...I don't know.

Sadie: Harlowwwwwwwww

Sadie: Marry himmmmmmmm

Harlow: Gotta go. Boss here.

CHAPTER 15

*T*he axe-throwing range smelled of artisanal nachos, wood chips, and hipster cologne. Harlow perched on a stool at the bar that ran along the back wall behind the throwing stalls and pretended not to watch Bishop's ass while he took his turn with the throwing hatchet.

"Bullseye." Bishop turned around, grinning from under the brim of a cheap trucker hat that he somehow made look like a million bucks. "And you said I couldn't do it underhand."

"There's a 'that's what she said' joke in there somewhere." Alice flipped her hatchet up and caught it by the handle.

"Watch, behind the back now." He twisted, flipping the axe without looking. It whirled through the air, hit the painted target on the log, and bounced off to the floor.

"Smooth, man." Dusty snickered, his hand slipping from Sadie's waist down to tuck into her back pocket. Harlow glanced away, grabbing her beer off the bar.

"I can't believe they let you BYOB to an axe-throwing range." Bishop vaulted onto the stool next to hers, letting the momentum carry him into a spin and then stealing her beer at the end of it. "I love this place."

"God bless Texas," she said, swiping it back before he got a sip.

"And food trucks out front? Brilliance. Bars and businesses should stop having kitchens at all and have rotating food trucks." He picked at the edges of their platter of nachos, going for the chips that only had a little bit of cheese melted down onto them. "Didn't you write that into your neighborhood plan?"

"I did." She couldn't believe he remembered that, from when she'd mentioned it maybe once in a passing text. "Food truck hubs with a rotating schedule."

"See? Brilliance."

Harlow's eyes strayed to his quick, long-fingered hands, and then she looked away.

"Speaking of my neighborhood that's not yet officially my neighborhood, I need to get going. The senior VP wanted Bill and me to both turn in preliminary maps of our plans for Sunnybrooke. Nothing final, just like a rough concept sketch of ideas. I've been working so many hours I'm starting to dream in ARC GIS."

Sadie and her date stepped up to the side-by-side log targets, and she frowned. "You really have to go? It's still early."

"ARC GIS doesn't sound that preliminary to me," Bishop commented.

"Yeah, well, I want mine to be better than Bill's, don't I? Anyway, I'd be done by now but my computer's running so slow it's acting like it's losing as much sleep as I am."

"I can fix that. Valedictorian dropout, remember?" He poked her in the knee. "Why didn't you tell me? Computers are basically the one thing I'm good for."

Alice reached across Harlow to get a nacho. "You know it's not as much humble as annoying when you say that after kicking our asses at axe-throwing all night."

"Yes, I'd like to thank the academy and years of video games for my perfect hand-eye coordination..." he intoned.

Sadie's axe bounced back from the target with a loud clatter. "One stick. Harlow, you can't go home until I get it to stick at least *once*. Seriously, what am I doing wrong?"

"You need to throw it harder, babe. Put your back into it." Dusty walked up to retrieve his own hatchet off the rubber mats on the floor.

"Do you like the two-hand throw?" Bishop asked. "Maybe you're a two-hander." He hopped off the stool and grabbed one of the hatchets out of the holder. He stepped up next to Sadie and showed her how to hold it in both hands and raise it over her head before releasing straight down the center.

She lifted the hatchet, letting it droop down behind her head. "Oh, this feels weird, like I'm going to throw it straight through the wall or something."

"Do it." Bishop's eyes twinkled. "The guy at the front desk would be telling stories about you for years. He'd put your picture on the wall of axe-throwing renegades who are no longer allowed in."

"Okay, well, that would be a little cool." Sadie turned, wound up, and shrieked when it hit the edge of the target. "Ooh, it stuck! It stuck!"

"Don't pull it out, get your picture with that bad boy!" Bishop looked around. "Where's your phone?"

While he snapped Sadie's picture, Dusty scowled at both of them. "I'm gonna hit the shitter," he muttered, and slumped off toward the restrooms.

Sadie glanced after him, then dashed back to the bar. "So, what do you guys think of him?" She lowered her voice so it was pitched below the thuds of axes hitting logs and laughter from the other throwing stalls.

"Well, he's um…" Harlow couldn't remember a thing about Dusty when Bishop had just reclaimed his stool next to her. She could feel that whole side of her body more vividly, like her nerve endings were being tickled by a delicious breeze. "He's cute!" she finally managed.

"Bzzzt." Bishop gave a thumbs-down to go with his buzzer sound. "He flinches every time his axe bounces off the target. I do realize I'm the third wheel here and I don't get a vote, but really…" He gestured at the plate of nachos. "He ate all the chips with the meat on them while you were taking your turn throwing. And when he went to get water, he didn't bring any back for you."

Harlow nodded. "Plus, he said you looked nice tonight directly to your boobs."

"Bishop's right," Alice said. "The guy kind of brings his own bib."

His whole face lit up, and Harlow caught herself smiling along with him as he hopped off his stool to high-five Alice. "See? I told you I was going to make it a thing."

"And technically," Alice said, "you're not our third wheel, you're our fourth."

"Which is way more useful than a third," Sadie pointed out.

"Especially right now," Harlow said, "when we need you to go to the men's room and distract Dusty for another minute so we can girl talk."

"You got it." He snapped off a salute. "Fourth wheel reporting for duty." He caught Harlow's eye. "When I get back, we can take off and go do the computer thing. I know it's late, but I'll be quick, and then you'll have it for work tomorrow."

"Yeah, if you're sure. You seriously don't have to. I could probably hit up the IT department at work, I just haven't wanted to give up my computer for long enough to let them work on it."

"No worries at all. I've still got plenty of bad karma to work off."

Her heartbeat bounded, remembering the last thing he'd offered to work off his bad karma. But he still looked relaxed as ever, not like he had been trying to remind her of what they did together, so she just rolled with it.

"Just how misspent *was* your youth?"

He waggled his eyebrows at her. "Trust me. You don't even want to know."

She watched him go, waiting for him to get out of earshot.

"Why'd you make him stall Dusty when we already voted him off the island?" Sadie said.

"Duh, because she wants to talk about Bishop."

Harlow turned back to her friends. "I think I'm going to kiss Bishop."

"Didn't you already—"

She glared daggers at Sadie, and before Alice could catch on, she said, "No, we haven't kissed yet."

"What about Andrew the stockbroker?" Alice tugged her stool out away from the bar so they could sit in a closer huddle.

Harlow picked at the label on her beer bottle. "I may have already told him I didn't want to see him anymore."

"What about the puppy?" Sadie sighed. "Those pictures were adorable."

"I know, I almost did a fourth date just to meet the puppy. Those soft little ears…"

Alice was not about to be distracted by a puppy. "I thought you said Bishop wasn't relationship material."

"He's not. He's all but unemployed right now, actually. But jobs and stability aren't everything." She checked the hallway toward the bathrooms, but the coast was still clear. She was pretty sure Bishop could keep that guy talking as long as he wanted. Talking was one of his many talents. "Look, I got drunk the other night and the only thing I could think about was jumping him. Like, it was the most pure *want* I can remember since I found out you could design neighborhoods."

"I should point out that people have been known to get horny when they're drunk." Alice redid one of the tiny clips holding her hair back. "I imagine it's been a minute for you."

"Yeah, but that's the thing. When I was sober again, I realized, Drunk Me was *right*. Jumping his bones is exactly what I want. Lying to myself about it is just…not really working any more. And it gets worse."

Sadie leaned in, avidly chomping nachos. "Yes. Please tell us all of the worse."

Harlow tried not to meet her eyes, since she was going to reveal part of something Sadie already knew about and Alice didn't.

"The other night I was super tired and over everything, and the only person I could deal with talking to was him. Like, everybody else seemed like too much work and even though I was schlumpy and tired, I still wanted to see *him*."

"Harlow, marrrrry himmmm," Sadie groaned. "At this point, I'm already worried about how I can juggle it to stay friends with both of you if you break up."

"Which is *not* exactly a strong argument that they should get together."

"Okay, but you saw them at brunch! They had this rhythm with each other, like they'd been dating for years. When have we seen anybody that fit that well with Harlow, basically ever?"

Alice hesitated.

"That's what I thought." Sadie sat back with a creak of her stool.

Harlow glanced between her two friends, an ache growing in her chest. She knew it was crazy. She was just starting to wonder if playing by the rules could really get her *everything* she wanted. Because when it came to romance, all it had gotten her was bored.

Alice turned to her. "It's not that I don't get what you're saying, or why you're saying it."

Harlow's breaths were suddenly the wrong shape to stuff into her lungs, as if Alice were about to take away everything she wanted. Not that she would, but even though Alice wasn't her oldest friend, no one else got her like Alice did. They were basically the same person, and she knew whatever Alice said next, it was going to be true. Even if she didn't want to hear it.

"But?"

"But when you want a guy *this bad* even though you can't see a future with him? It's not necessarily a sign that it's all going to work out in the end. It's just a sign that when it doesn't work out, it's going to really make you bleed." Alice glanced down. "I would know."

Heat flashed through Harlow and suddenly the thump of axes all around them seemed louder, more final. "So what, because it didn't work out with you and Rob, that means I shouldn't go for it with a guy I finally feel something for?"

"It means…I love you." Alice slid off her stool and hugged her. "And I'm here for you, no matter what happens."

CHAPTER 16

$\mathcal{B}$ ishop was back in Harlow's apartment.

He wasn't sure what bothered him more: the way her place looked like a magazine but felt like a hug and was the existential antithesis of his own sauerkraut-and-saggy-futon combo, or the fact that the last time he was here, he'd had his hand down Harlow's pants.

Oh, who was he kidding? It was the second, by a mile.

That was the thing with penance, though, wasn't it? It was supposed to suck. If it didn't hurt, it didn't really count. Which meant the memory of Harlow's soft panties heating under his palm counted. A lot.

He shook his head, disconnecting the cable between his laptop and hers now that he'd transferred the software he needed. He couldn't remember the last time he'd had trouble focusing when he had a computer in front of him.

"I can't believe you brought me a present when you're already coming over to fix my laptop." Harlow perched on the dining room table next to the laptops, playing with the colorful twelve-pack of bath bombs he'd bought her.

"Yeah, but I didn't know I was going to be fixing your laptop when

I bought the present," he said without looking up from typing. "And a bathtub like that deserves accessories."

"You shouldn't be wasting your money on that, or on buying nachos for everyone."

"Says the girl who paid the group cover charge. The least I could do was buy dinner. Besides, the food truck took PhonePay."

"Just because it comes out of your phone doesn't mean it's not real money."

"Right, yeah of course." And that was why he shouldn't try to type and talk at the same time. He searched for a way to cover his slip. "Sort of. I've still got money in that account because that's where the Match app pays me for the jokes, and you can't really get the money off the internet from there."

"You can if you link it to your bank account."

Which of course, is what normal people would do, who didn't need to keep their stolen money and their real name from being seen together in public. He changed the subject, and hit the last button to start her computer scanning for malware. "Hey, so this is going to take a minute to run, so what do you want to do?"

He flashed her a smile without entirely looking at her. Too dangerous. She was made for the soft golden tones of late-night lamplight, and right now, she glowed.

"Want to watch another episode of Veronica Mars? Or do you need to get to bed? I can finish up on my own if you don't mind me letting myself out when I'm done. I know you've got work in the morning."

She set down the bath bombs. She was looking at him in a way that made it impossible to stop thinking about kissing her. He closed his eyes. Why the fuck had he thought it was a good idea to invite himself over to her place after what happened last time?

He'd woken up in the middle of the night with her cuddled into his chest, smelling like vanilla and whiskey and arousal, and he had been so hard he'd seriously considered popping a Tylenol for the pain. He'd slammed three shots of whiskey instead, trying to feel anything else past the clawing desire to kiss her awake, and he'd ended up so drunk he had to sleep in her bathtub.

Classy move, dude.

"Bishop? Are you okay?"

He opened his eyes, intending to say something flippant to get them back onto safer ground, and the joke evaporated as soon as he realized how close she was standing. She saw it all in his face. He could tell she did because her expression changed and she took a step toward him.

He twitched and jumped out of the chair. "I should—"

She touched his cheek. Her fingertips sliding up the roughness of his stubble. Her other hand brushing his, where his fingers hung numbly at his sides. She twined their hands together, tilting her head as she looked up at him.

He had to move away. He had to step back and stop her and make her think he didn't want this. That he wouldn't give his right leg for her to keep leaning infinitesimally closer to his lips. From this near, she smelled incredible. Like fresh wood chips they'd knocked off the axe-throwing targets and this dark velvet perfume she'd only worn twice before. He wanted to inhale her, gobble her up, wrap her inside his clothes.

Their lips touched, and Harlow's breath sighed out as she swayed into his chest. His hand tightened on hers reflexively, but he was so dizzy with sensation he didn't know if he was steadying her or knocking them both off balance.

His heart punched him straight in the throat.

"Damn it," he growled, and shoved both hands into her hair, tipping her head back so the kiss went deep and harsh. She pressed up onto her toes, her lips bruising his between little gasps for air. A chair bumped his knee and he kicked it out of the way, barely registering the crash as it hit the floor because he was backing her up into the wall, and now the whole length of her body was rubbing into his.

"Shit." He slapped his palms against the wall, and weakly considered pushing away from her. "Throw me out, would you?"

She was grinning, her eyes shining like all the light in the world had gathered up behind them. "So you *do* want me."

He scoffed out a laugh. "You think?" That finally got him to take a step back, thanks to the reminder that he was Tylenol-hard again. It might be marginally less embarrassing if she didn't notice it only took a single kiss from her to get his dick to point straight to the space station. "Harlow, what are we doing here?"

She tucked a strand of hair behind her ear, caught between bold and shy, and he wanted to cuddle her for it. "Just so you know, I decided to stop seeing Andrew."

"Are you kidding? Right after he got a puppy?"

"Enough with the puppy already."

"I'm just saying, if you're dropping a dude who has two degrees, makes six figures, and has an adorable puppy, all so you can make out with me, it's possible you're getting the short end of the stick."

She crossed her arms over her chest, but her eyes were still luminous when she peeked up through her lashes at him. "I think that dude never kissed me the way you just did."

He wanted to give her every breath he'd ever breathed in his life. And out of the corner of his eye, he saw his laptop sitting there like a murder weapon about to drip blood on the table.

Why the hell hadn't he met this girl when he was twenty?

He took a step back, then another, and dropped into one of her dining room chairs, suddenly exhausted by his life. "Look, Harlow, I know I joke around a lot about my crappy choices, but pretty much all of it is true. You should know that. After the shit I've done, I don't have a lot of pride left. But I don't want to be the ex that a woman regrets. Especially not when that woman is you."

The light in her face changed, and she pressed her lips together. "What I regret is letting you talk me out of dating you in the first place. I think you're too hard on yourself, and I've been letting you get away with it because I'm secretly too hard on everyone."

He looked away, his knee jiggling with tension. He couldn't exactly explain to her why she was wrong, why she wasn't hard enough on him. But he couldn't agree with her, either.

"Seriously, Bishop, what makes you such a terrible choice for a boyfriend? So what if you didn't finish your degree? Do you think I'm that big of a snob? Or wait, maybe it's because you work your ass off at a ton of different part-time jobs so you can have the flexibility to be there for your little sister. Instead of taking one full-time job that would pay better, probably be easier, and leave your sister high and dry. Yeah, you're right. That's unforgivable."

She picked up the chair he'd knocked over, setting it back on the hardwood with a gentle click and sitting down with him.

"My parents are in prison."

"What?" He actually twitched, like the words jumped out and startled him. "Both of them? But when—" It had to be a long time ago, when she was a baby or something. Maybe she was adopted by a nice middle-class family. He couldn't picture a five-star citizen like Harlow being created by convicts.

"They got arrested my senior year of high school. I spent the last semester in foster care so I wouldn't have to move schools to stay with family out of state. I don't tell a lot of people because…" She took a breath, then let it out on a little laugh. "Well, because I worry they'll judge our family as harshly as I judge our family. Then the other day, listening to you talk about your parents and your sister and everything you guys have been through together, I don't know." She shrugged. "It reminded me that it's not always so simple as good people do the right thing and bad people do the wrong thing."

A laptop chimed that it was done, and he couldn't even remember what he'd set it to do.

"I think because of my parents, the mistakes they made, I've been trying too hard to be sensible in my own life," she said. "Picking guys based on their jobs and five-year plans and sneakily asking test questions like whether they ever bought renter's insurance. It's like I'm trying to plan an arranged marriage, but for myself. The results have about as much mojo as if I'd let my mom do the picking for me."

He really, really wanted to know what her parents were in prison for. It better not have been anything to do with how they treated her. If they'd been abusive, what he'd do in response was going to add

117

another big black mark to the bad person column of his personal ledger. But he also wanted to hear what this had to do with her deciding to kiss him.

"So what are you saying?"

She smiled, her gaze slipping back to his lips and heating. When she came closer, she did it slowly, like she was giving him the chance to turn her down. As if he had that capability left in his morally bankrupt body. All he could do was stare like he was a fish and he'd jumped right on her hook.

She swung her leg over his chair and straddled his lap. "I just realized the only person I really want to be kissing is you." She pouted, her eyes playful. "You gonna make me go back to boring kisses with other guys?"

He was so fucked.

Bishop slipped his hands up the back of her shirt, widening his fingers to span her waist. She sucked in a breath and he could feel the faint prickle of goosebumps under his fingertips. She was even prettier up close.

"You don't like flings. I'm a fling."

"Quit trying to talk me out of you."

"It's kind of my job as your official date screener."

"Well, considering your hand is up my shirt, I think you already gave yourself the green light."

His head fell forward, resting against her breastbone. "I'm so fired."

"Bishop."

"Yeah?"

"Get your head out of my tits and kiss me."

A laugh coughed out of him and he pulled her tighter into his lap, one arm around her waist and one hand sprawled at the nape of her neck. He meant to start slow, but his tongue delved deep with hers, and they were zero to sixty and breathless in an instant.

"I hate that you make me laugh," he whispered against her mouth.

"I can tell how much you hate it."

She rocked her hips against his growing erection.

"Oh that? That's just because you're hot. It's the making-me-laugh

118

thing that's really getting me in trouble." He kept coming back to her lips between every sentence, like he didn't want to stop kissing her long enough to talk, but he didn't want to give up talking to her, either.

"How so?"

He pulled back, his whole body blazing when he looked at her. This girl. *Damn.*

He didn't answer. Instead, he stood up and swung her into his arms and carried her down the hall, through the open door to her bedroom.

"I'm not assuming anything, by the way. I just need to get you out of my lap or I'm going to assume you all the way to next Sunday."

"How about let's extend it to the Wednesday after? The Wednesday after's good for me." She smiled sunnily, not looking at all like the nervous girl who confessed to him that it was hard for her to get naked with someone she hadn't known that long.

He flicked on a lamp and put a knee on the bed next to her, then paused as he glanced around. "Of course you have the prettiest bedroom in the world."

The bed was huge, with some sort of gently furry blanket the color of thick cream, with raspberry scrollwork around the edges and an antiqued brass headboard. In one corner was a reading chair with its own little lamp and oversized ottoman, a chunky knitted blanket thrown artistically over one arm.

"I want to come home and find you reading on that chair and then put my head under your blanket until you drop the book. And by the time I'm done with you, you can't look at that chair without blushing for the rest of your life."

"Whoa, that's...specific."

He dropped his forehead to hers. "Harlow."

"Yeah?"

"I'm way too turned on to be kissing you right now."

"Really?" She dragged her nails down his stomach and tugged at his belt buckle. "Can I see?"

"Definitely not." If he let her hands into his pants right now, it was all going to be over, and he really didn't want this to be over. Instead, he rolled her over onto her stomach and straddled her, threading his fingers together with hers to hold her hands over her head.

He bent and nuzzled his face into the caramel and vanilla colored waves of her hair, biting and then kissing the nape of her neck. "You have no idea how insanely much time I've spent thinking about doing this lately."

"Bishop?"

"Yeah?"

"Take off my shirt."

He released her hands to strip it off over her head. Sweet hell, all of her skin was burnished golden and silky and he couldn't think of a single thing except how to get his mouth on as much of it as possible. He left kisses all the way down the graceful line of her spine, the steam filling up his head getting thicker. By the time he reached the line of her pants, he bit the curve of her ass straight through her jeans.

She squeaked with a little gasp and he rose so he could rub his hands up the back of her legs. Letting his thumbs find the inside seam of her jeans and follow it up to the center. He rubbed a circle right there, watching her fists clench in the pillows, her hair wild across the fabric.

He wanted a picture of her laying like this, wanted to lock it into his mind and keep it like the best secret he'd ever have for the rest of his life. She reached back and popped the clasp of her bra, baring the last bit of her back, and he had to blink twice just to see straight. He pulled his shirt off over his head and dove down to her. She flipped over beneath him and her bra was a tangled mess of lace and underwire between them, the velvet tip of one nipple skimming his chest. He drove his hands into her hair, thrusting against her because it made him crazy to feel that heat radiating through her jeans.

The scrape of denim against denim brought him back to himself and he pulled away from her swollen lips with a choked laugh.

"Jesus, five minutes with you and you've got me back to dry humping like we're in junior high."

She hooked one leg around his hip. "I don't remember it feeling that good in junior high."

She tugged on his belt, unhooking it, and he thought there was a reason he should be stopping her but he couldn't remember it. Mostly because he was lost in the glory of kissing her throat. Her pulse pounding against his tongue, the last hints of that dark perfume lighting up his brain like a neon sign that said "Beautiful Woman, This Way."

Cool air hit his ass, and he realized she'd worked his jeans most of the way off. *Oh, fuck it.* He abandoned any hope of being a good person tonight, and rolled onto his side so he could shuck his pants. They got caught on the shoes he had completely forgotten he was still wearing, and he nearly ripped the laces straight out of his boots getting them off. He didn't totally get out of the second sock, but that was as much as he could manage before he rolled back on top of her, his skin bare against her jeans.

She'd gotten rid of her bra while he was busy hating his boots, and he got lost in the sight of her. He smoothed his palm down over the most perfect breasts he'd ever seen in his life, all the way down to where her stomach was fluttering just above her jeans. Which pulled his eyes back to her face, because he was breathing hard, too, but not that hard.

She had her head turned, not looking at him, and her cheeks were flushed pink.

"Harlow? You okay?"

She blew out a breath and rolled her eyes. "I'm fine. I'm such a *girl* sometimes."

He came up, covering her body with his and kissing the tip of her nose. "It's hard for me to understand you saying that like it's a bad thing."

"It's just first times, sometimes, for me. You know." She paused, still avoiding his eyes. "Can you...kind of hug me? Like you did on the couch?"

Pain thrummed in his chest. "Ah, sweetheart." He found her hands and kissed first the left, then the right, and held her palms flat against his neck so she could feel how fast his pulse was beating, too. "I've got you. I've always got you, okay?"

He rolled onto his back, letting his legs sprawl so she could lie between them and wrapping his arms securely around her. One hand cradled her head and the other covered as much of her bare back as he could reach.

"It doesn't have to be our first time tonight, you know. It doesn't have to be anything except whatever you want it to be. I just got a little wound up for a second there. In my defense, there are a shortage of perfect breasts in the world. It's not that surprising I lost my head on first sight of yours."

She smiled against his neck. "Was that a mangled *Princess Bride* reference?"

"If you wish."

"Also mangled."

He kissed the top of her head.

"Bishop?"

"Yeah?"

"I didn't want you to stop. I'm like 10.2 on a scale of 1-10."

"Hmm…" He nibbled her ear while he thought, and the way it made her shiver against him was distracting as all hell.

"What does hmm mean?" she asked warily.

"Hmm is me trying to figure out how to go down on you and hold you at the same time."

Her breath came in with a little stuttered catch. "I'm okay now. Promise. I just had a moment, that's all."

He turned them onto their sides so he could move, bringing her hand up to his mouth and nibbling a path along its edge. "What if I held your hands?"

She was panting again, her amber brown eyes dilated with arousal. He hooked a finger under the button of her jeans.

"Can I?"

She ripped it open herself, then jerked the zipper down. He laughed and curled his fingers into her waistband, pulling them all the way off. Unlike him, she'd kicked off her shoes as soon as they got home, so her pants went easily. Smart girl. He left her panties, partially to give her a minute to adjust and partially to torment himself. They were pale pink silk and lace and he was probably going to be thinking about them for the next six months of his life, at least.

He scooted down, nuzzling his face against her belly. "What if I promise not to look at your gorgeously naked body?" He kissed her belly button, reaching up to cover one of her small, soft breasts with his palm. "And I keep my tongue so busy you don't have time to worry what I'm thinking about?" He licked her navel, slicking the flat of his tongue in a slow, warm trail from the edge of her panties back up to her belly button. Her abs shivered and her nails scored his shoulders.

"You're officially my favorite friend I've ever had right now." She laughed breathlessly. "But you know way too much about me. I should never have told you that because now you know what's going on in my head when I'm trying to brazen out the hot-but-awkward first-time sex."

"I might have something that can help with that."

"Oh? What is—" Her question broke off into a gasp as he took the side of her panties in his teeth and tugged upward so the fabric pulled tight between her legs.

"First, turn up the hot part so the awkward part gets smaller." He slicked his tongue under the side band of her panties, then moved to press a chaste kiss right over the center. "Second, you don't have to wonder, because what I'm thinking is 'Oh God, she's so hot I'm going to come too fast and she's gonna hate me.'"

She laughed, shaking beneath him.

He squirmed, because her soft bedspread was doing great things to his cock, as was the sight of her mostly naked and laughing, with her hair spread out across the pillow like a sex-thrashed halo.

He hooked a finger through the front of her panties, rubbing her with the back of his knuckle. "You want these off or on?"

"Um, don't you need them off?"

"I can work around, if you'd be more comfortable." He kissed his way in from the leg opening, demonstrating with a rough rub of his tongue exactly how little they could be in his way.

"Oh wow. Off, though. Definitely off."

He dragged them down, settling one of her legs over his shoulder and smoothing his cheek against her thigh. "Ah, now, honey, how am I going to hold your hands if you're fisting the bedspread like that?"

She flushed and let go of her tight grip on the blanket. He caught her left hand, rubbing his thumb across her knuckles as he mirrored the movement with his mouth on a place a lot more personal.

She wasn't loud. Her pleasure came out in a series of sucked-in breaths and low moans that vibrated more often in her belly than escaped through her mouth. He liked her tiny sounds so much that even though he was excruciatingly turned on, he slowed down even more. Drawing it out until her orgasm was a slow cresting wave. Then he scooped his hands under her ass, lifting her and holding her to his mouth as his movements gentled, coaxing her to keep coming long after she should have dropped back down the other side.

When he let her down, she went completely relaxed. He crawled up next to her and tucked her into his arms. "Want more?"

Her hand closed around his cock and his hips jerked forward.

"I'm going to take that as a yes. Can I also take that as a 'you have a condom'? Hopefully? Because I did not in any way come prepared for this."

She twitched, moving slow and uncoordinated as she dug in the bedside table. Throwing out a novel, a flashlight, a rattling bottle of aspirin or something, and then coming up with a ripped-open box of condoms. She tore the square with her teeth and reached for him. His eyes closed and head fell back as her hand smoothed down over him, giving a squeeze to his swollen tip before she sheathed him.

He threw an arm over her waist and kissed her, brushing her hair back away from her face. Looking at her right now did something to him. Something unsteady and reeling that had nothing to do with the desire pumping through his every vein.

His voice came out rough when he said, "How do you want me, sweetheart?"

She blinked and hesitated, like she hadn't expected him to ask, then all in a rush she said, "Just like on the couch. Would that be weird?"

He caught her back against his chest and rolled her up on top of him, finding a pillow to support her head. The position thrust her breasts right into his line of sight, and her body was tormentingly warm all along the front of him. He was so, so glad he'd asked.

"I've thought about it so many times, what it would have been like if you just pulled down your pants and thrust up into me, how perfect and—"

He pushed up into her. No finesse, no waiting, just a jagged pulse as his whole body surged to get closer to her. To feel her wet and clasping him while she was saying those dirty, delicious things that he thought had only been in his own fantasies and *damn*. She felt even better than those fantasies.

"Ah—" She stuttered a breath of a sound and squeezed down all around his arousal.

He groaned, and she said, "Bishop, oh my gosh, you better not come too fast right now or I am really going to hate you."

He coughed on something that might have been a laugh if he had enough breath to do anything but rail up into her, every thrust melting delicious wetness all the way down his cock.

That roaring in the back of his head was already threatening, the edge too close. The feel and scent and sight of her getting him off way too damn fast. He reached around and cupped her between her legs, his palm getting slick and wet the first time his thrust from behind pushed her against his hand.

That time she moaned out loud. His other hand wrapped around her torso and thumbed her nipple, holding her tight and teasing more pleasure into her all at once. Her last orgasm was so close, it took almost nothing at all to push her into another one. The sound of her gasping out his name wiped his entire brain clean and beautiful.

He bucked underneath her, losing hold of his carefully slowed speed and lifting both their bodies off the mattress with a hammering rhythm that jolted him into climax, the lightning of pleasure streaking down his burning thighs and up his heaving abs, and making him choke on air he couldn't remember how to breathe as he collapsed back down with her whole weight on top of him.

"Oh wow," he wheezed.

Harlow turned, coming to rest on her side as her eyes found his, looking a little stunned.

He cupped her face and kissed her, even though he hadn't at all caught his breath enough for that, because he didn't want to miss his chance. Once he started, her tongue felt so good in the humming of his post-orgasm glow that he kept on kissing her until he ran out of air and had to pull back.

She still looked wide-eyed. "That was—"

He grinned, but it came out wobbly, like every part of him was staggering. "Something, right?"

"Something."

He ditched the condom in the trash can to the side of her bed. Then pulled the bedspread up to cover her, laying a kiss on her bare shoulder as he cuddled in behind her. Reaching out, he caught the switch for the lamp and clicked it off. She was already relaxing into sleep, but he knew how she was, and he was pretty sure if he let her drift off without saying anything, she'd get weird about this in the morning. Probably start to worry that because it was spur of the moment, that it was casual. As if *anything* about what just happened could be called casual.

He couldn't stay away from her, no matter what he'd told himself. As for how he could be with her without her finding out how he was paying his sister's bills, he had no idea. But he wanted to, more than he'd let himself want anything in a long time.

"Harlow?"

"Hmm?" She reached back, her fingernails trailing down the side of his neck and making his skin tingle. He hesitated, because he didn't know how to say this. Hell, he didn't even know if there were words for whatever was kicking him so sideways right now. But he definitely knew the words for what it *wasn't*.

"I didn't fuck you just because I'm attracted to you. If that's all it was, I would have made myself stop."

126

Her hand paused in its stroking, and her voice in the dark was tentative, like she wasn't sure what he'd say next. "Why didn't you stop, then?"

"Because you make me laugh. I'm a goner for a girl who can make me laugh." His grip on her tightened. "And when you asked if you had to go back to kissing other guys, I wanted to commit homicide."

"Hey, Bishop?"

"Yeah."

"If all I wanted out of this was to fuck you, well..." She paused. "I probably would have done it anyway. You're really hot."

He snorted into startled laughter, then grabbed her and growled a kiss against her shoulder. "You are such an asshole."

"Yeah." She grinned. "But I make you laugh."

CHAPTER 17

*H*arlow woke up happy and cozy when it was so early it was still dark outside. She stretched, confused by the fuzzy feeling of her bedspread against nude skin instead of crisp sheets and her pajamas. Then she remembered last night, and a slow smile spread across her face.

Bishop.

She'd scraped up her courage, and told her friends so she couldn't back out, and kissed him. And it had gone...well. Wow.

When she kissed someone for the first time, it usually didn't head straight from there to bed, but maybe that was just because all those other times, she hadn't been kissing *Bishop*.

She reached out, her grin broadening, but hit only empty bed. The bathroom was right across the hall and the door was open so she could see he wasn't in there, either. Her outstretched hand began to curl closed, but no. He wouldn't have run out on her. Not Bishop. Not the guy who woke her when she when she was already dozing last night, just to make sure she knew this meant more to him than only sex.

Except wait, last time he stayed over, he'd made her breakfast. Cinnamon waffles from scratch—who did that?—and eggs so fluffy she couldn't even tease him when he bragged about being a breakfast food virtuoso. He was probably already in the kitchen. She rolled over in bed, hiding her grinning face in the pillow for a minute. Her friends were not going to believe this. Two orgasms on their first time *and* gourmet breakfast.

There was something about this guy, the kind of "something" she'd been waiting for. Except now that it was here, it sparked so much brighter and more arresting than she'd been expecting. And smaller, at the same time.

She just kind of wanted to hang out with him more than anyone else, and his jokes seemed funnier than everyone else's, and he always got what she was saying without her having to explain it. They liked the same shows and he didn't like but *loved* brunch, and he knew where everything was in her kitchen without asking, because her mind just made sense to him. She was so freaking lucky she'd taken the leap to leave their friendship behind and go for it.

Maybe this was the kind of luck you got when you stopped being a judgy little asshole who wouldn't consider any man as a potential match unless he showed up with a 401(k).

She dropped her feet to the floor and thrilled inwardly when her toes found his discarded shirt. *Ha!* She knew he hadn't ditched her. The shirt went on over her head, the fabric arousing against her skin just because it was his. She padded into the other room, waiting for sounds of pans clanging. But Bishop wasn't cooking—he was asleep with his head on her dining room table.

Her laptop was closed, so he must have finished whatever magic tricks he was doing to it, and his laptop was open in front of him. His back was lean and muscular above the jeans he must have thrown on whenever he slipped out of the bedroom last night.

The clock on the microwave informed her that she still had thirty minutes before her alarm went off. Plenty of time to wake him up so they could say goodbye properly before work.

She bent over and brushed a kiss over his bare neck. "Good morning, handsome."

He twitched, his hand brushing the trackpad so the screensaver vanished to reveal a job hunting website full of computer-related words. She melted a little as she began to understand.

He was so determined that she shouldn't date a broke deadbeat that as soon as they hooked up, he got up in the middle of the night to hunt for what looked like freelance coding jobs. Just judging by how worried he was, it was clear he was nothing like her mooching exes. Not to mention the distinctly unselfish way he'd taken care of her last night in bed.

She rubbed a fond circle over his shoulders. "You're going to throw your back out if you keep sleeping in weird places every time you stay over." As she spoke, her eyes flicked across the second pane he had open. It was a spreadsheet, full of so many numbers that at first she assumed it was also some sort of computer thing. But then she saw the column of names, and the column of four-digit dates. Months and years only, just like...what the hell?

They were credit card numbers. *Other people's* credit card numbers.

Bishop sat up and her hand fell away from his back.

"Hmm?" he mumbled, and then he seemed to focus on the screen. He clicked fast to minimize the spreadsheet, then turned in his chair. As soon as he saw her face, he bolted to standing, his eyes wide.

"Please tell me there's a reason you have all those credit card numbers. A really good reason, like—" She stalled out, trying to think of any legal reason you'd have possession of other people's credit cards.

But the sadness in his eyes, the way his whole face fell when their gaze met...he didn't look like there was a good explanation. Harlow's body began to tingle dizzily at the edges, like she was about to get really sick, or have a headache that came on all in one bright day-erasing flash. She needed to sit down. She needed to know where those credit card numbers came from, and why he'd left her naked and alone in bed to go back to working on them.

"Hold on." Bishop looked around, then darted over and threw open the lid of her roll top desk. He pulled a notepad out of one of her carefully organized pigeonholes, snatched up a pen, and started scribbling.

"Seriously?" She gaped, tears starting to burn at the corners of her eyes. "You got a brilliant idea that can't wait, right *now*? For what, how to steal from more people?"

"No, just please—" He was still writing. "Let me do this, because…" He tore off the sheet and when his eyes came back to hers, her tears broke free.

He still looked like the person she knew. The guy who remembered more random details of her neighborhood plan than her boss did, who made up little catchphrase inside jokes that made her dating fails seem funny instead of heartbreaking, who brought her ice cream and egg rolls, and made her smile when she was too tired to go out. He looked exactly like that guy, but she didn't know him at all.

Proving her point even more, he crossed the apartment to the kitchen, put a piece of bread in the toaster, and pushed it down.

"After what I'm about to tell you, you're probably not going to be hungry, but you'll feel worse if you don't eat. And I know you're not going to believe anything else I say." He brought the paper to her. "So I wrote it down, so I at least get to say it, once." He swallowed, looking even more sick than she felt. "I lied to you, Harlow, yes, but not everything is a lie. How I feel about you has nothing to do with the things I've had to do for money."

There was no explanation coming. She could feel that empty truth wedging itself in between all the other words he was saying. The man she'd been falling for was stealing other people's money.

She knocked the letter away, letting it fall to the ground. "Don't. Don't try to excuse it. Everybody needs more money than they have, right? The rest of us work for it, Bishop. That's what you do. Because guess what? The rules apply to you. They apply to everyone, even when you think they don't. Sooner or later everything you've done will catch up to you and you're going to be so *surprised* when the consequences slap you right in your smug little face."

"No," he said quietly. "I won't."

She couldn't take the way he was looking at her. She spun away. "Just go."

"No, there's more that you—"

131

"I don't *care*, Bishop." She threw out her arms as she whirled back around. "Can't you see nothing you say is going to change anything?"

"Actually, it's going to make it worse." His perfectly chiseled jaw was tight, no trace of humor anywhere on his face. "But I need to say it anyway. One of the credit card numbers I stole was yours. Your card was the one I used to pay for my Match subscription, and I'm sorry for that, but I'm not sorry for meet—"

The toast popped.

Her breathing had gone jerky and inadequate, and tears blurred her vision. "Why the hell would you tell me that?"

"Because it's the truth and you deserve to know."

"I *deserve* a man who doesn't lie to me in the first place." She stomped back to her bedroom, snatched up his boots and brought them back to the living room, shoving them at him. She turned and ripped his laptop off the table, then grabbed the bath bombs he'd brought her last night. Out of guilt, probably.

I've still got plenty of bad karma to work off.

She stuffed the laptop against his chest, the fancy box of bath bombs denting in the strength of her grip as she stared down at it.

If he knew it was her card that had paid his subscription, that was probably the whole reason he'd gone on a date with her in the first place. Their entire relationship probably existed because he felt guilty. No wonder he'd been such a good friend, so attentive and sweet and charming. Not only that, this gift was almost certainly bought with other people's money. Stolen money.

Her fingers tightened and she hurled the bath bombs in his direction. The package hit him and jolted open. He yelped and jumped back as colorful balls went rolling in every direction.

"Okay, I get it! I'm going." He backed toward the door, clutching his boots and laptop against his bare chest.

Where was his shirt? Oh God, she was still wearing it. She reached for the hem and his eyes widened.

"No, hey, keep it. You don't—"

She ripped the shirt off and threw it in his face.

"I'd rather go naked than have anything of yours touching me."

His whole body sagged back against the door, like the flimsy weight of the tee shirt had tipped the balance and it was all more than he could carry. He wouldn't look at her.

"I'm sorry, Harlow. If you don't believe a single other thing I say, believe that." He flipped the switch in the handle so it would lock behind him, and slipped out.

Her throat twisted so hard that for a second, she wasn't sure if she was going to cry or vomit. She jumped forward and slammed the deadbolt closed, then fell against the door as her sobs shook her, her shoulder slowly sliding down its surface until she was on the floor. From here, all she could see were the bright bath bombs rolling in every direction, and a single piece of paper lying on the floor.

His note. Everything he'd needed her to hear that he knew she'd be too upset to listen to.

She bolted off the ground and snatched it up, then tore it into pieces.

CHAPTER 18

"*D*o you want coffee, hun?" the waitress asked.

Harlow didn't lift her head off the vinyl of the diner's table. "Yes. And water." She knew she looked like a wreck, and she didn't care. She couldn't eat yet, but even so, the smell of hash browns and pancakes was soothing.

"There you are. I thought this booth was empty. Did two rounds through the whole place already." Alice slid in across from her. "Listen, I know you said you needed butter and alcohol stat, but it's seven in the morning and I'm not a miracle worker. So, this place has plenty of butter, and I have your 'special smoothie'!"

Harlow lifted her head to see her friend giving her a perky smile and a waggle of a metal water bottle. Like a flask, only bigger and more innocent looking.

"I love you." She reached for the water bottle, but Alice pulled it back.

"Listen, I totally understand how getting a crush on a guy who turned out to be a credit card thief would put you in a position to need an infusion of butter and alcohol. No judgement. But as your best friend, it's my duty to mention at least once that it's a weekday, and you're in the middle of racing the boss's brother-in-law for a promotion. It's really not the time to risk calling in for boy drama."

Harlow waved a hand in front of her tear-swollen face. "Are you seeing this? Do you really think I can go into work looking like this and not ruin all those years of my reputation as the steady, consummate professional?"

Alice handed over the alcohol.

Harlow took it, casting another glance across the table. Thinking about her own blotchy skin, messy ponytailed hair, and red eyes only made it more obvious by contrast that Alice was looking especially good today. Her friend's eyes had a focused spark to them, her skin was luminous, and she was sitting up straighter, like her body didn't feel so heavy. Had she gone to a spa? Heavens knew she deserved one after the tough few weeks she'd had...but wait, she was also missing one earring.

"You had *sex!*"

Alice flushed. "Honey, we're here to talk about you."

"Who wants to talk about that? My life is stupid, and I was stupid, and you had sex so good you didn't even notice you *lost an earring.*"

Alice's hand flew up to cover the ear that still had an earring, which was deeply suspicious. Harlow launched herself across the table and started trying to wrestle Alice's hand down so she could see whatever her friend was trying to hide.

The waitress chose that moment to appear with Harlow's coffee and water. "Um, ladies, did you want—"

"Coffee." Alice smiled up at her, perfectly composed as she folded her hands back into her lap. "And water with lemon, please."

Harlow fell back into her seat, sliding the metal water bottle under the table so the waitress wouldn't start in about outside beverages.

As soon as she left, though, Harlow pointed across the table to Alice's earlobe. "The lilies! The sex was so good you lost one of your freaking *lily* earrings and didn't even notice." Then she realized the implications of that and cringed. "Oh no, Alice, do you think it's lost for good?"

"I did notice I lost it," her friend said. "And I did look." A smile started to peek through. "But I'll be back there again soon, and he swore not to vacuum until we find it."

"If that man's smart, he took the earring knowing you'd have to come back for it."

Alice looked down, and the hairs on the back of Harlow's neck prickled. A guy Alice just met wouldn't know the significance of the lily earrings she inherited from her grandmother, but *Rob* would.

Harlow sucked in a shocked breath and Alice jumped. "Don't be mad. I know what he did was terrible and I shouldn't forgive him or condone that behavior and I don't, but I—" Her eyes were pleading. "I couldn't stay away from him any longer. It was hurting me as much as it was him. Look, I know you're stronger than me when it comes to this stuff, but I..." She opened her hands, fingers stretching, but couldn't seem to find the right words. "I love him. It wasn't even a question of could I love him after what he did, because I just *did*."

Harlow opened her mouth, closed it again. Alice had been miserable without Rob, there was no arguing that, and she looked so much happier this morning. "Look, I can't judge you for taking him back. I clearly have no room to talk about falling for screw-up guys." A flash of Bishop's stricken expression seared itself into her brain, and Harlow dropped her head back onto the table. "He made me toast."

"What? When? Because I mean, that's nice but that doesn't excuse committing fraud."

"After I found the credit card numbers." She lifted her head to send a grimace Alice's way. "He didn't say a word at first, he just went and made me toast, and wrote me a whole letter. He said once I knew the truth, I probably wouldn't feel like eating, but I needed to." She fumbled, her shoulders curling forward as she tried to fight away the image of him quietly, quickly caring for her, when he knew she was about to be furious with him. "Alice, you have to go to my apartment and get rid of the toast. Please? I can't go back and...*fuck*. Why did he make me toast?" She dug her hands into her hair, pushing her fingertips against her temples. Her body felt like a bag of aches she was struggling to prop upright.

Alice came around the other side of the booth, pulling Harlow into her arms and tucking Harlow's head against her shoulder. "Oh sweetheart, of course I'll throw away your toast. Shh, hey, come on. Don't cry."

But Harlow couldn't stop, even though she tried holding her breath so no one would hear. Why had she come to a stupid diner? Now she couldn't stop smelling toast, even though her nose should be too clogged to smell anything.

"He made me toast and locked the door when I made him leave so I'd be safe, and I threw bath bombs at him. And he flinched, too, like it hurt. I've never been so violent in my entire life. I yelled, Alice. Me! Fully raised my voice in the middle of an argument and shouted, like I was on reality TV or something."

"Bath bombs!" Alice shook her head. "I mean, I admire your scruples, but why waste good bath bombs?"

"I couldn't keep them. They were bought with dirty money." Harlow sniffled.

Alice squeezed her tighter, and the waitress slowed next to their table, but Alice must have fixed her with a death-by-look stare because the waitress sped up and kept on going. "Tell me more about the letter. Is it like a Dear John letter? What did he write down that he didn't say out loud?"

"There was a letter?" Sadie's purse hit the seat of their booth with a thud. "You didn't say anything about a letter on the phone."

Harlow pulled back. "You called Sadie?"

"Why didn't *you* call Sadie?" Alice's eyes skewered her.

She avoided both of their gazes. She'd only called Alice because Sadie was the sweet one. If she talked to Sadie, Harlow would just give in and call Bishop and let him make excuses for what he did, and she'd take him back. She figured Alice would yell at her and make her strong, and remind her how stupid she'd been not to recognize the signs of ill-gotten money earlier than she had.

Except Alice was hugging her and smuggling her booze, and Sadie was here anyway, and Harlow was so screwed. None of this was working out the way she had planned, and if they guessed why she sometimes called one of them individually instead of both, she was pretty sure they'd both be hurt.

Maybe they'd think she was so upset, she forgot to call Sadie and there was nothing more to it.

"You know, I don't appreciate being volunteered as bad cop," Alice said.

Or maybe not.

"You love being bad cop," Harlow muttered.

"True, but I don't like being *volunteered* to be bad cop. Important distinction."

"He wrote you a letter after you threw him out?" Sadie broke in, impatient with their argument. She scooted into the booth across from them and grabbed Harlow's untouched coffee. "I thought this all happened this morning?"

"He wrote the letter before I threw him out."

"Like on paper, with no emojis?" Sadie slurped coffee without taking her eyes off Harlow. "Shut up, that's so old school romance."

"I tore it up."

"*What?!*" Sadie's screech was so loud a baby at another table started to cry.

Harlow lifted a weak apology wave to the kid's dad, then took a long drink from her illicit water bottle.

"I can't believe you got a breakup letter from a romantic thief and you *tore it up*." Sadie set the coffee cup down with a loud clunk. "If you didn't un-tear it, we are no longer friends."

"How would that even be possible?" Alice said. "Jeez, Sadie, go easy. Look at her. She doesn't need to be yelled at right now. Are you on his side or hers?"

"Hers!" Sadie moaned, then stretched her arms out across the table and fell onto them, hiding her face. "Which is why I desperately want her to have a romantic letter that will somehow make this all better."

"It won't," Harlow whispered.

"It *might*," Sadie hissed. Then she disappeared under the table.

"What the—" Alice leaned sideways to try to see where she went.

Harlow's purse disappeared off the bench on their side. "Sadie! Give that back."

Sadie popped up on the other side and began rifling so furiously through the purse that her black hair waved and shimmered in the harsh diner light.

"Don't read it!" Harlow yelped, and a fresh sob cracked out of her.

"So it *is* in here." Sadie rifled harder.

Alice put her arm around Harlow again. "Oh, sweetheart, don't cry…"

The dad from the screaming baby table got up and came down the aisle to them. "Hey, you girls want to take it somewhere else with your Kleenex commercial?"

Alice made a suggestion about where he could place his opinion that was so vulgar it shocked Harlow's tears into a full retreat.

Once the guy left, Harlow slumped, shredding the end of a paper napkin where it was still wrapped around a set of silverware. "I think I knew Bishop had done something wrong. Made mistakes. I knew it deep down when he kept insisting he was so undatable. But he never acted like a deadbeat around me and I felt like he cared. I didn't think he would do anything terrible to *me*."

Sadie looked up, her eyes luminous and wide. "He did care, Harlow. Oh my gosh, it was so obvious. But remember, he hadn't met you yet at the time he stole your card."

"Yeah, the card he used to pay for the subscription he's been using to date other women." She tossed down the silverware. "He had to put my name in to use the card. There's no way he didn't know what he was doing when he messaged me."

"Um, isn't the app on screen names?" Alice said, nudging the water glass closer to Harlow.

She took an obedient sip, because she knew Alice would keep hinting until she did. "Yes, but Bishop knew my real name, I—"

"Told him on your first date," Alice finished. "Right? So he didn't know. At least for the first date. Because *why on earth* would he go on a date with you, if he knew it was your card he stole? That would be stupid."

"Which is probably why he was so adamant about you two not going out again after the first date!" Sadie bounced a little in her seat, her eyelashes fluttering like a Disney princess high on an epiphany.

Alice snapped her fingers at Sadie. "Hey. I'm not kidding. If you're here on his side and not hers, you can get the fuck out. Go hang out with him wherever broke thieves spend their time."

"Look, you guys, you guys…" Harlow tried, but they both talked over her.

"Does she look happy to you right now?" Sadie drew herself up and glared right back. "Because she sure looked a lot happier last night when he was still around. So sue me if I wouldn't mind fixing that instead of hating on him and spending the next few months with all of us miserable while she tries to forget him and can't. Because I've seen that look on someone else recently, *Alice*, and that's not the over-him-by-next-Tuesday look." She stopped and leaned forward. "Wait, are you missing an earring?"

"Here's what I don't get," Harlow interrupted, with the only topic that had a hope of forestalling where the earring conversation was headed. "If he didn't know who I was on the first date, and he decided he couldn't see me anymore because of that, then why did he keep talking to me?"

Alice frowned. "I don't know. Wouldn't he want more distance between himself and his victims?"

"I hardly think I qualify as his victim." She shifted in her seat, uncomfortable with the label. "All he got off my card was the money for a subscription to the dating app, and a donation to that weird LegUp, remember? The one about the paw-less cat or whatever. The bank wrote off all the charges so I didn't actually lose any money."

"That's probably how he covered his tracks. LegUp is really flexible with how you can transfer money around. That way, if you're raising money for somebody's medical expenses, they can pay the bills directly, or get a check mailed to them, or connect it to their bank account. It would be a good way to launder card numbers into something else."

Sadie poked her straw down into the water she'd stolen from

Alice, the ice rattling with her jittering movements. "Okay, but more importantly—when was the first time you talked after the date? Did he contact you or did you contact him?"

"It was a message on the app." Harlow picked up her phone and started to scroll back through her messages with Bishop, but their thread was impossibly long. "Oh, you know what it was? This crazy stalker girl left Post-its all over his apartment, and he messaged me joking about how I'd ruined his dating standards. It really was kind of funny. I can see why he'd want to share it with someone."

Plus, who was he going to tell? He wouldn't want to text his little sister and freak her out about stalkers. Couldn't really talk to his dad, who was never around, or his mom, who was too busy with her own problems. After he'd dropped out of college, he didn't really have anyone else until her.

She looked up at her friends, her eyes raw from all the tears. "You know, I'm really glad I have both of you. Thank you for being here. I'm sorry I'm such a mess."

"Don't you dare apologize," Sadie said fiercely. "We love you, and I'm sorry this didn't work out. It's just so...weird. The way it all happened."

No friends since college. The thought was still tickling at the back of her mind. He'd dropped out and grown apart from his friends when his sister had to have surgery. A big *expensive* surgery. And LegUp could be used to pay *medical* bills.

She covered her mouth.

"What?" Alice said. "Are you feeling sick? We should get some toast in you to settle your stomach." She snuck the water bottle full of vodka out of Harlow's lap, then winced. "Not toast. Um, a biscuit! Or hash browns. Are hash browns too oily?"

Harlow wasn't listening. She was thinking back to the day in the doctor's office. At the end, Bishop had gotten up to do the co-pay. Which, okay, he was Daisy's accompanying adult. That didn't mean he didn't have a credit card or something from their parents to cover it. Except he hadn't reached for his wallet when he stood up. He reached for his *phone*. Which was how he paid for everything as far as she'd seen.

PhonePay and LegUp must be how he laundered his money to get things that weren't on the internet, like Alice said, but maybe he was also paying his sister's medical bills. Only her chemotherapy co-pays or everything? Whatever it was, he was definitely using the stolen cards for that.

The vinyl booth squeaked as she sat back.

"I think," she said slowly, "that he might be covering his sister's cancer treatments with those cards. That may or may not be why he started. He couldn't get the coding jobs he wanted without a completed degree, and he said he needed a flexible schedule to take her to appointments, hence all the side hustles, but..." She looked up. "It's not the only thing he bought with the stolen money, and there's no way of knowing when he started stealing or why, but the timing matches up."

Sadie was pressing her lips together so tightly she looked like she was bursting with the effort of holding in the words she wasn't saying.

"That would make a pretty good argument for stealing, if anything could," Alice admitted.

Sadie brightened and she started bouncing in her seat again. "You know what would tell us more? *The letter.*" She dug with renewed fervor through Harlow's purse, sending ChapSticks, tampons, and antacids flying in her enthusiasm. "Ah-ha!" She pulled out a piece of notebook paper, torn up and all pieced back together with scotch tape. "I knew we could still be friends." She smiled at Harlow.

Harlow's laugh came out as a sick-sounding throb, and Alice rubbed her back.

"Wait, why is this..." Sadie frowned at her. "These pieces don't match up."

Harlow reached for her silverware and started smoothing the torn edges of the napkin she'd shredded earlier. "I haven't exactly read it yet. I taped it back together face-down once I calmed down a little. I thought you guys could read it and kind of screen it for me? To see if it was anything I needed to know or just a bunch of excuses or something." She let go of the silverware and sat up straighter. "I think I'm okay now, though. I think I want to hear it."

If he really was stealing for his sister, he'd definitely mention that in the letter, and that...well, it wasn't great, but that would be an entirely different situation than him stealing for fun. He'd looked so broken when he left her apartment. Not exactly the picture of the remorseless laughing villain.

Sadie was carefully peeling the letter apart from its tape and re-arranging two of the biggest pieces that didn't match up.

"Do you want to read it, or do you want us to read it?" Alice asked, her hand still steady on Harlow's back.

She swallowed and gestured to Sadie. "You do it. Out loud, just rip the Band-Aid off. He thought it was important enough to write when I was flaming mad and trying to throw him out of my apartment, so there's got to be some kind of explanation in there."

Sadie smoothed the paper and held the pieces together in the places where the tape was ruined.

"Harlow, I never wanted to lie to you. I don't have people in my life because I—"

"Y'all need a warm-up on those coffees? Ready to order a little something to eat?"

"I will literally kill you," Alice said.

Sadie whipped out a ten-dollar bill so fast that she must have had it stashed in her bra, and smiled up at the waitress. "Thank you so so much. We'll just signal when we're ready, 'kay?"

The waitress took the bill, eyeing Alice warily, and nodded. She took her coffee pot and retreated. Sadie began again.

Harlow, I never wanted to lie to you. I don't have people in my life because I hate to lie. I've told you every truth I could, including that you'd be better off without me, even if it weren't for the stealing.

Except I failed at staying away from you because no one has ever clicked with me the way you do.

143

Sadie flopped her head onto the table. "Harlowwww, marry himmm..."

"I will literally kill you, too." Alice glared. "He is a criminal! He lied to her!"

"This is literally killing me anyway," Sadie said. "Romantic thief letter! I've never gotten a romantic thief letter in my whole life. The only way it could be better is if he were a highwayman."

"You mean if it was *armed* robbery? Your taste in men is seriously skewed, my friend."

Harlow couldn't speak. Her throat hurt, like it had been all yanked out of shape by the emotions rioting through her all morning.

No one has ever clicked with me the way you do.

She reached across the table to see if that's how it ended, but Sadie slapped her hands down over the paper.

"I'm reading, I'm reading. Stop with the death threats." Sadie cleared her throat. "Don't forgive me." She stopped, biting her suddenly trembling lip.

"I'll read it if you can't," Alice said.

Sadie didn't argue this time, just passed over the letter, turning it carefully so the pieces stayed together as she slid them across the table.

Harlow closed her eyes as Alice started to read, afraid to glimpse the ending before she had to.

Don't forgive me.

You'll be better at keeping us apart than I was, and that's what needs to happen. I only wrote this because I knew you'd assume it was all a scam, or some kind of lie right from the beginning, or that somehow, I only wanted you for what I could steal.

You ~~were~~ are irresistible to me. In all this mess, that's what's true.

-Bishop

When Alice finished, she reached for the water bottle full of vodka, and unscrewed the cap.

"What are you going to do?" Sadie whispered.

Alice was still drinking.

Harlow folded her hands on the table in front of her. Unfolded them. Her body felt insubstantial, like if she were outside, it would start to drift apart and slowly roll away on the wind.

"He never explains why he's doing it." She really thought he'd try to explain. Instead, all he said was, *Don't forgive me.* She tried to clear her head and think logically. "Even if he really is stealing for his sister's sake, he didn't say he was planning to stop. No matter why he's doing it, it's still illegal. He'll get caught sooner or later and go to prison." She looked up. "I can't go through that again."

Neither of her friends said anything. The waitress passed their table with her coffee pot and very pointedly didn't look their direction.

"But what he said in there, how he felt." She laid her hand on her breastbone, trying to explain. "I felt that, too," she finally said. "How with him, it was...different."

She looked at her friends.

"What if that was him? You know, the *one*. And he's a criminal, and that ruins everything for us. With my job and his life and just everything." Her voice wavered, the numbness starting to creep away. "What if I'm destined to only ever see the people I love during visiting hours at the prison?"

Alice's hand shot up, signaling the waitress. "We're gonna need some waffles over here. Extra butter."

CHAPTER 19

*B*ishop flicked his pencil so it whirled across the table and collided with the screen of his laptop, then came to rest atop a stratigraphy of papers. This was a waste of time.

After he watched the best woman he'd ever met dissolve into tears over him, he told himself it was better this way. His life was a bomb crater, and she was out of the blast zone now.

And then he nearly peeled his own skin off trying to live without her.

So he grew a pair and did something he hadn't done in years: he actually looked at how deeply he was in debt, and whether there might be a way out. The total was actually a full decimal point worse than he'd even suspected. Not that it mattered. He'd given up on having a future years ago.

With Harlow's tear-swollen eyes haunting him, he set to work figuring out if he could patch together a better life just for right now. All he'd done in the five days since then was apply for freelance jobs, crunch numbers, and come to the same conclusion in ever more depressing ways. There was no way he could give up stealing without also giving up eating.

Although conveniently, those results had killed his appetite.

If he got a regular job where he was paid as an employee, fully half of his wages would be garnished for back taxes and unpaid student loans. If he kept going with the independent contractor side hustle stuff, they couldn't garnish it, but he had to keep everything in cash because if he put it into a bank account, his medical bill creditors would yank every penny. So okay, cash. Except all those side hustles that paid direct added up to chump change, and then at the end of the year he was supposed to pay the government their cut. So far, he'd never had enough left to pay the taxes he owed. Which meant more back taxes, more garnishments, more penalties, so on and so forth. He could declare bankruptcy, but that wouldn't erase his student loans, and new medical bills came in for Daisy every day.

He also couldn't qualify for more loans to finish his degree without paying back what he owed. So really, all he had to find was a great job that didn't require a college degree and paid *double* what he needed, so he could cover his bills, Daisy's copays, and the garnishment, too. No sweat, right?

He heaved a snowdrift of scribbled-up paper off the table and shoved his chair back.

If he dumped his sauerkraut-soaked studio for even cheaper housing, and landed every freelance coding job under the sun, he could make this happen. He'd be working like a dog, though, just to live... well, like a dog. So at least that made sense. But even those numbers didn't add up unless Daisy finished chemo and went into full remission.

So basically, a miracle wrapped in four jobs, and never being able to have a bank account again or his creditors would take every penny. Cool.

Even if that diamond-studded act of God fell into his lap, Harlow was never fucking going to take him back. Not after he lied to her, stole from her. That was the part that made all his old financial problems seem an even deeper kind of hopeless.

He needed something he could *do*, some way to believe it wouldn't always be this bad. This lonely.

Bishop blew out a breath, stretching his tired fingers at his sides as

147

he bounced on his toes. He'd missed the free boxing classes at the YMCA this weekend, and that was maybe the only thing on earth that was going to take the edge off the memory of Harlow ripping his shirt off her body. Standing naked and sobbing as she threw it at him.

He turned in a circle once, twice. This apartment had never seemed so suffocatingly small as it did right now, with the futon knee-bangingly close to the card table, and half the floor covered in medical bills. This was not the healthiest way to cope, he supposed.

Five days of post-breakup financial spreadsheets in an apartment with a first warning of eviction notice on the door, interrupted only by trips to the pediatric chemo unit…yeah, that'd be enough to leave anybody depressed. He needed to get out of the house or pretty soon he was going to be listening to "Nothing Compares 2 U" and sobbing into his last paper towel.

Bishop stripped off his jeans and pulled on a pair of basketball shorts and sneakers. Grabbed his water bottle and barely slowed down enough to lock the door on his way out.

If he looked at his laptop right now, those other numbers would start taunting him again, the ones he'd never used. At the moment, he wasn't sure he was strong enough to hold out.

He had two ways of getting credit card numbers. The first was a neat little trick with the Wi-Fi. Sit down in any coffee shop with open Wi-Fi, and send a browser window to everyone else signed into it. It looked like a software update but instead it was a program he'd written that sent Bishop every keystroke they made. It usually wasn't too long before somebody did some online shopping and entered their credit card number.

That one was slow, and required skimming through large amounts of keystroke reports to find the card numbers.

The second way to get numbers was to hack into a consumer website and either steal saved numbers off user profiles, or download a record of all transactions. That one took a lot longer to get in, but paid off big when he was able to pull it off. It also sometimes came with other useful information, like social security numbers.

A batch of those, from a third-party company who made sure your utility bills got auto-paid every month, was how he got Harlow's card number and social security number. The first of which he'd used, the second of which he'd saved and forgotten like he did all the others he'd gotten. He had years of social security numbers stored up as his own little health insurance plan, in case Daisy ever needed more than quickly-cancelled credit card numbers could provide.

The wind was gusting hard outside, and it flapped his shorts against his legs as he hunched his head and strode down the sidewalk toward the gym. Dirt from the gutter whirled up and peppered the back of his calves. He didn't feel any of it.

Social security numbers were how you got the big money. You could apply for brand-new physical credit cards under other people's names. Unless they checked their credit report regularly—and really, who kept up with that stuff—you were home free. You could even get cash out with those. Apply for lines of credit. Do all sorts of stuff he could never manage in the two or three transactions he got through before fraud detection kicked in on his other card numbers. He could be rolling in cash if he was willing to use social security numbers.

Thing was, he'd also be fucking up people's lives. Credit cards were easy to cancel, and the bank absorbed the charges. Social security numbers were a whole other level of fraud, and a bitch to untangle once yours got swiped, even though technically you still weren't responsible for the charges. Assuming, again, that you checked your credit report and reported it in time. Which almost no one would.

Work like a dog for next to nothing, or double down on the sin he'd already committed and live like a king?

Bishop dodged around a fire hydrant and kept walking, his head bent against the gritty blast of the wind. Harlow wasn't going to forgive him no matter what. She wasn't the type to hang out with criminals, even once Daisy was finally better and he could live broke and legal again. Harlow's parents were in prison, and even if he didn't know why, he could tell from the tone of her voice that she'd never forgiven them. And they were *family*. He couldn't imagine anything he wouldn't forgive Daisy for.

Man, he hoped the scans came back clean this time. She deserved to be a kid again, with hobbies and awkward flirtations, instead of in pain and stuck in bed all the time.

The door of the gym bounced off his outstretched palm as he plowed inside. The whir of treadmills and bounce of basketballs echoed off the hard walls, and he took a breath of rubber-and-sweat scented air. So much better than sauerkraut. The ceilings were high here, the rooms not as empty, and the claustrophobia of his life eased for a second.

He scanned his key tag for the account he'd paid up a year in advance, and strode into the room full of hoops. From across the room, he caught a flash of bicep tattoos and an impressive jump shot, and a grin flashed over his face.

"Hey, who knew hobbits could jump?" he hollered across the room.

Samwise's ball swished through the net, and then he looked over, searching for the source of the voice. The taller guy laughed and waved for him to join, and Bishop rocked back on his heels, thinking better of it. They were already mid-game. He shouldn't butt in. He shook his head at Sam, then turned away, pretending to focus on finding a place to set down his water bottle.

He hopped into another pickup game that was starting, but even as he played, he swore he could hear the staccato bounce of Sam's basketball, distinct from all the others. Guy was *fast*. That Wednesday game would probably wring a hell of a sweat out of Bishop if he ever went.

As they all spanned out on the court, he could already see the guys on his team for the day were middle-aged and slow. Again. He glanced over his shoulder to where Sam was playing defense, guarding a whip-fast brunette with a long ponytail. He seemed like a good guy, Sam. The kind Harlow should be dating. With a future and a scruple or two left about how he lived his life. Judging by his limited-edition Nikes, he also had the kind of cash Bishop would only get from stealing other people's identities.

Bishop played like shit, distracted by thinking of how different everything could be if he started tapping into those social security numbers. Sam's game ended and he came over, shucking his gym bag at the edge of Bishop's court and waiting there.

Bishop dribbled harder, zeroing in on the basket so he could pretend he didn't feel Sam's eyes. If they started talking, he'd probably end up having to lie. He hadn't been able to show up to those Wednesday games yet, and if he dove further into identity theft, he probably never should. He'd have to withdraw even further from anyone who might get to know him well enough to uncover his crimes. But damn, at least he'd be able to afford a decent apartment. Buy Daisy a wig that actually looked real, some school clothes if she got to go back to school this year.

He shot and missed. On the way back across the court, someone else had the ball and he had to work harder to pretend he didn't see Sam, who lifted an arm to wave this time. Sam's hand hung there in the air for a minute before he finally lowered it, and pretended he'd been scratching the back of his neck.

Bishop jostled the ball away from the other team, aggressively enough that it was definitely a foul, but nobody called him on it.

On the sidelines, Sam picked up his bag and slung it over his shoulder. Waited another second, but when Bishop didn't acknowledge him, he took off. The water Bishop had drunk sloshed in his stomach. After the next basket, he waved to his team for a break. His steps slowed as he headed over to his solitary water bottle.

He was tired of feeling like shit. Tired of not having any friends. Tired of being fucking tired.

Most of all, he was tired of hating himself for doing everything in his power to keep his sister alive, because he shouldn't have to apologize for that. The medical industry in this country was totally screwed up, but that wasn't his fault. He shouldn't have to be slinking around, too ashamed to join a weekly basketball game. It's not like he was robbing old ladies to buy himself a Ferrari, for crying out loud. He wasn't *that* bad a person.

He squatted down, pouring a little water into his mouth then holding it there while he hung his head. He didn't want to steal even more. He hated lying, to anyone. If he was being honest, he hated that a lot more than he'd ever minded being broke, or working multiple jobs.

Bishop lifted his head and swallowed the mouthful of water, letting it fill his belly. Screw those social security numbers, and screw being rich. He couldn't get Harlow back, and he'd never be out of debt. What he *could* do was start working toward living clean right now, so on the day Daisy officially went into remission, they'd have two things to celebrate. He'd have to live like a dog to afford to feed himself without stealing, but at least he'd be an honest dog.

One who could maybe, as soon as the credit card scam was done, have a friend again.

CHAPTER 20

*H*arlow: Bishop, are you there?
Harlow: Please tell me you're awake.
Harlow: Nobody's answering their phones and I don't know who else to call.
Bishop: What's wrong? Are you okay?
Harlow: Oh, I'm so glad you're up.
Bishop: I never turn my ringer off in case something happens with Daisy. Is everything okay?
Harlow: Yes? No? I don't know. I'm on this really weird date and I kind of need a ride. Or just like maybe a buffer? I'm not sure.
Bishop: What's going on? You've had a lot of weird dates and not sounded freaked out like this.
Harlow: He's just being really persistent about making sure I get home all right.
Bishop: Okay? That sounds like a good thing.
Harlow: But he won't let me just get an Uber. He wants to come all the way home with me. I keep telling him he doesn't have to, but he keeps insisting.
Bishop: Are there other people around? Can you tell the staff or

somebody that he won't leave you alone and you need help until I get there? I'm getting my keys. Just send me the address.

Harlow: No, I mean, it's not that bad. I'm probably making too much out of it.

Bishop: Where are you? Are you safe right now?

Harlow: I'm in the bathroom at the bar.

Bishop: Okay, good. Start at the beginning and tell me what the deal is with this guy.

Harlow: Well, I found him on the app. His screen name is an inside joke from The Office, so I thought that was cool. Real name's Todd. Date went great, he was funny, I was a little tipsy. He's a big guy, used to play football, so we were joking about all the weird stuff with college sports and what they make you do when you're on scholarship. I was really ready for a date to go well, you know? So when he asked if I wanted to grab one more drink after dinner, I said sure! Anyway, we get to talking and boom, it's one in the morning.

Harlow: I take his # for a second date, but when I go to leave, he wants to see me home. As in drop me at my door even though he lives in the opposite direction and neither of us drove here. He was being really sweet about it. He says his mom raised him to see a lady home, especially if it's this late. But Bishop, I told him a bunch of times I don't need him to do that, and he's not budging.

Bishop: I don't like that you told him no and he's still on this.

Harlow: I know, me too. And I'm kind of like, if he's pushy now, once we're alone in front of my building, then what? So on the one hand I don't want to blow it if this could go somewhere with us. The date did go really well, and it's not crazy that he'd want to see me home safely. On the other hand, if he is a creep, by the time I know for sure I'll be on a dark street with no one else around.

Harlow: I know it's weird that I texted you of all people, after everything that happened, but I tried Alice and Sadie and my friend from work and my friend from the gym and it's Thursday night past one, and nobody has their phone on.

Bishop: No, I'm glad you texted, don't worry about it. I don't know what to think of this guy either, but if he's insisting hard enough to make you nervous, you're smart not to just go along.

Harlow: Whew, sorry, that explanation was long. I should have just called but the girl in the stall next to me is farting like crazy and it's gross.

Bishop: LOL Thx for saving me from that.

Bishop: Okay, here's what I think we should do. Pretend you called an Uber. I'll show up, all my rideshare stickers on the window, and play undercover chaperone. When I drop you off, I'll linger like the smell of that girl in the stall next to you.

Harlow: Ew!

Bishop: LOL

Bishop: Anyway, I'll stick around and either give him a ride back to his place if he wants that, or I'll take off once he sees you safely to your door and bows out like the gentleman you're hoping he is. If it goes south, or he tries to elbow his way inside, I'll be there to back you up.

Harlow: This is weird, isn't it?

Bishop: Not as weird as it would be if you put yourself in danger rather than call me.

Bishop: And let's have a signal. If something happens between now and then so you want to ditch him before he sees where you live, just work in the word BIB, and I'll get him out of your hair.

Harlow: Okay. Good idea.

Bishop: Are you going to be all right until I get there?

Harlow: Yeah, I'm sure it's fine. I'm feeling a lot better. I'm probably making a big deal out of nothing. I just figure, I don't really know this guy from Adam, it can't hurt to be careful, right?

Bishop: If he does anything to flip the scales to scary before I show up, go back to the bathroom, or ask the bartender for help. Bartenders live to play the hero, they'll love it. I used to be one, I would know.

Harlow: Thanks, Bishop, seriously.

Bishop: No worries. Be there in 20.

· · ·

155

Harlow shifted her weight from foot to foot, looking down the empty street in front of the bar.

"Are you sure your car is coming?" Todd asked again, his face lit up by the glow of his phone. "Because my app is showing an available rideshare only two minutes away and it's already been what, ten or fifteen? Since you said you ordered yours."

They were standing under a shallow awning, but the pavement was all puddled up and gritty from an earlier rain storm. The bartender had locked the door behind them after closing time, and the only other guy who'd been left in the bar was halfway down the street now, his stumbling walk fading into the shadows between stoplights. She took a big breath, hoping the rain-scented air would help her stop being so nervous when she had no good reason to be. But it just smelled like wet garbage and gravel out here.

"No, my ride's coming. You don't have to wait with me if you don't want to." They hadn't been clicking quite as well since she got back from the bathroom. Either he was picking up on her nerves, or he was irritated that she'd been in there so long. She wasn't sure which.

"Of course not." He touched her shoulder and smiled. "Just means I get to spend more time with you."

She tried to smile back, and then jumped when Bishop's car pulled up in front of them. "Look, there he—I mean, it is. The Uber."

Todd's smile dropped away. "You ordered us a pink car?"

"Uh, they weren't exactly categorized by color." She glanced up at him. "Is that a problem?" With his shoulders still as broad as if he wore football pads every weekend, it would be pretty sad if his masculinity could be threatened by the color of the car he was riding in. It certainly didn't seem to bother Bishop. It made his sister laugh, and that was good enough for him.

Bishop hopped out of the driver's seat and came around before they could approach the car. He looked thinner, his arms even more cut, and there was a tension to him as he sized up her date that made it look not only like he thought he could take the taller man, but that he was seconds from taking a swing and testing that theory out.

She took a step in between them. "Are you our Uber?"

"Yes, ma'am, if you're Harlow. Will that be one passenger or two? The app just said one but…"

"Two," Todd said before she could answer.

Bishop kept looking to her as if the other man hadn't spoken. "Ma'am?"

"Two," she confirmed, pasting on a smile. She was being ridiculous, letting too many scary internet headlines get under her skin when Todd hadn't been anything but a gentleman all night. Well, maybe except for the pink car crack.

"Ah, great." Bishop took a step back, that vibrating tension easing out of him when she confirmed that the plan was still on and her date hadn't done anything to freak her out while she waited.

Bishop flipped the hat in his hand up in the air, caught it, and dropped it onto his head. It was a black cabbie hat and it made his cheekbones look sharper, somehow. "Right this way, you two." He opened the car door. "Thought it was just going to end up being one, but lucky for you, I do happen to have a backseat. Help yourself to a bottle of water." He popped the latch to pull the seat forward and indicated the plastic sign he'd hung on the back of the seat with his Uber profile identifier and a reminder saying *Don't forget to five-star me if you liked your ride!* "Right this way, sir."

"Uh…" Todd said. "I don't really think I'm going to fit in the tiny backseat of your pink car, dude."

Bishop drew back. "Um, where else… I mean, it's always been my policy that the lady gets the best seat in the house. But I suppose if you don't mind that sort of thing, I guess you could make her take…"

"No, it's not like that," Todd protested. "I'm not trying to be a dick, it's just my legs are longer. You don't mind, do you, Harlow?"

"Uh…" She stalled. She didn't mind sitting in the back, actually, but she got the idea Bishop was taking her date's character for a little bit of a test drive on her behalf.

Bishop gave her a look. All disapproving frown and raised eyebrows like, *Wow, this guy*. And didn't try to hide it even the slightest bit. Todd scowled and started wedging himself into the back seat.

"All right then," Bishop said, cheerfully slamming the passenger seat back into his knees. "Whoopsie, sorry about that." He whacked them again, the five-star review sign swinging up and catching Todd in the nose. "Um, sir, you may need to tuck your knees in a bit. The seat has to go allll the way back to latch before we can move it forward again."

"Where the hell am I supposed to 'tuck' my knees to, into my—" Todd caught sight of Harlow's expression and broke off, then grumblingly raised his feet off the ground, folding his knees almost to his ears so the seams of his pants were visibly straining by the time Bishop got the seat to lock into place.

"There we go!" he said sunnily. And didn't slide the seat forward at all. "Ma'am?"

She slipped by him, caught between wanting to laugh and feeling guilty at the test gauntlet he was putting poor Todd through. She slid the seat forward as many notches as it would go, throwing Todd an apologetic look. He appeared sour, stuffed in the glove-box-sized backseat and still rubbing his nose where the sign had slapped it.

Bishop got back in and she sat up straighter, suddenly aware of her posture and sort of wishing she'd refreshed her makeup when she'd been in the bathroom. Was her shirt too low-cut? Bishop looked good. Tired, a little underfed, but also so handsome she had to force herself to stare straight ahead instead of looking over at him. Was he thinking about whether she looked different since their time apart? She tried not to think about how, the last time she saw him, she'd been naked.

He checked his mirrors and merged smoothly onto the quiet street. "You folks having a nice evening?"

"We *were*," Todd griped, still wriggling around to find a comfortable way to fit behind her seat.

He'd seemed more charming before. Or maybe she'd been tipsier before? Maybe he was just grouchy and tired now, since it was getting late. She glanced back at him, and his trimmed goatee and styled hair didn't seem as handsome as they had earlier. Especially when every cell in her body was currently tuned to the Bishop station. She thought she had some chemistry with Todd, but it was nothing compared to the tingly-skin, weight-on-the-chest transformation her body had undergone as soon as she saw Bishop's car pulling up to the curb.

Could she really see a future with Todd? He didn't seem like the kind of guy who'd even let her buy a parrot when they were old, much less learn to speak its private parrot language. He'd say it was too messy, or too loud. Or she'd want to name it something like Gabardine and he would insist on Ralph. Who the fuck named their parrot Ralph?

"So," Todd said. "Do you have one of those apartments with doors that open to the outside, or do you have an elevator or..."

Bishop glanced at her. His fingers started to tap on the steering wheel, but he stayed out of the conversation, letting her do her thing.

Harlow frowned at the weird question. "Doors open to the inside, but it's a walk up."

"Ah," Todd said. "I had better walk you all the way upstairs then, just to be safe."

"Sir, will you be needing a ride home, after?" Bishop asked. "We can schedule a second ride on your account instead of hers, if you'd like."

"Nah, I can call somebody when I get back down."

Harlow's stomach tensed. Even if Bishop waited down front, she didn't want to be alone with Todd in her hallway. Why was he pushing this so hard anyway?

This was stupid. She wanted a date to work out so badly right now, to prove she could feel something for someone who seemed like they had their life in order. Of course, if she didn't want to be alone with him, this wasn't going anywhere, anyway. She turned partway around, her gaze connecting with Bishop's before she pretended to turn her attention to the backseat.

"You know where we should have gone tonight? One of those seafood places, the ones with lobster and the little bibs."

Todd raised his eyebrows, taken off guard by the change in topic. "Um, okay? I don't like how your hands get all sticky at those places, though."

"Oh, why'd you have to say seafood?" The car's speed faltered like

Bishop's foot had come off the gas. "I had some earlier from this street cart and I don't know…suddenly it's not sitting too well."

"Hey man, TMI. You want that five-star review or what?"

Bishop put a hand to his stomach. "I don't know. Whoa. How far is it to your place again?" He glanced to his phone's navigation window and she noticed he'd set an address about two blocks away from her house. Well, that was clever. If he didn't use navigation, Todd would have wondered why the Uber driver knew where she lived, but this way Todd couldn't peep her address if she decided to call it early. Which she had.

"It's only about ten minutes, but you don't look so good." She wasn't totally sure what Bishop had in mind, but she tried to play along anyway. "Do you, um, need to come up and use my restroom?" Except then Todd would still end up with her home address.

"Ten more minutes… No, wow, I'm not going to make it that far. Listen, guys, we just passed my house and I think I gotta—no, I definitely gotta—this is gonna be bad." He jerked the car over to the curb. "I'm sorry, get out you have to get out, I need to get home. Just order another ride in the app, somebody'll pick you up."

"Are you fucking kidding me right now?" Todd burst out. "You're just going to leave us on the side of the road at two in the morning?"

"Oh no, it's coming!" Bishop yelped, and pounded on the steering wheel. "Ma'am, there's a lever to let him out of the backseat, can you —" His face was all twisted up into a fake grimace, but their eyes connected for just a second and she realized his plan.

Harlow leaped out. "Come on, I really don't want to see this guy get sick." She hit the lever. "Not the romantic date ending I was hoping for, right?" She forced a laugh, and the sly way Todd's face brightened at her words sealed the deal. Yup, he'd definitely been hoping for a lot more than to "see her home safely."

He grabbed the side of the door and un-wedged himself from the backseat, stumbling as he made it out onto the pavement.

Harlow dove back into the car and Bishop hit the gas before she even had the door closed.

"Look at his face!" Bishop crowed, pointing to the rearview mirror.

She leaned in to see in her side mirror that her date was standing in the street, waving his arms in exasperation. "He thinks you just chose the Uber driver with explosive diarrhea over him."

Harlow laughed longer and harder than it probably merited, out of relief and how much better she felt once it was just the two of them in the car. Rain started to pat softly at the windows, and she was happy he'd shown up with her ride before the next wave of the storm set in. She looked over to the driver's seat, and then she remembered and her hands flew up to cover her mouth.

"Oh my gosh! Your license! I completely forgot you don't have your license right now."

He shrugged, but his laughter faded and he shifted his weight in his seat.

"Here, just pull over, I'll drive."

"You said you were tipsy." He gave her a dirty look. "I'd rather me get nailed for driving without a license than you get a DUI. It'll be fine, I'll just go the speed limit and not attract any attention."

"You're driving *a pink car*."

"Hey, it's magenta!"

"Whatever you say." She tried not to smile at his indignation. "Seriously, I didn't mean to get you in trouble. I completely forgot."

"C'mon, Harlow, you know nothing was going to keep me from coming down here once you said that guy was making you nervous. You think I'm such an asshole that I'd leave you hanging because of a *driver's license?*"

She ducked her head, fidgeting with the hem of her shirt. Her creep-radar had been trying to tell her something, and she hadn't wanted to listen. What if she'd let Todd get all the way home with her? How hard had he been planning on pushing the issue?

Bishop pulled up in front of her apartment building and looked over. "Hey, you okay?"

She sort of wasn't all of a sudden. Her stomach was flipping and fizzing with the release of all the stress of a first date and oh, yeah, mostly because she was sitting in Bishop's passenger seat. She hadn't thought she'd ever see him again. How could he look that beautiful in a tee shirt and a simple flat cap?

He'd shown up for her. Without a second thought, when she'd pelted him with bath bombs, screamed in his face, and thrown him out without so much as letting him put his shoes on. She hadn't even eaten the toast he made her. Alice had thrown it away before she'd allowed Harlow back into her apartment, so it wouldn't make her sad.

Then again, part of her must have been sure that he'd come, or she never would have texted him at all.

She had a sudden flash of the way he'd held her, that first time on the couch. Warmth filled her, holding back the cold damp of the late-night rain, and then she blinked.

"Thank you for coming, Bishop, seriously. I—don't know what I would have done if you hadn't answered." She paused. "Probably convinced myself it was all fine and gone with him, actually. Which would not have been the right call."

"Hey, if you're in a jam with a creepy guy, you know I'll be there. Even for girls who completely hate me, I am universally on call for that. Once a big brother, always a big brother, right?"

He was talking a little too fast, and his thumb was rubbing at the gear shift so hard it looked painful.

"Bishop, I don't hate you." It came out softer than she intended.

He flicked a glance at her, his eyes burning bright under the brim of that cap. Looked away.

"It's late," she said, and pulled her purse into her lap.

"You sure you're okay?"

"I'll be fine now. Thank you again for the ride." How were you supposed to say goodbye when you weren't going to see each other again, but you weren't in the flush of anger anymore, and when the guy had just bailed you out in the weirdest, sweetest way possible? Harlow had no idea.

She opened her door and he took a quick breath.

"Harlow, um…take care of yourself, okay?"

"Yeah, of course."

She didn't look at him as she got out, but once she was standing on the curb, she hesitated. That wasn't what she'd wanted to say. It didn't seem like the right ending. That glance he'd given her…it was searing and yet over so fast she wished she could rewind it like a TV show, digging for all the layers of meaning that might have been behind it. She wished she knew what he was thinking.

His car was still parked behind her, the engine quietly rumbling. A layer of glass between them, just like there would be once he got caught for fraud and sent to prison. She hitched her purse up higher on her shoulder and went inside.

CHAPTER 21

*H*arlow: How's the gastrointestinal distress these days?

Bishop: PinkUber at your service, ma'am. Fictional food poisoning all healed from last week. Why? Got another live one on a breakfast date and need me to fake a peanut allergy attack?

[Three dots bouncing. Disappearing. Bouncing.]

Harlow: Got ditched for brunch and I'm all alone at the Tipsy Taco...

Bishop: I'm there.

Sadie: Hey, I can come to brunch after all! I told my mom you were sad from a breakup, and she said I could skip church to come comfort you.

Harlow: Um, I may have invited Bishop to brunch after Alice bailed and you said you couldn't make it...

Sadie: OMG BISHOP!!!

Sadie: Do you think he'll wear the cape?

Harlow: What cape?

Sadie: From when he SWOOPED IN LIKE A SUPERHERO TO SAVE YOU FROM TODD THE JERK! *heart eyes emoji *

Sadie: I have the creepiest feeling right now that Alice is going to psychically sense me saying nice things about Bishop, and she's going to call my mom and rat me out for lying to get out of church.

Harlow: You didn't lie. I really am sad from a breakup. If you can call it a breakup when we were mostly friends the whole time except for 1.5 one-night stands.

Sadie: How much do I love that Harlow, my most responsible and upstanding friend, had 1.5 one-night stands with a hottie thief who writes her love letters and makes her romantic toast?

Harlow: I'm going to take that to mean you're not mad I invited him to brunch and now have to un-invite you so I can talk to him alone?

Sadie: Not mad, but very, very curious about the change of heart. Was it the cape? I bet he looks killer in a set of superhero tights.

Harlow: I have to know his side of the story. It's driving me absolutely crazy. Like, I keep asking myself why my instincts were all waving red flags about Todd, who seemed nice but turned out to be pushy at best and date rapey at worst. And yet I felt safe with Bishop right from our first date, but he turned out to be stealing for a living, and lying to me about it.

Sadie: Like, maybe you weren't that wrong about him and there must be more to the story?

Harlow: Exactly! I'm sick of beating myself up about this because I'm NOT stupid. If everything between us was a lie and he's a heartless criminal, he wouldn't have gotten up in the middle of the night and risked driving without a license. Especially not to rescue me from a date that I told him was just a little uncomfortable, not even dangerous or anything.

Sadie: I couldn't agree more. Even if Alice is secretly monitoring our text conversations and she's coming to take away my stash of good chocolate for saying that.

Sadie: Text me ASAP when brunch is over. Unless sex. Then

text me after the makeup sex. OMG! If this works out, I totally get to be maid of honor at the wedding. And if he really is a thieving creep who just happens to be great at axe-throwing and writing love letters, then I will bow my head in shame and accept mere bridesmaid status when you find your real future husband.

Harlow: I told you, you and Alice get dual maid of honor status if I ever get a wedding. This is not a competition. Now, I'm starving and I need taco-related sustenance if I'm going to keep my head for this conversation.

Sadie: Yeah, don't swoon like you did in the car. Be tough! Channel Alice's murder eyes and scare the truth out of him.

Harlow: I didn't swoon!

Sadie: You said you started breathing all funny when he sat next to you!

Harlow: It was late. Maybe I was tired.

Sadie: Well, go mainline some coffee then, because if he sees how "tired" you are this morning, you guys are gonna end up having makeup sex on top of the waffles.

Harlow was loading rosemary-bacon scones onto her plate when Bishop sidled up next to her, his light cologne making her throat quiver when she took a long, long inhale.

"So, who was dumb enough to ditch you for brunch?"

"Alice and Rob are back together."

"Are we happy or sad about that?" He took a small pumpkin pancake and popped an orange slice on top.

"She's glowing so hard you can see it from space. Or you could, if they ever left the bedroom."

He stole a glance at her from under the narrow brim of today's hat, which was her favorite black fedora. "And how do *you* feel about that?"

"I feel like I want her to be happy, and I just hope it works out." Harlow came to the end of the buffet table and turned to face him. "Why are you so interested in Alice forgiving the ex you've never met?"

He held out his free hand. "Hi, is this the kettle convention? I think I'm the pot that's up for debate today."

The corner of her mouth twitched and she suppressed a smile. "Yes, I did invite you here. But this isn't a forgiveness brunch."

He smiled, his gaze warm on her face. "It's good to see you, so if an unforgiveness brunch is all I can get, I'll take it. I do, by the way, have a thing I want to say on that topic. In the meantime, you have to try the butternut squash, pumpkin seed, and pulled pork taco. Also the maple bacon mini waffle towers. You filled up last time before you got to the best stuff. I can't let you go astray twice."

"It's *all* the best stuff. This is my treat, by the way. I owe you for an Uber ride. And whatever the going rate is for risking a huge ticket for me."

"On the house."

"But if I don't pay for brunch, are you going to have to use stolen cards to pay your share?"

"Listen, Harlow…"

"Yeah, that's what I thought. Waffle towers first, then we talk."

He cringed. "On that note, if you need me, I'll be doing a face-first dive into the mimosa fountains."

"As long as you grab me a Clementine mimosa when you're done with your swim."

He gave her a wounded look. "Obviously."

It was colder on the patio than it had been last time, so Harlow slipped into her wrap sweater and belted it tightly, trying to stay strong. Sadie was right. As soon as she saw him, she just wanted to hug him, talk or no talk. And then once he looked right at her with those *eyes*, she wanted a lot more than a hug.

As soon as he sat down with their mimosas, she took a sip of hers and said, "So how long have you been paying your sister's medical bills?"

His hand stopped halfway to his mouth and the kimchi fell out of his street taco. "How do you know about that?"

"PhonePay. It's how you paid at the doctor's office, and the Door

Dart in the park, and when you bought nachos at the axe-throwing range, and the last time we came here to brunch. You said something about how you couldn't get cash out of there, but you can. Except then you have to either send a check to your real name or hook it to your bank account, which is again connected to your real name. That's how you funnel your stolen money, right?"

He ate his taco. Slowly, like he was trying to decide what to tell her. And then he just exhaled and admitted it.

"Yes. It is. I can launder nearly everything as donations through LegUp, transfer that to my PhonePay account, and then figure out what local stores and restaurants take PhonePay. Can't do it for utilities or rent or cash, though, which is why I manage and clean WebBnbs, drive rideshares, and write jokes for the app." He picked up his fork but didn't eat. "Fraud detection pings after a couple of transactions, so we never get ahead on the medical bills, but it's enough to pay her medications, co-pays, everything we need to fork over up front to make sure she's getting what she needs."

"You said we, but it sounds like mostly you." She was aching to reach over and touch his hand, but knew she shouldn't. "Why aren't your parents paying her bills?"

"They help, as much as they can." He tapped the end of his fork on the table. "When Daisy was nine and had to get her first big surgery, too many of the bills had gone to collections and they sued my parents, got a bank levy. They can't take your house for medical bills, but if you're in deep enough, they can take what you owe straight out of your bank account. They didn't even have enough time to declare bankruptcy."

"What? There's no law against that?"

"Nope. And if you can't pay your mortgage, how long do you think you get to keep the house? So I—" He stopped and looked at her. "This isn't an excuse, okay? I know none of this shit is right. I did the only thing I could think to do when my sick sister was about to be put out in the street. I'd just gotten my financial aid check for my senior year, and I used it to keep my parent's house. After that, I had to drop out because they prefer you to pay your tuition if you're going to take classes. We transferred all the medical bills into my name, because as long as Daisy was sick, the bills were only going to get higher. I didn't have anything the bank could take, so Daisy would always have a home."

Harlow went to pick up her mimosa, but her throat was too knotted to swallow. She reached for Bishop instead. He squeezed her hand, his fingers engulfing hers. His Adam's apple bobbed as he looked down at their hands. And then let her go.

"I know what you want me to say, Harlow. But I can't stop yet."

She pressed her lips together, her plate blurring as she forgot to blink. It was more than she thought. More than just the awareness and attraction between them, the easy banter. As soon as he showed up, she felt the jerk of something in her belly pulling her toward him. She needed there to be a way this could work. Hell, she had a whole plate full of delicious food in front of her and she couldn't even eat, her stomach was so churned over this.

Since when did she want any man more than a maple bacon mini-waffle tower? That was just *wrong*.

"I..." She couldn't believe she was about to say this. But it's what she wished she would have said to her parents when she still had time, because she'd been screaming it at them in her head for nine long years afterward. "If you care about me enough," she said, unable to force the catch out of her voice, "you'll find a way to stop breaking the law."

"Harlow..." Her name came out of him on a gusty exhale, and he came half out of his chair, then seemed to remember they were in public. Instead, he abandoned his plate and came around to her side of the table so he could sit close enough to grip both her hands. "What do you think I've been trying to do for the last few weeks?"

She looked up, blinking to try to shake off the humiliation of dropping such a revealing ultimatum to a guy she'd barely even been dating. "Wait, you have?"

"Harlow, if I could move heaven and earth for you, they'd already be in the U-Haul." He gave her a pained smile. "I've been doing everything I can think of to find a way out of this mess. I wasn't even bothering to look for coding jobs before, because they all want references or a degree. But I dug deep enough to find a few startups that can afford to pay so little they'll take a chance on me. But they have to be freelance, so that narrows the pool even more. Without rideshares, I've been stuck writing jokes for the app by the million and let me tell you, trying to be funny when you're...well, like I've been since you threw me out, is a very special form of torture." He tried to smile. "Hey, maybe you even saw one of my punchlines when you swiped right on Todd."

She ignored his attempt to distract her. "Why does it have to be freelance? You could get a full-time job doing computer stuff for the Match app, instead of writing their jokes. You were valedictorian, you were good. You can, I don't know, figure out the algorithm to put people together with their perfect match or something magical. Anything full-time has to pay better. It's not like you can take Daisy to her appointments anymore so you don't need the flexibility…"

He winced. "Remember the bank levy? We owe enough under my name now that they sued for my bank accounts, too. Now, I can't put a penny in a bank anywhere or it goes straight to the creditors. If I get a job as an employee where they withhold taxes, they garnish 50 percent of my check for back taxes and the unpaid student loans."

Her head was whirling trying to keep all the bad financial news straight. "Wait, why do you owe taxes?"

"If I work as an independent contractor, which is how most apps and side hustles pay, then the money comes straight to me. The catch is you have to pay taxes at the end of the year, because they're not taken out. And I needed every penny. So now, I can't work a real job or they take half and I can't make enough to live on what's left. Also, I can't have a bank account. Everything has to be in cash or hidden in PhonePay accounts that don't link to my name." He took a breath and his thumbs swept over the backs of her hands. "Sweetheart, I owe over a million dollars."

She choked. Tried to recover. "What about declaring bankruptcy?"

"Won't wipe the student loans, and as long as Daisy's sick, the medical bills just keep coming back. Even if I could have finished my degree and gotten the best-paying job out there, it would take me multiple lifetimes to pay off the debt, fees, and interest." He tipped his head to the side with a sardonic little smile. "But I also don't want to steal. I never loved it, but I could live with it, until I got spectacularly dumped by the most beautiful naked woman I've ever seen. So I've been...trying to find another way. That's the thing I wanted to tell you."

"Please tell me there's good news after that." She almost couldn't believe how deep in he was, how he could even still laugh when he was living under the weight of all that.

"My sister's latest round of chemo will be done in two weeks. If her scans go well and she's really in remission this time, then I won't have the copays or all the running around to appointments. I can try to get a real job and deal with the garnishments. I still need to find a way to live on half of what I can make, though, so I let my studio apartment go. Tried to move in with my parents, only lasted two days, so I got roommates instead." He grinned, but it was weak. "I live in a two-bedroom house with three drummers now. Very dedicated to their craft, unfortunately. But until the chemo is done..."

"You're still stealing."

"Yeah." He let go of her hands. "Even with roommates, everything I've been able to patch together isn't enough."

She took a breath, tried to think clearly. Tried to do anything but *hurt* for him and his sister and their impossible situation. The idea in her head right now was crazy, and she should be kicking herself for even thinking it, but like she'd told Sadie, she was tired of doubting herself.

She wasn't stupid. She wasn't crazy. And Bishop had always been worthy of her trust.

"Move in with me."

His hand glitched in the middle of setting down his champagne glass, and it tipped over and rolled on the placemat. *"What?"*

"I want you to be able to stop stealing," she said. "If you don't have to pay rent or utilities, all you have to worry about is the copays for the next couple of weeks until she's done in chemo. Your side hustles and freelance coding work should be able to cover that. After that, you can go looking for a full-time job that pays well enough to pay your bills even after garnishment. You've clearly got the skills, and the freelance work will help you get recommendations to make up for the lack of a degree, so bigger companies will be willing to take a chance on you."

She paused for a second, trying to gauge his expression.

"If you crash on my couch, you can stop stealing today." She looked him in the eye. "If you really mean it and you actually want to give up the easy money."

"There's nothing easy about that money, Harlow, not about living with it." His face darkened. "Even before the hell of having to watch you on a date with another guy, knowing he was free to be with you, and I wasn't."

"Then what do you say?"

His gaze fell, just for an instant, to her lips. "Are you asking me to move in with you as a friend, or as a boyfriend?"

She kept her voice level. "I'm asking as a person who cares about you, who thinks you're a good person in a hard situation who deserves a chance to make it right. That's all, for now."

He leaned his elbow on the table, propped his head in it, and studied her. "I don't believe you, you know? About not forgiving me. I don't think you'd ask me in to your home if you didn't forgive me."

"You let me judge you without knowing why you were stealing. That wasn't fair to me, and it sure as hell wasn't fair to you."

"Haven't you heard? Life isn't fair."

"No. But you did it to give your sister a second chance at life. And I think if she could do the same for you, she would. So I'm going to do it for her."

"It's not because you miss me?" He swiped a piece of bacon off her plate, popped it in his mouth. That playful spark was back in his eyes, the one that always tugged a smile onto her face.

"A little." She reached across the table and pilfered a mini muffin from his abandoned plate. "Or at least I did before you started eating my bacon."

"Or it's because you miss my amazing breakfast cooking." He nodded at the brunch buffet. "I see your attempts to replace me."

"You really can't believe I'm doing this, can you?" She laughed, the sound coming out like relief.

"I really can't."

Her smile faded and she looked down at the muffin without eating it. "I thought I knew you, before I knew about the stealing. Maybe I'd like to think I wasn't wrong."

CHAPTER 22

"There you are."

Bishop turned around to find Harlow leaning in the doorway of the bathroom, still with her purse and tote bag and laptop bag all hanging off her. The woman hauled half the contents of her apartment with her to work every day.

She was smiling, but when she saw what he was doing, it turned quickly into a groan. "Bishop! I told you not to be all guilty and trying to do stuff for me the whole time you're living here. It makes me feel guilty that you're guilty and then we're both uncomfortable."

He sat back on his heels, and tossed down the scouring sponge. "Don't take this the wrong way, because you're a very tidy person, but you live in filth. Your grout, Harlow. How can you not see that there are *things* in your grout? Growing things."

"Oh really?" She set down her laptop bag and folded her arms. "Better question. How can you care about my grout when your laundry is all over the living room? What if we had people over?"

"Uh, good point. I'll find a place to put that." He sprinkled more scouring powder on the wall behind the free-standing tub and kept scrubbing. "And I notice because I didn't get to be a 5-star janitor by overlooking the grout."

"You mean that whole thing where you manage people's WebBnb nightly rentals? You do the cleaning, too?"

"You should see me fold the ends of toilet paper." He air-kissed the tips of his fingers. "They don't teach that kind of detail work in the Ivy Leagues." He rinsed the section he was doing and tackled the last bit of tile. "I only ever had one unhappy customer."

She admired her now-glistening bathroom wall. "I'm guessing the complaint wasn't about your grout."

"No, for a while there, I had a couple that wanted it to be a real B&B, you know? So I'd go over there in the mornings and make breakfast for whoever was renting that luxury condo, chat them up. It was fun, paid well. Everybody loved it. Until a particularly adventurous couple mistook the nature of my services."

"They wanted to sleep with you?" She lit up, flushing a little but her eyes wide. "What did you do?"

"Them, obviously."

"You didn't!" She threw the hand towel at him.

"What? They were cute!" He rinsed the final section and grabbed his cleaning supplies. "Unfortunately, they mentioned it in their detailed—and might I add glowing—review and the owner wasn't having it. And that's how I got fired for a five-star customer service job."

He put away the scouring powder under the sink and washed his hands. Behind him, she was giggling. "You made that up."

He had not. But he would let her think that if she wanted, in case she was the type to decide he was a player because of one measly threesome. "Harlow?"

"Yes?"

"Have I told you lately how great your house smells?"

She snorted. "Every time you say that I'm tempted to buy sauerkraut just to see the look on your face."

He took her tote bag off her shoulder. She was so weighed down, she looked like a coat tree. Grabbed the laptop off the floor and headed back to the living room where she kept both of them.

"I don't do anything special, though," she was saying. "It's probably

175

lingering cinnamon from those apple pancakes you made me before work. Seriously, when do you sleep? You're up so late coding, and then I wake you up in the morning when I leave for work. So sorry I don't have more than a couch to offer."

He still had high hopes that with good behavior, he might earn back his bedroom privileges. Either way, though, Harlow's couch was a penthouse compared to sauerkraut central or his brief stint renting half a room in an apartment full of drummers.

"Coders are like vampires. We only need a couch because we live off the blood of our victims and only come out at night. But if you want to offer up your blood..." He made the mistake of glancing at her neck. It was slender and graceful and the skin there looked soft and *fuck*, he was going crazy being this close to her all the time and not knowing where they stood. It had been almost a week, which in wanting-to-kiss-her time was about seven years.

Harlow flushed, her gaze dropping to his lips. "No, but I could offer dinner. I'm even better at dinner than you are at breakfast."

"Not possible." He dropped her bags in the nook by her desk. "Apple pancakes, Harlow. Did you see the glory?"

"I saw every delicious bite disappearing into my mouth."

He went over and scooped up all his loose clothes, then dumped them into the suitcase he kept by the couch and flipped the lid closed.

"Oh!" She blinked at him. "Thanks for doing that already. I didn't expect..."

"It's not that hard. Just laundry."

A smile tickled at her mouth. "Yeah. I guess." She continued on into the kitchen and opened the fridge. "I'll be home late tomorrow. I've got an, um, errand to run."

"You know, if you wanted me to come with you to visit your parents, I would." He came over and grabbed one of the bar stools on the opposite side of the pale granite counter. "I know how much you hate it. I'm a good buffer, when I need to be." He gave his eyebrows a bounce. "Hey, if I can brighten up chemo, prison is almost too easy."

"How do you know that's what I'm doing?"

"You leave your bullet journal open on the table all the time."

When he'd first seen the thing, with all its font-perfect lettering and tiny hand-drawn icons and symbols and lists, he'd told her he hadn't known she was an artist. She blushed and stuttered and insisted it was only a planner, but she was too Type A and liked to make her own. Bishop was pretty sure you could just buy a planner and it didn't require fifteen different kinds of pens. What she did was definitely art, like a calligrapher. Only practical, because Harlow.

"How do you know I don't like visiting my parents?" She took out a La Croix and popped the top.

"Um, because you write it in in *black*. And then cross it out when you don't go. And then write it again in black with more exclamation points. I love the little swoopy thing you do under the exclamation point, by the way. You could make those journals and sell them if you ever get tired of designing playgrounds."

"It's fine. I've just been putting it off because last time I visited… anyway, it's fine." She grabbed a box of pasta out of the pantry, then turned back to him with a smile. "Want happier news? I turned in the proposal today."

"For Sunnybrooke?"

"The one and only. Maps, sketches, budget projections, everything."

"Did Bill turn in his on time?"

"As far as I know. There's no way his cost-cutting measures are as good as mine, though. Condos spread out the building costs over several different families without sacrificing any of the upscale nature of the neighborhood. Plus, it widens out our range of prices and our target market. Win/win."

"You're right." Bishop watched her dance around the kitchen, his smile growing as she listed out all the benefits. "There's no way Bill Dumpling thought of any of that stuff, because when most people are told to cut a budget, they just make everything suck more. Only Harlow Rimes would find a way to make it cheaper, but somehow even better."

"And more space-efficient, which is more efficient for materials and energy consumption," she said with her head inside a lower cabinet.

He came around the counter and pulled her back up to her feet, her hands warm in his. "Harlow. You've got to stop this."

She looked up at him, her eyes all golden smoky brown. "Stop… making dinner? You said yourself if it can't be made in a skillet, it's beyond you. We already had eggs for dinner once this week."

She was backed up against the counter and he knew he should let go of her hands and take a step back, to save his sanity if nothing else. She smelled like vanilla and caramel and he wanted to devour the skin of her neck to see if it tasted as good as it smelled. Also, she was trying to cook dinner again, because she was way too good to him.

"If I can't be doing stuff for you because I feel guilty, you can't be treating me like a guest. Even if Daisy's scan comes out clean in a week, it's gonna take me a minute to afford the deposit for a place of my own again. I hate the idea that you can't just relax and hang out because I'm up in your business all the time."

He let go of her hands and backed up, leaning his hips against the counter and hooking his thumbs into the pockets of his jeans.

"Actually…" A little hint of a smile tugged at her mouth. "I think I'm more relaxed with you here than I was alone. I'm definitely taking less work home."

"Seriously, what would you be doing if I weren't here?"

"I don't know…" She brushed her hair back, a strand catching on the hook of her littlest finger. "Maybe a facial mask and the latest Sally Thorne novel?"

"Okay, let's do that."

"I'd call your bluff, but I only have the one Sally Thorne."

"I have stuff to read."

Her look only grew more skeptical.

"What? I read." And now he was kind of offended. He went over to his suitcase and pulled out his paperback of David Sedaris. A little more digging produced a copy of Amy Schumer, and okay, it wasn't the *Brothers Karamazov*, but at least it wasn't Hustler. He waved them as evidence. "I just haven't had any nights free to read since I've been here because you're such a Veronica Mars junkie now."

"How can Veronica be so mean to Logan? His parents are awful and he's so lonely and he loves her..." Harlow moaned.

"He's a juvenile delinquent with a rap sheet." He focused on tucking his books back into his bag. "She's smart to stay away."

"Whatever. Seriously, Bishop, you don't have to do a facial with me."

"Harlow, you let a guy you've known less than two months move into your house. You're saving my ass." He came back into the kitchen, resisting the urge to touch her cheek. "Please believe I would let you put any amount of crap on my face if it made you happy."

"You say that now..." But she was already starting to smile as she grabbed his hand and started to pull him toward the bathroom. He didn't put up much of a fight. Harlow, in a tiny room, touching his face? Yes, please, and make it a double.

Until he'd been on the straight and narrow long enough to convince her—and himself—that he was a safe bet for her to date, he'd take any touch he could get. Even if it involved beauty products.

"Wait, is it going to get all gummed up in my stubble? Maybe don't put it in my stubble."

She pushed him up against the sink and patted his chest. "Nobody's putting anything in your stubble, tough guy. Now get that shirt off."

Bishop was starting to really, really like this roommate bonding stuff.

He pulled his shirt off and tossed it onto the floor. Harlow was dangerously easy to spend time with. Even easy to live with, surprisingly, considering how small her apartment was. The not kissing her part, on the other hand, did not fall under the category of easy.

But it was her call. If she ever wanted him back in her bed, she'd have to make the first move. Until then, he'd be right here. Making her pancakes, letting her put goop on his face, glorying in the gift of being allowed to be close to her again. Even while he hoped, all the time, for more.

179

CHAPTER 23

*H*arlow used to love her job. She could get lost for hours in planning future homes for people, in imagining new friends coming together in her parks and kids dashing down her sidewalks. But it had been much easier to focus at work when the only thing waiting for her at home was her couch and Netflix queue.

Now, she couldn't focus on her paperwork because she kept thinking about the guy who was currently occupying that couch, his mouth probably getting that adorable little frown-crease it only got when he was coding. Probably not wearing a shirt because he said he didn't want to drive up her bill by running the A/C all day. He didn't even leave his laundry all over the living room anymore, since she brought it up that one time.

It would have made everything easier if his laundry could come between them.

Instead, she was stuck with the reality of a devastatingly attractive roommate who she was not supposed to kiss. She was helping him get back on his feet. He was not at the right place to commit to a relationship. He needed to focus on his family.

She, on the other hand, could not stop focusing on that adorable little crease at the edge of his mouth. When they'd done facial masks together, she'd dabbed dark blue goo into the shadow of that crease, her fingertips almost touching his beautiful lips and she'd thought, *what would it hurt?*

But that's how she'd gotten into this mess. By throwing caution to the wind and kissing him just because she wanted to, and imagining nothing else would matter besides how good it felt. As it turned out, a whole lot of things mattered. Including felonies.

Harlow had an awesome job, good friends, and a comfortable life because she'd played by the rules and followed her head rather than her whims. Her parents had ended up in prison because they'd done the opposite. Just because she was letting Bishop crash on her couch didn't mean she had to jump back into bed with him.

Even if he had built her a snowman out of marshmallows this morning, and set it up so it was peeking out of her coffee cup when she opened the cabinet. And even if the snowman *had* been a little bit cute.

Her officemate cleared her throat and pushed away from her desk, and Harlow looked up. Emilia's earrings today dangled with tiny bells and they chimed softly as they swung against her cheeks. "Wanna go on a croissant-and-coffee run with me?"

"Love to, but isn't it a little early?"

"Nah, it's already ten."

Harlow frowned, glancing at her computer clock, but it really was just past ten. She was usually starving by this time in the morning. But in the past, she hadn't had a shirtless man making her sausages and waffles before work to go with her mug-dwelling snowman. "I'm actually not hungry, but you go ahead."

"Not hungry for croissants, huh?" Emilia squeezed her shoulder as she passed. "Don't worry so much," she said in an undertone. "Since when has upper management ever been on schedule for anything but their tee time? If they'd given the job away to someone else, we'd have heard by now."

The VP had said they'd have a decision by Monday, but here it was

Wednesday, cruising fast toward lunchtime, and there had been nada for news. Harlow managed a smile. "I know, you're right."

It wasn't that she thought Bill Dumpling had secretly gotten the promotion. Even if the board had told him first, it only would have stayed a secret for the time it took him to walk down the hall and say something smug to her about it. The thing was, her company couldn't afford to take extra days to make management decisions right now. After the money Hank stole, getting Sunnybrooke off the ground was the only thing that was going to keep them solvent. If there were more delays at this point, it might mean something darker.

Maybe they hadn't had enough money to keep going after the embezzlement, after all. How cocky had she been, offering to help Bishop when her own employer was hanging by a thread? If she couldn't pay the rent, they'd both be sunk.

Her phone beeped a text and she jumped, the sound incredibly loud in the small room.

Ellen: Do you have a minute?

Harlow's stomach plummeted, and she gulped for air. This wasn't necessarily bad news. It wasn't. It might not even be about the promotion—it could be about the right of way issue at the Horse Heaven subdivision. And if it was about the promotion, she had as good of a chance as anyone else. Or at least she had before they turned in their proposals. Why had she made her neighborhood plan so elaborate? She could have dropped the walking trails and parks, made it all cheaper and more basic. Just houses instead of a community designed to foster friendships and outdoor recreation. It wouldn't have been what she really wanted to build, but she had to pay her dues here.

Harlow: Sure! What do you need?

Ellen: Can you come up to my office?

She rose and smoothed her skirt. On the bright side, if she lost her job, Bishop would certainly let her crash in his car with him. He had grumbled more than she had when the Monday deadline came and went with no news.

She headed toward the vice president's office, trying to ignore the portraits of past neighborhoods that decorated the walls. If she didn't get this promotion, her version of Sunnybrooke would never get to exist. All the families that would have called it home would stay scattered in overpriced apartments across Austin, never meeting each other.

Instead, Bill Dumpling would build a checkerboard of square, cheap houses that made everyone who lived in them feel as forgettable as their beige siding.

The name plaque outside Ellen's office gleamed in the fluorescent lights. Harlow curled her hand into a fist, squeezing her fingers together to make sure they were steady before she knocked.

"Come on in, Harlow."

CEO Tony was leaning against the wall behind Ellen's desk, and her heart jumped. He rarely ventured out of his office for anything. His chin came up at her entrance, but he finished the text he was typing before looking up from his phone.

"That was a hell of a map you drew," he said, then grinned. "Those food trucks were the clincher, though. Barbecue is the fastest way to a Texan's heart. Gal like you really knows how to sell a *house*."

Harlow smiled tentatively. "Um, thanks? I mean, there aren't a lot of restaurants in the neighborhood yet, which can be a deterrent to families reluctant to move away from downtown. Bringing in food trucks seemed like the fastest way to transition—"

Ellen waved a hand. "It's not a thesis defense, Harlow. What Tony's trying to say is, we loved your proposal, and we'd like to offer you the job." She gave him a tolerant smile. "Which is normally the thing you say *first*."

He rocked back on his heels, the new leather of his cowboy boots creaking as he chuckled. "Right. What she said."

"I—" She fumbled, caught off guard by the unexpected presentation and how braced she'd been to be denied the thing she'd been working toward for her whole career. "So wait, I got it? I'm the lead for Sunnybrooke?"

"All yours," Ellen confirmed. "Your proposal package was very persuasive, as was the preliminary work you did before Hank's, um, departure. Very well-thought-out. We won't be able to afford all of your ideas, of course, but your addition of condo buildings was a very clever measure to increase revenue while decreasing costs. If this works out, we might let you try your hand at one of our more upscale neighborhoods, where there's more of a budget for amenities."

"I, uh—thank you." She smiled, but it felt wide and silly on her face. The news didn't feel quite real yet.

She'd more than half expected the good old boy's network to usher Bill Dumpling in ahead of her, with all his years of experience and safe ideas. But it had *worked*. All her preparation and hard work, never cutting corners. She'd followed the rules and done a better job and in return, she was about to get her dream job, a hefty raise, and an office of her own.

Her old boss Hank might be lounging on some tropical island somewhere, living off a stack of stolen money, but he'd never get to come home. Sooner or later malaria season would roll in and the money would run out, and what was he going to do then, get a job shelling coconuts?

Hank had taken the shortcut to riches, but she'd stuck around and done the right thing and was reaping the benefits now. And getting to make her city a better place in the bargain.

"You'll start to see the increase in your compensation by next paycheck," Ellen was saying. "However, given the unfortunate circumstances with Hank, the position does come with a few new strings attached along with—" Her phone beeped and she glanced down at it, then picked it up and swiped the screen open.

"Of course, of course," Harlow said. "I appreciate so much you giving me a chance and I'm open to whatever uh, strings you need. To feel comfortable." She had no idea what to make of the other woman's phrasing, but Ellen was typing on her phone now and didn't clarify. Harlow waited, shifting in her heels as the corner of her lips tugged and twitched, wanting to smile but feeling silly for smiling when she was the only one.

"I'm sorry," Ellen muttered. "I need to take this. Can we chat details tomorrow?" She was already lifting the phone to her ear.

"Absolutely. I have a million things I need to get started on." She flashed them another grin and did her best not to sashay out of the office. She couldn't wait to see Bishop's reaction when she told him the news.

CHAPTER 24

he door to Harlow's apartment banged open, and Bishop swiveled away from the lines of code on his laptop. She burst inside, flinging her bags down.

"Bishop, you're never going to guess what happened!"

He whipped off his fedora and Frisbeed it across the room to her.

"You got your promotion?"

She caught the hat, then paused, her face freezing in mid-excited grin. "Well, yeah, actually. I guess you can guess."

"Hell yes!" He bounded out of his chair. "What should we do to celebrate? We need a helicopter. Rooftop full of peacocks. Limousine." He snapped his fingers. "Champagne! Yes."

He headed for the kitchen.

She laughed, popping his hat onto her head and looking completely adorable in the tweed fedora. "Bishop, I don't exactly keep champagne on hand in case of emergency."

He winked. "Yes, but I do."

"Um, how do you just *have* champagne?"

"You said you were up for a promotion," he said with his head deep in the fridge.

"You didn't know I'd get it, though."

He turned around to give her an incredulous look. "Uh, yeah, I kind of did. There's no way they have more than one person at that company who's as excited about floor plans and bench placement as you are. And even if they did, I've seen your bullet journal. It's highly unlikely some old guy named Bill Dumpling can match your level of organizational skills. He probably has to have a secretary send his text messages."

He pulled a brown paper bag out of the fridge, with "Sausage" scrawled on it in Sharpie.

Harlow drew back, crinkling her nose. "Ew, that bag is bleeding."

"I drizzled some Worcestershire sauce on the outside so you'd be too grossed out to touch it." He pulled a bottle of champagne out and tossed the bag in the sink. "Get some glasses, Ms. Lead Designer. We've got serious celebrating to do." He grabbed the bottle and shook the hell out of it.

Harlow jumped to stop him. "What are you doing? Now it's gonna spray everywhere."

"Well, *yeah*. How is it a celebration if the champagne doesn't spray?"

"It'll get the floor all sticky!"

"Okay, come on." He grabbed her by the hand and dragged her to the bathroom and straight into the tub. He lifted her hand and held her steady so she could step over the tall side, giggling with her golden-brown hair falling forward beneath his hat. She was glorious. It put a catch in his throat to think that she was getting everything she wanted, everything she had worked for and deserved so much. He wasn't used to a world that kind, but Harlow had a way of making him believe again.

He gave the champagne another shake, determined to give her the celebration of her accomplishments that she deserved.

"Wait, wait!" She pulled the shower curtain around the tub.

"Harlow." He stopped to give her a dirty look. "There is nothing festive about a shower curtain."

She pulled off his hat and plunked it back on his head. "Shut up and open that champagne, roomie."

He twisted off the wire cover and set his thumbs under the rounded edge of the cork. "Ready?"

Her eyes met his, all warm melted-butter-on-toast-colored and bright with happiness. His thumbs jerked early. The cork blew out and hit the ceiling, pinging back down so hard he ducked, starting to laugh as champagne blasted everywhere.

Harlow shrieked. "Oh my gosh, it went up my *nose!*"

"That's good luck!" he improvised, choking on laughter at the startled look on her face.

The white button-down she wore to work was soaked and he was pretty sure he could see the outline of her bra through it, if he could manage to look away from the way she was licking champagne off her lips.

He held his thumb over the opening and shook the bottle again, spraying her so she squeaked and held up her hands to ward him off. She was fully soaked now, with her face lit up and cheeks sparkling with droplets. Her laughter had a little catch to it, and then her eyes started to shine with tears.

"Bishop, you don't even understand. It's crazy. I'm going to design where families live their actual lives. People don't get it, but the way you design a neighborhood changes everything, it changes *how* they live. It—"

"It changes the world," he said quietly.

She grabbed his shirt and hauled him across the tub, kissing him so hard their lips didn't even line up right at first. Champagne sloshed out of the bottle as he wrapped his arms around her, cupping the back of her head so he could kiss her even more deeply. The relief of finally getting to touch her mixed with all his happiness for her and her future, and Bishop went dizzy with the rush of it. His hat fell off and he picked her up, her whole body pressed tightly against him as her legs went around his waist.

"Bedroom," she gasped between kisses and he was so, so glad she wanted what he did because he was exploding with it. He stepped out of the tub, careful as he tried to balance their combined weight, and then he was kissing her again all the way across the hallway. He wished he didn't have this stupid champagne bottle taking up his hand when he had so many better uses for that hand, and that reminded him that all their clothes were soaked. He didn't want Harlow's fuzzy bedspread all sticky, so he boosted her up onto her tall dresser instead.

She giggled as he almost didn't lift her high enough, but then he bumped her up the rest of the way with a grunt. He left her long enough to sweep the covers back on the bed, which knocked her stuffed narwhal onto the floor. He rescued Henry the narwhal and propped him up next to the champagne bottle on the bedside table.

"Leave some for us, now," he admonished the narwhal.

That made Harlow giggle, and when he came back she was perched atop the dresser with her legs swinging and eyes shining and she was so beautiful he forgot he was supposed to be moving her and just kissed her instead. Her face was beautiful even with his eyes closed, her high cheekbones whispering against his palms, and her lips soft and happy, so that he was smiling into their kiss even before she pulled his shirt off. He surged back between her knees, skimming her shirt up and off her head so it joined his on the floor.

Her bra was white lace against the burnished gold of her skin, and he wanted to kiss a line all the way down to it. But by the time he kissed his way to the very center with her breasts swelling to either side, she was gasping and yanking at the button to her jeans. He took care of it for her, then the zipper, too.

"Lift up?"

She tipped her weight back on her hands and wriggled enough to let him pull her jeans and panties off, smoothing them the rest of the way down to her ankles. He kissed the insides of her knees while he unzipped her ankle boots and dropped them with twin thunks to the floor. Honestly, he could barely hear a thing over the roar of his heart right now, because she was trailing her nails up his neck and into his hair. It felt like the nicest thing anyone had done for him in years.

"Lean back." He shot her a look that felt like it ought to turn the air to steam between them. Considering how hazy her eyes got in response, it just might have. He kissed a trail down from her belly

189

button this time, but the angles were all wrong and she was still sitting up too straight. "Hook your knee over my shoulder, sweetheart."

She made a tiny sound at that, and then her bare skin was warming his shoulder and he turned to lay a kiss to her soft inner thigh before he scooted her to the edge of the dresser and dove in to taste her. Now she was making more than tiny sounds, and he was lost in the soft textures of her. The way he could feel her tremble and jerk under his mouth. The angles were still all wrong for him to reach everything he wanted, so he found her with his hand instead, pushing two fingers into her slick heat.

Her nails scraped the finish of the dresser. "Oh, Bishop—"

He rolled his tongue softly over her clit, giving her deep, desperate thrusts with his fingers because he wanted to be inside her in the worst way right now. He loved the way she squirmed and rode his hand when he curled his fingers forward and found her favorite little place. Even as he was thinking it, she went stiff, her legs clamping tight over his back and against his shoulder. He pushed deeper, letting her throttle his fingers as he slowed and drew out her climax. Laying small kisses across her lower belly more out of affection than any need to arouse her further.

Her hands found his shoulders and she pulled away, scooting back so she could curl into him and lay her forehead to his. "Oh hell," she whispered, then stole a kiss. "Why are you still wearing pants?"

"You are a very smart woman." He ripped his button open and shucked his jeans and boxers on the floor. Very thankful that he'd been barefoot in the house because that meant he didn't have to deal with shoes before he boosted her off the dresser and back around his waist, her bare legs clamping down with a strength that drew a groan out of him. Naked. Naked Harlow legs around his waist and oh fuck wow.

He dashed for the bed.

She rolled her hips with single-minded focus and he was standing so hard already that the tip slipped inside before he could stop her.

His arms clamped hard on her waist and back. "Condom," he panted. "Harlow, we need a condom."

"Bedside table," she half-whined, and he swore he could feel her pulse a little wetter as she reluctantly pulled away from the head of his cock. He dropped to sit onto the edge of her bed because he wasn't sure he could trust his legs when she was doing things like that. But then he didn't want to stop kissing her while his hand dug blindly for a condom, so it took some fumbling around before he finally found one and managed to shove it onto himself.

He took her by the hips, his whispered, "Okay?" bumping into her moaned, "Please…" so he didn't even have to pause before he was sliding inside her and it was *everything.* The sweet clasp of her around his cock, the way her nails bit heedlessly into the muscles of his arms, the break of her breath against his temple.

Laying down was really the thing to do. Would give him the space to buck up deep and hard into her, the space to see her naked and beautiful and riding him with her hair all wild and champagne streaked around her face. But he couldn't make himself let her go long enough to do it. He was clinging to her like no one had held him in his whole life and Christ, how had he not realized how lonely he was? He'd been fine, he thought, and somehow now that she was coming home to him every day, touching him, laughing with her feet in his lap on the couch at night…

He grunted, tears stinging his eyes as he buried his face in her neck and surged up deeper into her. He wouldn't let her go, didn't care. Would fuck her right here straddling his lap until his head exploded from how perfect it all felt.

He reached for her bra clasp and their fingers bumped as she went for it at the same time. His head fell back and they started laughing and kissing and somehow, together, they got it open. Lace fell between their bellies as her breasts finally pressed against his chest.

That felt *incredible*, and he kissed her again just because he had to. She tasted like champagne, happiness fizzing up in him until he could hardly stand it. He was grinning now as her hips rolled in his lap, her legs jerking him closer with small clenches of her muscles. That tide of pleasure was starting to pull him under like he needed to slow down right now or lose it.

She caught his jaw in her hands, flipping her hair out of her face. "I missed you." She kissed him. "Missed this."

Her words reached down deep in his chest and instead of forcing himself to slow, his hips leaped upward, the pleasure of her sharp and piercing, and he was coming like nothing on earth could have stopped it. Heat exploding up through him and her slender body clamped too hard inside his arms as he rose all the way off the bed until he was half-standing, hammering into her.

She gasped. "Don't stop. Oh damn, right—"

But he was finished a stroke later, and he fell back on the bed, rolling her beneath him and still breathing hard as he reached down between them to touch her.

She ducked her head. "Hey, I'm okay. That was amazing, and you don't have to..."

He didn't push, just left his fingers there as he kissed her, deep and slow with that tide of everything she'd made him feel that knocked him right over the edge without her. Her breath caught and came out against his lips and slowly, her legs relaxed and she arched slightly toward his touch. He started to rub just a little bit as he nibbled soft, wet kisses down her neck. Her head fell back and he concentrated on finding all the most sensitive places on her neck. Just at the edge of her collarbone, then scraping dull teeth over her shoulder. He was still hard enough to push in deep and grind against her G-spot, so he gave it some more attention. She inhaled sharply, and he kept up the slow rubbing, rocking, kissing until her body jerked tight and her shoulders came all the way off the bed.

It felt amazing like this, when the haze of his own orgasm had cleared and he could feel every wave of her pleasure as it took her, squeezing down on where he was still buried inside her. The hooks of her fallen bra were digging into his hipbone and he'd never been happier. He eased off his touch to draw out her orgasm, letting her ride it until she finally collapsed against the mattress, her arms flopping outward as she lost her grip on him. Only then did he leave her long enough to ditch the condom.

They crawled up to the pillows, and she flung her bra off the bed and collapsed onto his shoulder with a gusty exhale. "I'm so glad you came back. Nobody does that like you do."

"Absolutely what every man wants to hear," he teased. "But no need to butter me up. I'm clearly a sure thing."

"No, no I mean..." She rolled closer, pausing. He pulled the sheet up over her back so she wouldn't get cold. "There's something different about the way you touch me," she said quietly. "I don't know. That sounds stupid."

"No. It feels different to me, too."

His admission came out hoarsely. Bishop swallowed, feeling that same pressure in his chest as when she was locked into his arms and he didn't even want to let go long enough to lay down. But he didn't want to push, didn't want to say anything she wasn't ready for, so he didn't say more.

He cleared his throat. "Tell me something, Harlow."

"Hmm?"

"You design these communities, spend all this time on these houses and neighborhoods, and yet you live in an apartment. How come?"

"I don't know, I guess it doesn't seem worth it to get a place just for me. Thought I'd wait until I had a family." She was drawing on his stomach with one fingernail. "Plus, money. Everything in Austin's getting so expensive. I'll get a discount on one of the units in Sunny-brooke, but I don't have enough saved for the down payment yet. Though with this raise...hopefully in a few years."

"By then the units in Sunnybrooke will be gone." That was bullshit. She deserved a place there for free, for everything she was going to end up doing for it. "Your first community, your baby."

"I mean, probably. If I do my job right, they'll sell out every unit. But people will move, and I can still get a place when one turns over."

"Don't you get to customize them when you're the first to buy? I figured that's why you had so many carpet and tile samples in that tote bag of yours."

"Yeah. But it's okay, I'll get there." The pause before she'd said that suggested otherwise, but she changed the subject before he could call her on it. "What about you? What do you want to do with your life? Like, if you could do anything?"

His jaw flexed, and she looked up, her chin propped on his chest. "The question should be what I *did* with my life, Harlow, you know that. It's already done."

A shadow crept into her eyes. "Yeah, but just for fun. Imagine if your bills all disappeared tomorrow and your sister went into remission, what would you do?"

He played with her hair, tried to let himself actually consider it. It felt dangerous, like a wish that might cost something even to think it.

"Probably still something with coding. I really do fall into it like nothing else. The focus of it, the way you have to do it all just so. And that magic feeling when it's done and you made something out of nothing." He hesitated, and now, here with her, he thought of something else that hadn't entered his mind for a long time. "You know what else I used to think about? Stand-up comedy."

She smiled, at first slowly and then all at once, her eyes brightening. "Oh, yeah. I could see that. That would be amazing. Have you ever tried it? Up on a stage, I mean?"

"No, not myself. But I used to date a girl who was trying to break into it and we wrote a few bits together. I always went with her to open mics, and a couple of comedy festivals. It was the coolest thing, when a joke landed just right and everybody in the audience started to laugh. I'd always turn around to see the whole crowd just lighting up, nobody thinking about how they looked or what they should say to their date next. Just eyes glued to the stage and having the time of their lives. That would be the coolest, I think."

He squeezed her in a small hug, struck by how long it had been since he thought about anything other than the bills right in front of him, or how Daisy was doing that particular week. Imagining anything different had gone by the wayside maybe even before he left college.

"Show me your neighborhood," he urged. "All of it, not just the details you've mentioned here and there. I want to see your perfect place to live."

"You want to see the ARC GIS map?" She started to get up and he tightened his grip.

"Are you kidding? You're naked, I feel great, and there's no way we're moving." He put her hand back on his chest. "You can draw me a map the old-fashioned way."

She giggled. "I'm pretty sure the old-fashioned way had a lot more to do with quill pens and parchment than abs and fingernails."

"Sure, but don't abs sound like a lot more fun?" He flexed his to make them look more defined, and then shivered when she started to trace a path between the pads of muscle.

"Well, here's the main street, where all the other streets feed into so there's not too much through-traffic where the kids are playing in their yards." She edged it over to the cut of his hipbone. "We're going to add one street that connects to the elementary school nearby, so that parents will have a shortcut without having to go out to the highway."

"Smart." He nodded. Though if she didn't move this map further north, he was liable to get distracted.

She traced a line up his side, circling his pec with a light touch that left him halfway between goosebumps and ticklish and paying very close attention.

"This is one of the parks, with a stepped stone and lawn amphitheater so we can have outdoor concerts and summer movie nights. Encourage people to get to know each other as soon as they move in. That way, you can see your friends more often because they're your neighbors too, even this close to the city. Friends are really what makes the difference between a house and a home, a subdivision and a neighborhood."

He kissed her head, because he didn't trust his voice to say anything out loud. Not when sleeping on her couch and sharing meals with her had been the closest he'd felt to a home since maybe ever. He and his parents had never gotten along that well, and there was such a huge age gap between him and Daisy. He would do anything for her, always had, but they never got really close as far as hanging out until she got sick and they were at appointments together several times a week.

College had been a brief blip of parties and Frisbee and all-night pizza-fueled coding sessions, and he'd flourished there, with friends all around him. That might have been the last time he'd felt this good. Or maybe not even then.

He closed his eyes. Harlow was right over his heart now, drawing the reclaimed water ponds that would adorn the walking paths and provide habitat for migrating birds.

He murmured his approval and let her voice just wash over him, losing himself in the idea of a whole world built by Harlow's beautiful mind.

CHAPTER 25

*H*arlow hitched her laptop bag up higher and juggled her
tote to her shoulder, where it immediately slipped back to
her elbow. Her purse strap was half-choking her by the time she got a
hand free to reach for the door to her apartment building.

"Hey there, Ms. Lead Designer." Bishop jogged up from the curb, a
crooked smile lighting his face. "Let me get that." He grabbed the door
and slid her tote onto his shoulder, touching her back as she stepped
inside. Suddenly it felt like way more than her strangling purse strap
making the air feel thin in here.

It had been two days since their champagne-and-sex extravaganza,
and neither one of them seemed to know where that left them. He'd
slept in her bed that night, but the next he was back on the couch, and
she couldn't decide if she should take the easy out he was giving her
or not. There were so many reasons dating him could be complicated
or end up terribly, and only one vote in favor of it, really. Namely, that
she spent all her time wishing she were near him.

But then, as soon as she was, looking at him felt like it sucked all
the air out of the room. She took a gulp right now and tried not to
notice how wide his shoulders looked in that shirt as she followed
him up the stairs.

"Where are you back from?" she asked, keeping it light.

He scoffed. "The WebBnb I've been managing down the street. They couldn't figure out how to turn on the shower. Guy stood there in a towel through the whole tutorial, too. It was...awkward."

"Maybe he heard about your five-star customer service."

He gave her an aggravated look that made her giggle. "Should have known you'd hold that story against me." He pulled the key out of his pocket and let them in to the apartment so she didn't have to juggle her remaining bags to get it.

"Maybe I'm just proud to have a five-star roommate."

He held the door with one hand, lifting an eyebrow at her in a look so sexy it should probably not be allowed out in public. "Am I really earning all five stars, though, if you're not availing yourself of all the services on the roster?"

Her mouth went dry. Were they going there? She slid by him, her shoulder brushing his chest in the tight space, debating furiously about what she should say back. Before she could decide, her phone rang.

Hell.

Her laptop bag slid down her elbow, yanking at her blouse as she bumped the bag aside to mine her purse for her phone. It was Ellen, the VP from work, and now her pulse had a whole other reason to run rampant. Bishop lifted her laptop bag off her arm, taking her phone so he could slide it loose, then handing it back to her.

"Thank you..." She tossed him an apologetic look for the interruption. "It's work, so I'm going to take this in the bedroom real quick, okay?"

"Eh, don't bother. I'm gonna take a bath, so I won't hear a thing over the water." He deposited her bags in their usual spot by her desk and retreated down the hall.

"Hey, Ellen!" she answered. "What's up?"

"Hi there, sorry to call you at home. I know I said there were additional considerations to the promotion we needed to discuss, and I didn't get back to the office today until you'd already left for the day."

Harlow winced. She'd stayed an extra hour and a half, not wanting to look like one of those people that was already at the curb by 5:01. Clearly, it hadn't been enough for the workaholic VP.

"Anyway, I need to get this ball rolling. I didn't want to go into the weekend without letting you know what the next steps were."

"No problem, this is a good time to talk." Harlow slid into one of the dining room chairs, pulling off her work shoes as her gaze drifted up the hall to where the water was running in her bathroom. Where Bishop was taking off his clothes. That five-star comment had definitely been flirting, right?

She shoved it out of her mind and focused on the call. Ellen had made it sound like the promotion wasn't exactly a done deal, and the longer she listened, the more her heart sank.

When she hung up, she closed her eyes and leaned the corner of the phone against her forehead. "Crap. Crap, crap, crap."

Water swished from down the hall. "Everything okay?" Bishop called through the door.

"It's fine, it's just—" It wasn't, really, though. And actually, it was his business because it was going to affect him, too. She walked down the hall. "That was the vice president of my company. Apparently, the fine print on that promotion includes a background check."

She laid her head against the door, then softly banged it against the surface.

"Big background check. Huge. On me *and* my closest family and friends, about everything. Because of course my performance and ideas couldn't just be good enough that they'd just *give* me the job of my dreams. Oh no. There's always more." And it always had to do with other people. What Harlow wouldn't give for her life to be entirely her own, able to succeed or fail on only *her* choices.

"Is this about your ex-boss? Asshat in the Bahamas with the secretary and the gold-plated Speedo?"

"Oh, I really hope he doesn't think all those embezzled riches give him the right to wear a Speedo. But yeah, pretty sure good ol' Hank is the reason behind the policy change." She turned to lean her back to the bathroom door. "They're going to let me get started in the meantime, and she said it's just a formality. They already put the budget in an account for me to work with so we can finish the plans as soon as possible. Millions, Bishop. Actual *millions* of dollars. No wonder they're so freaked out about who they give access to."

Water splished. "Isn't that kind of dangerous? What if somebody else from your office takes off with it again?"

"Well, it's not the *whole* budget. It's just the starter money, before the cash flow from pre-selling units starts coming in. Everybody with access to the account has to go through the same enormous background check as me. Also, we have to use our personal social security numbers as mega-PINs. Unless we have a potential embezzler at work who is also running around with my social security number, I can't get blamed for anything." She tugged at her necklace, and let out a sigh.

"I don't know, it doesn't sound as big of a deal as that sigh just made it out to be."

"Well, it's a lot of things. It's..." She sighed again.

"Do you want to just come in here so we don't have to keep talking through the door?"

"Aren't you naked?" She shifted, not sure what entering the room would mean for the state of their very undefined relationship.

"Hold on, I'll make some more bubbles so you don't objectify me." The faucet turned on and then off. "Out of hot water. Maybe if I splash around, it'll get the bubbles to foam up. Hold on."

"Or you could just pull the shower curtain."

"Oh. Or that." Metal rings rattled on the rod. "Okay, I'm PG-13."

"I doubt you've ever been PG-13."

She cracked the door, and he tipped his head back against the back of the tub and smiled, but his eyes were worried. Around the edge of the shower curtain, she could see the sleek muscles in his chest, and the definitely-bigger-than-sleek muscles in his arms as they lay along the edge of the tub. His black hair dripped with water and his face glowed with the hint of sweat. But not even the sight of Bishop in a bathtub could entirely cheer her up right now, with her stomach churning with dread. She dropped to sit on the bathmat and hugged her arms around her knees.

"So, I'm guessing from the puppy funeral look you've got going here that a background check on you isn't going to come out quite so squeaky clean as I'd expected." He tilted his head to the side so he could watch her. "Lay it on me, Rimes. What's the deep dark baggage in your past you're afraid they're going to find? You shoplift a couple of nail polishes as a teenager?"

She shook her head, propped her chin on her knees.

"Get caught with a joint once?"

"You're getting warmer…"

"Pot? Seriously, Harlow?" He scoffed. "Pot's nothing. This is Austin, not Dallas. Your boss probably won't hold that against you. Especially not if it's on the juvenile record."

"That's the thing, Bishop. They will. They will and all the thousands of days I did exactly the right thing won't matter worth a shit because of who I was born to."

"Oh shit, the parents, the prison…" He's starting to put it together now. "They actually went to jail for pot? I thought they mostly just gave people fines for possession these days."

"It wasn't exactly a Ziploc full. They got caught with eighteen hundred and fifty-two *pounds* of marijuana, Bishop. Plants for miles in hidden tracts out in the forest, plus more screened in by corn plants behind our house. Second-degree felony. So yeah, I don't think my bosses are going to want to trust me with millions of dollars after they find out I was raised by felons."

She leaned her head back against the wall, staring up at the ceiling.

"That's why I had to finish my senior year of high school in foster care, and put myself through college. I mean, my roommate used to go home and her parents would do her laundry on the weekends. Can you imagine? She didn't even have to do her own *laundry*. And now I probably won't get the job I'm perfect for, the job I've earned, the job I care about a thousand times more than the other guy…because of somebody else's fuckup."

Tears began to gather in her eyes. Maybe if she got enough of the groundwork done before Bill took over, they'd make him use her plans to save time. Maybe Sunnybrooke could still get made, even without her.

"Harlow."

"It's fine, it'll be fine. I'm over it. It's better than failing because I actually did something wrong. At least this way I know—" Her voice cracked.

"Come here." Water swished as Bishop leaned over the edge of the tub and pulled her into a hug.

Her face pressed into his wet, warm shoulder and it was probably smearing her makeup all around, but she couldn't stop shaking. It was happening again. No matter how hard she tried, or how carefully she followed the rules, everything just got jerked out from under her. She lost her valedictorian status by a hundredth of a percentage point the last semester of high school, because her kleptomaniac foster sister kept stealing her textbooks so Harlow would pay attention to her. That never would have happened if she'd still been on her parents' farm, studying quietly in the tire swing by their old pond. Her shoulders shook even harder, remembering that tire swing she hadn't dared let herself think about for years.

"Don't cry," Bishop said gruffly. "You're going to get that fucking job. Nobody cares what your parents did. Just go in and tell your bosses the truth, and that your parents are incarcerated and have no way to access or affect the budgets for this job. They said this was a new thing, right? They never even used to do it to their previous neighborhood planners?"

"Yeah." She sat back, groping for some toilet paper to blow her nose.

"So I bet they'll give you a pass. Just be up front with them. Don't let them find out on their own through the official check. It only makes you look guiltier. I'll even move out, so they'll have no reason to look at me."

She jerked her head his way. "Wait, you've never been caught, right? For the credit card numbers?"

"No."

"And you're clean now, you're not doing it anymore, right?"

He looked slightly annoyed at that one, but he held her eyes. "No. I'm not."

She hadn't expected any other answer. It was weird, how something in her just trusted him, despite the big lie that had started their relationship. It was even more weird that she didn't want him to go. She loved her job and she should want to protect it at all costs. Losing her thief of a roommate-maybe-more shouldn't even tip the scales of that equation. But it did. *He* did. She didn't want him out of her life. And really, it was such a tiny chance that this background check could cause any trouble because of him. It was worth it, to bend just this tiny rule, for how important he'd become to her.

"Then why would you move out and maybe put yourself in a position where you have to *start* stealing again, when it'll probably be fine?" she challenged.

"Are they only digging into criminal records, or financial ones, too? Because the second would make more sense and if they find out you have a boyfr—" He glanced away. "A roommate whose finances are so deep in the hole, he should be living on the south pole...well, I can't imagine that would look too good."

Her stomach twisted anew. He'd almost said boyfriend, and now he wouldn't look at her, and suddenly she felt his nakedness on the other side of that curtain so much more acutely. "They didn't say they were checking credit scores. It's more the stuff with my parents I'm worried about."

"Harlow, they're not going to take the job away. You haven't done anything wrong. You're just freaking out because you want it too much and you're waiting for the catch."

She huffed out a bit of a laugh. "Am not." She totally was. How did he know that, when he'd only known her two months?

She shredded the tissue in her lap, stealing a glance at him. He was so good at that, reading her. And damn, did he look beautiful in her bathtub.

"And Harlow?"

"Yeah?"

"Stop looking at my penis."

She choked out of sheer surprise and almost blushed, but his eyes were sparkling, his hair messy and wet around his face. She started to laugh instead because he clearly wasn't upset about her checking him out. And despite his joking, most of him was actually still hidden behind the shower curtain. "It's not like I haven't seen it."

"Hey, I thought we weren't talking about that? My penis just snuck out of the friendzone twice. That doesn't give you a get-out-of-jail-free card to ogle it every time you get sad."

He kept giving her openings today, like he wanted to talk about it. Always light enough she could ignore it if she wanted, but it was kind of adorable how he kept bringing up the status of things between them. So different from the usual guy-in-his-twenties commitment phobia.

"It's been three times," she pointed out.

"You didn't see it the first time, so it didn't count."

"But I felt it."

His look went smoldering for an instant that took her breath away, then he covered it with a crooked smile. "Stop it, you're going to make me blush."

"I doubt Jenna Jameson could make you blush."

"Jenna Jameson could make me do anything she wanted me to do, including her laundry on the weekends."

She smiled, but it wobbled and sank away as she dabbed at her smeared eye makeup. She blew her nose. "You really think they won't freak out about my parents if I tell them the truth?"

"I think it's the best shot you have." His voice dropped, going serious and gentle. "And I think if they knock you out of the running just for that, you should go work for a different company. You're great at what you do, Harlow. Any company with a brain in its CEO's office would be stoked to have you."

Her throat went tight. "Stop it. You're gonna make me cry again."

"Please don't. The water's getting cold, and once that happens, I'm really not going to want you to steal looks at my penis."

She chuckled, the sound a little gaspy with her tears. "Thanks, Bishop."

"We're friends, right?"

She peeked up at him and smiled. One more opening. She didn't know when she'd decided, but her answer was just there, solid in the center of her like she'd known it all along.

"I kinda thought we were more than friends these days."

"I'll take that, too. Either way, no thanks required." He brightened. "Though I guess that means you can look at my penis after all."

He whipped the curtain back and reached out, rolling her right into the tub on top of him as she gasped and squealed with laughter.

"Oh my gosh, Bishop, my *clothes!*" But she didn't worry about her soaked work clothes for long, because every part of him was hard and naked beneath her, and he was kissing her like they'd just reached the swelling trumpets number of a romantic musical, and the spotlight was all theirs.

CHAPTER 26

The backseat of Bishop's parents' car was not a comfortable place to be. It had that plasticky new car smell, which must be coming from an air freshener, since the sedan was fourteen years old. His mom looked like bombed-out hell, her eyes all shadowed and sunken in her face like they got when she had one of her real-deal migraines. But she put on her biggest sunglasses and hadn't even tried to stay home from today's big appointment. Now she was making stilted small talk with his dad in the front seat while Bishop tried to crane his neck to see how close they were to the hospital.

He hated being back here and not being able to see where he was going, plus his knees were crammed all sideways because his dad had shoved the driver's seat way back. Did he really need that much space to drive?

Beside him, Daisy had on her most restrained wig—the one that was her natural deep brown, with only one or two streaks of blue. She was playing on her phone and just as he took a breath to tease her about the dangers of phone addiction, his dinged.

Harlow was in big meetings all day to get the street layout plans finalized, but somehow she'd managed to sneak away long enough to text.

Harlow: You doing okay? Crossing my fingers for all the good news.

Harlow: This one is for you.

It was a selfie of her blowing him a kiss off a hand with crossed fingers, her cheekbones high and beautiful and her eyes a smokey caramel with mile-long lashes. He saved the picture.

Harlow: This one is for Daisy.

The next one came in, and he laughed as zombie blood sprayed in a GIF of Michonne and Carol fighting side by side in The Walking Dead.

"Dais, Harlow sent you a good luck GIF."

"Who's Harlow?" his dad said from the front seat.

"Harlow's the woman Bishop's been seeing," Mom said, her voice pitched migraine-low and strained. "She's a city planner."

He almost corrected the specific job title, but she looked so miserable he decided it wasn't important. She must have heard about Harlow from Daisy. He nudged his little sister. "You little gossip."

She laughed. "You're the one who texted me to say she was your girrrlfriend now. Why'd you do that if you didn't want anyone to know?"

His face felt hot, but he was definitely not blushing. Men did not blush. Then again, how manly was it to be texting your little sister about your relationship status? He made a mental note to get himself a fucking life.

"You're always bugging me about her," he muttered. "Thought you'd want to know."

Daisy reached for his phone. "I wanna send a GIF back."

He handed it over, but then Daisy grinned and started to narrate as she typed, "Dear Harlow, Bishop loooves you and wants to have your babies…"

"Gimme that back, twerp."

He jostled her, trying to grab the phone, but she'd been off chemo for long enough that she was fast again. She hit send and crowed with triumph. He reached to mess up her hair in retribution like he once would have, but caught himself in time. It was a lot harder to comb the wigs back into place than it was with regular hair.

"Just for that, I'm naming my most annoying kid after you, after I start having Harlow's babies."

She handed back his phone and he rolled his eyes when he saw she'd sent a Carol GIF, and then a text that said, **My brother wants to make out with you.**

Harlow: Don't know what you're talking about. Your brother and I just nod respectfully at each other from across the room. Which is what I expect you'll be doing with your boyfriends when you start dating.

He sent her back a GIF of a flirtatious nod, then checked the time. Eighteen more minutes until their appointment. Which, in medical office time, was probably fifty-two minutes until they'd see the doc. His heart was bumping along about two notches too fast, and breakfast wasn't sitting too well. He needed to get his shit together before Daisy noticed.

It was bad enough their dad was actually in town and their mom had left the house. Talk about cues that things weren't normal. It was a wonder Dais wasn't biting her glitter-painted fingernails off at the tension in the car.

A soft touch patted his arm, and he looked down to see her reaching across to him.

"The cancer's going to be gone this time," Daisy whispered, low enough so their parents wouldn't hear. "I can tell. I feel so much better."

His eyes burned and he tried to swallow. Being off the chemo always made her feel better, and she didn't always feel different before new tumors showed up on the scans. He nodded anyway. "You scared that cancer away. No doubt about it."

She beamed, throwing her shoulders back in her best tough girl posture, and Bishop wondered if he could keep from throwing up for fifty-two more minutes.

~

They met in Daisy's doctor's real office, not the exam room, like they always did on Big News Days. He only had three chairs in front of his desk, and Dad went through this whole awkward thing about looking in the hall and trying to steal a chair from beside the blood pressure station, but Bishop stopped him. They needed that chair for the other patients. Which his father would know, if he'd been in a doctor's office since the last Big News Day.

Bishop leaned up against the wall next to Daisy's chair. Out of the corner of his eye, he watched her picking off her nail polish, the glitter flecks catching the light as they drifted to the floor. He had to hook his thumbs in his pockets to keep from fidgeting. His mom grabbed a tissue and dabbed under her huge sunglasses. Bishop clenched his teeth. Crying already and they hadn't even gotten past the preliminary speech. Couldn't she even *try* to hold it together for her daughter?

Dr. Crandall was droning on about how the chemo had gone and the side effects they could expect for Daisy as she shook off the effects of the latest round. Bishop caught his eye.

"Jim? Could we..." He nodded to the desk and the closed folder.

Dr. Crandall sighed. "Of course. Yes. Unfortunately, the chemo-therapy did not produce the results we were hoping for."

Everything stopped moving. His lungs, his blood, time. He thought he was braced for bad news but he hadn't been. Deep down, he really thought it was about to be over, that they'd made it through the worst. They had to have. It had been *years.*

"Chemotherapy isn't going to be enough and now, we need to look at removal options for the tumors we saw on her scans. In fact, one of them, given the placement, is going to be a very delicate process. There's a surgeon over in New Mexico that...his touch with this is near supernatural. If it were my daughter, that's where I'd take her. You'll have to check with your insurance, of course, make sure he's a covered provider under your plan, but I've seen his surgical results. I think it's worth the extra trouble and travel."

Mom crumbled in her chair. Dad started to ask a question but

Daisy interrupted. "Wait, so I maybe have to have surgery again or I definitely have to have surgery again?"

"Definitely," Dr. Crandall said. "I'm afraid at this point, my dear, it's the only safe option for you. I'm sorry, I wish—"

"No," she said, and Bishop pushed off the wall. "No!" she said louder. "I don't want to have surgery again."

He started to pull her into a hug but she shoved him away. "You said it wouldn't hurt!" she shouted right in his face. "You told me they'd give me stuff and it wouldn't hurt but it *did* hurt and I don't want to do it again."

"Dais—"

She ripped off her wig and threw it at the desk, her bald head gleaming in the fluorescent lights.

"I don't want to have cancer anymore!" she howled.

Bishop caught her when she started to run and she pummeled him, hitting his chest and chin and anything she could reach. He held her anyway. When her knees buckled, he went to the ground with her, rocking her as her hands went limp against his chest and she sobbed.

"I know, I know," he murmured. "It's bullshit."

She hiccupped. "It *is* bullshit." And she cried even harder.

"I'll uh, give you folks a minute," Dr. Crandall said, and let himself out.

Bishop's chest hurt too much to cry. Everything hurt. This couldn't be happening, not again. He looked up and his mom was sobbing, both fists stuffed against her mouth like she could stop the sounds from coming out. Dad was just...gray. Like a body that had been dropped in that chair without any life left in it.

For the first time in a long time, Bishop could see it. This was hard for him, but it was even harder for them. No matter how they dealt with it, no matter how he judged them for it, Daisy was their *child*, and they were hurting like holy hell. Just like he was.

Tumors. Surgery. Recovery.

All the words caught up to him at once. How could one eleven-year-old kid be expected to suffer all this for so long with so little hope? They were saying she still had a chance, but that's all it was: a chance. Not a life. Not the childhood she deserved, free of pain, and needles, and doctor's offices.

Bishop closed his eyes and tucked his cheek down on top of Daisy's head. He wanted to promise he wouldn't let them hurt her, but he couldn't lie to her this time. He listened to his mother cry, and didn't realize he was crying, too, until Daisy's bald head grew slick with tears under his cheek.

CHAPTER 27

$\mathcal{H}$arlow was not freaking out. Yet. She was starting to consider freaking out as an option for her near future but currently, she was still calm and collected.

Or at least collected.

Bishop hadn't answered any of her texts since he got to Daisy's big doctor's appointment. Which, okay, Harlow didn't know how long those kind of read-your-scans-and-next-steps appointments usually took. Still, by the time two hours had passed she was starting to worry. She had a full slate of meetings all day and about a trillion decisions to make, so that helped distract her for the next few hours. By the time five hours had passed since the start of Daisy's doctor's appointment, she started to consider the possibility that it hadn't gone well.

That made the next hour of meetings really hard. She spent the whole thing feeling faint and vaguely dissociated from her body. Like she had low blood sugar or was coming down with a really hardcore flu. She had to ask the CFO to repeat himself, twice.

After that meeting, she gave up on texting and called, but Bishop didn't answer that, either. When the city's planning representative no-showed on her last meeting of the day, she left work early. She debated for a long minute before turning toward her apartment. There was every chance Bishop was still at his parents' house, but she'd check hers first. Then she'd try everywhere else.

Her fingers drummed on the steering wheel as she waited through yet another hell-cursed red light, debating whether it would be too intrusive to show up at Daisy's doctor's office if he wasn't at her house or his parents' place. She knew where the office was. Maybe they were still doing tests, or whatever other doctor stuff you did for little kids who might still have cancer. If that was the case, Bishop needed to be there to support his sister and wouldn't necessarily want or need her to butt into the middle of all that. Except her instincts were telling her that if he wasn't answering his texts, it was because he really, really needed her.

Especially because of everything else this might mean for them if Daisy was still sick. All of their conversations about money and the future had revolved around the idea that Daisy would get done with chemo, and her scans would come back clean. She would be able to start the road to recovery and Bishop could start building a normal life for himself. If he needed more money than he could get past all his garnishments and bank levies, then…

Harlow couldn't even let herself think about that, that the goofy guy who had made her four-leaf clover pancakes this morning—for luck—would have to become a criminal by this afternoon.

A horn blared from behind her and she looked up to a green light going to yellow. She hit the gas too hard, trying not to think about the background check that was "just a formality" of her employment, and how much she couldn't risk dating someone who broke the law. Even if she could live with the idea herself.

Which you can't, she reminded herself. Things got too complicated when you bent the rules. You risked all kinds of terrible possibilities that law-abiding people didn't have to worry about. There had to be another way, even if Daisy was still sick. Harlow was making a lot more after her promotion, so maybe they'd let her help out a little.

They couldn't just…break up. Not so soon, not over this. If Daisy was sick again, Bishop would be so, so upset and he'd need her. Plus, he still didn't have a license and Daisy might need her to drive to some appointments.

How was *Daisy* taking the news, whatever it was?

Harlow parked in her apartment's lot and popped the door open so she could get a deep breath of fresh air. But it was windy today and the air just tasted like dust. It did nothing to settle her suddenly fussy stomach.

"You don't know anything," she told herself. "You're spiraling and overthinking and frankly, being kind of ridiculous." She smoothed her hair and straightened her blouse and gathered her bags.

As soon as she let herself into the apartment, any hope that she was overreacting disappeared.

Bishop was packing.

He didn't look at her when she came in. Strode into the bathroom and came back with his razor and shampoo, dumped them into his suitcase. He emanated tension like it was vibrating straight out of his muscles.

Harlow's elbows slowly unbent under the weight of her tote bag and laptop until the bags rested on the floor. She'd never really understood those characters in movies who threw up because they were so upset. It seemed melodramatic, like the kind of thing people talked about but nobody actually did. But the silence in the apartment twisted her stomach with a pain so sharp it felt like she was the one who needed to see a doctor.

"Were the scans—" She gulped. "How bad is it? Is it terminal?"

He stopped and braced his hands on the edge of his suitcase. "No, they don't think so. Or at least it's not terminal if the surgery is successful. Sorry, I guess I should have said the chemo didn't work, and she needs surgery again. It's a complicated one, because of where one of the tumors is located, so we need this hotshot surgeon from New Mexico. He's not 'in network' for our insurance, which also means if we want her to have the best care, it's all out of pocket. Daisy took it really bad." His head sagged forward. "We all took it pretty bad, actually. I need to get back there."

Was that all this was? Maybe he was packing to stay with his parents because Daisy was upset and she needed him. Harlow crossed the room and reached to lay a hand on his back but he jerked to his feet before she could touch him.

"Do you need a ride back to their house?"

"No." He bent over and yanked the zipper on his suitcase closed, jerking it hard when it caught. When he stood up, he met her eyes and they were more remote than she'd ever seen them. "I'll take an Uber."

She took a step back. She knew he couldn't afford Ubers right now. At least not legally. Her pulse started beating fast and that light-headed, sickly feeling came back.

Could she be with a thief?

Because she knew where this was going and the thought of letting him walk out of her life—today, right now, right this actual *minute*—was hurting her so much more than she could have imagined.

She tried to care about the money and the complications and whether this meant they were on a break or never going to see each other again, but what came out of her mouth was, "Are you okay?"

Pain cracked through his eyes, and she realized they were blood-shot and a little red in the lids, like he'd been crying. His bicep flexed as he tugged his suitcase up to his side.

"No." His voice was hoarse, as raw as his eyes.

"I can—"

"No." He cut her off. "It's bad enough that Daisy needs not just any surgeon, but a really *gifted* surgeon. It doesn't matter if the cancer is terminal when the tumor is this close to an artery and all tucked up into her vital organs. If I'm going to keep my sister alive, I have to steal, and my crimes can't be anywhere near you or your job when I do it."

"Bishop, you don't have to—"

"I sold out my future for her," he said, the words rolling out like a sentence being laid down, as final as a gavel's strike. "I sold my goddamn self-respect for her, and I'd do it again any day of the week, and twice on Sundays. But I won't risk yours."

His voice didn't waver but his face twitched, then twisted with anguish, tears slicking his eyes.

215

She went to him like she couldn't help herself, no idea what decision she was making with the gesture but knowing he needed her to hold onto him. Her arms went around his waist but his didn't follow. Instead, his hand came up, so gently, to cup her cheek.

"I love you, Harlow." Before the shock of those words fully sank in, he dipped his head and gave her a kiss that tasted of salt. His lips were rough and a bit cracked and gone before she was ready, the sweetness of the touch lingering even while he pulled away. "And that's why I won't take you down with me."

His thumb swept across her cheekbone and he let her go.

"Bishop, *don't*." She wasn't even sure it was him she was begging for mercy. There was no way the world could be this cruel, that *this* was really the choice laid in front of him. "People get sick all the time and they make it through without breaking the law. There has to be something else we can do. Bankruptcy, some kind of public assistance or grant or…we'll figure something out."

His suitcase wheels bumped over the edge of her rug and rattled onto the hardwood. "I've had years, Harlow. The only way out is a huge chunk of money and I've never had that in my life. Probably isn't gonna happen before we need that surgery."

"Don't you dare give up this easily." She wrapped her arms around herself and squeezed, trying to make that light, unreal feeling leave her body so she could feel okay again. God, had it only been this morning she'd been eating shamrock pancakes and feeling okay? "On us, on your own life…Bishop, at least stay and *try*. Let me help. I have some money saved, I could—"

"It won't be enough. Bills like this will gobble up every penny you've ever saved like it's nothing. I don't want you wrapped up in this." He turned back and his eyes weren't as certain as his voice. She could see there was still a chance there. He didn't want to do this any more than she did. "With that background check, and everything in your life finally paying off, now's not the time to take chances, Harlow. You've earned all of this and people deserve the Sunnybrooke you would build for them. Somebody ought to get the perfect life, somewhere, right?" His voice wobbled on the last syllable, and nearly cracked.

He said he *loved* her. They'd just gotten together, officially anyway, but it already felt so different from any other person she'd ever been with. Maybe this was what finding The One felt like. And if it was, maybe that's why the people in books were always throwing up. It was every part of you going haywire, like *everything* had changed, not just your emotions.

If he felt this, too, there was no way he could give it up so easily.

"Bishop, I *want* to help you. I want to be there for you and Daisy and be...part of your life."

She didn't want to say those three words, not right now in the crucible of the moment when it felt like she was being pulled apart. She needed to think, needed to be sure she was saying it for the right reasons, and right now all she cared about was that he didn't *leave*.

"But if you don't care enough to try and find another way..." Her voice quavered, trying to find some way to make him change his mind before he went down this path. "If you start stealing again, I can't be with you. My parents chose crime over me, and I haven't seen them outside a prison for my entire adult life. I can't risk that life."

"I understand." He opened the door. "Goodbye, Harlow."

CHAPTER 28

*H*arlow did not have time for an emotional breakdown. She'd just gotten a career-making promotion and dozens of people's jobs were depending on her. Considering the mess Hank's embezzlement had left, Sunnybrooke could very well make or break the whole company. She was not the type to drop a ball that big.

Harlow did her job. She went to work, she clocked in on time. She clocked out on time. She did not cry in between those times. But in the rest of her life? All bets were off.

It was a Wednesday, or maybe a Thursday or a Tuesday when Alice found Harlow in her apartment, doubled over between the couch and the coffee table, an old ketchup-smeared plate caught under one knee as she cried. Her friends had taken to stopping by a few nights a week to check in on her, probably because she'd become sort of erratic at answering calls and texts.

"Oh, honey." Alice rushed across the room, dropping her spare key on the coffee table. "Don't cry, sweetie. Or maybe cry but like, at least breathe a little in between." She tugged the ketchup plate out from under Harlow's knee and slid it onto the table, then dropped onto the floor and rubbed her back. "What happened? Did he call? Did something happen with Daisy? Oh Jesus, I hope they'd tell you if something happened with Daisy."

Harlow tried to explain, but all that came out was another sob, so she gestured to her phone on the coffee table.

Alice grabbed it and clicked it on, an exhale escaping her when she saw the So You Think You're a Match logo. "Oh, Harlow, you haven't been swiping again, have you?"

She nodded miserably.

"There's no way to even tell which jokes Bishop wrote! You're probably matched with half of Austin by now."

"I can tell." Harlow sniffed. "I can tell which ones are his."

"You just think the funniest ones are his."

"The funniest ones *are* his!" She started to cry again.

"They can't be that funny if they made you cry like this." Alice paused. "Hey, about that breathing. You promised me oxygen, remember? In your lungs, not just in your general vicinity, honey."

"They started to recycle," Harlow choked out. She grabbed the Kleenex box, which was empty, and then snatched a used tissue off the floor and blew into that instead.

Alice shuddered. "Okay, don't do that. We haven't sunk that low yet. Let me get you some more Kleenex."

Her friend went down the hall and cabinets rattled as she looked for more tissues. She came back with a roll of toilet paper and curled onto the floor with Harlow again. Her friend laid her head on the edge of the couch, leaving them at the same eye level. She tucked Harlow's hair back from her face.

"Now tell me what you were saying about recycled tissues?"

"Not tissues, jokes. I got the same one I've gotten before, about Prince Charming and the bag of dicks."

"What?" Alice cast a glance toward her phone. "That can't be right. They've got thousands. I swiped until I had to switch swiping thumbs the last time Rob and I broke up, and I never got a recycled joke. You'd have to be a real swiping addict to—" She broke off and said brightly, "Oh you know what, it's probably just a glitch in the algorithm, nothing to worry about."

Harlow squeezed her eyes shut and her eyelids were so swollen even that hurt.

"I can't believe I gave him an ultimatum. I was so scared, of him going to prison and of charges being brought against me as some kind of accessory. I was just trying to get him to slow down, you know? To think about other options, but he didn't even have to think. He picked crime, like it wasn't even a decision for him, just like my parents…" Her voice choked off for a second.

"Speaking of parents, have you been back?" Alice asked gently.

Harlow shook her head. After her dad said he wanted to find a way to start growing his plants again once he got out, she meant to keep visiting. Except every time she tried, she got so angry. Why couldn't one person care enough to pick her? Just one person who really mattered.

"The worst part is," she said in a small voice, "I think I would have done it. Kept dating him when he was stealing, you know? Or something. I don't even know what I would have done, but like…I could feel it. That I *couldn't* let him go. And he walked out like it was nothing for him."

"Yeah, but maybe that's exactly why—"

When Alice didn't finish, Harlow looked up. "Maybe what?"

Her friend looked away. "Nothing. But Harlow, it wasn't like he picked stealing over you because it was loads of fun. You know it was harder for him than that. Have you heard how Daisy is?"

"They got the surgeon they wanted, and the date for the surgery is set. I follow her Facebook. Her mom updates it like every 4 seconds. I donated to the LegUp fundraiser they did for the surgery." Harlow put up her hands as soon as she saw Alice's lips press together. "Anonymously! Don't look at me like that, I'm not creepy."

"Yeah, like they're not going to know who it was when they see the amount I bet you gave." Alice winced. "I thought you were saving for a down payment on a house."

Harlow let her head sag against the couch. "It's weird. I'm juggling these huge bunches of money every day for the Sunnybrooke thing, and none of it's mine or anything but...I don't know. It makes money seem somehow less real, but it's so, so real."

Money affected everything. It ruined relationships and even lives. Sometimes saved them. It felt like it shouldn't matter at all, compared to everything she was feeling, but it just kept mattering anyway.

Alice looked suspicious. "Are you high?"

"Do I seem euphoric to you?"

"No, but you're talking like a stoned person."

"I wish I were high. I wish I were anything but this." She hiccupped and when she caught sight of her phone, she started to cry again. Those jokes on the app were the last way she had to hear Bishop's voice, and now they were all used up. Gone. And she'd never hear him again.

Alice pulled her into a hug, their knees all tangling up together and the coffee table biting Harlow's elbow. "Oh, sweetie. Sweetie, please don't cry any more. Have you eaten? Can I get you something?"

"I don't want it, I don't *want* it!" That was all Harlow could get out before the sobs twisted her voice.

"What?"

"Love. If this is what it feels like."

"Oh, sweetheart." Alice squeezed her tighter, her voice dropping low. "That's exactly how you can tell it's real. This is what it feels like. I'm sorry. I'm so sorry."

CHAPTER 29

*B*ishop's parents' house was finally dark, and it felt like the whole building was sagging exhaustedly right along with all of them.

It had been a relief when his parents went to bed. It was so much harder to deal with them now, without the wall of his resentment to shield him from how much they were hurting.

He'd heard his dad earlier, hiding in the garage to talk on the phone to his mistress. Telling her goodnight and how much he loved her. Bishop really wanted to keep hating his father for basically having another family. Except he'd started to wonder if it helped Dad now, to know he still had one place to go where no one was dying and everything was okay.

His parents weren't perfect, but he didn't have much space to judge, considering he was sitting in their kitchen at one in the damn morning, staring into his girlfriend's bank account. Well, Sunnybrooke subdivision's account, with Harlow Rimes in the username line at the top.

There was less in there than there'd been on the day he left her apartment, but still enough to fix every problem in his life in one fell swoop. All he needed to access it was her social security number, which he'd stolen along with her credit card number before they'd ever even met. He could probably leave some electronic tracks just right so that her employers would be able to tell it wasn't her, and she couldn't get in trouble. It wasn't even *her* money that he'd be stealing.

He rubbed his eyes, his shoulders stiff from too many hours at his laptop. If he was actually going to steal the money, he would have done it the day he walked out of her apartment. Maybe he could have even made himself do it, except without that cash, she didn't get to build her dream neighborhood. Whether it was her fault or not, the scandal would probably tank her career so she wouldn't get to build anything else, either. He couldn't steal Harlow's dreams from her. Wouldn't.

Bishop used to think there wasn't anything he wouldn't do for his little sister, but it turned out there was one thing.

One person on earth he wouldn't throw under the bus to save Daisy's life. God knew it wasn't him. The remnants of his life were already smeared all over the tires of that proverbial bus. Probably splattered on its undercarriage, too. He didn't even know why he kept looking at this fucking account. It was stupid, leaving his IP address fingerprints all over it if anybody was watching.

For him, though, seeing her name on this screen was more consolation than stalking her lifeless social media accounts. She hadn't updated a thing since the day he moved out. For all he knew, she could have died in an accident. It's not like anybody would call him— the disgraced ex. But as long as money kept moving in and out of this account that was tied to *her* social security number, he knew she was still out there, safe and living out her dreams. It was like his fingers laid on her pulse, comforted by the steady pump of life through her veins.

"Why are you looking at Harlow's money?"

Bishop jumped so hard he knocked his elbow against the table. His long-empty coffee cup tipped over and rolled until it came to a stop against its handle.

"Daisy! I didn't know you were still up, kid." He hit the minimize button and turned in his chair. "You need a drink of water or something? You should be getting your beauty sleep. Or anyway, the internet says that's what it's good for. Not that I would know, with a face like this, but you should probably get some. Sleep, I mean."

Wow, apparently she wasn't the only one who needed rest. He couldn't hold up his end of the conversation with a hydraulic jack right now.

Daisy pointed to his laptop, undeterred. "Who are all those people?"

His head jerked back around and he realized what tab had been open behind Harlow's banking page. It was his master spreadsheet of stolen credit card numbers and social security numbers. *Shit.* He hit minimize on that, too.

"It's nothing." He tried to think of something. Anything. "Just, uh... phone numbers. I'm going to start doing telemarketer calls from home, for a job. These are the numbers they sent me."

She stared at him. He stared back, forcing himself not to glance away. She looked at his computer again and he couldn't help but check to make sure he didn't have anything else incriminating up.

"Those didn't look like phone numbers," she said.

She reached for the computer and he slammed it closed. She flinched, and he felt like the world's worst brother.

"Since when do you care about numbers?" He forced a laugh. "Trust me, you'll have to deal with all this boring job stuff all too soon anyway. Then you won't have to worry about how to get to sleep because your career will do it for you."

"Then why don't you want me to see it?"

"Because it's job stuff. People who don't work there aren't supposed to see it." Jesus, he thought she'd grown out of this twenty questions crap. She used to ask *why* about everything until Mom retreated upstairs with a migraine and Bishop bribed her with ice cream to stop.

"The first one you hid wasn't job stuff," Daisy insisted. "It had Harlow's name on top and it was the same bank as Mom goes to. Why do you have Harlow's bank on your computer?"

His head started to throb and he pushed his fingers hard against his temples. He was too tired to deal with this right now. "I still had her password. From when we were dating. I didn't take anything. I just miss her, okay?"

"Why would you take anything?" She looked even more confused. "And why don't you just look at her Insta?"

Oh wow, way to make yourself look even guiltier. He tried to smile. "Yeah, uh, I'll try Instagram next, I guess. For my pathetic ex-girl-friend moping. You want some hot chocolate or something? I hear that's good for sad breakups and also for getting little sisters to sleep."

"Why did you hide those pages?" She folded her arms, getting mulish. "You get that funny look on your face when you're lying."

"What, so now I'm *lying*?" He didn't even care that his voice was getting sharp because he needed her to back off right the hell now. He should have handled this better from the start, been quicker on the excuses. "When you're interrupting me when I'm trying to work and accusing me of...I don't even know what you're going for here." He barked out a short, humorless laugh. "I've got loads of numbers on my laptop, Daisy. It's computer programming stuff that I don't have time to explain to you and you wouldn't understand, anyway. You should be in bed. It's late."

She stared at him, her eyes starting to fill up with tears, and then she turned and fled upstairs.

He gritted his teeth and groaned, deep in his throat so it wouldn't wake anyone else up. That was...wow, he couldn't have covered that up worse if he ran around waving a flag that said THIEF in bright red letters over a skull and crossbones. Hopefully Daisy was young enough and tired enough that tomorrow, all she'd remember was how mad she was at him for yelling at her.

He laid his head down on the table and had a fleeting thought of sleeping right there. Except Daisy was probably upstairs crying right now and her surgery was in four days. If anything went wrong, anything at all...did he want one of her last memories to be crying herself to sleep alone in a dark room? Fresh pain twisted under his breastbone. He dragged himself out of his chair and went upstairs.

Her room was small and crowded with medical equipment, cheap wigs, and Walking Dead action figures and mementos. Above her headboard was the rhinestone-framed photo of her at the last Walker Stalker convention with two of her favorite actresses. The bed below it was empty.

His heart jerked in his chest. But then he looked to the open corner between her bureau and her bed, where she'd draped a blanket across the gap to make a fort. She didn't spend much time in there anymore—mostly threw her stuff under it when Mom made her clean her room. He peeked under the edge just to check. Sure enough, Daisy was balled up in the corner, hugging the pillow off her bed. She wasn't crying anymore, but she was doing those small sniffle-gulps of air that always took him to pieces.

"Hey, listen, Daisy." He clicked on the bedside lamp so he could see, but her face was still shadowed under the blanket fort. "I didn't mean to snap at you. There's a lot of grown-up stuff on my computer that I'm working on, and I'm stressed, but none of it's your fault, okay?"

"Why do you have a bunch of people's numbers, then?"

"They're clients." He sighed. "It's computer programming stuff, like I told you, okay?"

"You said it was for tele...markering." She fumbled the word.

Shit, he'd forgotten he'd said that. "Well, I mean, I'm doing that, too. I'm doing a lot of things right now to—"

"Are they bank passwords? Like you had to get into Harlow's page?"

Double shit. He hadn't thought she'd make that jump. And it wasn't right, but it wasn't exactly wrong, either.

"No, they're not bank passwords. Why are you so fixated on my computer tonight? Listen, I know you're having trouble sleeping. I get it, okay. I'm worried, too." He reached in and touched her shoulder, testing to see if she might be ready to come out for a hug, but she held very still.

"Because I don't get why you don't want me to see it. And you said it was phone numbers, and then you said it was computer stuff." She paused. "Is it...stealing?"

226

His feet tensed in his shoes like he was ready to push off into a sprint. Everything he could think of sounded suspicious at this point.

"It's not stealing." He had to force the blatant lie off his tongue. "It's just something I have to do, for work, that I don't like."

She was silent, and he knew exactly what was going to happen. She was going to ask Mom and Dad about it in the morning. They'd want to see the spreadsheet and it would be even harder to come up with a cover story for them than it would be to fool Daisy. This was exactly why he'd lived alone and had no friends for basically the entire time he was living off stolen numbers. It was a lot easier to avoid people seeing things over your shoulder when you were alone all the time.

"Listen, you can't tell anybody what you saw, even Mom and Dad. I'm...in a lot of trouble because I owe money. For school."

"And you have to steal to get out of trouble? To pay back your school?"

"No. I told you, it's not stealing, it's work. It's just I don't want Mom and Dad to know about the debt and be worried."

"Stop *lying*!"

"Shh! You're going to wake up Mom and Dad."

She crawled halfway out of the blanket fort, and now he could see how her eyes were red from crying.

"You guys keep saying I need to be tough and grown up, but nobody ever wants to tell me anything and I can tell you're lying. I'm not stupid and I'm not a baby."

He dropped from a squat to sitting on the floor, his head whirling. He had no idea what she'd believe anymore, and she was clearly not going to let this go.

"Shh, I'll tell you but you have to be quiet, okay?" He didn't have time to think. "I—what I've been doing isn't exactly stealing, okay, Daisy? I got in trouble because of school, because I dropped out and didn't pay for it."

He couldn't let her know any of this was because of her, so he stuck with only the part that was about his student loans.

"It's not stealing from other people, it's from... Well, not from the banks exactly but kind of. They can write it off, which is this whole pool of money that's kind of real money and kind of not real money because of the way tax breaks work and stuff. You have to promise, Daisy, you have to swear to me you're not going to tell Mom and Dad, or your nurses, or anybody because I'd be in way more trouble, then." This was awful. He was the worst role model ever. "Listen, I wouldn't do it if I had any other choice."

She thought that over. "Can you teach me to do it?"

"*What?*" He jolted and nearly came off the floor.

"Shh." She hushed him this time, as she curled against the end of her bed and hugged her pajama-clad knees. "Mom and Dad need money, for my surgery and to pay the doctors. They could use it, if you know a way where it's not taking it from other people, if it just comes from…somewhere else. I mean, if nobody else *needs* it, then you could teach me and I could help—" She stopped in mid-sentence, and stared at him. "You've been doing it for my doctor bills, haven't you? It's not for school. You haven't been in school for a long time."

"It *is* for school. I know it looks like I'm out of school but you have to keep paying for it even after you're done going. Remember, I told you about student loans?"

She did not take the bait. "I know you already used some of your school money to pay my doctor bills. Mom and Dad used to fight about it all the time. And whenever we go to my appointments, you're the one who goes up front to pay, even when Mom's there. If you took money from somewhere, then you would help pay all my doctors with it, I know you would." She shook her head. "You wouldn't just pay for school."

Dammit, dammit, dammit, why did he have to have a smart sister?

"No, it's not like that, it's—" He scrubbed a hand over his face, his teeth grinding together. "*Fuck.*" Tears hit his eyes so hard it felt like something popped.

"Show me how to do it, please?" She was whispering urgently now. "Then you don't have to do it anymore. You can go back to school for computers. Mom said you were really good at it."

He pulled Daisy away from her bed and hugged her. "I want you to listen to me, kid."

His voice was thick and it hurt to talk, and all he could think was *fuck fuck fuck.*

"You weren't supposed to ever know. I know you want to help, but it's not good, what I'm doing. I've been doing stuff they make you go to jail for, do you understand? Things only bad people do. And I never, never want you to do stuff like that. I don't want you to ever be like me, Dais."

"You're not bad!" she cried out. He tried to shush her but she just got louder, hitting his shoulder like that would make him listen. "You're *not* bad, don't say that. It's my fault and if I didn't have *stupid* cancer you wouldn't have used up your school money and—"

The bedroom door popped open. "Daisy? What's wrong?"

It was his dad, of all the people on earth he didn't want to see right now.

"Bishop's being—" she howled, then stopped. "I'm sad," she said instead, and a second later a fat tear rolled down her cheek.

Did Daisy know how to cry on cue? When had she learned *that?*

She sniffled loudly. "I don't want to get surgery and I'm scared and Bishop was trying to talk to me but I got mad and I yelled and I'm sorry."

That little con artist. His stomach sank, but he was impressed in spite of himself. She'd covered up better than he had, because now their dad was hugging her and his eyes were shiny, too, and nobody was paying a bit of attention to Bishop.

Except where had she learned to lie like that? Pretty soon, she'd probably start doing whatever bad things she wanted because she knew her big brother sometimes broke the rules, too. Not only that, she was eleven. It wouldn't be long until she slipped up in front of the wrong person about his stealing.

Daisy knew he was breaking the law, she knew he was doing it for her, and her first thought had been to ask him to teach *her* to steal. His hands shook and he stood up and stuffed them in his pockets so his dad wouldn't see. He knew he'd screwed his own life with this, but he'd never imagined he'd mess up *Daisy.* Not his incredible, quirky little sister who was supposed to have a clean slate, just as soon as she beat the cancer.

He couldn't keep stealing, not with her watching and thinking it was her fault. He had to find another way, no matter how impossible that was. Because if he ruined Daisy, what was the point of any of this?

CHAPTER 30

The bus was filling up quickly for a Wednesday afternoon. Bishop dropped his gym bag at his feet and leaned a shoulder against one of the cold center poles, leaving the last open seat for someone else. They'd been back from New Mexico for four days, but it was the first time he'd left his parents' house. Daisy was cranky, but recovering okay. The hint of infection that scared them all and kept them in the hospital an extra week had subsided quickly. The doctors said they'd gotten all the tumors this time, but he'd heard that before.

It was always hard to leave her when she was the sickest, all wan and barely speaking, but it was long since time he faced up to the facts. His responsibility extended much further than getting her through this moment, this illness. He thought he could save her life by throwing his away, but he couldn't have been more wrong.

Everything he did affected Daisy. He was her big brother and she was learning about life from watching him live it. He could try to spin it however he wanted, but just like when he snapped the laptop closed and tried to lie, she paid way more attention to what he did than what he said.

The bus lurched forward, and he bent his knees and swayed with the movement, keeping his balance.

At first, it felt like the walls of the whole world closing in around him, like he was damned in every direction. But when they took Daisy to New Mexico for her surgery, there was nothing to do but sit and think, in waiting rooms and cars and recovery suites. During one of those endless days, he remembered something Harlow had said to him in passing.

She had meant it as a joke, but if he could pull it off, it would fix everything. Since then, he'd been working until his eyes all but bled, running off hospital vending machine coffee and free Wi-Fi. He still didn't know if he could pull it off, but he knew he couldn't quit until he pulled off *something*.

It wasn't enough to try to stay afloat right now the way he and Harlow had planned. If he didn't want to be one bad doctor's appointment away from life as a credit card scammer, he needed to pay off everything and take his future back. For Daisy, because it turned out he really couldn't help her if he didn't help himself.

There was no ignoring that his bad choices had harmed the people in his life rather than saving them. His family still had a roof over their heads, at least for now, but he'd hurt Harlow and unwittingly saddled Daisy with the kind of guilt that could change the course of her whole personality. Assuming she wasn't already going to end up as a criminal mastermind after his fumbling explanation of how you could steal money that was sort of real but sort of not.

Needless to say, he was not holding his breath on the nomination for Brother of the Year.

The bus lurched to a stop. He picked up his gym bag and wound his way to the front, ducking his head against the blast of cold wind when he stepped outside.

Before everything blew up with Daisy, he hadn't ever let himself admit how much it hurt to drop out of college. He'd been good at coding—the top of his class for years, and the one all his friends went to when they had some glitch they couldn't fix. After he lost that, it was almost easier to believe he could never have any future rather than start to hope again. Especially in the midst of the emotional exhaustion from Daisy being so sick.

He told himself there was no other choice, but really, stealing had just been the easiest path at a time when he couldn't face anything else that was difficult.

Not that it was going to be easy to legally make over a million dollars as a broke college dropout, but Bishop had been able to pull off damn near anything with a computer, once. He was a little curious to see if he still had it in him.

He thought, if he could make his current plan work, that Harlow might be proud. She'd probably never know, sure, but he still liked to think about it. Even if he made a trillion dollars and he could fly Daisy around to her appointments in a helicopter, he'd lost his chance with Harlow. She'd made that clear when he left her apartment.

There weren't many laws left that Bishop respected, but a woman's no was at the top of the list. If a woman told you to leave her alone, you did. Period.

He scanned his way in at the front desk of the gym and headed for the basketball courts, trying to shrug off the pain that dug at him every time he slipped up and let himself think about her.

It wasn't clear what time this whole meetup usually went down, so Bishop dropped his bag near the wall and sat alone on the outskirts, turning down all offers to join a pickup game. He didn't want to be already tied up when the game he had been waiting for came along.

When Samwise finally came in, Bishop scrambled to his feet. The taller man was wearing a tee shirt that covered his tattoos today, and he didn't wave when he came in. Bishop hesitated, then forced himself to cross the open gym floor.

"Hey man, I uh—remember me?"

"Yeah, dickhead," Sam said easily. "I invited you to our Wednesday games months ago, and you blew me off." He took a shot from his water bottle. "What's up? Change your mind?"

Bishop chuckled, relief unwinding all at once like a spring in his chest. "Sorry, I kind of needed to get my shit together first."

"Oh yeah? How'd that work out for you?"

"Guess I realized if I waited until I had my life together, I'd never get to play ball."

Sam smirked. "Yeah, I hear that. You ready to get your ass handed to you? These players are a little faster than your usual crowd." He led Bishop across the floor. "Hey!" he called to a group starting to gather in the far court. "This is Bishop. Bishop, these are a bunch of assholes who just so happen to be half-decent at basketball."

Nobody said hi, but the girl with the long dark ponytail smiled and shot him the ball in a pass so hard it ached all the way into his elbows. Bishop already knew he was coming back again next Wednesday.

CHAPTER 31

Harlow: 911. You're not going to believe this.

Sadie: OMG are you okay? Do you want to talk about it?

Alice: They gave you a raise and you're gonna be VP? Because ABOUT TIME, girl.

Harlow: Yeah, not quite that good. Lunch today, Go☆ts on Main

Harlow pulled open the door of the coffee shop, setting off a jangle of star-shaped bells. The air inside was all layers of coffee beans, foamed cinnamon milk, and inexplicably, pine trees. Every table was already occupied except one, so she headed to claim it instead of getting in line at the counter. Her purse seemed about ten pounds heavier with the envelope hidden inside, and she tucked it on its own chair next to her, keeping a protective hand on top.

Alice was scrupulously punctual, so she probably wouldn't have to wait long, but Harlow only lasted maybe eight seconds before her fingers started to drum against her purse. To distract herself from reading the note again, she started counting goats and stars. The coffee shop's namesake goats were represented in adorable gamboling photographs and paintings, tacked everywhere on the reclaimed barn wood walls. But then the stars were hidden all over the place, which made for an even better distraction scavenger hunt.

Stars in the chandeliers, stars on the chair cushions, a star outline sifted in cinnamon on top of the latte belonging to the young mom at the next table, stars on…but why on earth had Bishop mailed her the envelope, after all these months? He could have called or shown up in person. She didn't think anybody even *used* snail mail anymore.

Harlow tried to pull herself back to counting stars, but she wasn't sure if she'd left off at twenty-one or twenty-three because her mind kept circling back to fifteen. Thousand. Fifteen freaking thousand.

"What am I not going to believe?" Alice pulled out a chair with a squeak, half-missing the seat when she sat down because she was looking at Harlow instead of what she was doing. She caught her balance and resettled herself on the chair, still waiting.

Harlow shook her head. "No, we've got to wait for Sadie. She'll—"

"I'm here I'm here I'm here!" Sadie clattered up to their table and threw down her purse.

"Do you guys want to order coffees first?"

Sadie gave her a murderous look. "Is it 911 or not? Because I didn't stop and grab lunch, so I'm looking at a whole afternoon of old desk granola bars for this, so the news had better—"

Harlow dropped a cashier's check for fifteen thousand dollars into the middle of the table, and Sadie squeaked into silence.

"Is it from Bishop?" Alice's voice came out low, and she was still staring at the amount.

"Yup. He also sent a twelve-pack of bath bombs, which I assume means they're lawfully purchased this time, and a note. Says it's for rent and everything else he owes me, and if it weren't for me, he never would have had 'the idea.' Whatever that means."

Sadie and Alice glanced at each other.

"If he sent you an apology, a gift, *and* money, why do you sound mad?"

"Because he also said to tell Alice he understands about the tires. Alice, care to speak to that?"

Harlow tried out a murderous glare of her own—she'd actually practiced it in the mirror before leaving work—but her friend just shrugged and didn't even have the grace to look guilty.

"Paint a car pink, it's gonna stand out. Could be a target for vandalism, I don't know."

"It's magenta."

Sadie's gaze bounced back and forth between them. "Harlow, before you get upset, I want to say for the record that I didn't help, I was only the lookout."

"YOU HELPED HER SLIT HIS TIRES?"

All around the coffee shop, heads swiveled to stare.

Sadie slid down in her seat and hissed, "I just said I was only the lookout."

"What exactly about him having to do...*very desperate things...*to pay for his sister's medical bills said to you that *four new tires* were a thing he should be scraping to pay for?" Harlow whisper-screeched.

"I'm pretty sure the whispering is drawing more attention than the shouting did," Alice said in a normal tone of voice, and flicked the check back across the table to Harlow. "And something tells me Mr. Magenta Car isn't having any trouble affording new tires these days."

Harlow pointed at Alice. "Okay, the fifteen thousand questions I have right now are taking precedence, and obviously I'm still coming over to help you move this weekend, but I just want you to know I'm very mad at you."

"Every time I saw you after the breakup, you ended up crying at least once," she said. "Until *Christmas.* If you're waiting for an apology on his behalf, you might be holding your breath until next Christmas."

"By Thanksgiving, Alice was going to lose it on something of Bishop's, whether it was his tires or something a lot more personal," Sadie put in. "I felt that letting her take it out on the car was the lesser of two evils. Just for the record. And the tires were super bald, anyway. For the record."

"Okay, so we know at Thanksgiving he didn't have enough money for non-bald tires, and now, he somehow has fifteen thousand dollars to spare." Harlow shoved the check away. "He sends me stolen money and then what? I don't know what I'm supposed to do with this. He left me so he wouldn't 'take me down with him.'" She air-quoted with heavy sarcasm. "Except the money isn't any less stolen if he's not here in person. Am I supposed to launder it? Did he already launder it? *How* does one even launder money? What in the actual fuck?"

"Um, now you might want to keep your voice down," Alice suggested, giving her iciest stare to a UPS driver who'd just wheeled a stack of boxes past their table and was now very pointedly *not* looking at them.

"I'll just get us some coffees," Sadie chirped.

Alice grabbed her arm. "No," she said in a gritted-teeth voice. "Let me."

"Oh, no, I don't mind!" Sadie smiled brightly. Very brightly.

"Uh, what's going on here?" Harlow said.

Sadie and Alice locked eyes, going from silent battle to silent conversation to silent *angsty* conversation.

"Spill it," Harlow said. "Whatever you're debating telling me, just tell me. Because I've got 15K of dirty money and thirty-three minutes before I have to be back at work, pretending I didn't spend the last hour having a very tense conversation with two vandalists who were supposed to be my best friends and not keep secrets from me."

"Vandals," Alice said. "It's vandals. Also, we thought you already knew."

"We thought that's what the 911 text was about."

"What's that supposed to mean?"

"Honey, have you been on Twitter in the last few days?"

"Seriously? You think I'm not sad enough already without going on Twitter?"

Alice and Sadie shared another look.

"I'll get the coffees." Sadie slid out of her seat. Alice turned on her phone, tapped twice, and flipped it around to face Harlow.

Former Joke Writer Sells Groundbreaking Algorithm for Seven Figures

"Shut the—" Harlow breathed the words, and then closed her eyes as tears began to sting. "When did this go up?"

"Monday. We've been dying over it—trying to decide if we should tell you, or wait for you to hear about it on your own, or just hope you somehow missed the whole thing and never had to re-open the wound." Alice's voice was flat. Steady. Someone who didn't know her probably wouldn't even recognize how angry she was. Harlow thought semi-hysterically that if Bishop had bought anything fancier than his old magenta car with a chunk of the seven figures, he'd better have invested in stab-proof tires.

"Well, I guess now we know what he'd do if money was no longer an obstacle for us." Harlow's voice came out too high, wavering despite her best efforts to stay stoic.

He paid her off, way more than he owed her. Guilt money. The question was, did he feel badly because of how he left, or because by the time he no longer had to steal, he didn't feel like getting back together with her anymore?

She kept her eyes closed, but a tear dripped out from beneath her lids anyway. "He said he loved me," she whispered. "Why would he say that and then, once he could again, he doesn't even call? Doesn't text. Doesn't *try*."

"Aww, sweetie…" Sadie's hand squeezed her shoulder and she sat on Harlow's side of the table this time, sliding a coffee cup in front of her. Sadie had gotten her a lot of whipped cream. Like, a *lot* of whipped cream.

"Why did this have to happen now?" Harlow burst out. "It's been nearly a year. I haven't even had to put Kleenex on my grocery list in months."

They looked at her.

"Okay, for one month, singular. But *still*. That's an improvement. And then he just…mails me a check like I'm a hooker he forgot to pay off."

"At least you're an expensive hooker?" Sadie attempted.

"Read the whole article." Alice clicked the phone back on. "Really. We'll wait."

Harlow skimmed it, slowing down on the details that were about him, like the paragraph where they described him as "the young entrepreneur who's wearing Prada, but clearly hasn't made time in his new busy schedule for a haircut."

He'd sold the algorithm to So You Think You're a Match. It was a Netflix-style algorithm, but instead of guessing whether you'd like some new baking show, it gave your percentage chance of compatibility with your matches on the app.

"Whoa." Harlow dropped the phone. "That's going to change dating apps forever. But how can he do that? Is it based on some kind of psychological profile or something?"

"Simpler than that," Sadie said. "The algorithm went live a few weeks before the big profile article on Bishop came out. If you say you've been on a date with one of your matches, it asks if you'd go on a second date. You give it a thumbs up or a thumbs down and it learns your taste. And the girl from my date last weekend? She was a 96 percent match, and yeah. Nailed it. We're going on a second date." Sadie glowed.

"Bishop invented the algorithm for true love." Harlow stared at the phone, even though the screen had gone black.

"He invented second-date prediction," Alice said. "It's hardly a cure for cancer. I could probably do the same based on bra cup size. How hard can it be?"

"Hard enough that no one has ever done it before." Harlow pushed her phone back. "Hard enough they paid seven figures for it."

She sat there, staring across the coffee shop at a big photograph of a shirtless, well-muscled actor holding a goat. Last time they'd been in here, she'd loved that picture so much that she and Sadie had taken selfies with it, but right now, it just seemed like so many meaningless shapes.

"I should be over him. It's been so long, and we only knew each other for a few months, really. It doesn't make any sense why there's still that *thing* in me that keeps jerking me in his direction."

Alice looked down and fidgeted with her coffee. She and Rob were moving in together this weekend and her skin looked like she should be starring in exfoliation commercials. How could love just…change your entire *skin*? Or set you off-balance for nearly a year of what should have been the best time of your life, when you were setting out on your dream career? What was it about one specific person that could get its hooks into you so deeply that you didn't even have a choice about it?

Harlow reached for her phone, and stabbed open the dating app.

"What are you—" Sadie started, then sucked in a breath. "Harlow, no, don't look!"

"I just want to see what our number is. For closure. It's got to help, right?"

Alice snatched the phone and pulled it out of her reach. "No, actually, it doesn't. He literally chose a life of crime over you. Zero percent is how compatible you are with a guy who gives up on your relationship without trying to find a solution that doesn't involve a felony."

Harlow took the check on the table and flipped it around to face Alice. "He did, though. He did find that solution."

"Except he didn't call you afterward," Alice said, and Harlow struggled not to flinch.

"It's been months," Sadie put in. "For all he knows, you could be engaged to somebody else by now. Maybe he didn't want to assume you were still interested, but this is an olive branch check. Like hey, I'm not a deadbeat and you can call me if you want to."

Sadie's argument made sense, but Harlow didn't want to let herself hope. If he had anything like the kind of feelings she still did, he would have made it clear he wanted another chance. The most personal thing he said in the note was that she should buy the home she'd always wanted. A home for *her*, singular. Not them.

She stared at her phone, hidden under Alice's hands. Maybe the compatibility number would explain everything. If it was really high, then it was no wonder she couldn't forget about him. But he clearly wasn't that into her. Then, she just needed to accept there had been a possibility there, but it hadn't panned out. Simple.

"So, if I haven't rated anyone, will I still have a percentage?" Harlow shot a look to Sadie next to her. "Or will it be blank?" She would not think about if Bishop had given her a thumbs up or a thumbs down. Or how many other girls he might have dated and rated since she told him she couldn't be with him if he was breaking the law.

"Everybody has the compatibility ratings," Sadie said. "Though obviously, the accuracy gets better the more people you actively rate."

"This is a really bad idea." Alice was still guarding the phone. "I mean, what are you hoping to get out of it, Harlow? He still didn't call. If he was here, begging forgiveness and asking for another chance, that'd be one thing. But the check is just basic decency for crashing on your couch."

"It's pretty high for couch rent," Sadie said. "I think fifteen grand counts as more than basic decency. That's at least deluxe decency, right there."

Harlow ignored her friends as they glared at each other. "If it was Rob," she said to Alice. "Would you want to know what your number was?"

"It's completely different with Rob! Everyone knows we're a terrible match on paper. Except in real life, there's just something about him and I *can't* seem to feel that for anybody else. Believe me, I tried."

Harlow just looked at her.

Alice handed over the phone. "Okay, I hadn't thought about it like that."

Harlow opened the Match app and clicked on Bishop's profile. She got a sinking throat-whirling feeling when she saw it was still active. The number glowed in red, right next to his crooked smiling picture.

Compatibility: 13%

"What? There's no way that's right," Sadie gasped, reading over her shoulder.

"What is it?" Alice leaned over the table. "It's super high, isn't it? Listen, Harlow, who cares what that app thinks. You can find another guy who you'll like—"

Harlow stopped listening. Tears filled her eyes and she squeezed them shut, not wanting to see all the people in the coffee shop around them.

She couldn't lie to herself anymore. It didn't matter that she'd been following all the rules and checking all the boxes, from college degree to renter's insurance to organic kale. She was miserable. Had been darkly, draggingly miserable for months now. And it was all over a man that even million-dollar math confirmed was a *terrible* match for her.

Sadie squeezed her shoulder, but Harlow cleared her throat and moved away, forcing a smile. It was absurd how many times they'd had to comfort her since Bishop left. She couldn't keep being *that* girl.

"I'll come over this Friday, okay?" she said to Sadie, her voice wavering but as normal as she could make it. "Help you get ready for your date with Last Weekend Girl. I'll bring a cheese plate."

"I mean, that would be awesome, and you know I'm never going to turn down cheese, but honey...are you okay?" Sadie looked lost.

"I've got to get going." Harlow pointed at Alice. "No more tire vandalism. I'll see you on Saturday, and I can save you some boxes. We usually have a bunch around the office."

She stuffed Bishop's check back in her purse and hooked it over her shoulder, and even took her coffee with her. It didn't help. She was simply not okay, and no matter how terrible the idea forming in her head was, she was going to have to do it anyway.

She knew she should have bought Kleenex again this month.

CHAPTER 32

*I*t was an indication of how bad Harlow's life had gotten
that "visit prison" was no longer the item on her to do list
that she was dreading the most. Which was why she'd come here
first.

She'd never meant to cut her parents out of her life, or even go a
full month without visiting them. It had just been easier to put it off,
those first few times after she got in a fight with her dad. Then, the
breakup with Bishop had happened, and she'd been so sad she
couldn't face anything else. After that, so much time had passed that
she wasn't sure what to say or how to explain why it had been so long.
Her dad and mom kept sending letters, more and more frantically as
the months ticked by, and she hadn't thrown them away. She'd simply
been putting them aside in a special folder for when she felt ready to
deal with them.

Which was pretty much what she'd done with her parents themselves. And Bishop. And all the other messy parts of herself that were
undeniably real but so inconvenient.

Her compartmentalization wasn't healing any of the things she
wasn't ready to face. They were, actually, starting to feel like they
were killing her. Nibbling sharp pieces out of her heart until the

visual of rat's teeth was so vivid, she'd started having stress dreams about rats climbing around in her rib cage.

Harlow took her keys and left everything else behind in the car, even her bullet journal and her phone. She'd checked the app three more times just to stare at their compatibility rating. Thirteen percent. Not only inexcusably low, but the unluckiest number in the entire hundred-point range.

She'd written it in her bullet journal in black ink.

Weirdly, it had made her smile to do it, remembering how Bishop had cracked her color-coding system. Her steps stuttered and she stared at the cactus in the flowerbeds beside the prison's sidewalk. He hadn't made fun of her, though. For the color coding or for being such a terrible daughter. He'd offered to come along and be a buffer for her parents, and he'd admired the hand-lettered fonts in her bullet journal. He had, actually, thought she'd traced those fonts at first because he couldn't get over how nicely they were drawn. He called them art.

She hugged her arms across her chest, torn about whether she was allowed to think of him fondly again now that he wasn't stealing anymore, and she was no longer trying to pretend she could get over him. It would just hurt more to remember the good times if he turned her down once she found him. But then, would it?

She started walking again. She had been doing all these things to make it hurt less, and she'd still escalated to the Kleenex of the Month club and dreams about rats eating her heart. Maybe a fond bullet journal memory or two wouldn't kill her.

The process of security only ratcheted up her anxiety, and for a distraction, she let herself binge on happy memories. Bishop's duck print pajama pants. The way he'd unknowingly brought her favorite flavor of Ben and Jerrys to their Netflix-and-chill night that was supposed to not be code for sex but turned out to be code for sex after all. Because he'd known she was aroused just by looking at her.

He'd known which drawer held her silverware. He might be a genius, her pretty ex with his excruciatingly sharp jawline, but not even his algorithm could predict a guy who matched her so well he knew which drawer held her silverware on his first trip to her apartment. Who'd slept in her bathtub so he wouldn't puke on her rug, and invented ginger-lemon-raspberry pancakes because they were her three favorite flavors.

Harlow paused outside the visiting room and closed her eyes. She really, really didn't want to go through with this confrontation. In a last fit of self-indulgence, she went back to her very favorite memories. The way he'd held her that first night on the couch when he slipped his hand down her pants. The way he'd cradled her cheek when he told her he loved her.

The memories were weeks apart and in such different contexts, but they blurred together because they felt the same. That cradling, gentle hug that reached deeper into her than any other touch ever had. Had he loved her, even a little bit, all the way back on their Netflix night? Or maybe she already loved him, and that's what made it feel so different to her.

That *thing* must have already been in her back then. The thing that felt so different from liking him or enjoying his company or even the sharp rush of infatuation. The thing that only grew stronger with time, and made your skin glow, and made you do crazy things until you didn't even recognize yourself any more.

That thing called love.

She opened her eyes. The same thing that hauled you back to a prison you hated, month after month, year after year, for people you thought had betrayed you.

She went inside and her dad came bolting out of his chair when he saw her.

"Harlow!" He said it hoarsely, like he might cry. She stepped forward and hugged him quickly, both of them stiff and his hands clutching too hard at her back.

"I didn't—when they said you were here I couldn't—I'm so sorry." He started speaking fast, before she'd even sat all the way down. "I didn't mean what you thought I said last time you were here. I was never going to break the law again, once I got out. I've been writing and writing, but I don't know if you—"

She couldn't take it. It felt like her torso was going to crack all the way down the center, and she reached out and took his hand. "It's okay, Dad. I know."

"Hey!" One of the guards took a step closer and gave her the stink eye. She quickly moved their linked hands above the table, opening her palm to show they hadn't passed anything.

"I didn't mean to be gone for so long. I was angry, and then...a lot of things happened. I'm sorry, I shouldn't have taken it out on you."

"Well, of course you were angry, Love Bug, thinking we'd gone through all of this and I was going to get us right back in the same pickle. Believe me, once I get out of here and get to be with you and your mother again, I'm not going to so much as cross the street without a crosswalk. It's been terrible in here without—" He cut himself off. "Anyway, that doesn't matter now. Tell me how you are. What happened with your job and Hank running off with all that money and the promotion you wanted?"

She had to look down and swallow a couple of times, twisting her crystal ring on her finger. She'd ignored her own father for months, and the first thing he wanted to know was how *she'd* been. She couldn't even believe he remembered the promotion, after all this time.

"No, Dad, we can talk about that in a minute but let me apologize. I shouldn't have stopped visiting, especially when it's not like you two could come to me. That wasn't fair of me. I was angry and I didn't listen to what you had to say, because..." She paused. "Well, I mean, I think we both know I've been angry this whole time. Expecting you to make it up to me, somehow, for everything that happened."

He sat quietly, but his chapped fingers wrung hard at each other atop the table. He looked thinner than she remembered, older already.

She looked at his hands, so many thoughts swirling around in her head. "People say that if you don't live your life and do what's important to you, nothing else matters. And that sounds fine and obvious, but when you go through it firsthand..." She paused. "When you really try to live without something you love, it sinks in a lot differently."

She met his eyes.

"Listen, Dad, you're great at gardening. You can do things with soil and cover crops and nutrient cycles that I can't even fully explain to people. I understand how passionately you feel about the medical benefits of CBD oil and some of the other applications. I get now how truly important that stuff is to you. But I...saw that very differently for a long time."

"Harlow, I know you think your mom and I chose pot over you," he jumped in. Her eyes widened and he waved a hand. "The guards know what I'm in for, you can say it out loud. The thing you have to understand is that yes, we believed in what we were doing and why we were doing it. We were helping people with chronic pain and anxiety and all sorts of different things that are more important than getting high. But no, we wouldn't have done any of that if we thought for a second it stood a chance of actually landing us in prison, away from each other and our daughter."

He leaned forward, raising his voice slightly to be heard over a crying baby at one of the other tables.

"All our friends who'd ever gotten possession charges or were caught with plants just got fines or community service. We had no idea we'd both get such a hard-line judge, or a parole committee with a zero tolerance policy for drug charges. Given the choice, we would have chosen you, Harlow. We would have chosen our family."

She nodded, blinking rapidly against tears. "I know, Dad." She said it simply, but she hadn't listened, much less believed him, for ten long years before today. In her heart, she'd thought he had his chance to make a choice and he'd made the wrong one.

What she hadn't realized was that sometimes, you couldn't make yourself stop loving someone just because you didn't forgive them. You kept loving them, and the pain of it punished both of you for it every single day until you let it go and accepted you were going to love them anyway. Whether they did the right things, or the wrong things, or nothing at all. Maybe if she'd been a parent herself, she'd have figured it out faster. Instead, she hadn't grasped it until Bishop crashed through her life in all his imperfect, irresistible glory.

She had cut all the messy people that she loved out of her life and all it had done was make her a mess instead.

She was ready, now, to try letting them back in, if they still wanted her. The process scared the crap out of her, and she was pretty sure it wasn't going to work out all that well. They'd screw something up, and so, most likely, would she. But the bar was pretty low right now, and that gave her some much-needed courage. Trying to deny the people she loved had hurt so much that it *had* to be worse than anything they could screw up in the future.

"Listen, I know you and Mom are both being released in the next few months. I, well, I did get that promotion. I also came into a little bit of money, so I bought a new place."

His face lit up. "You did? You got the job, and a house, too?" He reached to hug her, and had to stop himself and sit back down when the guard looked over, because hugs were only allowed at the beginnings and ends of visits. "I knew it! I knew they wouldn't give that job to anybody but you."

She couldn't help but smile at his reaction, and how much it reminded her of the celebratory bottle of champagne Bishop had hidden in her fridge before the winner of the promotion was even announced.

"It is good news, though that's not what I came to tell you. But thank you. What I wanted to say was, I'm keeping my old apartment and I'm going to leave it furnished, so you'll have everything you need. The rent is paid until springtime. I want you and Mom to have a place together where you can go while you adjust and get back on your feet again. And I would like...to have the time and space for us to learn how to be a family again. Now that I'm an adult and we can all be together for the first time in a decade."

"Your apartment and all your furniture? Love Bug, are you sure? I know how you feel about your things. You were uh, pretty particular, even as a child."

"Do you mean uptight? You can say uptight."

"I just don't think most eight-year-olds want to refinish their own desks when they get scratched. That's not bad, of course. It was very... responsible of you."

"It had the perfect pigeonholes! I still have that desk, thank you very much, and you better believe it's coming with—" She paused. "You know, actually, now that I'm thinking about it, maybe it would do me some good to have a few less pigeonholes in my life."

"Uh-huh." His lips twitched but his face stayed mostly solemn. "Well, we'll take good care of it for you, in case you decide you can't live without the perfect configuration of pigeonholes. I know how you feel about your organization systems, Love Bug." His eyes were shining, and she swore his skin looked younger than it had when she'd first arrived. "Thank you, Harlow. The apartment would be a big help. And thank you for coming back here today and giving me another chance when I know it was hard for you."

"Never mind that. The really important question is, do you have a bad pun I can pass along to Mom? I bet she's really missed them." She bit her lip, and a smile crept out in spite of her efforts. "And oh, Dad? Don't freak out because there are prison guards watching you, and also there's a small chance he hates me, but I should tell you that I met a boy."

CHAPTER 33

The house lights in the comedy club were turned down, and a comedian was mid-set when Harlow tiptoed in through the back. No one took notice of her, but her heart drummed like she'd stripped naked and streaked for the stage. Her shoes were sticking and then peeling off the floor with every step, as if more than one beer had been knocked over in here. She was picturing that they'd been tipped over from laughter, not thrown by hecklers. Or at least she hoped so for Bishop's sake.

For the three weeks since she'd found out about his algorithm, she'd been cyber-stalking Bishop. Mostly out of old-fashioned pining, but also for practical reasons. She wanted their big reunion to be in person, and she had no idea where he was living now. She'd straight-up given him an ultimatum, and now she was straight-up going to eat her words, along with a healthy portion of humble pie.

The cyber-stalking was how she found out he had a set tonight at a comedy club. Not headlining, but listed as one of the named comics. She didn't know much about the comedy biz, but she thought that was pretty impressive, considering he couldn't have been doing stand-up for more than a few months.

He could be with someone else by now, and Harlow figured a

normal person would be freaked out about tracking down her ex to confess she still had feelings for him. Instead, she felt rock solid. There was something in them that had always matched, despite that damned thirteen percent compatibility rating, and she just...didn't believe Bishop had stopped loving her. She wasn't even nervous.

Or at least she hadn't been until she showed up here.

Now she was huddled at a tiny table in the back, staring up at a stage where she was about to see the man who was hardwired into her heart. And it was all sinking in. He had a *stage*. In the time since they broke up, he'd become a millionaire *and* followed his dreams to do stand-up comedy, while she'd been a tear-sodden mess.

Except no, that wasn't exactly true. Just this morning, she'd walked through her neighborhood, bringing muffins to the construction crew for the favor they'd done for her in setting up her big surprise. She still couldn't quite believe Sunnybrooke was real. That she'd made it happen.

"The next comic we have for you tonight has recently become something of a national celebrity. But I promised him I would leave all of that out of it, so folks, we here at Laugh Tracks know him as the Millennial Deadbeat. Please give him a warm welcome!"

Bishop appeared from backstage with a quick wave and self-deprecating smirk. It had been so long since she'd seen him in real life that her chair legs gave a little bark from her involuntary movement.

He wore a black tee shirt with a charcoal gray vest and a deep gray fedora, with just enough stubble she wanted to actually lick his perfect jawline.

She could imagine the texture against her tongue, that's how far gone she was. *Jesus.*

"How's everybody doing tonight?"

Bishop stepped up to the microphone and waited through the quick round of applause.

"Anybody on a first date and already know this shit ain't gonna work out, but you still have to sit with him through the rest of the show?"

There were a few snorts of laughter as he peered out into the darkness of the audience.

"Just pretend to be super offended by my next joke," he whispered into the microphone. "Tell your date you want to go home." He paused, looking around as the snickers spread. "No worries if you're a bad liar, I'll make it so offensive *everyone* will buy it."

They began to laugh.

"Just for you, ladies. Don't say I never did anything for you."

He pulled the microphone off and draped his other hand over the stand, looking like he'd been hanging out on a stage since infancy.

"So, when I told my family I was going to do stand-up, they made me promise on my manhood that I wouldn't talk about them."

Harlow held her breath, not wanting to miss a syllable of his set.

"I promised, of course, but joke's on them because I didn't have much manhood to lose." He flicked the brim of his fedora. "I got my hair from my mom's side of the family, which means from my dad's side of the family I must have gotten my…" He looked pointedly down at his pants, then whispered into the microphone. "Wow, sorry, Mom."

The front row coughed into the kind of sound where the joke was dirty enough you almost didn't want to laugh at it. Bishop grinned, relaxing enough to let people know he was kidding and it was safe to be amused.

He turned away, then peeked back toward the audience and whispered, "Dirty enough to get you out of those bad dates, ladies? Or should I have actually dropped the word 'micropenis'?"

Laughter *roared*.

Harlow clapped out of sheer delight at their reaction, even while she blushed at both the word and from the realization that she was probably the only person in this room who knew firsthand how very non-micro Bishop's penis was.

He strolled away from the microphone stand, flicking the cord up around his wrist. "Anyway, they'll never know if I make jokes about them. If I had the kind of parents who showed up for things, would I be *this* desperate for attention?"

That got an easy laugh rolling through the room.

"No, no, folks, relax, I'm just kidding. No daddy issues in the house tonight. Everybody knows we all became comedians for the health plan."

Harlow snorted at that one. She found herself watching the audience, a grin stretching her face at the people's eyes all trained on him. His timing had always been good, but on stage, it was spot on. She had no idea how you could even learn something like that.

"So, since I clearly have no parental issues, I figured I'd make jokes about my little sister." He bobbed his eyebrows. "She's twelve and she's the funny one in the family, because she has cancer."

That only knocked free a couple of isolated chuckles, and Harlow scowled, shooting an indignant look at the tables around her.

Bishop didn't seem bothered. He sauntered toward the right end of the stage, holding an arm out to the audience.

"Hey! I'm allowed to make cancer jokes. I have my cancer-by-proxy card. And if I'm lying and she'd really be deeply offended, you'll never know." He grinned, all mischievous as he peeked up from under the brim of his hat. "Because she's never gonna get into this club with the crappy fake ID I got her."

Harlow was laughing and shaking her head, then brightened even more when she realized the rest of the crowd was laughing with her. Bishop waited until it was all quiet again, then one beat longer.

"So, I met a girl." He propped his hand back up on the microphone stand, the cord playing through his fingers. "Hot girl." He looked out at the crowd. "Hottest girl in the mother-loving world. And you think, right, a hot girl like that, a guy like me? She's gonna hate me, probably think I'm a deadbeat."

Harlow's pulse gave a hiccup.

"Oh, I am, though. I am a deadbeat. I've got more side hustles than hotel sheets have pubes."

Everybody laughed right on cue like he'd paid them. Harlow beamed, pleased with the audience again.

"But ah, wait." He held up a finger with a charming smile. "She doesn't know that yet. So we go out a few times, I buy her a nice dinner, I woo her with pillow talk about my student loans..." He let it hang for a moment, then shrugged. "Then yup, she hated me."

The rest of his set whirled by and it seemed like only seconds later, she was applauding his big finale. Some of his jokes landed better than others. Sometimes, she could see where his timing got thrown off because the audience laughed less than he expected, or sometimes more. And okay, maybe she was biased, but she couldn't believe how relaxed and professional he seemed. He looked like he'd been doing it for twenty years or something.

She couldn't even focus on the other comedians once he finished because her head was in a whirl. Had that hot girl joke been about her? And if it wasn't...

The nerves were definitely back in force now, and her knees jittered under the table, trying to sort out how she was going to find him. The way she'd imagined it, she talked to him at his comedy set, but somehow she hadn't figured in a backstage area. Could she ask a bouncer for access? Did comedy clubs have bouncers?

She sat through the whole next set, debating. When the waiter came by to ask if she wanted another drink, she looked up to respond and that's when saw him. Bishop, not the waiter.

He was over at the bar, hat tipped back on his head and vest open now. Not a person was talking to him, like they didn't even recognize him from being *on stage* barely ten minutes ago.

She got up and headed his way without answering the waiter, and then remembered she hadn't paid and had to backtrack to throw a twenty down. Then, Bishop didn't notice her standing behind him. She had to actually reach up and tap him on the shoulder, feeling like a gawky fangirl.

He turned with an absent look on his face and when he saw her, his eyes flared. He startled so hard he bumped the barstool at his side.

"Holy shit, Harlow!" He swooped in to embrace her, and then stopped. "Can I—Will you knee me in the balls if I hug you right now? Oh fuck, it's worth it, I'm going for it. Sorry, balls."

She ended up laughing into the shoulder of his shirt as he squeezed her tight. On the in breath, she caught a whiff of a light, new cologne she didn't recognize but immediately loved. Then, he was letting her go before she had a chance to fully absorb what it felt like to be held by him again.

"Holy shit," he said again, taking off his hat and ruffling his hair, grinning so big he damn near developed dimples.

Wow, doing comedy made him really happy. He looked amazing. She pushed back the quick twinge of jealousy.

"What are you doing here? Of all the gin joints in the world, you walk into mine..." He looked skyward for a minute, then shook his head. "Jeez. How've you been? Sunnybrooke's incredible, by the way. I definitely don't cyber-stalk its website all the time. Just lightly, on the weekends, for a hobby."

"Uh, yeah, it's going pretty well. Phase One is, yeah, we're uh... building things." Apparently, they'd lost the ability to keep up a conversation, but standing here beaming at each other was a definite go. She squeezed her purse in front of her. "How about that algorithm, huh?"

He laughed, bright and relieved, and sat back on the bar stool behind him. "All your idea, remember?"

"I think I said something about figuring out the math behind people's perfect match. I didn't think anyone could actually *do* that."

"They can't." The bartender showed up with his beer and Bishop nodded to Harlow. "Buy you a drink? Least I can do for making me a millionaire."

"Seems like a fair trade." She winked so he'd know she was joking.

"Red wine or a whipped whiskey?" His eyes sparkled and she got goosebumps.

He remembered.

"Oh, definitely whipped whiskey." It seemed ridiculous that she could have ever been nervous about coming to see a guy who would drink whipped whiskeys in duck print pajama pants with her.

"Okay," Bishop said to the bartender, proudly sliding a debit card across the counter. "We need two shot glasses, two-thirds whipped cream-flavored vodka, one-third dark bourbon, and there's an extra five in it for you if you never—and I mean ever—tell Barbara I drank anything with whipped cream-flavored vodka in it."

He turned back to Harlow, who was trying not to look like a person who cared who Barbara was.

"Anyway, so the algorithm is stupid simple, which is I think why it predicts so well. It's all ones and zeros, flawlessly binary. Of your matches, did you go on a date or not. Would you go on another or not. Simple, no room for confounding variables, so it points straight as an arrow." He grinned. "The ripple effects are incredible, even though it's only been on the app for a few weeks. People are pairing up faster, though that might be because the numbers give them confidence. The really cool part is, the rate of people ghosting on dates is down forty percent."

"Forty percent already?" The bartender brought their shots back and she held hers up for a toast. "I don't know how you did that, but oh my gosh! Forty percent is huge."

"I know, right? Everybody wants their number to be the most accurate in terms of prediction, so they're dating like crazy. Every time the website crashes from traffic, my boss swears she's going to give me a bonus. The woman is in heaven."

"Wait, they gave you a job? I thought you sold the algorithm, free and clear."

"Yeah, I did, but now they've given me this whole team of specialists to make the algorithm better. Can you believe it?"

He knocked back his shot and she remembered she hadn't touched hers. She didn't want it to be gone so quickly, so she sipped to enjoy the weird contrast of flavors.

"So another funny story: my friend Samwise? Turns out he's a statistician. We're trying to figure out what profile variables predict longer-term matches, going beyond the second date. We have a team of interns going through the literature, then our sociologist, Barb, figures out which variables are worth testing. I build them into the website, and Sam finesses the numbers so…" He screws up his forehead. "It's hard to explain, but there are different ways to analyze the same data to give you increasingly more sophisticated results. Sam's a master, seriously. We're so lucky he was willing to quit his other job and join the team."

"Oh wow, I didn't even know you had a friend named Samwise. Or a team. Or…a sociologist."

"Oh yeah, Barb's great. She's the headliner tonight, got me my first slot at this club, actually. Turns out that sociologists are pretty much the funniest people on earth."

Finishing her shot suddenly seemed like a good idea. So much had happened in his life, and in hers. She felt so out of sync and at the same time, she just wanted another hug. To feel the scrape of that delicious stubble along her lips and— She signaled the bartender, and pointed to the wine this time.

When she turned back to Bishop, she caught him watching her, and she had to clear her throat. "I don't think I've ever heard you sound so excited about work before."

"It's nice, yeah. I kind of get how you feel about playground benches now."

"What about Daisy? I mean, I saw on Facebook that her scans came out clean this time but is she…"

"Remission Day!" He pumped his fist in the air. "Yeah, she's doing great. Started back in real school this fall. Made a ton of totally shit friends that Mom and I both hate. Normal teenager stuff." He focused more intently on her. "I'm done with all that other stuff. The cards and everything. You know that, right?"

For the first time, he sounded a little nervous. Maybe it wasn't only her who was trying to figure out how to take the verbal leap from how-have-you-been to hey-maybe-do-you-still-love-me?

"All the debt is gone. Oh, Bishop, that must feel like heaven."

"Uh, not exactly." He snorted. "Would you believe I still owe ten grand? Nine thousand, seven hundred and fifty-six dollars, to be exact. I'm making monthly payments."

"You sent me fifteen!" she blurted out, then bit her lip. "Why'd you send me that exact amount if you still owed ten? You could have been five thousand in the clear and…" That money was gone, signed away in so many different pages of paperwork that she didn't have the first clue how it could be reversed, but she couldn't just *take* it now that she knew he wasn't rolling in millions. "Do you want me to—"

"Don't even try." He waved her off. "I looked it up. That was the amount you needed for a down payment on a place at Sunnybrooke, and it's really fine, Harlow. I've got a day job now, and the app people have been really good to me, so payments are no big deal. I just think it's ironic. I've been trying to write a bit around the whole thing, but there's almost nothing funnier to say about it than the thing itself." He waved the beer he'd ordered before she showed up. "I made over a million dollars and I'm still in debt. Ever since the news about the deal broke, I lead with that whenever women approach me. It's like gold-digger repellant."

"Ah, so that's where the hot girl bit came from." She played with the stem of her wine glass, not looking at him as a wave of laughter rose from the crowd in front of the stage. "So um, so then...are you seeing someone now?"

"Oh, no the hot girl bit is about you, actually." He paused. "It's a little funnier with you in the audience, isn't it? Turns out a lot of my jokes are about you. There's something universally hilarious about a guy being shot down by a girl way out of his league. You know, relatable."

Whatever post-Rob glow had transformed Alice's skin seemed to be currently taking over Harlow's whole body. Starting, inexplicably, with her toenails and warming her all the way up with a buzzy feeling that hummed in her bones. Was he saying he was still into her?

She scoffed and struggled to hide a blush. "Right, out of your league. Except you're a millionaire and I'm in middle management."

"*Former* millionaire, and don't feed me that crap. You're Charlie and the Chocolate Factory, making dreams come true."

She took a breath and went for it.

"Speaking of, want to see my chocolate factory? Sunnybrooke, I mean."

"Yeah." He looked at her, his eyes all quiet and intense. "Yeah, I really do."

She squirmed on her bar stool, her gaze falling to his lips. Could she kiss him now? Or maybe she should wait until her big surprise. He was *so* close, his knee bumping hers, and he seemed excited to see her, as if he remembered every detail of their time together just like she did. It didn't even feel like taking a risk. Being with him felt almost too easy, like it always had. She moved to slide off her bar stool, in the same instant that he started to fidget.

"I mean, for old times' sake, obviously. Um, right?"

"Right!" She jerked back onto her barstool.

Was he giving her an out, in case she didn't want it to be a date? Or did *he* not want it to be a date so he was clarifying?

"I just meant because you heard me talk about Sunnybrooke so much and it's a real thing now and I thought you might like to—"

"I would! I mean, I always thought you had the coolest job. I wasn't just pretending to be interested because I was into you, just so you know. I've been following the website but there haven't been many pictures and, anyway, that'd be great." He smiled, a little too brightly, it seemed to her. "When do you want to get together?"

Well, there was her answer, right there in his use of past tense. *Because I was into you.* She took a deep breath to steady herself and damn him, she could smell that mouth-watering new cologne.

Crave by Calvin Klein. For those special ex-girlfriend torturing occasions.

"Is tomorrow good for you?"

To undo her grand romantic gesture, and pretend platonic was all she wanted, too?

Harlow pushed away the thought and slapped on a smile. "Yeah, tomorrow's great!"

CHAPTER 34

*B*ishop was walking next to the actual Harlow Rimes, practically hand in hand. He couldn't quite convince himself she was real, because he'd had so many reunion dreams over the last few months. In some of them, she was kissing him, sometimes yelling at him, and on one notable occasion she'd been an elephant. He wasn't sure if that was because of the whole "an elephant never forgets" thing, or because she loomed larger than everything else in his mind. Either way, she'd made a cute elephant.

In none of his dreams had they been making awkward conversation about a orthodontist's office.

"Nice to have health care offices nearby, right?" He swallowed. This was not how he'd pictured this going.

He needed to be witty, brilliant, lovable. Forgivable. Walking next to him was the only woman who'd ever felt so much like *his* that it made him understand the phrase "starting a family." Because she felt like the beginning of one. And she wouldn't even meet his eyes.

"Yeah, uh, the Sunnybrooke brand is all about is urban living in a suburban space. A lot of how we create that atmosphere is by finding ways to group services together so people drive less. Hank and I battled the zoning committees hard for our vision for this neighborhood, but now the homeowner's association also owns the associated office parks. The commercial rents from the doctors, hair stylists, and daycares help keep the homeowners' association fees down."

He nodded, trying to figure out how to stop talking about zoning so he could tell her that she was the centerpiece of every dream he'd had about a better life, now that he could finally stop stealing. Except that made him sound like he was expecting something. That was why he'd sent the money instead. To pay her back and let her get *her* dream. And yeah, to hold out a hand in case she wanted to reach back. Which she hadn't, until this awkward walking tour of a mostly-still-dirt neighborhood.

It had been so weird, the way she'd invited him to come here. He'd thought she'd meant it as a date, and then he realized she hadn't said that. He didn't want to assume and look like one of those guys who thought being "just friends" with a girl was some kind of punishment. Like he wouldn't want to see the neighborhood she'd invented unless it was part of something romantic. He was interested in everything when it came to Harlow: her work, her friendship, her love...he'd take anything he could get but when he'd tried to say that, he'd fumbled it and now he was left with absolutely no idea of what *she* wanted.

He was so aware of her next to him that he could barely solve the whole leg-foot-leg-foot equation that walking had suddenly become. He couldn't decide if he should make his move and risk alienating her, or try to play it safe and friendly so he could keep her in his life in any role at all. The idea that today might be his only chance made every passing minute feel like it was whooshing by, carrying pieces of him away along with them.

"This is where the park is going to be." She gestured to one side of the street.

"With the outdoor movie screen." He nodded. "Last time I saw that park, you were drawing it in just left of my nipple."

She laughed, but instead of following his turn down memory lane, she peeked up at him. "Alice is sorry about your tires, by the way."

"She isn't, actually." He smirked, the pressure on his chest easing a little at the thought. "It's one of the things I like best about her."

"How'd you even figure out that it was her? I mean, it happened months after we broke up."

"Easy. I watched her do it from the basement window."

"What?" Harlow stopped walking and gaped. She was wearing a light sweater that kept slipping toward her right shoulder, and he had to stop himself from smoothing it back up over her skin. "And you just let her do it? To all four of your tires?"

"Sure. First off, I knew I deserved it. Second, those tires were shot, I didn't have a driver's license, and I gave very few fucks about anything at that particular moment of my life."

Her eyes flickered to a darker brown, and she glanced down.

A smile tugged at his mouth, remembering that night. "Third, it was one of the cutest things I've ever seen in my life. They should make Hallmark movies out of that shit."

"Out of my friends slashing your tires? Don't know if that's quite the Hallmark brand."

"If it's not, it should be. Sadie was full-on cat burglar, down to the black beanie. Alice was just in regular clothes, not bothered at all. I think her coat might have even been red. Sadie kept going from giggling to squirming all around. She would flinch and sort of half-scream every time another tire blew, and when they left, she actually patted the car and apologized to it."

"Oh my gosh, of course she did." Harlow hid her face in her hands, cringing, but she was laughing a little too, so he kept going.

"Whereas Alice was just stabbing those tires, no hesitation at all. It took a lot of force and she was *into it*, boy." He chuckled. "I wish I had watched more closely, but I missed a bunch because I ran upstairs to get a better view, so I could see if maybe you'd come with them and you were waiting in the car or watching from across the street or something."

"Bishop! You thought I would not only condone vandalism, but come along?"

"I hoped you might."

"You hoped I would *slash your tires*."

He tucked his hands into his pockets. "I really missed you."

There were so many things flickering through her expression he couldn't read them all. Or maybe he was afraid to, because she'd tracked him down at the comedy club and the only thing she'd asked was how he'd been. She invited him here, but then all they'd talked about were parks and car-related vandalism.

A cool breeze kicked up, prickling at his skin as the late fall chill battled with the bright Austin sunshine. Harlow took a breath, then held it like she wasn't quite sure how to say what she was thinking.

He looked away. Harlow was a good person. Of course she would want to smooth over the terrible note they'd ended their relationship on. That was all this was, and he was lucky to get that much.

His gaze fell on the buildings they'd been walking toward, and he squinted against the sun. "That's weird." All the Phase I buildings were just skeleton frames of lumber or open foundation pits. Except the one directly ahead of them had a full brick entryway built and a small roof atop it like it had crossed some invisible boundary into finished reality before the rest of its building. "Do they always build them like that?"

"Uh, not exactly." She was fidgeting with her purse. Yup, he'd definitely made her uncomfortable by bringing up how much he missed her.

Don't blow this, Riley. If you pretend you meant to keep it platonic all along, you've still got a chance to see her maybe twice a year at group brunch.

"Are these the condo buildings you added as part of your budget overhaul?" He led the way across the street, trying to give her an easy subject change while wrestling with himself.

Twice a year is better than what you have now. You can live with that. You can, damn it.

"That's them. Luxury loft condos, so we get the lower price point but hit the same marketing demographic. I'm hoping they'll become the millennial version of a starter home."

"What even is a luxury loft condo?"

"Basically a studio apartment, only with a ladder, granite counter-tops, and a bigger bathtub."

He looked around the flawlessly finished entryway, trying not to think about how much fun they'd had in her bathtub.

"And doorbell buzzers with cool brass plaques. Very New York City. Except look, this one has a boo-boo." He laughed, pointing to the top buzzer, which had a square of gauze taped over it with electrical tape. It looked like it had come out of someone's personal first aid kit, not a Home Depot.

"Um, that's nothing. Want to see where the amenity center and gym will go?" She grabbed his arm and the contact zinged through him, distracting enough that he let her tug him away a step before the clues clicked into place. He dug his heels in and brought them to a stop.

"Wait, Harlow is this place yours? Did you buy a condo, is that what you brought me here to see? Dang, and you got penthouse level, too!" He grabbed her in a hug and swung her around, his heart pounding at how close she was, how perfectly natural it would be to kiss her right now. Instead, he set her back on her feet and reminded himself she'd tried to drag him away rather than show him the condo. That probably just meant that she was uncomfortable about taking the down payment money he'd sent her when he was still in debt.

He grinned, keeping it casual to hopefully put her at ease. The money was nothing, and he'd wanted her to have the home she was so obviously meant for. "Let's do the big unveiling, hey?" He ripped off the gauze cover to the doorbell, and then stopped when he saw what it said on the brass plaque underneath.

Rimes & Riley

But that was his...their...

He looked at her. She began to turn a deep, mottled red, her mouth opening and closing like she wanted to sputter something but didn't even know where to start. She turned away and he caught her arm.

"Please, wait. Don't go."

His mind raced, but he couldn't quite make sense of it. It had only been last night when they talked at the comedy club. She could have gotten the brass plaque engraved this morning, but he had a hunch that the doorbell thing explained why this entryway was the only part of the entire neighborhood that was built to finished quality already. That would mean she'd pulled some strings to get the entryway finished and set this whole thing up with his name literally chiseled in it *before* she'd even seen him for the first time in months.

None of that made sense, considering she'd held him at awkward arm's length for this entire walk, and tried to distract him from seeing the doorbell with both their names on it. What had he said to make her change her mind after she'd already set up this incredible gesture in brick and brass? If he hit his knees right now and begged, could he take it back?

"Harlow…" He had to ask, because he was too lost to make the pieces all fit on his own. "What is all of this?"

"If you missed me so much you wished I'd slash your tires, why did you say you only wanted to see me today for old time's sake? Why didn't you call instead of sending a check I never asked for?" Her hands opened and closed at her sides, half pulled up into her sleeves. "No, actually don't answer that. This was all stupid. Our compatibility rating is thirteen freaking percent. That's enough of an answer in itself."

It was completely ridiculous that she could doubt how he felt about her. He needed to explain, but right now all he could do was smile. She put his name on her home. She'd checked their compatibility number.

"Sure, but Harlow, your app numbers are all wildly inaccurate right now because you haven't rated anyone."

"You don't know that." Then she stopped. "Wait, have you been creeping on my data?"

"That would be unethical, and I happen to be an extremely law-abiding citizen these days. Also, a chicken. I made Sam look."

"You did not." She looked shocked, but her blush was subsiding.

"He checks once a week. He's supposed to break it to me gently when you start to date." Bishop stuffed his hands into his pockets so he wouldn't reach for her before she was ready, but his whole body was glowing like the smile had spread beyond his face and reached all the way down to his toes. "By the time I got enough money to stop stealing, I wasn't sure you'd still want to see me, and I didn't feel like I had a right to ask. So I sent the check so we'd be even, and to test the waters. After you didn't respond, I told myself I had to move on. Well, actually, Sam told me I had to move on, or he'd dump my moping ass and I could find a new statistician."

She eyed him. "I'm not sure I'm a fan of this Sam."

"He also tried to take me ring shopping the instant he found out you tracked me down at the club."

"Okay, maybe I'm a little bit of a fan of Sam."

She was still hugging herself, standing half between the doorway and the curb like she wasn't sure what to do next. He went down to meet her.

"Harlow. Sweetheart." He brushed a wisp of hair tenderly back from her cheek. "You bought us a luxury loft condo. And engraved my name on the doorbell when you hadn't talked to me in a year. Can you just look at me? Please?"

"I was making a romantic gesture!" she squeaked, her face getting all flushed again as she squirmed. "I rehearsed a whole speech, about how you can plan traffic flow and park benches but you can't plan love. But then I wasn't sure if you still liked me that way, and then you saw the doorbell too early, and now there's no room for a speech, and I can't just say I love you for the first time without a speech."

She was the most adorable thing he'd ever seen.

Bishop tugged her a little closer, trying not to smirk. "I derailed your planned speech about how you can't plan love?"

"See, this is why we're only thirteen percent compatible," she mumbled, burying her face in his shirt.

He held her, his chest shaking with silent laughter as he pressed kisses to her hair.

When she peeked up at him, abashed and beautiful, he ducked his head and kissed her lips. Sweet and slow, and long enough so it was like he could feel every day they'd ever spent together sailing through his head in app messages and laughter and whirling axe throws, and every day of their future rolling out toward the horizon. Starting right here in the doorway to their future home.

He pulled away and leaned his forehead against hers, trying to remember what shape his lungs used to be.

"I don't know," he murmured. "Feels like 100 percent to me."

EPILOGUE

Three years later

$\mathcal{H}$arlow hiked up her billowing white skirt and tried to run faster, but her heels kept sinking into the grass.

"And now one more shot of the groom's side of the family!"

"Keep running," Bishop ordered. "I think they just released the hounds."

"We should have gotten married in an older park!" she huffed. "The seedling trees are all too small for decent cover."

"I see a spot. This way!" He grabbed her hand and pulled her the last bit, the band of his new ring brushing her fingers and making warmth burst up through her belly. They ducked behind the row of hedges just as the photographer's voice rang out again.

She glanced behind them. "Nice. I think we're covered from both sides."

The hedges lined both sides of a walkway that separated the lawn with its flower-draped arch from the paving stone patio. Pictures were still happening over where they'd had the ceremony, and on the patio, their guests were grouped around the three citrus-bright mimosa fountains.

Bishop crouched next to her, still holding her hand. "It was so smart of you to plant hedges at the edge of the venue lawn."

"Well, I knew somebody would need to hide from their family at some point."

"You think of everything."

She peered through the gap in the hedges at their wedding party and relatives grouped around the photographer. "Everything except to wear flats when your wedding takes place on a lawn. Oh! There goes Sadie again." Her friend's heel sank abruptly in the grass and she caught herself on Bishop's Aunt Mildred's jacket sleeve, then patted the sleeve as she apologized profusely.

"Ugh." Bishop winced. "Aunt M is a grouchy old bat. She's not going to take that well. Maybe I should go—" But then Mildred broke out into a beaming smile and Sadie said something else that drew an actual laugh out of her. "Wow, Sadie really has a gift." He shook his head. "I can't believe you wouldn't let me have Sadie as my best man."

"I can't believe your best man was a hobbit. I'm just waiting for the toast later where he disappears into mid-air before the cheers."

"That was Bilbo, not Samwise. And it's not cool to make fun of his name." Bishop gave her a look from worried blue eyes and she bit back a laugh.

"You do it all the time!"

"It's different when I do it."

The giggles were teasing up the corners of her lips now, but she fought them back down. She couldn't even with how fussy Bishop got about protecting his new bestie. Even three years in, he mentioned Sam multiple times in any given conversation.

"You know it's not cool if you love him more than me."

"No? You gonna fight him for me?" Bishop perked up.

"No, I'll just send Sadie after him so he falls in love with her instead. She already got your Aunt Mildred. Sam will be a cinch."

"You sure you didn't already?" Bishop pointed through the gap in the hedges.

Harlow tried to lean forward without tipping over. Crouching in heels while wearing an off the shoulder mermaid-cut gown wasn't the easiest thing to do but she didn't regret the dress. She hadn't been able to resist the swirling lace of the illusion sleeves. Or the long row of pearl buttons trailing down her spine. Plus, crouching in heels was definitely preferable to posing for another camera.

The photographer had been stuck on getting shots of Bishop staring lovingly into her eyes...which kept making both of them crack up. So now they had a million pictures of her hanging onto his arm while they laughed themselves silly, and about half a million of Alice fixing her eye makeup after she laugh-cried it off again, and no loving gazes whatsoever. Ah, well. Hopefully the photographer had gotten the moment in the ceremony mid-way through the vows where Bishop's eyes had gone shiny with tears and he looked at her like he couldn't believe they were really here.

Harlow was pretty sure she could last to a hundred and fifty if she could see him looking at her like that every day.

She clucked her tongue as she followed Bishop's pointing finger to where Sadie was laughing at something Sam said, and Sam was tugging at his collar and blushing a little.

"Wait, didn't he show up with a different girl?" Harlow asked.

"That's just Allie," Bishop said. "They've been friends since they were kids. And you should never—and I can't stress this enough, Harlow—*never* let them play on the same basketball team. Or it will be a slaughter."

She laughed. "I'll keep that in mind."

Bishop was peering through the gap in the hedge again, eyeing the way Sadie's hand had landed on Sam's sleeve. "I thought they'd met before, at some point. Were they like this last time?"

"They met, but he wasn't wearing a three-piece, then. She's a sucker for suits, especially if there are tattoos underneath. Does she know about his tattoos?"

"Uh...maybe we should go run some interference." Bishop shifted his weight, his dress shoes creaking.

She poked him, smirking. "Are you jealous? You *do* love him more than me."

"You must be kidding. I couldn't love anyone more than the girlfriend who was cool enough to let me buy a parrot." He leaned forward and stole a slow kiss that wobbled her balance so he had to catch her before she could grass stain her dress.

"Girlfriend?" she teased. "Where's this girlfriend? I'll fight her."

Bishop's face warmed with a slow smile, his blue eyes bright in the dappled sun coming through the trees. "Sorry. Wife, now."

Harlow swallowed down the sentimental lump in her throat and waved a hand, hoping Alice wouldn't have to fix her eye makeup again. "That's true, I am pretty cool about our new pet. Especially considering you bought the only non-talking parrot in existence. Hmph."

Bishop still believed it had been his idea to buy a parrot. She thought that was adorable.

"Gabardine doesn't need to talk," he argued, almost as fussy about their parrot as he was about Sam. "She communicates in other ways. I'm convinced she's invented a next level dialect of American Sign Language. Or Morse code head bobbing."

"We'll figure it out. We've got like seventy years or so. Parrots live forever." As would she, as soon as she got the photographer to print that one perfect picture of Bishop so she could carry it with her everywhere like a complete sap.

She dropped a steadying hand to the grass to lean in and kiss him again. It felt different today, since the wedding. She basically couldn't stop kissing him, trying to figure out exactly what had changed. But then pain tweaked through her calf muscle and she winced.

"You okay?" His hand rubbed down the embroidery of her almost-invisible sleeve.

"I'm starving. Also, I really need to sit down, but if I grass stain this dress, I will cry myself to sleep. I'm never going to look this amazing again in my life and I'm not missing it for anything. Not even cramped calves." She shot a look past the hedges. "Maybe we should bite the bullet. Go back out there. Appetizers are at stake."

"Now you're just talking crazy. Here." He shrugged out of his black jacket and spread it on the grass for her. "Ruin that. Why I thought I should wear a jacket in May in Texas is beyond me anyway."

Because he looked insanely hot in it, that was why. Wide shoulders and slim waist and that *jawline* of his, all perfect above his crisp collar. But she didn't argue, just collapsed back to finally sit down. Besides, the charcoal vest he had on underneath fitted even more beautifully than the jacket.

"Cover me," he said. "I'll make a run for food and if you see anybody stop me, call out my name to give me an exit excuse. If we wait any longer, they're going to eat all the avocado toast appetizers, and then *I'll* cry myself to sleep."

She grabbed his arm. "Wait. Is the taco bar out yet?"

"Doubt it. That's supposed to be the main course, but the mini bacon biscuit things are fair game. You want a mimosa or our signature cocktail?" He grinned.

They'd named it a Netflix and Chill, but it was really just a whipped whiskey with a vanilla bean garnish and the bartender had informed them that absolutely *no one* would drink them.

"Mimosa." She winked. "We all know what happens when I get into the whipped whiskeys, and I didn't plant enough hedges in this park to hide that kind of risky business."

"I um, might need that jacket back now. For reasons."

She giggled and pushed him away. "Think clean thoughts, husband of mine. Clean thoughts about how much food you're going to score for us. Oh! And stick a couple of those bath bombs in your pockets. I really should have ordered more, and I want some for myself before they run out."

"Okay, okay, but if Alice catches me stealing the wedding favors, you have to rescue me."

"Deal."

She draped her arms over her bent knees and watched him go, still smiling. She'd heard wedding planning was supposed to be hell, but they'd had loads of fun planting inside jokes all over the ceremony and reception tables and getting the Tipsy Taco to cater the brunch buffet reception. For the other stuff that neither of them cared about —flowers and monogrammed napkins, whatever—they just picked the cheapest thing and went with it. Not that they needed to worry about money so much these days, with Harlow planning a bigger neighborhood and Bishop's new job. They could mostly afford what they wanted, so the only real wedding planning argument was when Daisy wanted magenta for their wedding color and even Bishop wouldn't cave.

The centerpieces were her favorite touch. Her stomach rumbled again, protesting from beneath where her strapless bra was digging into her ribs. Well, no, the taco bar was going to be her favorite. But the stuffed narwhal centerpieces in honor of Henry were definitely her second favorite. Henry was their fairy godmother, according to Bishop. He'd told her it was the picture of her laughing and hugging her stuffed narwhal that had made him decide to message her in the first place. He said he thought she looked fun.

She teared up a bit, thinking of it. Of all the forks in the road where they might have not ended up together. If she'd posted a gym selfie instead, or if her credit card number declined when he tried to pay for the dating subscription. If she wouldn't have texted him about that terrible date with Bib Boy, or if Alice had answered her phone so Harlow didn't need to call Bishop for the rescue that ended up bringing them back together...

Her new husband burst back into their hideout, balancing two tiny plates in one hand and three mimosa flutes in the other, his pockets bulging with bath bombs.

"I got you rosemary grapefruit and Meyer lemon, because I wasn't sure which one you'd want first," he said. "And this is the last bacon scone already. Can you believe how fast those went?" He paused. "Harlow, what's wrong? Don't cry, I was totally going to let you have the last bacon scone."

She shook her head and dabbed at her eyes. "Nothing, ignore me. I'm just happy, that's all."

He set down the plates and sat cross-legged behind their screening hedge, balancing the mimosas on the winding sidewalk beside them. Then he reached for her, stroking a soothing hand over her knee. She took a breath and suddenly her strapless bra wasn't poking her quite so hard anymore. He had a way of doing that, of touching her just right. He always had, but the longer they were together, the better it worked. Like their connection worked its way deeper into her bones with every passing year.

He was still watching her, but he didn't ask, just lifted her hand and pressed a kiss to the inside of her wrist.

"You know, you had a funny look on your face earlier, too. I meant to ask you about it, but I haven't been able to get you alone."

"You're going to have to be more specific. Thanks to that bossy photographer, I think I've had *every* funny look on my face today." She broke the bacon scone down the middle and passed him half.

He smiled at her offering. "Now that's love."

"Twu wuv." She quoted *The Princess Bride* through a mouthful of bacon scone and he snickered.

"It was right before you turned down the aisle," he said. "Like you were going to sneeze, maybe. At least until you saw me and transformed into full Disney princess mode. I think the first time you smiled, flowers sprouted out of your hair and all the birds in Austin started to sing."

She scoffed to hide her blush. "Exactly how many of those mimosas have you had, pal?" She took a sip of hers, lemon bubbling over her tongue. "Oh my gosh, I remember now, it was my *dad*. He thought I was going to be nervous so he was spouting wedding-related dad joke puns all morning."

Bishop brightened. "Do you remember any?"

"Mmm, at least thirty. I don't even know if I would have gotten nervous, because I was so busy being annoyed." She swallowed the last bite of scone. "How about this one: you know about the spiders who got engaged?"

"Nah, tell me."

"I hear they met on the web."

He snorted into genuine laughter. "I like your dad so much, it's probably unhealthy. I can't decide if it's because he's so wholesome, or because we're both criminals."

"EX-criminals."

"Don't get too attached to the ex part of the criminal equation.

275

Because apparently Daisy has a boyfriend, and I might need to kill him."

"She told me. At least seven times just today." Harlow scowled. "I hate everything about him including his name."

"His name is the least of it. She showed up today smelling like cotton candy. Again." Bishop's mouth twisted. "I can't believe the best this generation's bad boys have to offer is cotton candy-flavored vaping. So depressing."

"I know, right?" Harlow waved her champagne flute. "What happened to motorcycles and sexy leather jackets? At least they were the fun kind of dangerous."

"I'm telling you, if we went through all this shit to get her into remission just so she could give herself lung cancer vaping with some fourteen-year-old punk, I am going to end him."

"Nah, we'll sic Alice on him instead. She won't get caught."

"True. That's a better idea." He fed her a bite of avocado toast. "I'm starting to see why people call their wives their better halves."

"Oh, you're just now starting to see that, are you?"

"Well, I've only had a wife for about two hours, in my defense." He took a sip of his mandarin orange mimosa, then nearly spilled it down his shirt when a disembodied water bottle peeped over the hedge. "What in the hell?"

Alice's head popped up. "Take it, quick, before they see I'm talking to you."

Harlow grabbed the water bottle and Alice turned away, pretending to idly survey the reception area, then flipping a pack of tissues over the hedge, too.

"Stay hydrated," she murmured through a smile as she waved to someone at the bar.

"You're the best maid of honor in the world," Harlow vowed, taking a gulp of water and realizing she was way thirstier than she had thought.

"Nice try, but I know you said that to Sadie, too."

"Because you're both the best maids of honor in the world, and I got both of you."

"*Selfishly,* she kept both of you," Bishop griped, and a real smile flashed across Alice's face before she smoothed it away, putting on a bored expression as she pretended to hang out by the hedge for no particular reason.

"Do I need to toss over a condom, too, or are you two behaving yourselves back there?"

"Depends. You volunteering to keep watch, General?" Bishop asked.

That cracked another smile out of her before she hid it. Alice loved that nickname, and spent a lot of good time and energy pretending not to love it, which Harlow found adorable.

They kept bickering back and forth while Harlow smiled at them.

She couldn't prove it, because Alice wouldn't admit a thing, but she thought Alice might like Bishop even more than Sadie did. Her husband certainly did. Rob and Bishop got along so well that he'd actually ended up a groomsman in their wedding six months before. Back when it was Harlow's turn to keep the bride supplied with tissues, water, and wrestle her away from the crowd for regular bathroom breaks. Sadie seemed to be heading toward the altar with an ex-ballerina graphic designer she'd met on the app, but then they'd broken up this winter.

Judging by the flirting she was doing on the other side of the hedge, Sam was firmly in her sights now. Harlow hoped Sadie liked statisticians.

"Father-in-law, two o'clock," Alice broke off mid-banter to say. She swiveled in that direction. "No worries, finish your snack. I'll ask him if he's heard the one about the two cell phones who got married."

"The reception was terrific," Bishop finished as Alice walked away. "Your dad has heard that one."

"It's so creepy that you know that."

"Hey, you'd better be happy I love him, because I could have married you right away if he'd gotten his ass out of prison faster."

"You didn't need to marry me earlier," she scoffed. "Three years is a reasonable amount of time to date before getting married. If we'd done it right away, I couldn't have eaten cheeseburgers for six months because everybody'd spend the whole day looking for the baby bump."

"Correction. I *did* need to marry you earlier than three years into our relationship. You would not let me."

"I was being sensible," she said. "*You* were being romantic."

He shrugged. "Sounds like us."

"It kind of does, doesn't it?" She squeezed his hand, the ring on his finger giving her a rush all over again like she couldn't believe this was all real. That this was actually her life.

To ground herself, she looked around at the park she'd planned, and back to the love she hadn't planned at all. A soft smile spread across her face.

"Sounds like a perfect match to me."

<<<<>>>>

If you enjoyed Harlow & Bishop's story, please consider leaving a review online. Reviews are the #1 way you can help the authors whose books you love. Thanks for reading!

Already missing Harlow and Bishop? When you sign up here, you'll get an exclusive bonus scene of them clowning around together when they first became roommates.
Sign up here to get your bonus scene and a free book!

http://michellehazenbooks.com/newsletter/

Did you like Bishop's friend, Samwise the statistician? Well, he's about to embark on his own story...

THE MATCHMAKER PACT

Childhood best friends make a matchmaker's pact to find each other's true love. Make one a sex therapist and one the statistician for a dating app, and things are about to get interesting...

When Allie gets dumped, she runs to her usual—Emotional Support Karaoke with Sam. They've been best friends since she bonked him over the head with a Fisher Price microphone during the infamous Nickelback dispute of 1998. But not even karaoke can sing away the blues of the fact that they're both approaching the dreaded single-at-thirty milestone.

With every passing year, Allie's choices in boyfriends only seem to get worse. The agoraphobic spelunker. The arms dealer. The tattoo addict. Meanwhile, Sam's dating perfect-on-paper guys and gals...and dumping them all anyway. So Sam and Allie make a pact: instead of going on their own—clearly terrible—instincts, they'll do a better job if they swap and choose mates for each other.

But it quickly becomes clear that the stakes are higher than their individual happiness. Sam's a statistician working for a dating app and racing to find the algorithm for long-term compatibility. Allie's a sex therapist with one couple she just can't crack—they're as compatible as peas and carrots but she just can't get their sex life revved and they're about to run out of insurance benefits. So Sam and Allie agree that not only will they find each other lasting love, they'll use their dates to settle the truth of attraction and save both their jobs in the process.

Matchmaking hijinks ensue. Some well-intentioned. Some maybe the teensiest bit passive-aggressive. Only one arrest, but two fountain incidents. But by the time the bail is paid and the birthday cakes are being baked, Sam and Allie are starting to realize the only person they really want to spend time with is each other.

$\sim$

Coming soon!

Sign up here to be notified when preorders go live.

http://michellehazenbooks.com/newsletter/

Or scroll down for your first peek at Sam and Allie's story…

SNEAK PEEK AT THE MATCHMAKER PACT

Data point: Martin had revoked the power cord to karaoke.
Working hypothesis: Without karaoke, Allie would be sad.
Conclusion: Martin had to be neutralized, at any cost.

Sam planted both hands on the bar. He didn't have to attempt to look threatening. Generally, the height and the tattoos did that for him.

Martin edged back, holding up his hands. "Mate, you know I've got a strict two Phil Collins policy."

"You don't want to go there with me, Martin. Not tonight. Not over a couple of sad songs."

Sam threw a glance back at their booth, where Allie was looking two tequilas past sunrise, and starting to sniffle into a cocktail napkin with the Nickel and Mongoose logo stamped on it. In their favorite neighborhood bar, the wood came pre-distressed and the ceiling was stamped tin, but the whiskey was rough enough and the floor sticky enough that it passed for real Texas. And okay, they did have one tap paying out cold brew on nitro, but it hadn't gone completely hipster. Not an artisanal kombucha in sight.

Martin's hands twitched, wringing the bar towel hard enough that the scent of bleach started to tang the air. "You know I can't take it when the pretty ones cry, and singing Collins always makes her cry."

"Without karaoke to distract her, she's only going to cry more."

"Yes, but not on stage. In a quiet booth, where she's your problem and not mine."

Sam's gaze sharpened. Allie had been his best friend since the great Nickelback Debate of 1998 and she'd just been painfully dumped. If karaoke was what Allie wanted, he'd move heaven, earth, and fussy Aussie bartenders to make sure she got it.

"Okay, man, just remember you made me do this. Your liability insurance is up to date, right?"

"Sam. No. Not with a hump day crowd in here. Listen, mate—"

Sam picked up a cocktail napkin, ripped off two pieces, and balled them into his ears. "I gave you an out. You're the one who chose not to take it."

He scanned the bar. He could feel Allie's questioning look on his back but he ignored it for now. There were two groups of girls that were potentially young enough, but—oh yes, there. He chose the one at the end of the bar, and strolled their way.

They looked up with bright eyes and tentative smiles, and he gave them a crooked smile. "Hey, sorry to be the asshole that interrupts, but you won't even believe who I just saw. I had to share it with somebody."

He leaned in and whispered, and the resulting squeal split through the buzz of every conversation in the bar.

"OHMYFREAKINGGOD NO WAY!"

The tallest girl shot to her feet, whipping around to face the bartender. "*You* were in Werewolf High?!"

Martin was busy undermining his own acting credentials with a terrifically conspicuous attempt to block his face by scratching his ear with the bleachy towel.

The girls shot in full stampeding herd to the other end of the bar, a glittery purse catching Sam in the stomach on its way by. "Oof!" he grunted, then cringed as the squeeing intensified. The wads of napkin had not been big enough. He made a mental note to bring real earplugs the next time he needed to invoke the nuclear option.

Sam flipped up the bar pass-through and sauntered through, collecting the power cord to the karaoke machine and giving a two-finger wave to his victim. The bartender glared murder at him over a sea of waving cocktail napkins waiting for his autograph. While Sam was back there, he grabbed a glass and pulled himself a fresh beer. Out of the carnage, a Sharpie went flying and pinged off a bottle of Longbranch.

Sam stifled a laugh and made his escape back to the booth in the corner, checking the clock as he went. If he could turn this night around in under an hour, Allie would get enough sleep to counteract the headache from all that crying, and he might even make it to work on time in the morning.

He slid across slick vinyl into their booth. Hot wings: untouched. Allie's skin: extra pale. Assessment: his victory over Martin the retired werewolf heartthrob had come in the nick of time.

"That was risky." Allie lifted her glass in salute, sniffing quickly as if he wouldn't notice her reddened eyes. "I would have pegged those girls as a decade too old to remember Werewolf High."

"Yeah, but one of them was wearing the Darlene jacket." Sam sipped, not above a small amount of bragging. "Dark green leather, asymmetrical lapels. Figured there was a 73% probability of super fan, probably only a 12% probability of total cluelessness."

"Mmm." She nodded sagely. "Probability curves are all fine and good, sailor, but what's your t-value?"

"The real question, Allie, is never about your t. It's always about your—"

"N," they finished in unison.

She snorted at the old joke, but didn't quite make it to a laugh. "Leave it to a statistician to be obsessed with his sample size."

"Leave it to a sex therapist to twist old fashioned good science to be about her phallic fixation."

When she didn't volley back, something tugged in his chest. She might be worse off than he thought. He only had fifty-two minutes left before they were into overtime for a work night, but Sam wasn't sweating it.

If there was one thing he knew how to do in this world, it was cheer up Allie Greer.

He stood up and offered the rolled karaoke cord from his back pocket. "Your chariot, milady?"

Allie lit up. "That wasn't just a revenge mission?"

"Nope. Full tactical sortie to enemy territory."

"Ugh, you're way better at talking statistics than talking jarhead."

"What? You just add tactical before everything. Nothing to it."

"Just keep telling yourself that, Shaggy." She jumped to her feet and reached up to ruffle his hair.

"What's wrong with my hair?"

"Not a thing, champ. Let's just say there's a 20% off coupon to Great Clips in it for you if you're good tonight."

He trailed her to the tiny stage, kneeling to reconnect the machine while she went for the list of songs. Karaoke night was usually Tuesday, or whatever night Allie decided to plug in the karaoke machine in the corner. Which Martin normally let her get away with, as well as sneaking cherries out of the garnish tray, because it was Allie and she had that effect on people.

Her hair slipped past her shoulder, brushing the laminated pages of the song binder. The smile sagged from her face and her eyes started to well. "This was our song."

Sam straightened, brushing the curtain of her dark hair away from the page so he could see what song had stirred her up. "No, it wasn't."

"What?"

"*I Want to Know What Love Is* was your song with Dave, remember? By Foreigner. Something about how it was playing at the mall when he bought you the world's biggest cinnamon roll."

Personally, Sam thought that the bar for impressing a woman should stand higher than purchasing her an item for $4.67. But he'd keep that observation to himself, at least for tonight.

"Wait, you're right, that was our original song! Maybe I should sing that one. Or the new Adele. More alcohol is required for this decision." She pulled the binder off the podium and started toward their table, grabbing his hand on her way by.

He let her tow him along like she was the world's tiniest ski boat, while he threw a glance toward the bar. The crowd around Martin had only grown, and he smirked at the babble of female voices. *Is it true they're doing a reboot? Is Colter really that cute in real life? Can we get a picture please please pleeeeease?*

That would teach the bartender to cross him on one of Allie's breakup nights.

She flipped through the binder. "I've already done all these."

"Well, yeah. There have been quite a few Emotional Support Karaoke nights lately and—" He stopped before quoting exactly how many, and how none of the recent ones had been for *his* breakups. When she was already down was not the time or the place to address that.

She dropped her head to the table and groaned. "What am I doing wrong, Sam?"

"Well, you're a little flat on the G…"

"Not with karaoke, with men. You're a man. You should know where I'm screwing up here."

"Maybe you're not pretty enough," he said helpfully.

She lifted her head to scowl at him.

"Or it could be your personality?"

"I hate you."

But she snatched up a hot wing and started to eat, so he counted it as a win.

"Also, it could be that instead of looking for an equal, you're always picking up strays who need you. You never date anybody that's even half good enough to be a real partner to you."

"How is that any worse than what you do?" she accused.

"You mean stirring up fangirl havoc in hipster-y dive bars, or having a devastatingly effective jump shot?" He gave her his most charming smile. She appeared immune.

"I mean dating the most perfect people on earth and then inexplicably dumping them."

"The court objects. I've never dated a perfect person."

"You dumped a woman who cured epilepsy in *babies*." Allie slurped at the melting ice cubes in her drink.

"To be fair, it wasn't a cure. It was just the most effective clinical treatment yet developed."

"And she also happened to be Miss Texas."

"Former Miss Texas. She passed down the crown before she got her second Ph.D."

Sam tried to catch Martin's attention over the heads of his adoring public. The fangirls appeared to have called in reinforcements from somewhere. Martin had signed away all the cocktail napkins and was now autographing a takeout box. When he sent yet another dagger-eyed look their way, Sam nodded to Allie's empty cocktail glass but mouthed *beer*. The bartender raised a middle finger in acknowledgment.

"You're really not refuting my point here," Allie said.

He gave his table mate a level look. "C'mon. I think we can both agree she was way too good for me."

"She cried so hard when you dumped her that she burst a blood vessel in her eye."

He winced. "Okay, that sucked but it clearly supports my conclusion. Way too good for me."

"What about the yoga instructor who was also a stand-up comedian?"

"Meh. You're funnier than he was."

"But not more flexible."

"Apparently not." Sam looked pointedly at the karaoke binder she wasn't sharing.

"Admit it. You're no better at picking dates than I am."

"I will not. Because I've never dated an arms dealer."

"He said he was import/exports!"

"What about the agoraphobic spelunker?"

She cringed. "I could have lived with a lot of cozy nights in with Netflix, but the cave was a deal breaker."

Martin stomped past the table, dropping off a pint glass of pineapple IPA for Allie and revoking Sam's barely-half-finished porter without leaving anything in its place.

Allie sighed, her gaze distant now. Sam tensed, but before he could change the subject, she said, "I just...Dave used to rub my feet when I woke up. I thought if a man rubbed your feet, it meant he thought you were...that I could be..." She was huffing big breaths now, avoiding his eyes like she could hide the tear that had slipped down alongside her nose.

"That you could be what, Allie?" His forehead creased. This was new.

"Something!" she burst out. "To someone. Something special enough to stick." Another tear snuck out to join the first. "What if I end up like my parents? You remember how it was, Sam. The sound-track of my whole childhood was a fork scraping against a plate in a silent room because they didn't have a thing to say to each other."

She waved a hand at him.

"The whole reason I *became* a therapist was to figure out how couples could keep that spark alive because I knew no one should ever be stuck with what my parents had. A bare minimum partnership that was all about whose turn it was to take the kid to ballet. But I keep ending up in relationships that start out exciting but fade so quickly that even the sex stuff I do isn't enough to—" She cut herself off, gulping a breath. "TMI, I know, sorry, I know you don't want to hear about that."

He rubbed his twitching temple and tried not to think about Allie doing sex stuff to please guys she barely knew. If he pictured that for long, he was going to disturb the peace of this bar even more than the herd at the bar, currently screaming, *"Do the accent again! Do the accennnnnnt!"*

He slipped a napkin across the table. Quietly, so Allie could pretend she wasn't all the way crying. "The problem with that theory is that half the time—okay, more than half the time—you're the one who gets tired of them."

"Because when I feel it start to fade, I don't want to stick around to the bitter end. No matter what I do, it always starts to head that way, Sam. It's like my fate is a whole future of fork-scraping dinners because I'm intrinsically, I don't know, *boring*."

He choked. Her head snapped up, but now he couldn't hold back the laughter. "Yeah, you're boring. That's your problem."

She threw the napkin at him, glaring but with a tiny smile peeking through. "You're the worst. I should have called Harlow and Bishop instead."

"You really should have," he agreed. "Your mistake entirely." He reached for the karaoke binder, changing tactic. "I think I'm going to sing *Unbreak My Heart*."

"Seriously? Are you *trying* to make me cry?"

"I have work in the morning, so...yeah."

"What's that supposed to mean?"

"On Emotional Support Karaoke night you always arc from upbeat pop to girl power anthems to 90s heartbreak ballads and I've got to be up at five. You're never ready to go home until post-Toni Braxton so I figure why fuck around?"

She gasped, widening her damp green eyes at him. "How dare you try to fast-forward my emotional processing!"

"Quick question." He selected a hot wing. "Isn't Emotional Support Karaoke *designed* to fast forward your processing? Also, I was serious that we can't stay out too late. Work has been nuts lately."

"Money problems at the app still not any better? Come on, Austin is packed with singles. I do not understand how a dating app could go bankrupt here."

"Yeah, you invited me here to cheer *you* up so I vote we skip talking about my work problems. I've got a better idea." He flipped open the karaoke binder. "And it ends with a Carey and starts with Mariah."

Allie winced. "That bad, huh? I mean, I kind of thought that job was too good to be true when I saw what it paid. But tech is exploding right now. There have to be plenty of places looking for statisticians if this app doesn't make it."

"Right." He scowled at her. "I hope it's as easy to get a new best friend, considering Bishop vouched for me to the CEO, and not only did I not finish the algorithm they hired me for, I sunk their whole company."

She poked him. "*I'm* your best friend. Bishop's just the guy who's platonically infatuated with you. And your brain. Which he hired because he knows it's the very best brain."

"If I had the best brain, we wouldn't be in this situation. Look, I have the numbers right here." He leaned under the table. He'd brought his laptop in because he'd come straight from work and hadn't wanted to leave it in his car, downtown after dark like an invitation to a smashed window. He opened the lid and spun the screen toward Allie. "See? If the compatibility algorithm was ready tomorrow, revenues from new sign ups would rise quickly enough to offset the cash flow problem within only two months."

"Did you seriously put together a presentation to show how much your fault the company's financial problems are?" She rubbed her forehead. "Sam, you have issues."

"Not to show how much my fault it is. To convince the execs to give me more time because if I finish the algorithm, we won't need a buy out." He flicked to the next slide to show her the dates. "New ownership brings in money, sure, but it usually comes with a lot of other crap, too. Layoffs, restructuring."

She laid a hand on the back of his wrist. "Sam, everybody's jobs aren't your personal responsi—"

"See, this is why I didn't want to bring it up when you were already sad." He clicked out of the presentation and started to close all the windows of what he'd been working on when she called about that nitwit Dave. *Why* had he told her how bad things were? Especially tonight. Sam made a mental note to start lying to his best friend more.

"Just because I got dumped doesn't mean you're not allowed to have problems, too, Sam. I don't need you to pretend—wait, what was that?"

"Nothing!" He snapped the laptop closed. He forgot he'd opened that project back up to add the Dave data.

"It had my name on it."

"It's for, um, your birthday!" he fumbled. He hadn't expected to make good on his resolution to start lying more to Allie quite this soon.

"Of course you're already working on my birthday when it's still four months away." She rolled her eyes fondly, but then her smile shifted to a furrowed brow. "But wait, it looked like a PowerPoint. Why is my birthday present a PowerPoint?"

"Don't look a gift horse in its PowerPoint. You'll ruin the surprise." He snatched up her beer, making a big show of stealing a sip so that she'd start scuffling with him to get it back.

She narrowed her eyes, ignoring the beer. "Don't think I don't know what you're doing. One peek at my surprise birthday present isn't going to make me magically forget how sad I am."

On the word "sad," her voice began to wobble.

"Stop," Sam warned, with some alarm. "You know Martin can't handle it when you cry."

"I'm not!" she protested, another tear already welling up.

His heart wilted in his chest.

"Okay, okay, if you're already going to cry, I might as well be singing poorly when you do it. Two birds, one microphone."

He marched away from the booth, leaving the binder behind because he knew the code of the song he needed by heart. He'd heard her belt it out for a Tom, an Avi, a Bryndon, a Brandon, and a Malik. And that was in the last year alone.

He punched the buttons and vaulted onstage with one long-legged bound. He was already past his self-imposed hour, but nobody was going home when she was still feeling this bad, even if he had to stay long enough that they were *both* hung over for what he had planned tomorrow. He took a deep breath and began to sing about how hard it was to make someone love you.

His extra-high falsetto hurt his throat, Bonnie Raitt's lyrics tangled his tongue, and Martin had to stop mid-autograph to rip a cocktail napkin in two and stuff it in his own ears.

But the indignity was all worth it because over in their corner booth, Allie was starting to smile.

Coming soon!

Sign up here to be notified when preorders go live.

http://michellehazenbooks.com/newsletter/

THE SEX, LOVE AND ROCK AND ROLL SERIES

This award-winning series follows a rock band on the rise from bar rooms to the big time. Meet the fiery female drummer, the intense bassist with a sensual secret, and the charismatic lead singer with a dark side. Come along on the ride of their lives as they chase their dreams. Who will they meet along the way that will capture their hearts?

From spit-out-your-coffee funny to so heart-wrenching you'll be snatching up a napkin to dab at your eyes, this series will give you ALL the feels.

You can hop online and grab the boxed set to save 33%, or you can turn the page to check out Book 1!

A CRUEL KIND OF BEAUTIFUL:
BOOK 1

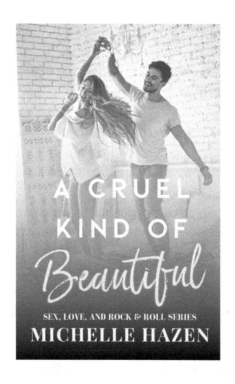

Escape into this friends-to-lovers romance that reviewers are calling "hot, humorous, and honest" and "a chocolate high."

Jera McKnight loves music, swoons for hot guys, but sucks at sex. Jacob Tate is her perfect storm: a pun-loving nude model with a heart as big as his record collection.

When a newspaper-delivery accident lands him in her living room, he's almost tempting enough to make her forget she's never been enough for a man—in bed or out of it. Sure, he laughs at her obscure jokes, and he'll even accept a PG-rating if it means he gets time with her, but he's also hiding something. And it has everything to do with the off-limits room in his apartment.

Jera pours all her confusion and longing into her drum kit, which pays off when her band lands the record deal of their dreams. Except just like Jacob, it might be too good to come without a catch.

She doesn't know if her music is good enough to attract a better contract, or if she's enough to tempt a man like Jacob to give up his secrets. But if this rocker girl is too afraid to bet on herself, she might just end up playing to an empty house.

One-click this heart-warming and swoony romance today!

Winner of the Great Expectations Award

"The indie music scene reads as authentic, the pacing keeps the story humming along, and the big twist is one readers won't see coming." - Publisher's Weekly

"I was already laughing by page two! Hazen has wit in spades and I can't seem to get enough of her writing." -Alexandra K, Amazon reviewer

"I'm blown away by Michelle's ability to take the rock band genre and breathe new life into it. Definitely an all-time favorite series for me." - KAS621, Amazon reviewer

UNBREAK ME: A HURT/COMFORT FRIENDS TO LOVERS STANDALONE ROMANCE

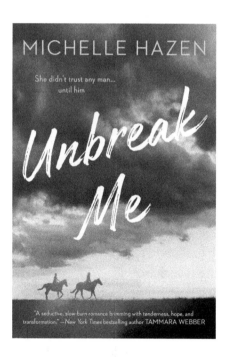

What could two troubled souls from different walks of life have in common? Maybe everything.

Andra Lawler lives isolated at her family's horse ranch, imprisoned by the memories of an assault in college. When she needs help training her foals, she hires a Haitian-Creole cowboy from New Orleans with a laugh as big as the Montana sky.

LJ Delisle can't stand the idea that Andra might be lonely—or eating frozen TV dinners. He bakes his way into her kitchen with a lemon velvet cake, and offers her cooking lessons that set them on the road to romance. But even their love can't escape the shadow of what they've been through. Despite their growing friendship and his gentle rapport with the horses, LJ is still an outsider facing small-town suspicions.

Before they can work through their issues, LJ is called home by a family emergency. In the centuries-old, raggedly rebuilt streets of New Orleans, he must confront memories of Hurricane Katrina and familiar discrimination. And Andra must decide if she's brave enough to leave the shelter of the ranch for an uncertain future with LJ.

"Hazen's well-developed characters, soft and steamy love scenes, and exquisitely detailed settings makes this a winning love story." -Booklist (starred review)

"A seductive, slow-burn romance brimming with tenderness, hope, and transformation."—Tammara Webber, *New York Times* bestselling author

"Hazen writes with grace and compassion about life after trauma, smoothly addressing racism, sexual assault, and large-scale disasters without pat answers or platitudes." - Publisher's Weekly (starred review)

"This is a book for intelligent people who also like hot romance." - Faith, Amazon reviewer

Available now in ebook, paperback and audiobook!

BREATHE THE SKY: A GRUMPY-SUNSHINE SLOW BURN STANDALONE ROMANCE

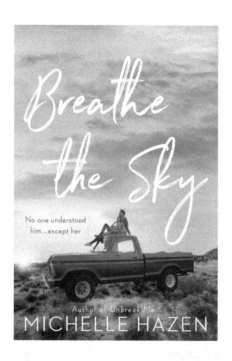

Two strangers start out saving animals and end up rescuing each other in this heartwarming romance from the author of *Unbreak Me*.

Mari Tucker is a wildlife biologist who scoops bunnies and endangered tortoises out of harm's way on construction sites. Still haunted by her past, she takes the most remote jobs in the Mojave Desert to avoid people and hide from her ex. It's a simple, quiet life filled with sweet animals and solar-powered baking until she ends up assigned to Jack Wyatt's crew.

Construction foreman Jack Wyatt's loud, foul-mouthed temper keeps even the most rugged of men on his crew in line. No mistake is overlooked, because out in the desert it could mean life or death. In his opinion, the job site is no place for sensitive biologists, especially one as shy as Mari. But instead of wilting from the heat and hard work, Mari wins over Jack and his crew one homemade brownie at a time.

Jack and Mari find a comfortable rhythm, building a friendship that's rare for both of them. After Jack's rocky childhood, they have more in common than they'd imagined. But even the Mojave sun can't chase away the shadows when the past is determined to track them down...

"Hazen's latest heart-melting and intensely passionate contemporary romance is a balm for the soul for anyone who has suffered abuse and survived to love again." - Booklist (starred review)

"An achingly beautiful romance that rumbles like a quiet thunder across the desert with the promise that love can reach even the weariest of souls." --Mary Ann Marlowe, author of *Some Kind of Magic*

"Hazen (*Unbreak Me*) sets this extraordinary tale of unexpected love in California's Mojave Desert. The slow-burning romance and Hazen's vivid descriptions of the desert keep the pages turning. This sweet, sensual contemporary is sure to tug at readers' heartstrings." -Publisher's Weekly (starred review)

"Gruff, secretly sweet man + reserved, intelligent woman / (working through past trauma) x (genuine respect) = the most adorably heart-warming love story I've read in ages." -Margaret T, Netgalley reviewer

"This books has cute turtles/tortoises, hot construction workers, brownies, and sweet love. WHAT ELSE COULD YOU NEED??" -Alexis, Netgalley reviewer

Available now in ebook, paperback and audiobook!

ABOUT THE AUTHOR

Michelle Hazen is a nomad with a writing problem. Years ago, she and her husband swapped office jobs for seasonal gigs and moved out on the road. As a result, she wrote most of her books with solar power in odd places, including a bus in Thailand, a golf cart in a sandstorm, and a beach in Honduras. These days, if she's not hiking or rock climbing, she's probably writing fanfiction, watching *Veronica Mars*, or driving an indefensible amount of miles to get to a Revivalists' concert.

She is the critically-acclaimed author of Unbreak Me, Breathe the Sky, and the Sex, Love and Rock & Roll series.

Come find Michelle in the wilds of the internet:

Website: http://michellehazenbooks.com/
Newsletter: http://michellehazenbooks.com/newsletter/

f facebook.com/MichelleHazenAuthor
🐦 twitter.com/michellehazen
📷 instagram.com/michellehazenauthor
BB bookbub.com/authors/michelle-hazen
a amazon.com/author/michellehazen

ACKNOWLEDGMENTS

Thanks to Sara Burns, Devri Walls, and Laura Lashley, for the Twitter-spiration for this book and the joke messages in its dating app. Sara, careful what you say to a writer. Your wish might just become a book ;)

Thanks to Morgan at @Morvamp for the post-it bad date idea. Can't believe that's real.

Eliza Gillie for helping with city planner details.

Katie Golding for alpha reading and her enthusiasm for the early chapters, and for sticking with me through all these years and all these books. But especially, for making the most perfect cover and graphics in the world for this book!

Margaret, for loving Bishop and voting on ten million rounds of everything, for everything. Muskrat Knife Fight Book Club is the best book club.

My brother, for being so awesome that now I have to write adorable older brothers into every book. Listen, I don't make the rules.

My mom, for being a killer publicist and also a pretty killer mom.

My husband, for always making me laugh when I least expect it. POTATO!

Naomi Davis, my brilliant, badass agent. Someday, I'm going to run out of books to write, and words to write them with. But I am never going to run out of words to talk about how grateful I am that you're in my life. It takes so many completely contradictory skills to be not just a good, but a great agent. You have to be friendly and outgoing and professionally detached and charming and analytical. You have to be creatively open-minded and keep your eye on the bottom line. You have to be fierce and persistent and sweet and assertive all at the same time. It's too much to ask that any one person be all of these things, and yet you are. No one could do this job better than you. No one.

To Bookends Literary, separately, because I wanted to say that I was already delighted to be a client of this agency because of its reputation and amazing list of authors. But to see how you treat writers of *all* different skill levels with respect, and how you donate so much time as an agency to help not just your authors, but the writing community as a whole...you are an organization I am proud to be a part of.

Thanks to Mary Helen for keeping me going on the hard days, and for being a crack metaphor-hunter, and for reviews that make my toes curl with happiness.

Thanks to my wonderful beta readers for this one: Gwynne, Sandra, Jen, and Margaret. I love you for your insightful notes, but mostly for your personalities. Thanks for living inside my phone and brightening all of my days. Extra thanks to Gwynne for hyphenating my compound adjectives and being a chill but scrupulous proofreader.

A heartfelt and cookie-bolstered thank you to the Veronica Mars fandom. You guys got me revved up to write again, and this book popped into being as a result. Thank you to all my readers, for every review, every email, and every way you've supported this crazy career of mine over the years.

NOTES

NOTES

NOTES

CPSIA information can be obtained
at www.ICGtesting.com
Printed in the USA
LVHW081159220821
695822LV00009B/272